GUNSMOKE & Glamour

A NOVEL BY

HILLARY MONAHAN

Fireside

Edited by Brian J. White
Copyedited by Shaun Duke
Cover illustration by Eli Hoyt
Book design by Pablo Defendini

Published by Fireside Fiction Company
Brooklyn, NYC

Fireside has two goals:
to find and publish great stories regardless of genre,
and to pay creators well.

firesidefiction.com
ISBN: 978-0-9987783-7-2

CONTENT NOTES

Fireside provides content notes for its books to guide readers who may wish to seek out or avoid particular story elements. These content notes may contain spoilers.

Gunsmoke & Glamour contains instances of transmisogynistic abuse, and a few instances of ableist language.

A current list of all the elements covered in our content notes can be found on our website: ***firesidefiction.com/about/#content-notes***.

CONTENTS

For Eric, who always goes where the tingling goes.

AUTHOR'S FOREWORD

Gunsmoke & Glamour is a book in which I take the alpha-male cowboy trope and kick it in the junk as many times as I possibly can. I have a deep-seated love of westerns. One of my favorite books of all time remains Larry McMurtry's *Lonesome Dove*, and for a long, long while I'd devour any Old West narrative I could get my hands on—books, TV shows, movies. But there was always an asterisk on my enjoyment. The books weren't friendly to women or marginalized identities.

This book is a product of that love and frustration.

One thing I'd like to touch upon before anyone delves into this story is the character of Irene. Irene is a trans woman existing in the Old West—a place not exactly known for enlightened viewpoints. You can imagine that comes with a lot of complications, the least of which is that Irene is sometimes forced to hide her gender simply so she can live her life. Irene sometimes presents as Seamus Miller out of a need for safety. This presentation does not represent a change in gender; Irene is not genderfluid, and her pronouns are always she/her.

Certain instances of transmisogynistic abuse warrant a warning for readers. I'm fortunate to have trans people in my immediate circles and family, and they were kind enough to help me navigate these waters with as much sensitivity as possible. It is not, of course, a catchall, but I'm hoping I've given Irene as much respect as I possibly can given the difficulty of her circumstances. My goal is to always do more good than harm.

There are also a few instances of ableist language some readers may find triggering.

Thank you again for supporting my books, and I hope *Gunsmoke & Glamour* allows you to experience some good ol' fashioned cowboy fantasy in a new, fun way.

—HJM

CHAPTER ONE

NOW

"Pardon my language, Clayton, but you're fucked."

Clayton Jenson took the news remarkably well for a doomed man. He tilted Doc's rickety chair back until the front legs were a foot off the ground and the caned back touched the wall. The only indication Clay'd heard his prognosis was the faint lines framing his eyes. He was a man of leisure otherwise; his long legs sprawled out before him, pants easing up just past his ankles to reveal alligator-skin cowboy boots. The white shirt beneath his purple brocade vest was open at the neck, and his guns hung crooked on his hips. His duster jacket pooled on the floor to his sides in lazy piles of caramel-colored leather.

"Damn," was all he said.

Doctor Irene Miller—or Doc, as everyone called her—swirled a blood sample around inside a test tube, her face impassive despite the bizarre phenomenon playing out before her. Fat crimson droplets rose from the crest of the glass, the dollops suspending mid-air and shining like scarlet pearls. Doc pulled the goggles from her forehead to her nose to get a better look, sliding an extra lens down and around to do… whatever it was Doc did. Clay didn't ask. He was too busy frowning at the ridiculous-looking headgear. The goggles looked like two shot glasses tied together with a leather string. The six or seven multi-colored lenses protruding from the sides like spider legs didn't help the aesthetic much neither.

"Those things are ugly, Doc."

"Glib even when your blood is defying the laws of gravity?" Doc lifted a second tube, and then a third, tilting them to the window so she could peer at them against the late-day sun. "This is fascinating in a completely horrible way."

"Fascinating ain't the word I'd use," Clay said.

"Of course it isn't. Speaking as your friend, it's disturbing. Speaking as a scientist, it's remarkable." Doc jerked her head back as one of the blood drops sailed toward her face, almost inserting itself into her nostril. "Unfortunate, but still remarkable."

Clay grunted and rocked his seat back and forth, letting it teeter on two legs.

Fucking blood.
Fucking witches.
Fucking fairies.
Fucking Cora.

"How *did* it come to this?" Doc asked, returning the test tubes to the rack on her workbench. She flicked her finger at a flying blood ball, and it exploded upon contact, sanguine rivulets blossoming across the pad. A second later, another droplet rose from the glass to replace its predecessor, fatter than the last and daring to float higher from the tube.

Clay let the chair drop to the floor with an unceremonious thud. "How do you think it happened? Betsy Lynch! Goddamned warty witch."

Doc swept the goggles off of her head and ran her fingers through her hair, creating lumpy tracks in an otherwise finely slicked, blond head. The cowlick at the crown was a nice touch. Doc wasn't at her most fashionable at the moment—she was wigless and wore boy clothes too big for her bird bones, her pants so long on her short, spindly legs she tripped on the hems. Her shirt was wrinkled, and her suspenders tended to slip off her shoulders to dangle around her elbows.

She didn't like her boy disguise, but sometimes it was safer that way. Doc had learned that the hard way a time or forty before.

"I told you not to go alone," Doc said. "And she can't help the warts, Clayton. Don't be unkind."

"She cursed me with the bad blood! I can be as unkind as I want to be. Goddamned Lynches. Ain't nothin' but trouble." Clay spat on the floor to punctuate his statement, his annoyance escalating when wads of his expectorate rose from the ground. Seemed all his fluids were acting ornery today. Better be careful where he pissed, or worse yet, where he dropped his seed. Flying spunk would scare the bejesus out of Delilah's whores.

"Maybell Lynch is a fine lady." Doc snagged cork stoppers and wedged them into the remaining blood vials. "I'll talk to Betsy tomorrow. She made the curse, she'll have the cure. If she's difficult, I'll ask Maybell to right you."

Clay tilted his hat down and grunted, his eyes skittering to the corners of the room. His fingers ducked inside his duster to reach for his tobacco bag. It was velvety and soft, a gift from Cora during their better days. He pulled it out to roll himself a smoke. He assembled the cigarette without having to look at it, his fingers nimble as he pinched, stretched, and folded the crinkly yellow paper.

He wedged the cigarette between his teeth, the weight against his bottom lip a comfort even without the smoke. "Can't do that."

"Why not?"

"Shot Betsy dead."

Doc's frown was so severe she looked like one of those sniffer hounds Clay's father kept back on the farm. Clay did his best to ignore it, but whenever Doc got that look, it made Clay all squirrelly and uncomfortable, like he'd stepped in a cow pie and tracked it all over the laboratory.

Again.

"*You bloody idiot,*" Doc screeched. "Instead of one witch, four will be jockeying to skewer you. Are you *stupid*?"

Clay struck a match and puffed, wishing the blue-gray smoke was thick enough to swallow him whole. There were fogs down in the bayou that did that—rolled in to sweep a man away with the dusk. Course, those folks were never seen again, but avoiding this conversation might be worth death by swamp gas. "Seemed like a good idea at the time. Bad blood makes me a dead man. She's just dead sooner than me. It's fair, if you ask me."

"*Fair?* Who cares about fair? I can't exactly ask Maybell for a cure when you've gunned down her sister!"

Clay pushed himself from his chair with another deep suck from the cigarette. He ambled towards the door, swinging it wide on its squealing hinges so he could eyeball the Houston horizon. It was a summer scorcher with no sign of breeze coming in from the Gulf. He wanted a poker game and a bath. If he was lucky, there'd be a soft bed and a softer woman to wind out the night, but he wouldn't push his luck. "Good to know when my life goes to shit, the good Dr. Miller finds my mortal blow fascinating. Then she goes and yells at me for killing my murderer. Best kinda friend to have, if you ask me. You gonna crap on my tombstone, too?"

"Bugger off, Clayton."

"That's downright rude. Why you gotta be so rude?"

"Yes, it's *so rude* of me to spend time figuring out how to save your miserable life," Doc spat.

Clay grinned. "Well, in that case that's right kind of you, Irene! Thank you muchly."

—

Hindsight told Clayton it was stupid to shoot the witch, and for it, hindsight could go to Hell.

Clay would never admit aloud that he fucked up, but now that he was alone, walking back to his hotel with the dust crunching beneath his boot heels and the cicadas screeching at the dusk sky, he couldn't ignore the tension behind his eyes. A bad blood curse was… it was bad. One of those things that started small and got worse fast. He felt fine now, but in six months, he'd be lucky if he could wipe his own ass without falling over.

Problem was, curses were tricky. He'd been lucky enough to avoid them 'til now, but he'd witnessed enough to know that every curse was as individual as the woman who cast it. Unraveling another witch's intricacies—the very flavor of her magic—could be a real pain in the backside. A skilled witch could untangle a novice's spell given some time, and Maybell Lynch was one of the greatest witches in Texas, but—

Well. She was probably furious with him. Rightfully so, too. He wished Betsy'd had the foresight to tell Cora to fuck off when she jingled her blood money. If she had, Betsy'd be vertical and Clayton wouldn't be contemplating his mortality. If the curse didn't kill him, a pack of angry Lynch witches would, and either scenario was a poor way to meet his maker.

Clay headed for the Rattlesnake Saloon at the center of town, his mind hard at work. He'd met dozens of witches over the years, some of them so strong they could turn his whiskers white when they got their scary on—real hellraisers when the circumstances called for it. Surely one of them could break Betsy's magic. He knew Marie could, but she was all the way down in N'Orleans, which might be worth the ride if it guaranteed he'd see his thirtieth birthday.

"Guess I'm goin' down to Delta town," he murmured, lighting another cigarette. No local witch would do the work, not with Maybell's sway. No one crossed the eldest Lynch sister on a good day, never mind a bad. She was just too scary. It was too bad, too, because Clay'd done a lot for the witch community over the years. Admittedly, it was his job to help them, but that shouldn't matter. Living witches were better than dead witches any day, and he helped make that happen.

Clayton Jenson was a certified lawman. The embossed papers he carried from the Office of United States Marshals said "Marshal Clayton Jenson specializes in legal matters pertaining to individuals of the magical persuasion." In Clay's mind, that made him a glorified bounty hunter who sometimes got to save the weirds instead of shoot them, but at least he got a shiny star on his lapel and a fancy title to impress the ladies.

It impressed the Pinkertons, too. They'd been trying to hire him for a few years now, mostly 'cause there weren't a lot of gents stupid enough to track the fairies, witches, and necromancers that needed attending, but Clay wasn't interested in the private sector. His setup worked. The pay was decent, and he got his pick of the jobs—a dozen a year was enough to put a roof over his head and food in his belly. The rest of his income he wrangled up from card tables as far east as Savannah and as far west as San Antonio.

It wasn't glamorous, but Clay didn't mind. He was as lazy as his lifestyle would allow for, and really, most law-dogging boiled down to talking to a lot of different people in a lot of different places. And he could talk—oh Lord, could he talk. The trick was knowing what to say and to whom. Clay had quite the colorful list of contacts thanks to Sterling and Cora, and his good looks and—to use Doc's term—"bollocks-born charm" got him the rest of the way. He had an especially good rapport with the fae. Every fairy Clay'd ever known was hung up on pretty things, and Clay passed for plenty pretty with his slate blue eyes, a shadow of dark stubble on his chin, and a lazy half-smile.

That probably meant dick-all after what went down in Little Rock—no fairy would forgive him for betraying one of their own—but Cora'd gone too far.

Clay pushed his way through the double doors of the Rattlesnake Saloon with the familiarity of a man who'd been there a time or twenty. He hauled himself onto the corner barstool, ignoring the "come hither" look Lola cast him from the corner. She was a busty blond with freckles, and he'd taken her friendly overtures for a sweaty tumble in the past, but thinking about Cora had soured his already-pissy mood. Last thing he wanted was skin that tasted of stale-flower perfume instead of Cora's sweet, spring rain. She may have been the most morally ambiguous woman he'd ever had the misfortune of knowing, but once he had her in his head, no other woman compared.

Figured. Not only had Cora of the Gales managed to kill him through the Lynch witch, she'd ruined tonight's potential bed sport, too.

Why you gotta be such a bitch, Cora?

—

The Rattlesnake wasn't a fancy place, but it was functional and sturdy, and what it lacked in decorative niceties it made up for in efficiency. It was two stories tall, the downstairs sporting a good-sized bar and half a dozen round card tables with cast-iron lanterns at their middles. The heads of dead carnivores loomed over the patrons, their tongues hanging out like they were salivating for man-flesh. The upstairs consisted of a single long hallway of closed doors behind which Lola, Delilah, and the rest of the girls worked their mattress magic.

Clay liked it here—the floors were meticulously swept, the rafters cleared of cobwebs, and it didn't stink like unwashed cowboy all the time. He grunted and waved at the barkeep, a one-eyed, one-balled brown man named Little Eagle who claimed that his single eye was twice as good as a normal eye because it had to do twice the work. It was shit; Clay had to pound his fist on the bar to get Eagle to notice he was there half the time, and waving from Eagle's blind side didn't do a whole lot except leave Clay with a dry whistle. But if that's the story Eagle wanted to tell, who was Clay to question it?

"How's your one ball?" Clay asked in greeting.

The story of how Eagle had lost the other testicle was epic and involved hand-to-hand combat, six enemies, and a raging battle on a cliffside. Eagle told it at least three times a week.

Eagle brought down his top-line whiskey, half-filling a glass and sliding it over the glossy, wooden surface of the bar. It struck Clay's waiting hand, and Clay promptly drained it, reveling in the burn seeping through his guts. Eagle topped him off again, and again Clay swallowed it down in one gulp. Eagle took the hint after the third pass, leaving the bottle at Clay's elbow.

"Bigger'n your two balls combined and twice as potent. Constance is pregnant again," Eagle said, flashing two lines of teeth that looked too white.

Clay smirked. Eagle was as big a bullshit artist as Clay was, but Clay was glad to call him friend regardless. He'd been born to a white pastor father who'd married a Sioux girl up in the Dakotas and then promptly dragged her down to Texas. Eagle'd grown up the oldest of thirteen children—all who lived to see adulthood, despite Texas' best attempts at killing damn near everything that touched it. When he'd matured, he'd joined the army, and when he'd done his time there, taking a bullet in the leg for a country that systematically murdered his mother's people, he'd taken his savings and opened a bar. Almost one year to the day after opening, he married one of the very girls he'd hired to whore on his second floor.

"Virile my ass. Constance has bigger balls than both of us for putting up with you," Clay said.

"Not going to argue that. A weak woman couldn't carry my child."

"It'd bust straight through a regular gal's womb, I'm sure." Clay whirled the amber liquid around his glass, willing the drunken haze to take him away. It hadn't hit yet, but he could feel that sweet fogginess encroaching upon the edges of his vision. Just three more drinks, maybe four, and he'd be there. He'd be free to put the day behind him. For one night, he could pretend the samples of his blood weren't trying to float away from Doc's test-tube rack. Tomorrow he could deal with this latest bizarre catastrophe.

A red rag swam circles across the bar surface to Clay's right, and he watched it from beneath his hat brim, finding the motion oddly soothing.

"You all right, Marshal?" Eagle asked. "Looking like you were shot at and missed, shit at and hit. And you're packing away liquor like Lola packs away peckers."

Clay's hand hesitated halfway to his mouth, but he shrugged his shoulders anyway. Even when his world was a heaping pile of cow chips, he didn't want people to know it. Doc could, but Doc was family, so that was fine. "I'm a'right."

"If you say so." Eagle tossed the rag aside and leaned over the bar. The turquoise beads of his drawstring tie clicked as they brushed against the oak counter. "Why don't you stop by the house tomorrow after church? Constance's cornbread is a gift to this outhouse of a world."

Clay swallowed his whiskey and eyed the poker table to his right. Jasper, one of the local bankers, had taken a seat along next to the mayor's new secretary, Roger. A thin, blond man with a red silk suit also lingered nearby, eying the empty chairs and gathering players. He didn't belong there. He was too tall, too pretty, and too… something. Off. He was off in the way that all magical things were off. Clay knew it as he knew he'd draw breath. And knowing it made him surly, which in turn required more whiskey.

"Love to, but I can't. I'm leaving in the morning. Got business in N'Orleans. Not sure when I'll be back."

The words sat on his tongue like a brick. He'd enjoyed his stay in Houston, had come to like the people during his sojourn. But thanks to the Betsy situation, he'd have to pack up and head east before Maybell wore his cock around her neck like a war trophy.

"Damn, White Man. That's not friendly news," Eagle said.

"Nope. It ain't. And I'll be sad to go."

Clay didn't loiter to discuss it any further. Roger shuffled the cards and looked around the bar, his gaze settling on Clay for an extra moment or two. If the invitation got any clearer, someone from the post would have to hand-deliver it. Clay gathered his whiskey and headed for the card table. The moment he circled a seat, the man in the ridiculous clothes closed in on the last free chair. Clay smiled at him, tipped his hat in greeting, and wolf-grinned over at Roger. "You shuffle them cards any harder, the queens'll lose their tits. Deal."

CHAPTER TWO

TEN YEARS AGO

Harland Jenson eyed the ugly hen scratch he pretended was penmanship with an assessing frown. "Nails for the fence. Bullets. Flour. That nag of yours needs shoes next time we come to market, Clay. Remind me."

Harland kept right on talking, and Clay went so far as to nod at him like he understood, but the fact was the din of the Atlanta market drowned the rest of Pa's words. The square was overrun by carriages, livestock, and the sweat-slicked bodies of shoppers brave enough to dare the June sun. The current fashions weren't keeping anyone comfortable neither; most of the ladies were covered in layers of linen and cotton, their skirts and bustles uncomfortable nuisances. Only their ruffled parasols and full-brimmed hats stopped them from melting into puddles on the ground.

The men didn't fare much better. Some of the fancier gentlemen wore long coats to their knees, and fine, thick trousers that probably made them feel like they were walking through a swamp. Rivulets of sweat poured from beneath their tall hats, their waxed mustaches droopy and lacking their pomp.

Fortunately for Clayton, his father was playing at being a farmer these days, and that meant Clay got away with lightweight pants, a thin, white shirt plastered to his lean frame, suspenders, and the black Stetson his mother gave him before disappearing into the fairy lands. She'd been smart enough to buy it big so Clay could grow into it, and grow into it he had at six feet, two inches. He was still a scrawny worm otherwise, no bigger 'round than a string bean, but Harland said not to worry—he'd fill out in time. Clayton wasn't so sure. His mother was tall and willowy thanks to her fae blood, and he more resembled her than his thick, burly father. If Harland didn't shave for a day or two, folks mistook him for a grizzly bear dressed in people clothes.

"Clayton, you listening to me?"

Clay tipped his hat and nodded. "Sure I am."

"Sure y'are. You're somethin', kid. Tie off them mules and don't get into trouble while I'm gone," Harland said, tossing the reins to his son. The leather cords whacked Clay in the shoulder before dropping to the ground. Clay gathered them up, lifting his head just in time to see his father maneuvering through the crowded street. He disappeared behind the Anderson Store's double doors a moment later. Clay wouldn't see hide nor hair of his old man for a good hour.

He had time to wander.

He dragged the mules out of the sun and into the shaded alley separating Jonah Livingston's barber shop and the apothecary. There was a water trough near full to the brim, and though the stupid animals tossed their heads and stomped their feet without drinking, Clay could tie them off knowing they had what they needed. He left them to their cool patch, pushing his way through the grimy, sweaty throng of shoppers, his eyes skittering from table vendors to stores. There were farmers and bakers and cobblers and people selling hats and clothes. A few folks stood on tall boxes to yell proclamations at the passing crowds, some preaching the Word of the Lord while others shared their unpopular opinions on rekindling the War of Northern Aggression.

Clay ignored the politicos. Harland fought during the war and had actually survived two separate gunshot wounds over his four-year enlistment—one in his biceps and one in his leg. He was lucky he still had all his limbs, though the leg gave him trouble from time to time, leaving him with an awkward gait. He didn't discuss his war experiences much, but when he did, he said no sane person would court war if they really understood what it was like to see their friends blown to bits.

As Clay had spent half of his teenage years holed up with his grandmother, great aunt, and female cousins in Missouri, he was none-too-anxious to see the war years return. He hated Missouri; summer months there were like living in a sweaty armpit.

Clay abandoned the main drag for something less claustrophobic. The side streets were so narrow they were barely big enough for an ambling boy with his hands in his belt, never mind a hauling cart or proper carriage. The store fronts were rundown, some the victims of war-time looting, others the victim of bad placement in an otherwise bustling downtown area. Cobwebs hung from the dilapidated infrastructure like ghostly veils.

He was peering at a web twice as big as his head when something silver flashed from the corner of his eye. It was a gloomy place, dark and creaky. Nothing should have caught the light like that, and he walked toward the shiny thing, his hand hovering above his six-shooter. His father had just given it to him on his last birthday, had just allowed Clayton to wear it on his hip in public. It'd come with all of the appropriate lectures about responsibility and manhood, and—remembering the speeches—Clay eased down, thinking himself ridiculous for reaching for it in the first place.

Until he felt the hum. It sent tingles down his body, his toes curling in his boots as the hair along the back of his neck prickled to standing. His hand went right back to the gun, fingers slipping around the grip and squeezing.

Mama'd told him nine years ago that because he was her son, he was special, and that he'd see things and do things other boys couldn't. Her promise hadn't manifested in spontaneous levitation or the ability to blast fire out of his ass like childhood Clayton had hoped, but rather with an extra sense. He could feel magic. He knew when something near him or around him was made of magic, casting magic, or had recently been saturated with magic. And following that shiny silver light had put him in proximity to the otherworldly.

His reaction to it was neither good nor bad in the same way that sneezing was neither good nor bad. The lead-up to the sneeze wasn't pleasant, but there was relief when you actually expelled the air and spittle. This was similar. The magic made him tense, but once he got past the initial discomfort, the thrum wasn't awful. It flowed over him like invisible water, like a layer of moving air that slipped beneath his clothes to glide across his skin.

Another flash of silver careened across the street. Clay followed it, his hand gentle on the weapon but ready to pull if necessary. He shouldn't pursue the magical whatever-it-was, but Clay'd always been too curious for his own good. It was how he'd gotten kicked in the head by his father's dapple gray when he was twelve, and how he'd lost his virginity to the Thomasville girl back in Saint Louis when he was fifteen. She was two years older and had quite the snaggletooth, and the moment the lights went down at the Spring Planter's Ball, she'd dragged him back to her father's hayloft so she could play leap frog on his cock for the better part of the night.

He remembered that girl fondly. Sort of. He'd forgotten her name, but that wasn't the point. The point was sometimes risks were worth taking, like following the magic to see where it went.

Clayton Jenson went where the tingling took him.

He looked both ways so he wouldn't be run over by midday Atlanta traffic. The magic was stronger now, closer, and he let the buzzing sensation lead him into another alley diagonal from the one he'd just abandoned. It wasn't as dark or as run down as its predecessor; the sun was able to creep in over a low-rise roof. There was a trellis above, a cross-section of hacked lumber that intersected in a series of big diamonds. Hanging from the overlaps of the beams were bottles of various shapes and sizes, each tied off with twine around its neck. It resulted in a splash of colors and diamond across the opposing wall, which is where he discovered the source of his magic.

Standing behind a booth with strange, metal devices surrounding her was the most beautiful girl in the world—at least in his estimation. She was no taller than his chin, with hair to her hips that started as white-blond at her scalp but turned ice-blue by the tips. Her skin was ivory, her eyes the gray of thundering skies. She had a narrow nose, a chin with a tiny cleft in it, and a naturally rosy mouth, her lips plump and tipped into a gamine grin.

She was dressed strange—strange for this weather anyway—with black gloves that stretched to her upper arms. Black lace covered her from chin to chest, though the dress went to gray satin at her bosom and fell to the ground in thick silk layers.

"Aren't you hot?" Clay asked in greeting.

If the girl was offended by his candor, she hid it well, her lips parting to reveal a line of perfectly straight teeth. "No. Are you, Puppy?" She had a lovely voice, a little deeper than most women, but feminine all the same. There was a music to her words that he liked very much—she had an accent he couldn't quite place, but then, he wasn't the worldliest person. It was European for sure, possibly British, but there was a little trill on her Rs that suggested something else. Scottish, maybe. Or perhaps Irish.

"I ain't no dog," Clay said, looking down at his boots so he wasn't stupefied by her beauty. He knew she was magic, but what type of magic? He didn't know a whole lot about the weirds, only that they came in all shapes and sizes and couldn't be trusted like normal folk, but he'd heard enough about his mother's people to suspect that this girl was something fae. She was too pretty to be real. Most fairy creatures used glamour to some degree—they were born with the ability to enhance or alter their appearances however they wished. The really talented ones added an allure component to it, too, making them hypnotic to those fortunate—or unfortunate—enough to look upon them.

Armed with that knowledge, Clay braced for the fairy's worst. Harland Jenson had raised no fool, and though the girl had a pretty set of melon-sized... eyes, there was no way Clayton would fall prey to fairy chicanery.

She leaned over the table, tilting her head so she could peer under the brim of his hat. "No, you're far too pretty to be a dog, but let's just say you're not ripe yet. A few more years and you'll break every heart you stumble across."

"Doubt that. I'm too skinny." He looked away from her mostly so he could remember how to breathe right, and that was when he spotted the bizarre *thing* on the ground. Shaped like some weird rodent and only six inches tall, it appeared to be constructed of multiple layers of hammered silver. Flaps of leather jutted out from under its arms, and at its middle was a glass shield that allowed a glimpse of cog-and-gear guts.

He stooped to get a better look. When it did nothing except continue to lie on the dusty ground, its green-gem eyes staring blankly ahead, he picked it up. It was light despite the mechanism's insides, and he ran his fingers over the curve of the glass to see if the panel opened for a better examination.

The girl tutted at him from behind the table.

“Be careful with Frederick. He gets sour if you handle him too long,” she said.

“Frederick?”

“The squirrel.”

“So that’s what it is.” He turned it over, and sure enough, there was a big “fluffy” tail on the backside made of metal wiring and pale brown hides. Metal discs attached to the back of its head, too, like someone had fashioned a pair of ears for it. “Now I can see it. Looks like a squirrel this way.”

“I think you’ve insulted me. Yes, Frederick’s a squirrel. What else would he be? A flying rat? A flapping possum? “

Clay shrugged. “I dunno. Some fairy creature. It’s what you are, ain’t it?”

“What? A fairy or a creature?” she asked dryly.

“Fairy.”

“Sarcasm’s not your strength, is it?” She plucked the squirrel from his hands to place it at the edge of her table, tail-side pointed in his direction. He wasn’t sure if that was an unsubtle kiss off, but he wasn’t going to worry about it neither. If she wanted him to go away, she’d make herself clear. Shyness didn’t seem to be part of her repertoire.

“And to answer your question, yes. I am a fairy—not that it’s any of your business,” she said.

“Guess it ain’t none, no.” He focused on the rock between the toes of his boots instead of on her pretty face. He wanted to look at her. Deep in his bones he had the need, but he was afraid to, too, like she’d steal his soul for her own if her stormy eyes caught his for too long.

“Oh, don’t mope now.” Before he could move away, she reached for him, her gloved fingertips gliding over his biceps. Contact was electric, a zap of lightning to his magically-saturated skin. He recoiled, actually stumbling back and conking his head against one of the overhead bottles. He whacked it away and pretended he didn’t notice when it swung right back to bounce off his hat two and three more times.

“Dang, girl. Give a boy some warning.” It was shameful how good her touch had felt, and he wasn’t sure if he should be embarrassed by the twinge in his pants-giblets or not. Stupid fairy probably knew exactly what she'd done to him. His mama said most of them were immoral perverts with insatiable appetites.

Well, Ma said it like that. Harland said that's why he married his mother in the first place.

"Sorry. Didn't expect you to jump high enough to touch the sky." She smiled and started fiddling with the buckles on her corset. He said nothing, just watching how her ministrations made her roundy plump parts jiggle in a most pleasing way. She pulled a pocket watch from a fold of dress fabric, the edges adorned with decorative wire wrap and lacy filigree. It was real fancy, like she'd bought it in a jeweler's shop, and that made him think she was rich. Richer than he was anyway.

"And what are you, if I may ask?" As quickly as she'd brought out the watch, it was hidden away beneath a corset flap. "To see through my glamour? There must be something different about you."

"Oh. My mama's a fairy. Sidhe." He took a deep breath and lifted his face, fixing his attention on the bridge of her nose. "I can sense magic. Chased after something silver and found you. Felt you." He frowned down at the squirrel, wondering if that's what he'd seen flashing a few minutes back. "That explains how you found me, but not how you saw through my glamour. Is my hair blue or blond right now?"

"Both."

She frowned at that, her tongue slicking out to wet her bottom lip. He tried hard not to notice how it made the rosy flesh sparkle in the sunlight. And failed. At this rate, he'd have to repurpose his Stetson to cover his lap. This girl was good at genital unrest.

"I don't know how to feel about that. You'd give my sister heart palpitations, that's for certain. She prides herself on her glamour." She reached out to tap his nose, and he reared away. Her fingertip glided beneath his chin instead, and he felt his heart go thick in his chest as another surge of shock-contact boiled his blood. He felt his flush stretch from his cheeks to his ears.

Clay shrugged, unsure of what to say and unable to say it anyway thanks to the lump in his throat. The girl flounced down into a fabric-covered chair, her hand reaching beneath her table to retrieve a tall, frosted glass of lemonade. He had no idea how she'd gotten ice to rim the edge—maybe more of her fairy magic—but he had a sneaking suspicion that whatever spell effect was keeping the drink cool also worked on her body. Otherwise, her heavy clothes would be unbearable in a southern summer. She was twice as dressed as any other woman he'd passed on the street, and they all looked close to expiring.

"Thirsty?" She offered him a sip, and he shook his head, concentrating on her goods instead of the comeliness of her person.

The gizmos were far less unnerving than the woman hawking them. Metal something-or-others covered the tabletop, the bases circular with long, skinny rods rising from their centers. The heads had three menacingly-curved blades, but they didn't look like any weapon he'd seen before.

Perhaps they served a more practical purpose, like chopping vegetables or slicing pieces of meat.

"You should buy one," she said as he reached for one of the devices. The metal was surprisingly cool against his fingers for such a warm afternoon. "For insulting Frederick. I made him, too, you know."

"What is it?"

"I call them wind machines. Behold." She put her lemonade aside and reached for a dish of flat, rounded rocks—the kind he'd skipped down the stream when he was a kid. She placed one at the base of his machine, and the next thing he knew, the blades at the top of her creation spun. He was afraid it'd slice his face to bits, and he stretched his arms out so he didn't sacrifice his nose to her ingenuity, but then he felt it—the current of air—and he froze. It was weak at first, but it quickly grew in intensity as the blades whirled faster, making a whomphing noise with every rotation. Subtle breeze became a gusting wind, and he felt the sweat along his temples dry.

It was glorious.

He narrowed his eyes and smiled, enjoying the relief, until she reached out to snatch the rock from the plate and the blades died. He frowned and peered at the thing, wanting to shake it to make it go again, but clearly the rock acted as a catalyst. "How much?"

"For the machine? Fifty cents." She held up the rock. "For this? A dollar."

"A dollar!? For a rock?"

"'A rock,' he says. What rocks can do this, hmm?" And he watched as she took her rocks from the basket to put them on the flat metal bases of the wind machines. They all blazed to life, their combined power enough to make his clothes ripple around his body. He'd been in one of those nasty wind storms once, the type that ripped up fences and tore roofs off barns. This reminded him of that, especially when his trousers were pelted with alley dirt and the bottles above his head swayed on their strings.

The girl looked terribly satisfied with herself, like a sale was assured. The problem was, Clay's father's warnings about fairies rang in his head. He put the first device back onto the table, smiled at her, and then feigned snatching a rock from one of the plates in the middle of her collection. He didn't actually take it, instead easing one from the plate closest to him. He watched the machines for an immediate change, and sure enough, the fan he pretended to take the rock from dwindled while the other kept on going.

The little liar.

"Think I'm gonna have to pass," Clay said, holding up the rock so she could see it. He pointed down at the plate he feigned stealing from and then the other he actually stole from. "Your eyes might be blue, but they oughta be brown, if you know what I mean." He tossed the rock back at the device and watched all of them die out one after another, the breeze fading with them.

The girl's chin lifted and her hands sailed to her hips, agitation evident in the rigidity of her spine and the deep V of her pale eyebrows. "Just who do you think you are?"

Clay shrugged and ran his sweaty palms down over his trousers. "Man keeping his money, I suppose. Nothin' more."

"More like a baby keeping his money. And now I get to live with the knowledge that an infant outsmarted me." She scowled at him, and then looked away, her nose crinkling in distaste. "Twit. Handsome twit, but a twit all the same. Oberon's balls."

"Well, this baby should get moseying. You have a good day now," Clay said, tipping his hat. He'd have liked to banter more or ask her to socialize later someplace they could get cozy, but that was probably overreaching. She was annoyed for one, and she was probably some decades older than him for two; his mama was real old but looked a human thirty. Fairies lived a real long time.

He'd just turned back for town when she snatched his wrist again, her fingers manacling and sending sizzle shocks along his arm. He winced, lifting his head to peer at her, trying to ignore the pleasure-pain radiating through his lean body. Her expression had shifted, her annoyance replaced by something else.

Assessment, maybe? Reluctant approval?

Maybe I'm not overreaching? She's confusing.

"A clever puppy. I like that. I don't find too many men that can keep up with me, never mind outsmart me." She'd started stroking the back of his hand with her gloved fingers, but a loud, barked "CORA" from the other end of the alley made her flinch. She jerked away, and Clay ran his palm over the skin where they'd touched.

A handsome, silver-haired man with a curved mustache and big guns walked their way, or more appropriately, jingled their way thanks to his spurs. The fancy way he dressed, the newness of his hat made Clay feel self-conscious about his own appearance, and he fidgeted with his shirt to tuck it flat into his pants. The stranger eyed him and then the girl behind the counter, his thumbs dug into his trouser pockets.

"What are you doing, Cora?" The man smiled when he asked the question, but it didn't quite reach his turquoise-blue eyes. Clay could tell by the creases around the man's lips and across his brow that he wasn't all that happy to see her—or, for that matter, Clayton with her.

"I was demonstrating my machines to my friend," she said.

"Were you now?" The man turned to look at Clayton, tipping his head back so he could give Clay a steady once-over. "And what's your friend's name?"

"Clayton. Clayton Jenson," Clay said, right as the girl said, "Donald Evans." The silver-haired man smirked, the fingers of one hand tracing along the curve of his mustache, the other hand splaying over his middle like he was holding his guts inside.

Wouldn't want to soil them finely-polished boots, Clay supposed.

The man extended the mustache hand to Clay for a shake. "Well, Clayton Jenson, let me introduce myself. My name's Sterling Cole." The man pulled his black coat aside to show off a shiny silver star on the lapel of his vest. "Marshal Sterling Cole. And this fine piece of work seated across from us is Cora. Or Nancy. Or Pearl depending on the day. And she is a charlatan. So, while I'm plenty glad to make your acquaintance, might I suggest you get rambling while the rambling's good? Or, to be more frank—" He paused to give Cora a disapproving scowl. "—while your pockets are still full."

The girl sniffed and tipped her pert nose in the air. "I preferred Donald," was all she said, and Clay felt the heat returning to his face. Standing before the marshal made him feel like his Pa had called him on the rug for misbehaving. He was a man of eighteen, not eight, damn it, and if he hadn't been associating with this little criminal, he wouldn't be in this situation.

"I gotta get back to my mules," Clayton said, spinning on his heel and leaving the alley without a second glance.

"Have a good day, son," the marshal said to his back.

"Nice to make your acquaintance, Puppy! Why don't you come back when you've got a few more years on you? We'll go out sometime, all right?"

Clay didn't answer. Hell if he knew what to say to a woman like that.

CHAPTER THREE

NOW

The blond man with his red satin clothing was terrible at poker. This was a good and bad thing. Good for the obvious reason that Clay had taken a few dollars off him over the course of two hours. Bad because that meant if he wasn't a poker player, he was at that table for another reason, and not knowing why ruffled Clay's feathers. Betsy was friendly before she'd gone and cursed him, too.

As his father liked to say, "Fool me once, shame on you. Fool me twice, shame on me." Clayton was done being a fool.

He didn't see the harm in playing the night through, though. He was confident enough in his quick-draw skills that if the skinny shitheel tried anything suspect, Clay could put a hole between his eyes without too much trouble. Even with Eagle's top shelf whiskey swilling around his gut, he was a better shot than everyone there—on that he'd put money. Spending his formative years in Missouri shooting bottles off fence toppers and keeping the seasonal help from humping the ewes paid off in surprising ways.

"Fold," Jasper said, throwing his cards down in disgust.

Roger followed suit, pulling a watch from the confines of his vest to check the time. "I ought to get home before my wife accuses me of losing our savings to Marshal Jenson. Again."

Clay eyed his cards. Aces over eights, Hickok's dead man's hand right down to the spades and clubs. It was the very definition of irony. He'd met Hickok once, right after the old man's sight started to give out and he'd gone full-time gambler. He was a cantankerous bastard, and a liar to boot, but Clay had liked him enough to play a few hands with him. That was one day Clay lost hard, mostly 'cause Hickok spent so much time talking that Clay'd been too busy listening to tall tales to pay attention to the game.

Good strategy, that. Clay'd used it a few times since.

Clayton lifted his eyes to the stranger, trying to get a read on him. The blond looked left at Roger, who was gathering up his change and dumping it into his pocket, and then right at the recently vacated seat of the banker. He squirmed in his seat like he had a weasel wedged up his ass. Clay took that to mean he had something decent, but was too craven to ante up. Seemed the shiny gentleman needed a little encouragement. Or a kick in the pants. Whichever came easier.

"You in or out? I'm getting old over here," Clay said, gnawing on the stub of the cigarette smoldering between his lips. The stranger peered at him awhile before sighing and throwing his cards on the table, his frail shoulders lifting in what was supposed to be a frustrated shrug, except the frustration never reached his eyes. The sly son of a bitch didn't give two damns that he'd just given away a pile of money.

What should have been an uncomplicated poker game had officially gotten complicated.

Clay dropped his cards and collected his last pot. By his estimation, he'd tripled what he'd put down tonight, but he couldn't relish the victory. He was too busy inspecting the stranger. If he concentrated, he could feel the subtle magic riding that body. There weren't a lot of ways to hide like that—weirdly, it took *more* magic to appear *less* magical. It was a layering effect of spells or glamours over the aura. Marie'd explained it to him once, and he'd nodded like he'd understood, but he'd walked away from the exchange no wiser than, "It's complicated stuff." And this stranger was complicated stuff. A quiet thrum emanated off of him, which meant Clay was picking up on a subtlety spell instead of an actual magical imprint.

It was perfume over a bad stench, and just like perfume over a bad stench, once you got past the flowery bullpucky, you couldn't ignore the rank reality.

"Where you from?" Clay demanded.

"Oh, here and there. You know. A migrant." The man's smile was as tepid as whorehouse bath water. "Alabama most recently. Florida before that."

"That so?" Clay stood from his chair, his fingers reaching out to trace over the hooked iron handle of the lantern on the table. The stranger followed his hand with his eyes and flinched.

Clay knew right then what kind of weird he was dealing with: fairy for sure. Probably one Cora sent to finish the deal. Fae didn't like iron. It burned them raw on the outside, and, from what Cora told him, melted their insides if it got past the skin. Clay was lucky—his human blood trumped his fairy blood and he could touch the stuff, but he'd seen what it had done to Cora's fingertips when she worked with it. He reckoned if he swung this lamp around, this fairy would sizzle like bacon on a fry-pan as soon as he was struck.

Clayton was in a foul enough mood that he was tempted to do it on basic principle, but that'd just leave a mess for Eagle later, and Clay'd like the barkeep to think of him fondly, not as that asshole marshal who'd mucked up his floors.

"Why don't you tell me what you're doing in town, stranger?" Clay picked up the lantern and let it drop back onto the table with a thud. The fairy jumped, and Clayton dug the last of his cigarette into the ashtray on the table edge. "Gonna be real honest—I've had a pisser of a day. I'm half-tempted to shove this thing down your throat and watch you writhe."

"It seems I've overstayed my welcome. Thank you kindly for the cards." The stranger stood so fast, his chair toppled to the floor behind him. The moment he turned for the door, Clayton's hand dove for his holster to retrieve what was technically a gun, but was probably more appropriately called a hand cannon.

Gayle.

Gayle was the gun Cora crafted for Clayton two years ago, and there wasn't another like it in the world. Double-barreled and weighted just right, Gayle was all dark, gleaming wood, gold filigree around the grip, and special mechanisms. Cora claimed the mechanisms made the weapon more accurate, and though Clay didn't know jack or squat about science, he had to admit it was the finest thing he'd ever owned. It was big, but not so big he couldn't use it in close quarters, and the brass lens along the top helped him with distance shots. He could shoot a leprechaun's pecker off from a mile away with it.

He pressed the barrels to the base of the slight man's skull. "You move one crotch hair and I'll splatter bits you didn't know you had across the floor. Who are you?"

Every muscle in the man's body tensed. "I'm sorry. Don't—I'll go."

"You're stuck now, Slick Ear. Your glamour's good—real good. Too good to be nobody, so that means you're somebody. Question is who? Ain't no house brownie, that's for damned sure."

"Hey, White Man," Eagle said, his voice deceptively mild. "You need me to close shop?"

From the corner of his eye, Clay saw Eagle walk around the bar. The barkeep had his own shotgun aimed at the stranger's back, his red towel tossed casually over his shoulder. Nothing said loyalty like a willingness to kill someone just 'cause Clayton looked like he might.

"Depends on what the slick ear says. Better yet, depends on who Slick Ear is. Show yourself, Fairy."

"Fairy?" Eagle asked. "Like, from the fae lands?"

"You bet. This one's gussied himself up in normal skin." Roger and Jasper still milled around the door, their faces studies in morbid fascination. Clay lifted his free hand to shoo them off, and they both nodded, but neither of them seemed all that interested in vacating.

They walked outside and turned the corner to peer in through the windows, Roger's puffy, red face distorted in the wavy glass panes.

Even Lola'd crept upstairs at the first sign of trouble, but instead of squirreling herself away in her room, she had knocked on Delilah's door to let the madam know something was amiss. Both of them leaned over the second-story railing, their pale bosoms threatening to spill over the tops of their threadbare gowns. Neither of them bothered to tuck their areolas away, which Clay would have appreciated had he not been contemplating murder.

Clay jabbed the stranger in the red suit with Gayle again, right at the top of his spine, and the man jumped, his hands flying up into the air as he whimpered. "Don't, Clay. Stop. Please."

Clay tilted his head at the familiar use of his name. "Clay? So we know each other now? 'Cause I'm fair-sure we ain't been properly introduced."

"Oh, shut up. I came to check on you, you ingrate. I'd have been quite content to leave it alone if you'd left it alone." It was amazing how the newcomer's sentence transformed. The beginning part was said in a tenor that turned into a soft alto at "shut" and then a soprano by "ingrate." Gone, too, was the southern drawl, the speech now Boston American with a twist of Irish curl. The body changed thereafter. The fairy shortened, going from six feet to five, the red silk suit turning into a red silk dress that enveloped skin the color of moonlight. The short blond hair went gold, then brown, and finally ended in lush red locks that swayed around broad, curvy hips. Her ears elongated slightly, the tips going pointed at the top and tilting away from her face.

She didn't even need to turn around—there was no mistaking that particular hair or that particular build. Adelaide WhisperWind was a one-in-a-million girl, and though she'd presented as a man not a half minute ago, now she was all wonderful woman with all the proper wonderful-woman parts associated therein.

Clay jerked the gun away to holster it. "Goddamn it, Addy. I nearly killed you. Why didn't you show yourself?"

"Because I'm Cora's sister and you two are squabbling? I figured it'd be best to keep a low profile. Or try to, anyway."

Clayton glanced at the men still staring into the window. Where before they'd been transfixed by the thrill of potential blood-spill, now they were transfixed by the vision of a short, fat Seelie girl with tits the size of wagon wheels and a face to rival Aphrodite herself. Clay shooed them off again, for all the good it did him. "Go on home to your wives. It's just Addy. I assure you, she ain't got nothing you two can handle." Roger managed to pull himself away, but Jasper continued to ogle right up to the point when Clayton jerked the Rattlesnake's drapes down to block his view. "Head on home, Jasper."

"Right. Yes. That woman was a man, Marshal," Jasper said from outside the saloon.

"I'm aware."

"Is that normal?"

Clayton eyeballed the short fairy. She'd crossed her arms over her chest, the posture squishing her fleshpillows together so they nearly touched her chin. Her eyes gleamed emerald fire and her cheeks were pink with flush. Addy was right-pissed, and for some reason, that comforted him. "Normal as Addy can be. Now go home."

—

Addy grabbed Clay's whiskey and poured herself a glass. She parked at his table without an invitation, too, like she had every right to take his drink and his seat because *they were such good friends, and wasn't this a lovely social visit*. Clay did like her, but she was right to be cautious around him; she was still Cora's sister, and circumstances being what they were, the timing of her arrival raised an eyebrow or two.

He circled to the other side of the table and spun a chair, straddling it with his arms over the backrest. His chin touched his forearms. His eyes peered at her from beneath his hat brim. "The hell are you doing here, Adelaide? You're a day out from Betsy Lynch laying a curse on me. Not gonna say I'm not glad to see you, but not gonna say it's not suspect timing. You've been gone for what… a year? Two?"

"Do you know how long I worked on that glamour? Months. MONTHS. And you tore through it. Cora said you were the best witchsniffer she'd ever met, but that's just plain ridiculous. You're ridiculous. I hate that about you." Addy took her whiskey shot and poured another one, her head shaking back and forth and sending those long locks tumbling around her arms like garnet silk.

"Glad you're listening to me," Clayton murmured, though he couldn't quite hide his smile. "Self-centered harlot. Any rate, take pride that I didn't know who you were right off. When Cora glamours herself, I see her, not her spell. You? I see the spell. Can just sense the underlying magic, too, is all."

"Small victories, I suppose, but I still think you're a brat. Now then, how about you admit you've missed me and give me some sugar?" Addy grinned and pursed her lips for a kiss she'd never get. Clayton certainly appreciated Adelaide's allure, but he knew when he was outclassed, and she was too much woman for him. She'd traveled the world for hundreds of years, had been the mistress of dukes, the paramour of emperors, and—last he heard—the concubine of an Arab prince. She claimed to have taught Giacomo Casanova himself the carnal arts, and from what Cora said, it wasn't idle boasting. Addy really had taught the Master of Fucking how to fuck.

It took a certain hugeness of ego to think one could venture into Addy's bed and emerge unscathed. Clayton Jenson was a brave man, an arrogant man most would say, but he was certain that even he would succumb to the man-devouring teeth that undoubtedly lurked inside Addy's well-traveled love tunnel.

She scared the hell out of him in the best way possible.

"It's a good thing I'm in love with your sister or I'd be a kissing fool right now," Clay said. "Mind, I'll probably have to shoot her next time I see her, but that don't change the fact I love her. 'Cause I'm not too smart."

Addy sat back in her seat, her rosebud mouth maintaining its cheeky smile. "And as much as I'd like to tie you into knots and ruin you for the rest of your days, I could never do that to Cora. Your friend, however—*who* is your friend? He's delicious."

Clay glanced at Eagle. The barkeep's gun remained pointed in Addy's direction, but thanks to how Clay'd seated himself, that meant it was pointed in his direction, too. Normally, Clay wouldn't mind it—he and Mistress Fortune used to have something of a torrid love affair going on. He left a lot of things to chance that other, more-cautious men couldn't ignore. But after what happened with Betsy that morning, he was pretty sure Fortune had packed her shit and moved on to greener pastures. He didn't need to up the ante on an already shitty day by courting a hole in the gut. "Stand down, Eagle. She's an old friend."

Hearing his name snapped Eagle out of his stupor. He retracted the gun and shook his head, his attention never leaving Adelaide. Unlike Jasper, who stared at Addy because he wanted to dive between her bosoms and bathe in her ocean of quivering flesh, Clayton knew Eagle well enough to say the man watched her because he was scared. It was obvious he hadn't seen fairy magic at work before, and with a pastor father preaching the word of God at him from the time he was dragging on the tit, he probably thought she was evil incarnate.

"You have strange friends, Marshal," Eagle said. "Some really, really strange friends."

Addy watched him slide behind the bar, a feral glint in her eye. She wriggled in her seat and patted her knee, her skin taking on an ethereal shimmer that highlighted the pink of her cheeks. "Aren't you cute? I could just eat you up like a buttery biscuit, and I have an *insatiable* appetite." Addy giggled, and that sent the whores in the balcony above her to tittering as well.

Clay'd almost forgotten about his precariously-dressed audience. He glanced up at them, surprised to see a half dozen girls lining the railing like a bouquet of dusky flowers. There'd been only Lola and Delilah to start, but now there was Scary Mary with her awful teeth, Jessica, Lizzie, and little Amy who looked far too young for her profession but was actually the oldest of the bunch. She was also the cleanest, which made her one of the local favorites.

"Who's the newcomer, Marshal?" Delilah called down, waving a hole-ridden handkerchief in Adelaide's direction. "Is she looking for a job? We'd make bundles of money with her."

Most women would be insulted at being mistaken for a trollop, but not Addy. She threw her head back and laughed, her hands slapping on the tabletop in front of her in delight. Her glamour faded, the dazzle of her magical allure absorbed back into her skin like lotion. Clay was glad for it. There was no resisting Addy when she had her love magic going, and he would have had to intervene on Eagle's behalf if she'd made a real play for him. He owed Constance that much—her cornbread was the best in the west. Handing her husband over to Addy for a night of carnal abuse was outright disrespect.

"I'm honored by your consideration, Lady Madam, but I'm afraid I must decline. I have to keep Clayton out of trouble in my sister's stead. I'll chat with you before I leave, though, hmm? See if I can't give you a few tricks to up your rates."

Delilah looked a little taken aback at Addy's insinuation that anyone could spread better'n she already did, but she was smart enough to keep it to herself. Delilah liked making money, and if the fairy knew something that'd help her do it more efficiently—even if it was quarter sucks and handjobs—she was all ears. "I'd be glad to discuss it with you. Over tea like real ladies, even."

"Make it bourbon and we have a deal."

Delilah smirked. "Sounds divine, Red. Come see me when you're done with the marshal."

The madam turned to shoo the girls into their respective rooms so they could prepare for the late-night rush, barking at all of them to "scrub their thatches 'cause men don't like dirty monkeys." That sent Addy into fresh giggle-snorts, and Clay had to snap his fingers under her nose to pull her attention back. She blinked at his hand before snapping at it, one of her sharper-than-normal canines nicking him on the side of his thumb.

"Ow! Why are all the women in your family bloodthirsty? Cora's gone and killed me and you're trying to cannibalize me."

Addy blinked at that, her smile fading to a solemn frown. "You mentioned a curse. What happened? Cora hasn't squeaked a word about anything."

Unless Addy'd taken up bullshitting since the last time he'd seen her, she had no idea what Cora'd done. He was willing to give her the benefit of the doubt—sure, she used glamour, but that was a different sort of untruthfulness. Bald-faced lying wasn't her thing. He lowered his voice to reiterate the dirty details, from how Betsy'd lured him over with a letter to the *Probably Stupid But Also Totally Justifiable* bullet he'd put between her eyes when she wouldn't reverse the curse.

"Well, isn't that utter shite? What are you going to do?" Addy reached for the back of his hand. The contact sent a shiver through his body that made him flinch. It wasn't the same as touching Cora. Cora was pure energy, an electric storm followed by a soft, undulating wind. Addy was cold air, like mountain-crest air that felt good in your lungs, but not necessarily on your skin.

He rubbed the spot to snuff the tingling. "Visiting a witch in Louisiana to see if she can fix me. Doc thinks Maybell will sic the rest of the sisters on me sooner or later, so I gotta get while the gettin's good. Plan on finding Cora and taking some of this out on her hide, too."

"When are you going?"

"I'd like to be out of here tomorrow morning, but that depends on Irene." Clay ran his fingers down the corners of his mouth and grunted. "Always waiting on her."

"Doc'll rush, don't you worry. As for Cora—" Addy took a deep breath and collapsed into her seat, her nose crinkled like she smelled something foul. "—I knew she could be vindictive, but I never would have guessed something like this. She was breathing fire after Little Rock, though. She couldn't even say your name without the skies going dark and lightning hitting—she burned down a church in Raleigh because I asked about you. Not on purpose, but you know how it gets when she's riled. It's why I came after you. I wanted to warn you that she had her temper up. I'm sorry I didn't get here sooner."

"No need to apologize. She did it, not you." He stood to stretch before sauntering over toward the bar. Little Eagle alternated between running his rag over the bottles lining his liquor shelves and casting suspicious glances Addy's way, but he managed to tear his gaze away from her when Clay leaned over the bar to offer a hand. "May our paths cross again, Little Eagle, but if they don't, take care of

Constance. Make an army of fat babies and promise to keep Delilah in line. She's a handful, that one."

Eagle hadn't heard what Clay'd said to Addy, which was how Clay'd wanted it, but that meant the weight of the goodbye took Eagle off guard. His dark brows dipped into a V, and he grimaced, his thin, brown fingers closing around Clay's paler, more-calloused ones. "I hope you'll make it back this way again, Marshal. It'll be strange having another asshole smelling up my corner stool."

"Hope to be back one day, my one-balled friend." Clay broke their hold to empty his pockets of poker winnings, crumpled bills and coins skittering over the polished surface of the bar. There had to be twenty dollars in total, but he found it a fitting tribute to his favorite saloon. Sad thing was it felt final, like that money was his swan song to everything he loved about Houston. The thought made his heart heavy, and he made for the door before his face could wear his strain.

"Clayton," Addy said from behind him.

"Yeah?"

"I'm going to talk to the Madam like I promised, but be a love and check on Montague for me? I'm two doors down from you on the right at the Whistling Widow. Number four. I'll be back before dawn so I have time to pack. I figure you'll want to leave before noon."

That lent him pause. He whirled on his heel, his spurs jangling as they struck the wooden floor below his feet. "What the hell's a Montague? And I don't recall inviting you along."

Addy stood and slapped at her red gown, smoothing the sides of her skirts until every layer fell in flowing rivers of silk to the floor. Her fingers trailed over the trim along her sleeves and bust, flattening the thick, ivory lace until it lay just right. "I don't recall asking to go, but that doesn't change the fact that I'm going. Cora's in a snit." She flashed him a blazing smile before flouncing her way toward the stairs. "And I am well-equipped to handle my sister's snits."

CHAPTER FOUR

EIGHT YEARS AGO

Harland Jenson stood shirtless on his porch deck, his suspenders hanging around his hips, his gray-flecked chest-hair matted to his torso with sweat. He removed his hat to fan his face as he barked orders at his eldest child and only son. "Keep your hands in your pockets so you won't get robbed. No loose women or you'll get itchers. No guns, and for God's sake, tie off your horse somewhere you can see it. Don't want no one taking off with it."

"Twenty years old, Pa. Not twelve. Go take care of Mama."

Clayton hauled himself into the saddle with a grunt. Ever since his mother'd come back from the fairy lands a year ago, his father'd begun talking to him like a kid again. It wasn't really Harland's fault—he was just parroting his wife—but between the two of them, Clay grew more and more convinced it was time to strike out on his own. His mama, Lucille, left when Clay was still short enough to tuck his head against her shoulder. When she returned, her son was five inches taller than her and had a shadow of whiskers on his chin. He smoked and drank and had women throwing their ankles over their heads whenever they saw the chiseled lines of his face and the blue of his eyes. Lucille did her best to come to terms with his adulthood, but sometimes, she couldn't quite wrap her mind around the lost years.

The overbearing parenting was annoying, but Clay didn't feel right complaining about it, mostly 'cause Ma just spit out his first and likely only sibling. Elise was born the first day of spring, and though he'd been fairly horrified his fairy mother still had her breeding chops at who-knew-how-old, the moment he set eyes on the perfect, pointy-eared bundle of pink fury she'd launched from her loins, he'd shut his mouth.

Clay guided Gus toward the road with a squeeze of his knees. The ugly, old horse was plenty strong despite his twenty years, but Clay didn't push him too hard out of respect for their two decades of companionship. Well, that and Clay liked to think if he was easy on Gus, Gus'd be easy on him and not bite a chunk out of his shoulder when he turned his back. It wasn't true—the horse had near ripped off his ear only last month—but Clay was an optimist. An idiot, maybe, but an optimist all the same.

The Georgia summer was hotter than Hades already, and it was only June, but he could look forward to it cooling off after sundown. Normally, Clay'd be wandering any which way but the city at this time of the day, but there was a special carnival visiting the outskirts of town he didn't want to miss. It was one of those controversial affairs that got a bunch of locals in an uproar about the "inherent indecency of such a debauched form of entertainment," which translated to Clayton as a hell of a good time. Not because he loved carnivals and the weird, freakish things they encompassed—fact was he'd never been to a carnival—but because *it got him out of the goddamned house.*

Anything that saved him a night of being talked to like he was eight years old had to be worthwhile.

It only took him an hour to get to the carnival grounds. For a penny, Clay could tie Gus to a fence with the other smelly horses and wander the tent-and-torchlight village the travelers erected for their show. This carnival thing was more organized than Clay'd anticipated, but the ratty-looking horse-handler with the lopsided mustache assured him that this was a *lee-git-o-mite* business venture, that the exhibitors were people who'd worked with P.T. Barnum himself up in New York. As Clay'd never had the opportunity to be morally affronted by Mr. Barnum before, it sounded like a right fine shindy.

They were set up on a flat, green field just outside of Atlanta proper. It was a rainbow-colored townscape complete with walkways, vendor tables, and a couple of stages near the northern and southern exits. The workers were dressed in garish costumes that looked good from afar, but up close, Clay could see they were faded and in need of a good wash. There were patches sewn onto the elbows of their outfits and the heels of their shoes could use a good cobbler.

It was the most threadbare glitz and glamour he'd ever seen.

Clay started on the eastern side of the camp, entertaining himself with the freaks of nature tent first. Inside, looking bored and hot, was a two-headed calf. Next to it was a six-legged pony, and next to that was a pair of conjoined twins who were singing a duet and playing fiddles. There were a couple of little people standing on boxes for good measure, too—one of them putting on some comedy act with a trained monkey, the other dressed like Lincoln and performing magic tricks.

As Clay passed the last row of exhibits—green-tinged jars filled with nature gone wrong, mostly—his skin prickled at the telltale rush of nearby magic. It was outside of the tent, along his left side somewhere, and Clay froze as he recognized that particular flavor of weird. It was *her*. It was that girl who'd pitched him the fraudulent wind machine a couple years back. Every magic felt a little different when he first sensed it—his mother's was warm and smelled like roses, which she attributed to being the descendent of a love goddess—but the girl was the air before a storm. It was stillness and electricity, and he found his feet shuffling her way before he could talk himself out of it.

There was no doubt in Clayton's mind that it was stupid to seek out a conwoman, but the girl was beautiful, which put the brain in his head and the brain in his pants distinctly at odds with each other. Acknowledging that fact did nothing. He ducked around two rows of screeching showmen to find the northern stage, looking at signs as tall as his own person that advertised "Private Dances from The Sultan's Jewel! A Nickel for the Dance of Seven Veils!" One of the posters showed a woman dressed in foreign garb, a bunch of silk scarves hanging from her waist to flit around purple slippers curved at the toes. She wore a strange gold top that covered her breasts, but showed off a scandalous expanse of midriff. A veil covered the lower half of The Jewel's face, but he could see sultry eyes lined in heavy kohl above them. Her hair was covered by a weave of colorful ribbons that fell from an ornate, gilded headdress decorated with peacock feathers and gemstones.

The Sultan's Jewel was not his conwoman.

The announcer sashaying her way onto the stage, however...

"GENTLEMEN, GATHER 'ROUND TO SEE A MYSTERY OF THE EAST UNVEILED—" She paused to waggle her eyebrows for effect. "—for your pleasure! She's traveled the world and graced the couches of king and commoner alike! She's been a concubine of a grand sultan and knows *all* the secrets of the Orient. From the heat of the Sahara desert all the way to our great Confederate Georgia, The Sultan's Jewel dances for your pleasure. Come, see her exotic charms, and know that you set your eyes upon the most glorious flesh in the world!"

Clay felt himself shoved forward as a few dozen men gathered near the stage. By the way their lecherous eyes looked past the announcer to the thick, purple curtains behind her, he presumed the blond had glamoured herself plain. He couldn't tell for sure because he could see past her magic, but no red-blooded man would dismiss such a pretty woman, not even with the promise of a concubine swinging her jubblies around.

Cora looked almost exactly as he remembered, and didn't that just make his chest go tight, like there wasn't enough air to be breathed? Her hair swayed around her hips in gentle, blue-tipped waves. She wore a white blouse that opened at her neck, the voluminous sleeves cinched above the elbows with black leather straps and bronze buckles. Her red skirts belled out from her hips to swish around her feet while she paced the stage, her finger wagging as she addressed the impatient masses.

"Are you ready for the dance of a lifetime, Gentlemen!?" When the crowd roared, she tilted her head back to cackle and shout. "I can't hear you, SIRS!" Clay nearly clapped his hands over his ears to block out the shrill whistling of the watchers to his sides. They were worked into a tizzy, their energy frantic and dangerously wild, as if they'd tear the stage apart to see the promised prize if she made them wait. The blond was smart enough to stop dallying. She waved her arms toward the curtain as reedy instruments wailed from the colorful backdrop.

A thick, velvet drape inched up to reveal a short, fat girl wearing diaphanous pink pants, a half-vest with gold trim, and about twenty veils hanging from a coin-laden belt at her waist. Unlike the picture, The Sultan's Jewel showed her hair for this performance, and it was garnet red—thick and silky and gleaming purple in the sunset. The moment she swayed toward the men, all sound stopped save for the music. The cheering cut short as the girl turned her eyes upon the crowd, her arms weaving hypnotically above her head. He felt the dancer's fairy magic for the first time then—similar to the blond's, but colder, too—and so much stronger than anything he'd encountered before.

He flinched away, frowning.

The Sultan's Jewel was hypnotic not only because she was a living, breathing embodiment of every earthly desire a man could have, but because she was glamouring them—all of them. There had to be almost three dozen men in attendance, and this new, strange fairy wound them around her fingers like threads on a weaver's loom. Clay tilted his head back to eye the crowd and saw a stupefied mass swaying in time to her movements, each of them standing with their mouths agape, their eyes glazed over in lusty appreciation.

Which is why they didn't notice the silver, flying thing. Clay caught the flash as it whirled around the last row of spectators. It jumped from man to man, twinkling like a star as it hovered waist-high and then dropped to boot level, only to fly back up right afterward. Clay watched it sweep to and fro, recalling how he'd followed a similar light the first time he met Cora—if that was her real name—at her table of wind machines.

He narrowed his eyes and the thing went still, like it sensed him watching. Clay stooped to get a better look, but the moment he edged the tiniest bit closer, the shiny ball sailed away and hid behind a farmer's legs. Clay straightened again, afraid to scare away whatever it was. He suspected Cora's goddamned squirrel, but he wouldn't know for sure unless it came nearer, and it wouldn't come nearer unless he pretended to ignore it.

Clay alternated between watching the woman undulating on the stage, her hips shimmying and her arms waving above her head in twisting spirals, and the silver light. It was bizarre, but he found the latter more enthralling—knowing the redheaded woman was glamouring everyone made her less interesting. It was cheating, and he wasn't a fan of cheats.

A minute later and the mystery thing ventured out again. It leapt for the front row, attaching itself to a man three bodies down from Clayton. It worked its way from his waist to his boot, swooping and soaring in long, fluid arcs. It was now close enough for Clay to discern its features, and his eyes widened in surprised recognition. It was the squirrel—that silly silver toy that Cora claimed to have made. The creature was scaling up pants legs, so light that no one could feel it, and pulling out paper money from pockets. Once the little thief absconded with a dollar bill and opened its mouth to propel the rumpled contraband down its throat.

It would inevitably wait for elegant gloved hands to empty its contents. It was another con. The dancing was a way to distract people while the squirrel robbed them blind.

Clay frowned and watched the stage, his hands wedging into his pockets to keep a grip on his money. He felt a faint swish along the hem of his pants a moment later, and he looked down in time to see the animal scaling the seam of his trousers. It could have easily been mistaken for a twist of wind, especially by a bunch of men transfixed by pale, glowing flesh. Clay peered at the creature, and upon locking its green-gemmed eyes with his, it froze. Its metal disc-ears tilted back on the hinges, reminding Clay of a scared cat. He reached down to swipe at it, hoping to call attention to what it had been doing, but before he could get his hand out from his pocket, the squirrel jumped for the dusty ground to bob its way behind the wooden platform of the stage.

"Little thief," he muttered under his breath.

Imagine his surprise when a deep, familiar voice from behind him said, "Ain't she, though?"

—

Sterling Cole looked much the same as Clayton remembered—a well-tailored suit jacket, a matching hat, and new boots. The last time they'd crossed paths, the marshal wore black from head-to-toe and somewhat resembled a preacher, but this time he wore pale gray that brought out the gleam in his silver hair and mustache. His shirt was starched white, his guns shiny and black in their holsters. He had a very polished, sophisticated demeanor, save for one small thing Clayton couldn't quite overlook—a woven hemp ring on his index finger that looked like it had seen better days. The edges were black with grime.

The marshal spit between his teeth, very nearly catching Clay in the ear, and Clay stepped to the side to avoid any future sprays. "Fancy meeting you here again. It was Jenson, wasn't it? Clayton Jenson?"

"Yes. Good to see you again, Marshal." Clay tipped his hat and cast his eyes down, feeling like he'd been caught doing something wrong. He was innocent—it was the danged squirrel—but if he said that, he'd probably sound like a crazy person. "Didn't know you were an Atlanta fixture."

"I'm not. I'm Cora's shadow—where she goes, I go. Trying to save the world from her sticky fingers, but she's hard to catch. She running the squirrel again I take it? Little bugger's a damned good pickpocket." Clay knew he should nod or say "yes," but his eyes swept up to the stage first. He looked past the beautiful redhead to the blond in the back, who lingered near the curtains with a self-satisfied smile playing around her lips. He ought to screech her crime to the heavens, but for reasons he didn't like to think about, he hesitated, his tongue thick in his mouth.

Sterling laughed and clapped a hand on his shoulder, giving it an encouraging squeeze. "It's all right, son. I think you can see now why she's so damned elusive. But that gal up there's run cons as far north as Boston and as far south as Baton Rouge, and I've never been able to pin a single one on her. So do yourself a favor and put a lock on your heart or she'll run away with that, too. She's merciless."

Clay snorted and immediately regretted it; sweet smoke wafted from the stage. The lanterns along the stage's edge had oil in them, and the air smelled like heavy, spiced vanilla. "She's a damned fairy. I know better. My ma's a fairy, and I love her, but she's real honest about her folks. Troublemakers." Clay waved a finger at the redhead. She was bowing to her audience, but the audience was too enthralled thanks to her magic to do anything other than gaze at her adoringly. "She is, too. Fae, I mean. She's using glamour. It's why everyone here's slack-jawed and drooling."

The marshal reached into his jacket to pull out a flat, wooden container with his initials embossed in the top. He opened it to offer Clay a pre-rolled cigarette, which Clay gratefully accepted. "They're slack-jawed and drooling 'cause Adelaide's gorgeous, though I won't deny that the glamour helps. She's Cora's older sister, you know—helps out with her games from time to time." Sterling struck a match off the sole of his boot and lit his cigarette before waving the flame beneath Clayton's nose. "I remember Cora saying that about you—that you sensed the weird. Just fae or all magic?"

"All magic. My ma said it's all the same stuff anyway, just used different—fairies use it one way, witches another." Clay watched the woman called Adelaide glide towards the velvet curtains of the stage, both she and Cora blowing kisses at the audience. The further Adelaide got from the men, the more normal they got, some of them starting to holler, stomp their feet, and throw their hats in the air in appreciation of the show. Clay doubted they'd be so appreciative once they figured out they were a few bucks short.

The noise escalated until Sterling had to shout to be heard over the ruckus. When even that wasn't adequate to make conversation, he put a hand on Clay's back and guided him away from the stage and around the corner, where Clay could see the field backing up to the fairgrounds. There was a cluster of brightly-painted wagons parked there, all arranged in a circular formation. That must have been where the performers slept, and he wondered which of the rainbow colors housed the thieving fairy sisters.

"Can you shoot?" Sterling asked, seemingly out of nowhere. Clay stopped looking at the pasture and blinked, nodding stupidly.

"Yeah, I can shoot. Good at it, too."

"Good. You married?"

"No, Sir. Bit too green for that."

Sterling nodded, his eyes pinching in that thoughtful manner Clay'd seen on his father's face when he was considering something important. "Don't often do this, and I can't say I think you'd be real smart to accept, but I'd like to offer you a job, Clayton Jenson, if you'd be interested." Sterling motioned at the stage where Cora stood, her gloved hand waving at the dwindling crowd. Clay watched her crouch low, the silver squirrel hopping out from behind the curtain to scamper onto her wrist. It clambered up her arm to perch on her shoulder, and she turned her head to make kissy faces at it, clearly attached to the tiny, mechanical atrocity that had done all her dirty work.

Clay smiled in spite of his good judgment, and Sterling let out a guffaw beside him, his elbow whacking Clay right in the side of the ribs. "Maybe you would be interested at that. Can't say I'm surprised. Can't even say I blame you. But keep in mind, son, she's a liar and a thief. If you can stomach the thought of putting her behind bars, this might be the job for you."

CHAPTER FIVE

NOW

Clay strolled back to the Whistling Widow Inn, his thumb brushing over the pointed edges of the star on his lapel. He should have taken it off three months ago if he was perfectly honest with himself, but he couldn't bring himself to do it. Splitting with Cora had done a number on him, but he hadn't been willing to give up the comfortable familiarity of his job, too.

Now, with that whole squirming death thing ahead of him, it was time. He plucked the badge from his chest and slid it into his pocket. He wasn't going to say he'd never wear it again, but for the time being, until he got himself righted or buried, it was better to put it to rest. He was on personal business now and the government could kiss his round and furries if they didn't like it.

Clay expected to feel something removing the star: regret, relief, guilt. There was nothing except quiet acceptance that this was the right thing to do. Sterling told him once that Clay could be the law so long as he had the gumption to send Cora to jail when she inevitably crossed the line. Clay'd agreed, but by the time he was faced with "too far," he loved her so much and the circumstances were so murky he'd called Sterling out of retirement to arrest her in his stead. It was a coward's move, no doubt, and on some level, Clay couldn't blame Cora for being mad at him—he was still mad at himself.

Didn't justify his slow and painful murder, though. A sound kick in the family jewels and maybe a bucket of horse piss to the face, sure, but not a curse that'd eat him alive.

He lit himself another cigarette and navigated the thin, maze-like streets of Houston to get to the inn. Drunken cowboys puked in the alleyways while painted ladies hoisted their dresses to show off pale, limber legs, but he continued on without pause. He would miss The Whistling Widow when he left it. He'd slept in enough rundown shacks with holes in the roof to appreciate the Widow's clean sheets and polished banisters. When he and Cora were traveling together, they never stayed anywhere too long. She got fidgety and wanted to "follow the winds," as she said, and he'd been more than content to hitch along for the ride, especially considering the travel he had to do for his job. They slept in rooms fit for royalty some nights, and—when the good places were full—they slept in rooms that doubled as ogre outhouses other nights.

It wasn't until he was halfway through the Widow's foyer that he remembered Addy's request to check on Montague. He didn't mind, though it'd be embarrassing if Montague turned out to be some foreigner she kept chained to her bed for stud duty. After that time in Baltimore with the contortionist albino and his disappearing bottle trick, he put nothing past her. She wasn't exactly a paragon of virtue when it came to her playmates.

"Goddamn it, Addy." He climbed the steps and approached her door with all the enthusiasm of a man going to the gallows. He pounded on the wood in hopes that her sheet warmer—or warmers, if that was her game—would have the decency to put on some britches before he barged in. The only answer to his knocking was a deep, warbling groan that started loud and tapered off to a whine. Clay's hand slid to his gun. People made lots of funny sounds during bed sport, but something about this was downright wrong. He rapped again, and again there was a guttural moan that ended on a grunt.

Either Addy'd fucked this Montague so raw he needed a doctor to recover from her fire cooter or someone had beaten that gentleman within an inch of his life. Whatever the case, Clay was a charitable man, and he couldn't abandon someone gurgling their death rattles on the other side of a door.

"Coming in." He twisted the knob and thrust the door wide, Gayle sliding from her sheath to gleam pretty in the hall lamplight. He pointed the barrels dead ahead, his eyes scanning the room from left to right in case Montague had a perpetrator lurking in the shadows. Nothing that he could see except...

Welp. That. Nothing he could see except *that*. And *that* was hard to miss.

The groaning wasn't from a man of the traditional sort, unless you considered monstrous wildlife traditional. Sprawled out on a hand-knotted rug was a surly looking behemoth, its body seven feet from head to rump. Golden eyes fixed on Clay, the creature's tail an enraged, stripy serpent whipping around in agitation. A plate-sized paw waved in the air, and then slapped down on the floor, long, flesh-shredding claws extending from its toes to menace the scarred wood beneath.

"You're a tiger," Clayton announced in case the tiger happened to be suffering an identity crisis.

The tiger groaned and stretched, its huge head smacking the floor as it flopped onto its back to show off a fluffy white belly. Its tail continued to waggle, waving like a flag as the animal rolled around to scratch its back against the rough wool carpet. Clay didn't holster his gun because a man would have to be stupid to drop his gun in the presence of a man-eating carnivore, but damn, if that thing didn't look almost cute.

"What the hell, Addy?" Clay shook his head and stepped back into the hall, slamming the door before stomping to his own room. Next time Addy asked him to check on someone, she damned well better tell him who or what he was checking on.

A tiger.

Women.

—

Packing took him all of fifteen minutes. His clothes fit in two thick saddlebags he could throw on his mare without worrying about over-encumbering her. Squirt wasn't as ornery as her father, but then, nothing was as ornery as Gus. He'd lived to the ripe old age of twenty-eight, though Clay'd retired him to his father's farm after Sterling's job offer. Sterling had taken one look at Gus and laughed himself to tears at the notion of a horse that old trekking across the country. Twenty minutes later, Gus'd taken a chunk out of Sterling's arm that required a needle. Clay thought of it as Gus's way of telling Sterling to piss off.

Through the Widow's thin walls, Clay could hear stirring in the room next door. Doc was back from playing in the laboratory. Clay snagged his hat from the foot of his bed and rounded the corner to knock on her door, waiting for the grunt that'd tell him it was safe to enter.

"What?" he got instead.

Clay said nothing, instead letting himself in and moseying over to the desk chair by the corner. He felt Doc's eyes on his back. Clay tended to leave Doc alone at night in case she indulged in a gentleman caller, but there were things they needed to talk about.

He forced a big, shit-eating grin as he lifted a ruffled dress from the chair and tossed it onto the bed. It landed with a *fwoosh!* of taffeta, the skirts cascading over the side like yellow rain. Doc rushed over to right it, tutting as she flattened the bodice. "There's girl shit all over the place," Clay said. "Why you need so much stuff?"

"Because I like dresses, that's why." Doc's chin jutted up, her feathers well and truly fluffed. Clay used to exploit Doc's reactionary nature for his own personal amusement, but then one day, Doc'd gotten sick of it and thrown a mortar at his head. The hole it left in the wall was big enough for Clay to put his fist through, so he'd cut the crap after that.

"I'm just giving you shit, Doc. Calm your britches. Came to say we gotta get out before the Lynches find me. Tomorrow morning, unless you'd like to be delivering my eulogy this time Monday."

Doc paled looking around at the room. Whereas Clay's room was kept sparse and orderly, Doc's looked like a lace-spewing monster had vomited everywhere. The floor was hidden by stockings and underskirts and dresses and shoes with little bows on the toes. The bureaus were full of feminine frippery that spilled over the tops because there simply wasn't enough room to contain it all. Combined with Doc's medical gadgets, a desk of books and papers, and a collection of colorful bowler hats for bad hair days, packing everything in a single night was a miserable prospect. "Tomorrow?"

"Yep. Oh, and Addy's around. Nearly shot her at the Rattlesnake tonight. She insists on helping with Cora, but who the hell knows how that's gonna go considering she's got an enormous tiger in her room." When Doc eyed him like he was insane, Clay nodded for emphasis and pointed at the hall. "A tiger. Over there. Had to be six hundred pounds."

Doc sank onto the bed, butt crushing the very dress she'd so painstakingly adjusted moments ago, fingers covering her mouth as she looked around in horror. Clay expected a tantrum about such a last-minute departure, but Doc surprised him by setting her jaw and nodding. She tugged the goggles from her head and flung them onto the bed before marching to the closet to retrieve her traveling trunks. "Fine. Tomorrow. But you need to get the cart and horses. I won't have time."

"I know, I know. It's not like this is the first time I've traveled with you."

"Good. This should only take me a few hours, but I have to clear out the lab, too. I can be ready by tomorrow afternoon for sure, but the morning..." Doc's voice trailed as she fluttered around the room, bouncing from dress to dress like a hummingbird sipping nectar from blossoms. Soon, her arms were overburdened with satin.

"You need help packing? I'm sure I can break all sorts of important shit," Clay said.

Doc snickered as she stuffed the gowns into a case, her fingers fussing with the skirts so they'd lay flat. "I'd rather break my own things, thank you very much. And it's not proper for you to see my underthings. We're not courting. I'm a traditional girl."

"Whatever makes you happy, Doc. Feel free to keep your unders to yourself." Doc gathered her blouses and skirts from the floor, brow crinkling with worry lines with every swoop. "I can ask Addy to come help you when she's done talking to the whores, if you want?"

That Doc didn't register the whore comment as aberrant said a lot about Addy's lifestyle. "That'd be appreciated. Where are we going anyway?"

"New Orleans to see Marie. She can help me with the curse, and then she can help me find Cora. She helped Sterling with the same back in the day."

Doc glanced up, her scowl so severe it looked like the corners of her lips might stretch past her jaw to hit the floor. "Why do you want to find her? She's trying to kill you. She might succeed if Marie can't undo Betsy's curse. Let her go."

Clayton knew good sense when he heard it, but it wouldn't change a damned thing. He tipped his hat down and plucked at the threads on his vest. His mouth felt dry, the half-bottle of whiskey he'd guzzled a scant hour ago a distant memory. "I gotta see her. I know it's a fool's errand, but I gotta try."

"But it's her fault you're dying."

"Yep." Clayton didn't want to talk about it anymore. It made him feel vulnerable, and when he felt vulnerable, he shot things. If the Lynch predicament taught him anything, it was that shooting things because you're in a shit mood wasn't always the best course of action even if it felt damned good at the time.

Doc sighed and shook her head, retrieving her hats from the top of the bureau. "I understand, Clayton. I wish I didn't, but I understand. If my opinion counts for anything, I think it's a rubbish idea. You two have danced this dance for too long. It's time to hang up your dancing shoes. Get cured and get out."

Clay turned on his heel for his room, his hand plunging into his coat for another cigarette. "Noted. For now, though, I'll leave you to your packing. I gotta get the stink offa me before I hit the sheets."

—

The morning began with a high-pitched, female scream. During happier days, that would have meant he'd found the golden nugget inside Cora's treasure trove, but today it meant bolting up in bed with his hand sliding under the pillow. Gayle waited for him, her double barrels a faithful, reassuring weight. The scream came again, this time more distinctly from the hall, and Clay stumbled out of bed to pull on some pants. He didn't sleep raw—too many bedbugs nibbling on his dangler in the past had taught him better—but he did strip down to his drawers, forcing him to hop around on one leg with one hand tugging up his pants, the other gripping his enormous gun.

He burst from his bedroom door with his buttons undone. The moment his feet touched the carpet, a woman threw herself at him, her arms wrapping around his middle as her face pressed into his bare chest. She sobbed on him, her entire body quivering in terror. He stared at the top of her head for a minute, willing his sleep-addled brain to kick into gear and remind him who she was.

Nope. Not a working girl. The cleaning gal. He left her a quarter every time she turned his bed.

What was her name again?

"Oh, stop. He's a friendly little kitty-cat," Addy said from down the hall.

For the first time since Clay could remember, Adelaide had dressed herself like a proper Southern lady. She wore white from head to toe, her dress a fitted bodice of lace and silk ties, her skirts belled out from her hips thanks to layers of petticoats. Her hair was tucked under a wide-brimmed straw hat and her hands sported delicate gloves that ended above her wrist. The parasol above her head was cherry-blossom pink with beads dangling from the edge. The tiger she held on a leash at her side…

Oh, right. That was the problem. The tiger.

"Why do you have a tiger, Addy? Ask me to check on the goddamned thing and don't bother mentioning that it's a Hellcat. Little bit rude, don't you think?"

Addy looked from Clay to the big cat stretching at her side, the cat's muscles rippling underneath his striped orange fur. "Why shouldn't I have a tiger? And it's not rude. You need to be more open-minded."

"It's six hundred pounds of death! Who's open-minded about that?"

"Montague is most certainly *not* six hundred pounds of death. More like seven hundred. But that's beside the point. He's harmless. I've had him since he was a baby. He was a gift after I performed the Dance of the Sea Snake for the prince. Which I made up on the spot, by the way, but he liked it." She scratched under the big cat's chin, her voice scaling as she crooned to it like a child. Montague had the audacity to rub his head against her glove for more pats, a low, rumbling groan warbling from his throat.

"Before you danced all over *his* snake, too, no doubt." Clay gently pushed the maid away from his chest, the poor girl sobbing her apologies as she skirted around him to escape down the back stairs.

Clay watched her go, his hand streaking down his face from his nose to his mouth. The tiger let out another appreciative groan and Clay eyeballed it over his shoulder, his finger itchy on his trigger. "Still not hearing a good reason to keep a tiger around, especially when we gotta travel fast."

Addy shrugged. "The short answer is, 'Because I want to.' The longer answer is, 'Because I bloody-well want to, so leave it alone, Clayton.' You sound just like the innkeeper when I checked in. Do you know how much it cost me to convince him to let us stay here?"

"I'm gonna go out on a limb and say a suck and fuck?"

"If only! Twenty whole dollars, only ten of which I'll get back upon checking out. Safety deposit, my arse. Now, stop fussing and get dressed. I was good enough to make our travel arrangements while you drooled into your pillow all morning. Irene mentioned needing a wagon when I got home last night. Poor thing was still packing at midnight, but she's making her way downstairs already, because she's brilliant. You're slow." She tugged on Montague's leash before swishing her way toward the steps, parasol held high over her head. The tiger padded at her heels like a dutiful dog, stopping only once to cast Clay a long, assessing look, like it knew he didn't trust it. Clay waved Gayle at it for good measure, but the cat just blinked and descended the steps, one fluid motion oozing into the next.

Damn thing didn't even know a threat when it saw one. People downstairs did, though. The other patrons started screeching the moment they laid eyes on it, the cacophony made all the worse by Addy's less-than-ladylike insistence that they shut up and leave the cat alone.

"Stupid tiger." Clay stepped back into his room to get ready, wanting to get downstairs to Doc as fast as possible, just in case. Whenever she raised her powdered head, there was the potential for the shit to hit the wall in a spectacular way. Irene liked folks. Folks often didn't like Irene. The world wasn't ready for her particular charms because people had opinions, and those opinions were often heaping piles of garbage.

He gave his face a quick wash and combed his hair. With the amount of road dirt he had ahead of him, he kept his dress simple—no vests or jackets or fancy anything. The lighter his clothes, the better, even if it made him look like a pig farmer. He wasn't trying to impress anyone, least of all Addy, her enormous tiger, and Doc.

Doc.

He sighed while thinking about her and shoved the last of his possessions into the bigger of his two saddlebags. He fastened his holster around his hips, Gayle on the left, a normal six-shooter on his right. It always made him feel lopsided to have a hand cannon on one side versus a dinky li'l gun on the other, but he was afraid two Gayles would make people think he was overcompensating for something. Plus, Cora'd hurt herself good making the first Gayle. He never would have asked her to repeat that particular torture.

Well, now he might, but that was 'cause she'd tried to kill him.

Clay gave his room a last assessing look before heading out—his last goodbye to The Whistling Widow. The loveliness of this place had helped him heal after things went to shit with Cora, and for that, it'd be remembered fondly. He reached into his pocket for his billfold, pulling out fifty dollars and laying it on the pillow for the cleaning gal. Once she was over her tiger-born terror fit, she'd come in to clean up after him, and that'd be waiting for her. It was more than she'd make this whole year, but she'd treated him right, and Clay's Mama always told him to pay kindness with kindness.

He was halfway down the Widow's front stairs when he heard the ruckus in the street. There were angry shouts and sneers, a few nasty catcalls, and Clay's casual trot became a full-on run, his lean legs skipping stairs to double-time it outside. His heart pumped faster as the anger rose in his gut, every nerve in his body tingling in anticipation of violence. Doc'd been spotted, and Doc brought out the worst in some. It wasn't her fault, just how the world was, but that didn't make it right.

There was the sound of breaking glass and a cry as Clay burst through the Widow's front door. His hand was already at his guns as the first rock sailed by his head. It was followed by a second and a third, but none of those rocks were aimed at him. They were aimed at the woman huddled down by a pair of haul horses fifteen feet away. In the time it took for Clay to get dressed and get downstairs, a crowd had amassed in the street, twenty or thirty strong, and they were closing in on Clayton's wagon or—more appropriately—the woman curled into a mint-green heap in front of the wagon.

Doc Irene's skirts looked like a decorated cake against the brown dirt beneath her. Her head was shielded by a parasol similar to Addy's so she could protect herself against any projectiles heaved her way. Clay couldn't see her face, but he could see her gloves on the parasol handle, and there were bloodstains near the thumb. Someone had hit her or thrown something that'd hit her, but Clay couldn't assess the damage from here. She was too compact and her umbrella too well-held.

"All right, everyone just calm the hell down," he shouted, but another rock sailed past him anyway to strike Doc in the shoulder. She let out a terrified shriek, trying to crouch lower like she could will the ground to swallow her whole. Another rock flew out from her other side, this one missing her entirely and striking one of the horses in the leg. The great animal neighed and reared up, shaking the cart attached to its flanks. Inside the cart, Addy let out a yelp and sat on the driver's bench, her hands gripping the reins in case the beast took off. Montague stood up behind her to make an awful, ear-splitting roar, which only spurred the horses into a worse panic. They danced in their tack and swung their heads around, their brown eyes wildly flitting in search of the predator. Clay had no idea how Addy'd gotten the tiger loaded without spooking them in the first place, but the cat's presence was definitely not helping matters now.

The horses pranced, their hooves stomping down hard and kicking up clouds of dust and grit. Each strike came perilously close to crushing Doc's head. If they ran, they'd trample her to death, especially with that loaded haul-cart behind them. If the mob threw another rock, they'd bolt for sure, and that wasn't a risk Clay could take.

"Doc!" he shouted, but there was no answer, and Clay gritted his teeth as he lifted his gun above his head to point it at the cloudless sky. "Irene! Move now! To me, behind you."

Irene let out a sob as she propelled herself off of the ground and at his legs, landing in a pathetic pile by his boots. Clay pulled the trigger on Gayle and the horses shrieked at the thunderous boom. They darted forward, their heavy feet coming down on the spot Irene had been not a moment ago. Montague roared in response to the jostling, and that was it—the horses took off, pulling the wagon, Adelaide, and her tiger with them. He could hear her shouting at them as they barreled away from The Widow, and he hoped she could get everything under control without too much trouble. He didn't want to have to go on an Addy hunt later.

Clay was about to drop his gun when he felt a rock pelt him in the chest. It didn't shred his shirt, but it did whack him hard enough that he'd probably be bruised tomorrow. He grunted at the sting and leveled Gayle at the offender. It was a young man about twenty years old, his face dusty, lips cracked and pale like he hadn't had a drink of water in weeks. His clothes were drenched in sweat, his shirt stuck to his chest like it'd been painted on. Grease plastered his brown hair to his scalp, an unattractive divide splitting east from west all the way to the back of his head.

Seeing the gun, the young man froze, the fingers of his left hand curling around the other rock he was ready to throw. He hesitated now, though, looking between the gun and Clay, his feet shuffling back and forth in nervous anticipation.

"Throwing rocks at an armed man is stupid," Clayton said.

"... n-no Sir. No it ain't. That there's a freak by your feet. I'm doing what the Good Book says."

"The Good Book says throw rocks at people? Put it down, son. For that matter, everyone put the rocks down or I swear I will shoot every last one of you." Clay wagged Gayle around, looking at the twenty faces surrounding him. Some of them were unsure of what to do, their eyes skipping from Irene to Clay and then to where the wagon had disappeared down the street. Others just looked angry that someone dared to thwart their murderous mob.

"Kill it! Kill the freak!" another man shouted from the right side. He lifted his hand to chuck his stone. Before the rock left his fingers, before he even got his arm up half a foot, Clay tore the six-shooter from its holster and squeezed the trigger. There was a blast and then a scream as the man's shoulder exploded, a smoky, bloody gash marring the flesh above his arm. If Clay had used Gayle, it would have taken the damned limb off, but this was just a flesh wound—something that could be sewn tidy by anyone with a steady hand. It was a warning to the man and anyone else who thought it would be a good idea to continue with their fool plan.

The man dropped to the ground, a few of his cronies closing in around him to see to his wound. Clay eyed the rest of the observers, his mouth pinched in a thin line. Irene steadied herself against his leg before standing up to straighten her skirts. Clay could see the extent of her injuries now; a thick cut bisected her cheek and curved down to her jaw. Whoever had struck her had damned fine aim; she was bloodied all the way from her face to the girly little bows on her bodice.

"You all right?"

"I'm fine," she said, her voice cracking on the "fine."

Clay eyed the crowd and grunted, putting the six-shooter away but keeping Gayle in hand in case anyone decided to be a hero. "Get our horse so we can find Addy. Putting Houston behind us would be a good idea." Irene nodded and scurried off, her parasol kept open in case of further attacks. No one moved a muscle save for the young man with the cracked lips. He frowned at Clay and motioned at Irene's retreating back. Pebbles fell from his fingers to skitter over the ground.

"What are you doing defending that thing? It's unnatural."

"Open your pie hole one more time and I'll fill it with lead. We clear, boy?"

There was no reason to say so to a crowd of pea-brained ratbags, but that so-called "thing" had saved Clay's hide more times than he could count. Doc was Clayton's best friend, no matter if she dressed like Seamus Miller to stay safe in a world not ready for her, no matter if she appeared with her frills and charms as her true self, Irene.

CHAPTER SIX

SIX YEARS AGO

"So what do you know about slick ears?" Sterling asked from behind a fanned hand of cards.

Clay grunted and played his trump, neatly snatching the trick with a high club. The riverboat gave an uneasy quiver thanks to the storm outside, and Clay's stomach flopped like a catfish on a hook. They'd been traveling the Mississippi for the better part of three days, and he thought he'd gotten his legs under him, but then the skies decided to vomit rain on their heads. Every lurch and rock made him queasy to the point that Sterling said he was as green as the felt on the poker tables. "What's a slick ear?"

"You know—your mama. Fairies."

Clay peered at Sterling and shrugged. "What everyone else knows, mostly. She didn't talk about it much. Said most of her folks were troublemakers and I was better off in the human world." They'd been law-dogging together awhile now, and this was how a good majority of their conversations started. Sterling would ask Clay what he knew about something, Clay confessed ignorance, and Sterling would regale him with stories of one weird creature or another, usually over inn food and glasses of whiskey.

By the time the tales ended, Clay was usually drunk and Sterling had forgotten half of what he had set out to say, but at least Clay learned stuff from the early parts of the talks.

"Well, there're two different kinds of fair folk. Seelies are royalty types who consider themselves the true fey. They're the pretty lord and lady Sidhe you see in the picture books. Unseelies are much more diverse 'cause they'll take anyone. That's where you find Fairy's monsters—redcaps, goblins, and the like. They got lookers, too, but that's not all of 'em. Not even half of 'em."

Clay nodded, his fingers drumming on the table while he waited for Sterling to play another card. The old man jawed so much sometimes he lost track of what he was doing. One time, he stopped pissing mid-stream because he got to talking about the migratory patterns of wendigos. "Well, Ma's Seelie. That's why she goes home every ten years. If she refused to split her time between here and Fairy, they'd boot her out of the court for good. Almost did anyway 'cause she married my father, but I guess they forgave her when she reminded them he'd only live sixty years."

"Smart gal, your ma. Frankly, I'm surprised they didn't disown her. That's what they do if you break the rules. She's lucky." Sterling threw a card and guzzled his drink, his eyes narrowing as Clay's cigarette smoke wafted toward his face. "That's why Cora's Unseelie now, you know. She and Addy got evicted from the propers a while back—before the States split from the Brits. They came over when Adams took office, and they've been conning their way through the country ever since."

Clay wasn't sure what surprised him more: hearing Cora's name after so long or that she was old enough to have settled in the States almost a century ago. When a fledgling America opened its doors for business, the Unseelie court announced its presence to the world by sending six emissaries to George Washington's doorstep in the spring of 1791. They'd been hidden in the fairy mounds of Wales with their prettier counterparts for millennia and were tired of the power struggles and wars that took place beneath the emerald hills. They sought independence from what they called "King Oberon's tyrannical ruling fist" and wanted to experience this life, liberty, and pursuit of happiness thing everybody was talking about.

Washington embraced the fair folk on the conditions that they abide by all common laws, pay taxes, and defend their country during times of national threat. The emissaries readily agreed, and The Fair Folk Act was drafted in January of 1792.

Cora'd been around for that, and that was almost a hundred years ago. He'd assumed she was older than him, but not by that much.

Hot damn.

Clay grunted and shifted in his seat, moving his hearts in front of his clubs and then back again. He hadn't responded to Sterling, which made the old man tilt his head and peer at him.

"Figured you'd have something to say about that," Sterling said.

"About what? Cora? I don't give a damn about her."

"Sure you don't." Sterling grinned from ear to ear, his lip pulled back so far Clay could see where one of his upper teeth turned gray along the gum line. "Well, Mr. Ambivalent, not like you'd care, but this riverboat is Louisiana-bound specifically because of Cora. Leroy Tarrens spotted her and told Skunk Miller, who told Robert Cook, who told me."

Clay didn't like Sterling's smile. He liked even less the way his stomach did an odd clenching thing at the thought of seeing the fairy girl again. It'd been two years since she'd bolted from the Atlanta carnival without a trace, and he'd met—and ridden—more than a few beautiful women since. In fact, he'd taken so many gals to his bed, Sterling said his parts were going to turn pimply and rot off. Hadn't happened yet, and it wouldn't because Clay preferred a higher class of lady, but no man with his hat hung up on a woman would spend that much time drilling between pillowy, feminine thighs.

Unless he was trying to forget someone.

Damn it.

Clayton's blatant discomfort amused the hell out of Sterling. The older man slapped his cards down on the table and howled in laughter, one craggy, gnarled finger pointing at Clay's chin. It wavered close enough to Clay's mouth that Clay could have bit the tip clean off if he wanted to. As tempting as that notion was, he refrained, but only because he was already gnawing on the end of his cigarette.

"You should see your damned face. She's got her hooks into you and you haven't even *touched* her. I warned you about her, boy. You better come to terms with the reality that her fine, fairy flanks might have to go to the clink sooner or later here." He sniggered and drained his whiskey glass before motioning at the barkeep for another. "And just so we're clear on the subject, no poking her after you arrest her. Looks bad for the rest of us."

"I'd nev… shut up, Sterling. Just shut the hell up."

Sterling smirked and retrieved his cards, his thumb sweeping over their faded backs before throwing an ace on Clay's king to steal the round. "I'm pulling your leg. 'Sides, you shouldn't let me off that easy. What if I'm a hypocrite? I might be following her around because I'm as in lust with her as you are."

As unkind as it was to admit, Clay's mind immediately skipped to, "You're too old for a girl like that," but the reality was, Cora was old enough to be both of their grandmothers. She only *looked* the tender side of twenty. "Why do you chase her?"

"You ever read *Moby Dick*?"

"Think I heard about it. The fish book?"

"It ain't about the damned fish. It's about obsession. This captain chases a white whale to even a score from long ago. In a way, I sympathize with Ahab—the chaser. I know Cora's breaking the law. Whether it's selling bad machines or that little shit squirrel of hers stealing or passing fake money, I can't catch her. Never, not once. Even when I think someone might have something on her." Sterling paused in his diatribe to cast Clay a sly look. "They won't testify. So I gotta do what I can to bring her in on my own."

Clay shifted in his seat, the wooden chair beneath him squealing like a pained piglet. Sterling had never indicated it before, but it was evident he knew Clay'd seen the squirrel con back in Atlanta. He knew Clay'd lied about it to protect Cora, and yet he'd taken him on as his deputy all the same. The question was "Why?" It seemed counterproductive to hire someone who'd protect the very criminal he sought.

As if reading his mind, Sterling snagged his trick and played another card. "Fact is, son, I want to catch her, but there's a bigger part of me that don't. She's too damned entertaining. And ain't that just a pisser."

—

They arrived at the Riverside Hotel near dusk. It was nice to look at with its tall, floor-to-ceiling glass windows and woven carpets from some sandy place Clay'd never heard of before. Dark paneling gleamed on the walls while plush couches invited guests to sprawl. On the right side, an arched doorframe opened up into a common room with cherry-topped tables and fine, velvet seats. The place catered to moneyed folk. That wasn't much of a surprise; Sterling didn't waste time on rundown shanties or boarding houses. He always opted for the best beds around because, as he put it, "I risk my life with this job on a monthly basis. The least I can do for myself is get a good night's sleep." Clay thought it was an extravagant waste, but there wasn't much sense in saying so. Sterling had a mule-thick skull on occasion, plus he was paying.

After they checked in, the woman behind the front desk slid Sterling an unopened envelope with his name printed across the back. He wasted little time breaking the red wax seal. Whatever was written there made him grin, and in grinning, the wrinkles around his eyes deepened to crow's feet. "You still itching to take that bath, Clay?"

"Yeah. I got a week's worth of swamp sweat on me. Why?"

"Leroy Tarrens' note. He says Cora and Addy were seen around Beverly's Auction House. Clean up so we can pay a visit." Leroy was not only Sterling's oldest friend, he was also another weird-hunting marshal operating out of Nashville whose quarry sometimes led him down into this neck of the woods. Clay'd met him a few times and liked him despite not being able to get a word in edgewise when he and Sterling got yammering.

Clay mumbled under his breath and climbed the stairs. It took him an hour to scrub his body, trim his beard to a dark shadow, and dress. He'd visit a barber to get rid of the dark locks that curled around his neck, but until then, he tamed the mess with a comb and two palms of tonic. The Stetson, his six-shooters, and a rolled cigarette for accessories, and he met Sterling in the common room. The older man gave him a once-over, his hand reaching out to swipe some lint from Clay's coat shoulder and adjust the lapels of his brown jacket. It was indicative of Sterling's avuncular fondness for him, and though Clay liked him plenty, he smacked Sterling's hand away anyway. He could adjust his own coat. He wasn't ten years old, damn it.

"Beverly's is around the corner. We won't need the horses," Sterling said, leading Clay out onto the cobblestone streets. Now that the sun had dipped past the horizon, N'Orleans was alive, its denizens throwing open their doors, chatting on corners, and walking hand-in-hand under the gas streetlights. Carriages careened by at breakneck speed, and Clay flattened himself against the hotel front to avoid being squished.

They were a block away from Beverly's when Clay first sensed Cora and Addy, their magics prickling over his skin with goose bumps. He was probably the only one in all of Louisiana feeling a breeze right then, but that was because the sisters together in such close confines emanated raw power. He shivered and rolled his shoulders, and from the corner of his eye, he could see Sterling worrying at that ugly old hemp ring of his.

"They're close," Sterling said. "Up that way."

"I know that, but how do you know? You ain't a witchsniffer."

Sterling lifted his hand to wriggle his ring finger. "I don't wear this ugly ol' thing 'cause it's pretty. It's woven from Cora's hair. Lets me see through her glamour and get a feel on her when she's near. Friend of mine made it for me." That explained why Sterling wore it, but that left Clay with another question. Why would Sterling ask Clay along as a witchsniffer if he could already track down Cora?

Again, as if he had a line on Clay's thoughts, Sterling said, "'Cause I gotta retire one day and I'm not sure how many rings Marie's willing to make. You're a natural."

Clay grunted before spitting the smoldering stub of his cigarette out onto the ground. "I hate it when you do that—read my mind like that. It's like you're a weird yourself."

Sterling smirked. "Hardly. It's my business to know other people's business and you wear your heart on your sleeve, son."

They walked into the auction house without another word, their hands looped in their belts. It wasn't until Clay's boot crossed the threshold that he sensed the third magic in the room. Unlike the fairy magic, this was primal force, like the fierce, whirling energy at the center of a tornado. The strange part was it also felt contained—something had bound that power into a very small space, which accounted for why he needed to be so close to feel it. His eyes skimmed the room. Two dozen people were seated in high-back chairs, all of them pointed toward a small stage at the back. Cora and Addy sat in the second row, not yet clued in to his presence. An auctioneer with a twisted, gray mustache stood at the front of the room with a statue on a pedestal beside him. It was a Chinese lion carved out of some green stone Clay'd never seen before. He thought it might be the source of the magic, but no, the energy came from behind it. On a long table with a rich purple tablecloth, five relics waited to be auctioned off, the golden box at the front the culprit. The thing practically vibrated with power.

"Sold!" the auctioneer said, pulling Clay's attention with the deafening thwack of hammer on podium. He pointed at a gentleman in the front row who let out a whooping cheer as the Chinese statue was ushered offstage and out of sight. The auctioneer then turned toward the table, and much to Clay's chagrin, motioned at the gilded box. A pair of young men lifted it and guided it forward for its turn on the block.

"Don't! No!" Clay shouted it before he could think better of it. Every head in the house turned to look at him, including Cora, her sister, and Sterling. Clay shuffled his feet and lifted his chin, his eyes straying Cora's way. She was as blond and perfect as he remembered, even if she was dressed funny with her high collared white shirt, black suit coat, and slacks. She must have glamoured herself up to look like a boy. Knowing that should have detracted from her appeal, but she was right fetching in those gentleman's clothes.

Clay forced himself to look away from her, but it was damned hard because she'd smiled at him, her eyes sweeping over him from hat to vest to hips and boots. A hot flush crawled up his neck and spread over his cheeks, and, God have mercy, he was pretty sure he was blushing. He cleared his throat and removed his hat to wave it at the box. "I'm sorry, folks, but you don't want to auction that off. It's weird. You know, magical weird."

The auctioneer stared at him blankly for a moment before faking a cough into a white handkerchief. "Pardon? That's a box from the reign of Louis XIV, and I assure you it's… "

"Fulla magical somethin'. Somethin' ain't right with it," Clay maintained.

"I checked it myself this morning during its initial assessment, and I assure you, there was nothing lurking inside of the…" The auctioneer's voice cut short as the box quaked. It was barely noticeable at first, just a shimmy, but then the top flipped open and closed of its own accord. The audience gasped and scampered back, most barging for the door with panic on their faces. Even the man who'd bought the Chinese lion made a hasty exit, his trophy abandoned in the wake of the unnatural shaking. People knew that fairies and magic were honest-to-goodness things that existed in their world, but that didn't mean they were comfortable having firsthand accounts of their shenanigans.

Then there were Cora and Adelaide. The sisters maintained their seats, unflinching even when the box trembled hard enough to make the podium beneath it teeter. They were so unresponsive to the phenomenon that Clay couldn't help but grow suspicious. According to Sterling, fairies may be hard to kill, but they bled just like everyone else. If this thing was a danger, shouldn't they be scared? Shouldn't they react like this was something surprising?

"What'd you put in the box, Cora?" Sterling asked, his voice mild despite his hand reaching for his gun.

"What? Why would I do something like that?" She stood and put her hands on her hips, forcing the buttons on her man-shirt to strain and reveal a flash of creamy bosom skin. Clay wished he hadn't noticed that. But he had.

"Oh, I dunno. To clear out an auction house so you're alone with the goods?"

Cora gasped, her hand grasping her neck in feigned consternation. "How dare you cast such aspersions upon my character? In front of my sister, too. Adelaide, you know Marshal Cole, and—I haven't set eyes on him since he was a puppy, but that there is Mister Clayton Jenson. Isn't he just delicious?" Her eyes flicked to the star on Clayton's lapel and she groaned, her fingers covering her heart like she'd been struck with a mortal wound. "Pardon me. *Deputy* Clayton Jenson. Just my luck."

Adelaide cast them a huge, gleaming smile before leaning over a polished, knob-top walking stick. She gave Clay an earthy look, an appreciative whistle hissing from between her front teeth. Without the silly costumes of the Atlanta carnival, Clay could see the redhead in all her glory now, and though he still preferred the blond, a man would be a fool to kick Addy out of bed. Almost a foot shorter than Cora, round where her sister was lean, big plush cheeks and sparkling green eyes, Adelaide was gorgeous—probably the prettiest woman he'd ever seen in his life. And undoubtedly as much trouble as her sibling.

She proved that assessment when she said, "Oh, Cora. If you don't want him, I do. Twice."

Sterling snapped his fingers to draw their attention, but both women ignored him, instead leering at Clayton like he was a piece of pecan pie. "That's my deputy you harpies are talking about. Keep your britches on. And stop avoiding the subject. What'd you put in it, Cora? Tell me true and I won't arrest you this time."

"Psh. You won't arrest me anyway. But because I'm a helpful lass, let's just say I think there might be a swamp bogey inside."

Clay hadn't heard of a swamp bogey before, and he glanced at his superior to see if this was a bad thing, a badder thing, or a baddest thing. The strain lines furrowing Sterling's brow resembled the rivers drawn on a map, meaning it was somewhere between badder to baddest. Either that or Sterling suffered some killer indigestion.

"How do we kill it?" Clay asked.

Sterling opened his mouth to answer, but then grunted instead, his feet retreating from the box as he lifted his gun. "Can't quite recall. Earth from its swamp mixed with dust from a desert... no. Not dust. That's for a golem. Well, *shit*."

The box jumped on its pedestal as if huge, invisible hands shook it. A single green tendril of bubbly gook oozed from the left corner to drip toward the floor in a stream. It reminded Clay of when he was a kid and he and Tommy Mayfair would have contests to see how far they could stretch their drool before it splashed to the ground. Tommy was damned good at that game. One time he near hit dirt before sucking the whole string back into his mouth. That skill probably hadn't gotten him far in life, but a six-year-old Clayton had certainly been impressed.

The dribble kept pouring. It pooled on the stage and seeped down the steps, the puddle soon turning into a quaking lake of viscous sludge. The color was the most unnatural thing Clay'd ever seen. It was bright, eye-piercing green with veins of golden yellow swirling throughout, like two paints mixed together but not completely integrated. And the smell...

Lord, it was rank.

It was musty herb cellars and rot, like mud, bad food, and outhouse all thrown together. Clay cupped his hand over his nose to block out the stench, but it didn't do any good. This thing was scat and low tide and every other awful smell he'd ever had the misfortune of encountering lumped into one stinky monster. He felt sick being around it, but he had to endure. He had to keep his guts in check and not puke on the floor. If he didn't, Sterling would never let him live it down. For that matter, Clay'd never forgive himself; he didn't want Cora thinking he was a lily-livered peckerwood.

The last of the slime bubbled over the box top with a repulsive belch, the mass churning and writhing before rising into a pillar almost as tall as Clayton's chin. It only took a half a minute for it to adopt a man shape, the quivering ooze growing arms, legs, and even a rectangular head. The creature's "body"—if that's what Clay could call it—was constructed entirely of the goo, save for a strange, black mass floating mid-chest. It looked like a piece of coal or maybe a rock, but Clay couldn't really say one way or the other. The jelly surrounding it was too thick.

The bogey teetered on its newly formed feet, its head whipping around to send green goo flying. The bottom half of its face split into a crude mouth that warbled through a shriek. It was awful and shrill, and Clay lifted his gun to shoot at the thing in hopes of silencing it. It was a waste of bullets. The liquid body absorbed them, sucking them deep into its torso. With another series of glass-shaking wails, the bogey lurched forward, its arms stretching long until they reached almost four feet away from its body. It knocked over the podium on the stage, sending the golden box toppling to the floor.

Shooting it may not have hurt it, but it certainly pissed it off. It advanced on Clay with flailing, gelatinous arms that struck the floor hard enough to make the boards bow. Clay scurried out of reach, his boots carrying him all the way to the back of the auction house. Before he could plunge through the double doors, Sterling ran at him to shove him aside, sending him sailing over the last row of chairs and sprawling on the floor.

"Stay inside. We can't release it on the public," Sterling shouted. "And Cora, if you have any ideas on how to put it away, I'd recommend you chime in now. I *will* haul your ass in if a civilian gets hurt."

"My memory seems to be faulty at the moment, Marshal. A pity, too. It looks like a rather big bogey. If it's any consolation, I have the utmost faith in you and Deputy Jenson," Cora said, shouting to be heard over the marauding monster.

Clay's eyes flicked her way. Instead of being upset or afraid or any other number of reasonable things, she looked amused by the situation. A devilish smile twisted her lips, her eyes dancing as the bogey staggered about and screamed. It threw a chair at the wall, the wood disintegrating to bits mere inches from her head, but she never flinched. Nor did her sister; Addy sat in a chair at Cora's side, a small mirror in one hand and a fluffy brush in the other. A bogey screeched not fifteen feet away, but Adelaide chose that time to rouge her cheeks.

"What is wrong with you two?" Clay demanded, finding his feet again to circle the enraged slime. The girls said nothing as the monster whirled on him, its freakishly long arms sweeping chairs aside like they weighed nothing. Clay shot it again, this time aiming for its rock heart, but there was too much gunk between the creature's "skin" and the rock. The bullets broke apart only to be swallowed by green jelly.

"Don't you think you ought to run?" Cora, from somewhere behind him. Clay almost told her to shut her mouth, but he had to dive across the floor to avoid another sweep of the bogey's arms. Being pissy would have to wait until he wasn't so busy getting mauled to death by an odoriferous swamp beast.

"That's what you want, ain't it? So, no," Sterling said. He didn't bother wasting bullets on the monster. Instead, he picked up a chair and smacked it on the back. As soon as the wood made contact with its body, half of it was swallowed by goo while the other half jutted out from its side like a four-legged tumor.

The creature whirled on Sterling then, another cringe-worthy scream blasting from its mouth before it charged. It moved faster now, clearly having found its bearings, and whipped a long, wobbling arm at the marshal's head. Sterling attempted to duck beneath it, but it clobbered him on the temple, the impact lifting him off of the floor to send him flying. Clay's heart stopped as Sterling slammed into the wall and crumpled, folding in half like a discarded dolly. His hat was torn from his head as the monster let loose with another furious punch, this time missing Sterling altogether but leaving a fist-sized crater in the wood panels above him.

For a horrible moment, Clay thought Sterling was dead. He stared at his chest, willing it to rise and fall, willing the old man's body to show some sign of precious life. Nothing. Clay didn't know what to do; his stomach was so low it swung by his knees, and he was pretty sure he'd forgotten how to breathe. This was his friend—one of the smartest, most entertaining men he'd ever had the pleasure of knowing. He couldn't be gone. Not this fast, not this way.

Come on, Old Man. Come on.

Clay wasn't much for praying—what with a mother descended from a pagan god or two—but his mouth moved in a holy litany that would have done any devout church marm proud. Well, 'cept for the part where he begged Allah, Buddha, and any other gods who might be listening for a hand. Church marm would string his ass up for being such a heathen piece of bullpucky if she knew that.

Sterling's body convulsed, one blue eye flying open to reveal a dilated, unfocussed pupil. "Sterling!" Clay shouted in relief, only vaguely aware that he had an echo. It wasn't until the sisters sailed to his side that he realized they'd gone from calm to panicked in the time it took Sterling to slump down the wall. Cora leapt in front of the monster to protect Sterling's prone form, her legs bent at the knees like she was ready to pounce the creature if need be. Addy screeched before unloading the contents of her purse at the thing, throwing the mirror, then her hairbrush, and finally her pots of cosmetics.

Everything stuck to the creature upon contact, glued there thanks to the viscous sludge that constituted its body.

It probably would have been funny to look at if the monster hadn't been so homicidally inclined.

"Move," Clay said, waving his gun in the thing's direction. "You're a civilian and I can't let you… "

"Hush, Deputy. I can do more against this thing than your silly bullets. Stay back. And whatever you do, *don't touch it*." Clay stared at her all stupid-like, his gun hanging weakly in his hand. Who did she think she was to boss him around? She'd already mucked up everything by jumping between Sterling and the bogey before he could. That was unsafe and illogical. At no point during Moby Fish had the whale taken a hit for Old Ahab just because, yet there Cora was screaming at the slime thing to—

Clay didn't even know what she was saying. What the hell was a pickle-sniffing fuckwit?

"Cora—"

"I have this, Clayton. Please, step away." Freezing cold winds erupted around her, her long blond hair streaking across her face as her clothes snapped taut to her body. The power emanating off of her intensified, and Clay's senses ignited with it. He sizzled, the hairs on the back of his neck and arms standing on end, his bladder twinging. It was uncomfortable being near her, which was probably the point; she was trying to bully the bogey back toward the stage with the force of her magic.

"INTO THE BOX!" she hollered at the thing.

The creature screeched in reply and lifted its wobbling arm, ready to let loose with another thundering strike. Seeing what the monster's strength had done to Sterling, Clay could only imagine what it would do to a girl Cora's size. Even if she was a fairy, her bones would snap or her head would come clean off her shoulders. He couldn't let that happen. He'd already nearly lost Sterling to the thing—he wouldn't lose the infuriating girl that gave him a near-perpetual hard-on, too.

He tackled it. The chair mashed into his gut, but he wrapped his arms and legs around the gelatinous monster's middle in spite of the discomfort. The thing roared and thrashed its anger, staggering back and forth in an attempt to shake him off, but Clay rode it out. When he was twelve, his father'd taught him to break horses. This wasn't so different. Sure, the monster was a giant made of magical ooze and smelled like wet dog ass, but its frantic bucking wasn't so different from a spring filly or a green stallion. He'd be fine so long as it didn't throw him into the wall or wallop him with one of its jelly fists.

Or so he thought.

The burning was almost immediate. Something sour and smoky joined the already-unpleasant swamp stench molesting his nose. It wasn't until Clay's skin went molten hot and his shirt fell apart that he understood its origin; the bogey's body was toxic. There was something in that bizarre, green sludge that was actually eating through his clothes and—by the agonizing pain now shredding across his chest—his skin.

Clay tried to fall away, his arms and legs dropping, but the thing was so tacky, he was glued to it as effectively as Adelaide's pots of rouge. Not even the creature's panicked thrashing could dislodge him. As the first blister as big as the pad of his thumb appeared on the side of his neck, he felt a set of hands grab onto his hips and attempt to pry him off. He didn't go anywhere, stuck as he was, but it was nice of somebody to try and save him. And was that Adelaide or Cora? He couldn't tell. His brain was growing as hot as his body, and he felt nauseous thanks to the bogey's bucking. His vision whirled with the monster, the world around him rushing by in a rainbow of colors. He was pretty sure he was going to pass out soon. Too bad he hadn't listened when Cora'd told him not to touch it. She probably had a reason for it. Like he'd burn his skin off if he did so.

"You're a moron, Clayton Jenson!" That penetrated the fog in his head. It was right next to his ear and said with a breath that was as cold as a Montana morning. He liked the cold—it felt good on his feverish skin. He liked Montana, too. There were mountains there and sunrises pretty enough to make the gods cry. "Look at me, Deputy."

Cora! That was Cora, and she was near. Such a fine-looking blond. Too bad he never got to poke her. Clay shook his head and willed his swimming eyes to find her, but it was near impossible. His cheeks felt warm and his eyes stung. He knew what it was like to be a lobster in a pot now. Unlike the lobster, though, no one had been kind enough to put him into the water head first. No, this was fire that started in his chest and blossomed out to the rest of his extremities.

"CLAYTON!" Cora's next screech helped him focus, though her pretty face undulated like a desert mirage in front of him. He smiled despite the pain and he felt something crack at the top of his cheek, wetness seeping over his skin from the blister's pop. More cool air blasted him in the face as a pale, little hand brushed across his forehead—a singular relief to this molten agony.

"Listen to me, Deputy," she said. "Reach for the heart and crush it. Do you understand? It's hollow, so crush it and it'll die."

Sure, he understood that. What was not to understand about such a simple thing? He forced another smile, a second blister going taut and crusty as he maneuvered his arm around to the bogey's back. The monster dropped to a single knee, tilted forward as it pounded its arms on the floor in frustration. It seemed it wasn't smart enough to attack its rider with its whaling fists, which was probably good for Clayton's well-being. Boiling alive was bad enough, but adding a whipping to it was insult to injury.

Injuries. So many of them. He ached all over.

Plunging his arm into the bogey's body hurt—less because of the toxic spooge and more because it stretched his raw skin. His scream was pained and primal, a howl exploding from his clenched gut as he punched his fist into the bogey's chest. He couldn't see anything, but he remembered where that rock-like mass was inside the creature's chest. It didn't take him long to find it. His fingers closed around it, his arm quivering as a thousand poisonous stingers needled his flesh.

With a mighty roar, he gave it a squeeze. It broke with almost no pressure, the shattered pieces wooden and frail and crumbling to bits like walnut shells. The bogey's enraged wail cut short as its body burst apart, the goo flying to paint the walls, the ceiling, and the floor. Clay was dropped on his back with an unceremonious thud, the chair that had been embedded in the bogey's side clunking to the floor inches from his head. His skin was on fire, and his mind was clouded with fever. The world shrunk to darkness as convulsions wracked his body. He was going to sleep now and wouldn't that be nice. No more pain, no more problems.

But before he could fall into oblivion's sweet embrace, someone with the bedside manner of a pillaging warlord wrenched him off the ground. He was tossed around like a sack of wheat, his agonized back striking something squishy yet solid as arms snaked around his middle. Cold air blasted against the side of his neck as a harping female voice spat into the shell of his ear, "I told you not to touch it, you bleeding idiot."

—

He woke to the smell of lilacs. He loved lilacs. His mother used to put vases of them all over the farm. "To get rid of the manure stink," she'd say. For the most part, it worked—the foulest smelling thing inside the house was usually Clay or his father after a long day's work. Ma never let them stay that way long, though. She'd nag them into the tub with threats of rose soap if they didn't wash good. As Clay didn't want to smell like no frilly underwears, he always double-scrubbed behind his ears and kept his crannies as clean as could be.

This lilac smell wasn't fresh-cut flowers, he realized, but perfume. It was still nice. He pictured Cora in his head with her lovely, long hair and her uptilted nose peering down at him in his sick bed. He hadn't noticed her gentle scent before, but it suited her. A pretty smell for a pretty girl, which is how it ought to be.

A wet cloth glided over his scorched skin, relieving some of the burn. He was bare-chested, so the little vixen must have stripped him raw sometime after he'd...

Ah, hell. Sometime after he'd passed out on her while covered in bogey jelly.

He could hear the cloth getting wrung out beside his head. Another waft of lilac hit his nose as something lacy skimmed over his chest. The wipe-down continued, this time on his upper arms and chest. He hadn't let himself consider what it'd be like to have Cora's hands on him before, but now, with the coolness of the water soothing the blisters on his body, it was nice. Relaxing. Enjoyable even. He could think of other ways he would have liked to have experienced her touch, preferably without the mind-numbing burns and the stiffness in his joints, but everything started somewhere.

He attempted a smile but failed, the skin of his face too thick and leathery to allow for expressions. The best he could do was skim his tongue over his scorched lips and wince a little. "Feels nice," he whispered, thankful that his voice didn't crack or squeak. He hurt in places he couldn't name, but he'd be damned if he showed it again. He'd made enough of a fool of himself after the bogey.

"It would with this many burns. I think I managed to prevent too much scarring. You may have some on your chest and the backs of your hands, but your face and neck will be all right."

Clay had two problems with this reply. The first was that it was said in a deeper voice with an English accent. The second was that Cora wasn't English and therefore some stranger was touching him—some stranger who smelled like lilacs and wore lacy sleeves. Clay's eyes shot open to get a better idea of who was doctoring him, and much to his surprise, there was a strange woman hovering above him, a cold washcloth poised in her hand.

"Who are you?" Clay demanded.

"Irene. But you can call me Doc Miller for the time being. Cora said you needed emergency treatment. Normally, I wouldn't take a patient during tea hours, but she said this was dire. And you were—are—dire," she said.

Clay's sleep-drenched brain took a minute to comprehend what was going on. Irene had rouged cheeks, painted lips, and an ornate wig the same red hue as a strawberry on her head. She also had an Adam's apple. Clay stared. He couldn't help it. He'd heard about people like this before, usually in relation to French folks and some real interesting fiction choices, but he'd never actually encountered anyone. He had no idea what to do, and so he did nothing at all.

Irene—or Doc Miller—didn't seem to mind Clay's incredulous look, or if she did, she didn't show it. She swept her wet cloth over Clay's chest before applying thick, yellowish salve to his many blisters. For a moment, Clay thought about telling her not to touch him, but the ointment worked fast, numbing most of the pains in his chest. Clay hurt so bad he would have taken doctoring from the devil himself at that point.

And this might actually be the devil herself.

"I understand that I'm something of an anomaly, a woman trapped in a body she rejects," Irene said, tucking Clay's sheet up over his chest. "But please keep in mind that I saved your life. Cora gave you into my care, and I will make sure you are righted. As such, shooting me would be poor payment for my kindness."

"She left?"

The doctor looked surprised by the question. Maybe she expected Clay to scream or rant or rail or threaten violence, but Clay was too sore and too tired to fuss. And she was right. She'd saved his life. Clay's mama taught him too good to be an ingrate, especially not over something that had no bearing on him.

Irene cleared her throat and washed her hands in the basin, a smile on her face. "Yes, as soon as I told her you and the marshal would be all right. Something about not wishing to be arrested. But, if it's any consolation, she left a gift for you."

"She did?"

Irene leaned to the bedside table to retrieve a piece of paper. Clay couldn't reach for it himself, so Irene held it over his face so he could get a better look. Seeing it made him smile—well, he tried to smile anyway. It was a crude drawing of a heart with the word "idiot" written through the center.

"I think she's taken with you, Deputy. The marshal only got a regular apology. You got art. Terrible art, but art all the same." On a normal day, Clay would have said something sly like "she can't help but be sweet on me" and swaggered off to bask in his victory, but as he was flat on his back and may very well have wet his drawers recently, he internalized his gloat. Of course Cora was taken with him. He was tall, dark, handsome, and slick.

The little lady never had a chance.

Okay, yes she did. Me, though? I didn't really stand a chance.

"Thank you for saying so, Doc. She's something else," Clay managed.

"Yes, she is—trouble and lots of it. But I suppose that's part of her charm." Irene swept away the paper so she could go back to checking on Clay's burns. It wasn't until she adjusted the bandages around his hands that Clay realized he was wrapped from elbows to fingertips. He looked like one of them Egyptian mummies he saw in the traveling circus.

"Damn. How long am I gonna be here for?"

"Until I deem you healthy enough to leave."

"And when's that?"

Irene clucked her tongue and collapsed into a chair near Clay's bedside, her skirts spreading around her like layered doilies. She plucked at the lace overskirt and tutted. "It could take some time, I'm afraid. I don't want you losing skin or succumbing to infection."

Clay would have frowned about it, but that required him to make facial expressions, and the smiling experiment had already gone sour. What was he supposed to do all day when he was stuck in a room with an English doctor he didn't know? "Damn. This is gonna be boring. I can't even play cards."

"I could read to you, if you like. To pass the time."

Clay perked up a little at that. "You would? You got the whale book? Sterling was talking 'bout that one. He said good things about it, though he called Cora a whale. I had some big girls in my day—softer the cushion the better the pushin', if you know what I mean—but she's little. Sure, she's got some hips, but that don't mean…" Clay stopped talking when the doctor started laughing. Irene had tilted her head back so far, her ridiculously tall wig teetered back to reveal slicked, blond hair and a makeup line along her brow. It righted itself a moment later, the wig slapping back into place with a puff of white powder.

"Ha! I believe that was a metaphor, Deputy. And sadly, I don't have *Moby Dick*, though I do… pardon me." Irene took a moment to dab imaginary tears from her cheeks. "I do have some other books. Let's see what's on hand, shall we?"

"… a'right. Don't know what's so funny, though."

"No, you wouldn't. You Americans are so very literal sometimes." Irene shuffled off to paw at her shelves, moving beakers and other strange jars aside to procure a leather-bound book far too thick for Clay's liking. She settled back in again and cleared her throat, licking her thumb as she turned one of the thick pages. "Ah. This is a good one. Charles Darwin, to be exact. He's somewhat controversial, but as you can likely tell, I don't mind a little controversy in my life."

Clay'd never heard of Charles Darwin before, but he nodded and twinge-smiled, grateful for the Englishman-woman's courtesy and company. "It exciting? I like exciting books."

"Oh, in my estimation it's the most exciting story ever told."

"Thanks, Doc. You're a real gentleman. Lady. Sorry. I don't mind that you dress like a gal at all."

Irene smirked and cleared her throat. "That's kind of you to say, Deputy Jenson. For the record, I *am* a lady. I don't just dress like one, but let's get on with it, shall we? *On the Origin of Species* by Mr. Charles Darwin. 'When on board H.M.S. 'Beagle,' as naturalist, I was much struck with certain facts in the distribution...'"

CHAPTER SEVEN

NOW

Doc didn't look much like any gal Clay'd ever known. Her frippery and paints were girly, sure, but that didn't quite hide the squareness of her jaw or the dusky stubble shadowing her cheeks. But looking pretty wasn't the point as far as Clay understood it. Irene *was* Doc. There weren't two separate personalities or nothing—Seamus Miller was simply the costume Irene Miller sometimes hid in to keep herself safe from folks who cared too much about something that was none of their business. Why Doc's bloomers mattered so much to strangers, Clay couldn't say, but in his opinion, Doc was Doc, and Clay liked everything about his best friend.

It was too bad not everyone saw it the same. People looked at Irene and saw something strange, and just like any strange thing, they wanted to beat it, drown it, or light it on fire because they didn't understand it. Their prejudice certainly wasn't fun to deal with, but it was predictable, and therefore he could work around it. If Clay'd seen one horde of Irene haters, he'd seen them all, and if he had enough notice that it'd be a silk and lace sort of day in Docville, he could prevent a catastrophe with a few well-placed stink eyes and a big gun. The problem in Houston was that he found out about Irene's grand entrance minutes too late. She'd gone downstairs before Clay could set the precedent, and for it, she'd bled.

He didn't relish the idea of telling her not to go anywhere without him, but for her safety, it was looking like he'd have to. Now was not the time to say as much, though. Doc looked miserable enough without Clay demanding to be a perpetual babysitter.

"Remember that awful book you read me the first time we met? About birds on some island somewhere?" Irene's sole answer was a noncommittal grunt. Clay couldn't blame her for being unfriendly—she was bruised all over and her bodice was stained with blood. Plus, they were forced to ride together, and the close confines were more than a little uncomfortable. After the cart took off, Clay hauled Irene onto Squirt and rode away before anyone got any more ideas. There'd been a lot of awkward shuffling and rearranging as Clay'd slid his arms around Irene's waist to hold the reins.

Clay squeezed his knees, angling Squirt west. He couldn't see Addy yet, but he felt her from a mile and a half away, which shouldn't be possible. He could always sense Adelaide's magic when they were in close confines, but once fifteen feet or so separated them, she disappeared off his witchsniffer map. Unlike Cora, whose weird fluctuated from small, tickling winds to tornadoes depending on the day, Addy always masked her magic. If she didn't, she blazed like frozen, blue fire.

Either the horses jolted her concentration enough that her glamour faulted, or she'd let it go so Clay could find her. Whatever the case, he knew where she was. He had better things to do than scour Houston for a missing fairy the rest of the day.

Like leaving town before he got a face full of furious Lynch sisters.

"Addy's over yonder. Hoping that cat of hers ain't eaten the horses," Clay said, not expecting Doc to answer but filling the uncomfortable silence all the same.

Irene shifted in the saddle and patted her wig, her fingers fussing with a fat curl of blond hair. "I cannot believe she expects us to travel with a tiger. She has bollocks bigger than yours, and that is saying something. Goodness, I hate horses. This is so uncomfortable."

"Don't think you're well-versed enough in my bollocks to say one way or the other. Unless you been peeking, y'old pervert." Clay braced, knowing as soon as the words left his lips that he probably should have kept his trap shut. Irene was volatile when she was in a funk, and an ill-timed joke could be construed as Clay being "insensitive to her moods"—she'd vivisected him in the past for what he thought were innocuous ribbings. However, if the planets aligned just right, there was the slight possibility he could make her laugh, and if she laughed, he'd done some good. A chatty, happy Irene was far preferable to the brooding, short-tempered one sitting uncomfortably in his lap.

This time, instead of dressing him down like a wet-nappied boy, Irene jerked her elbow back and slammed him in the gut. Hard. The air was knocked clean from his middle, making him sputter like that laundering machine Cora'd made a few years back. "You flatter yourself, *Marshal*. You're not my type. The sanctity of your bollocks will remain intact, I assure you."

Clay swallowed a groan and rubbed his stomach, trying to keep the wheeze from his voice when he dared to speak again. "True. I ain't dark enough for your liking."

"No, you're not. Your complexion is like milk porridge, and frankly, I loathe milk porridge. It reminds me of my mother, and she was a horrid woman." Irene snorted and pulled a handkerchief from her beaded purse, spitting on it to dab at the rusty stains on her dress. "Oh, I meant to ask, where are we staying tonight? For all that you've regaled me with your terrible cowboy poetry about starry nights in southern skies, I'm terrified of rattlesnakes. Tell me we're not sleeping on the ground."

Clay shuddered, though not from mention of rattlesnakes. Addy was close now—a beacon of power in an otherwise drab, magical landscape. Her frigid magic made his skin feel like it was wriggling away from his flesh. He wanted to scratch at himself to kill the itch, but that'd accomplish a whole lot of nothing other than making his milk porridge skin turn red. "Nah. So long as the cart's intact, we should be able to hit the Sanderson boarding house by sundown."

"Ah! Lovely. Let's hope the tiger didn't ruin everything, then."

"Not the tiger I'm worried about. Addy's blazing." Clay gave Squirt's reins a little slack, doing his best to ignore how the horse's canter forced Irene's bottom to bounce against his lap. This wasn't awkward at all.

No, ma'am.

They found Addy standing on the driver's bench of the haul cart, the reins clutched in her white-knuckled hands, her temples dotted with sweat. The horses had wedged themselves between two tall buildings, the cart too wide to penetrate the alley. By the lazy swishes of their tails, Clay was fairly sure neither nag was in any rush to change its situation. There was a tiger behind them, after all, and faced this direction, they didn't have to worry about it. There was a reason you had to cover a horse's eyes to get them out of a burning barn; they might have big heads, but those creatures had tiny brains. If they couldn't see the fire, it ceased to exist. This dumb shit philosophy apparently extended to tigers, too.

"Move. Back up. Do something, you stupid things, or I'll feed you to Montague," Addy squawked. Sometime during her mad dash, her pretty straw hat had flown off and her hair had come free from its pins. Red corkscrews frizzed out from her head in an enormous halo of hair. The parasol was gone and the laces on her bodice were so loose her heaving bounties practically flopped over her neckline. She was flushed, sweaty, and agitated, so much so that she was muttering to herself in Irish—something she only did when she was worked into a fine frenzy.

"Having troubles, Addy?" Clay kept Squirt a few feet away from the bottleneck. He couldn't see Montague over the cart's ledge, so he had to assume the cat was lying down amidst the trunks. Maybe they'd gotten lucky and it'd run off, though Addy would probably be screeching to the high heavens if her pet carnivore went missing.

"Horses are stupid. Horribly stupid. They're stupid, and they ran into this alley."

Clay swept his hand over his mouth to hide his grin. "So what I'm getting here is that you think the horses are stupid."

"Dún do bhéal, Clayton."

"Eh? You're talking funny again, Addy. Musta got dirt in your mouth or something."

"Goodness. Leave the poor woman alone," Irene said before sliding off of Clay's lap. She hauled herself into the cart in a very unladylike manner, her triceps bulging against the sleeves of her dress. She vaulted the baggage pile like she'd vault a saw horse, landing in the middle of her trunks and bags with an indelicate thud. Something she saw there—and Clay was willing to bet it was their striped, meat-eating friend—made her retreat a few steps, her hand sailing up to grip her throat. "Adelaide, dear, is this thing going to eat me?"

"NO! HE'S HARMLESS."

Montague decided to show exactly how harmless he was by raising his head and growling, which made the horses prance and whinny between the buildings. Irene scampered away from the Hellcat, clearly unconvinced that the enormous pussycat was anything other than murderous. Unfortunately, her heeled boots, the hem of her dress, and a maze of trunks, sent Irene sprawling into a pile of burlap sacks. They were stuffed with her undergarment collection, so they were soft, but that didn't mean she was pleased about it. Clay could hear her grunting and sighing as she fumbled to find her feet again.

He slid off Squirt's back to lend a hand. The moment he climbed into the cart, he could see the tiger staring at him, its golden eyes flickering between him and the prone Irene. Its long, pink tongue even had the gall to sweep over its fangs like it was telegraphing exactly what it wanted to do to the two strange humans in its midst. "Addy, I'm not saying this to be a prick, but so help me, if that thing tries to take a bite outta someone, I'm making me a rug."

"He won't. He's just a vocal cat. Now, help me get these horses out so we can leave this hellhole. I'm tired of Houston already, and I've only been here three days." Clay didn't have to be told twice. He righted the toppled Irene before climbing over Montague, Addy, the bench, and the two horses to get into the alley. The horses weren't good about the whole backing up thing, so it took him a while to coax them out, but an hour later they were back on the road. Addy drove the cart with Irene while Clay and Squirt trotted along at their side, blissfully passenger free.

"Hoping none of this sets us back too bad. Ruckus like that draws attention," Clay murmured, a fresh cigarette pinched between his teeth. He blew twin coils of smoke out of his nose, his hands busy stuffing his tobacco bag back into his coat. "Last thing I need is a Lynch finding out I'm leaving."

"I am sorry for the delay. Such a silly fuss," Irene said. Clay eyed her from beneath his hat brim. She sounded real sad again—all guilty-like—and that wasn't even a little bit what he'd been after.

"Aw. Hell, Doc. Ain't your fault folks're stupid. It's gonna take us a good week and a half to get to N'Orleans anyway. Couple hours probably won't matter. I'm just thinking too much is all."

"My apologies all the same."

She went quiet after that. For all that she'd perked up on horseback, she was somber and miserable now. As they rumbled their way past the Houston city limits, Doc began the brutal process of dismantling Irene, shucking her identity piece by piece. First was her wig, followed shortly thereafter by her lipstick, rouge, and powder, the cosmetics smeared in a rainbow across a soiled handkerchief. The gloves were discarded, the earbobs tucked into a silk pack. Each accessory, blood-stained or not, was painstakingly returned to the trunks until all that was left of the once-glorious woman was a miserable, skinny not-man pretending to be a man in a ruined dress.

Doc ran her fingers through her flattened hair and slumped, her eyes pinched to slits as she watched the terrain pass by. Clay said nothing. It wasn't that he didn't care, but what could he possibly say that'd make Doc feel better? Thanks to paints, silk, and lace, Doc went from her hated boy disguise to a butterfly in the span of a few hours. And butterflies weren't mean to return to their cocoons. They weren't supposed to tuck away their wings and go back to being caterpillars. Irene had to do that with Doc Seamus Miller, and it always felt unnatural—not just for Irene, but for everyone around Irene, too. Seeing Doc thrust back into a presentation she loathed was sobering.

Between Doc's depression, Addy's sour disposition, and Clay's general unease, it was shaping up to be a doozy of a day. They'd left Houston late and loud. With a haul cart and so much baggage, they wouldn't make great time, and any Lynch hell-bent on revenge would catch them by dusk. And then what? There'd be trouble if one Lynch came. There'd be a disaster if four of them did. For all that Clay was good with his guns, they were equally as good with their magics, and he wasn't sure how much help Addy and Doc would be under pressure. Sad to say, the tiger was likely his best ally in that eventuality.

The same tiger who was—at that moment—getting scratches under the chin from Addy and waving his enormous feet around in feline pleasure.

Yep, they were fucked. This trip was going about as well as a gnome rodeo, and after seeing one of those in Jacksonville once, Clay could say with some certainty that wasn't very good at all.

—

They got to the Sanderson place an hour earlier than Clay expected, and they did it without a Lynch lighting them on fire along the way.

Sanderson's used to be a dairy farm with all of the proper farm fixings—a big house, a huge barn, plenty of grazing land—but then Levi Sanderson's heart gave out when he was adulterizing with the pastor's wife after Sunday service three years ago. Gemma Sanderson, widowed and with four hungry mouths to feed, said God may have struck her husband down for being a slimy-cocked sinner, but she would prevail. She sold her livestock and converted the farm to a boarding house, opening her doors to the Texas traveler for the bargain price of a dime a night. It wasn't a particularly fancy get-up, but it was comfortable and clean and had easy access to all of the major travel routes.

Those reasons alone were enough to keep her beds rented out every night, but add onto it her near-legendary chicken and biscuits dinner smothered in thick sausage gravy, and she was a traveling man's wet dream.

Usually Gemma was more than glad to have Clayton stay on her farm. She claimed having a marshal there added an air of respectability to the place, and that was good for business. But hearing that he was traveling with a tiger had changed the business dynamic. A lot. She was irritated with him, her normally red face near-purple.

"He ain't coming in," Gemma insisted, her eyes drifting from Clayton to Addy and then to the cart outside. "I won't have one of my kids et."

"Your kids won't be 'et,' I assure you," Addy said, trying for her pleasant, temperate voice while her eyes burned rot-in-Hell fire. Every few moments, she'd twitch, though that probably had less to do with business negotiations and more to do with sitting on the cart's wooden bench all day. She'd been pissing and moaning that her ass was asleep since mid-afternoon. Clay'd offered to beat it back to life for her, but she'd gone and ruined it by telling him she considered that foreplay. "He's a sweet boy. Come meet him?" Addy pressed.

"No. I won't come meet him. Neither will my kids. No tigers."

Clay's molars ground together. He was tired, his back ached, and if he didn't eat something, he'd resort to cannibalizing Addy or Doc—probably Addy 'cause she was fatter. Doc was all stringy and would taste like coyote jerky. "What'll it cost, Gemma? Anything. I'm exhausted, and Addy here's starting to look like a pork chop. She's a goner if you don't feed me soon."

"... five dollars and the cat stays in a stall away from the horses."

"Done."

Addy glared at Clayton, but he brushed her off with a small tip of his hat. "Best you're gonna get, Girlie. You're the only one in Texas who thinks traveling with a tiger is a good idea."

"I will have you know he's a lovely animal. But FINE. If Montague stays in a stall, so do I." Addy threw her money onto the counter and stormed outside. There'd been a few hours there where her magic had been tucked under the veil of her glamour again, but now it was back with a vengeance. It was hot enough to boil oil outside, but standing near her was a dunk in an arctic lake—Clay wanted a blanket, some whiskey to warm his gut, and a hearth fire.

After he had chicken dinner that was.

Priorities.

"Two rooms then, I guess. One for me and one for Doc Miller. Then food, if you'd be so inclined."

"Plenty inclined. The doctor's with you tonight?" Gemma took her five dollars and tucked it between her bosoms. She was a short, squat thing, as wide as she was tall and whose mountain of flesh probably hid all sorts of goodies. Clay had to wonder if she'd ever lost something of value inside those creamy folds, but it was probably rude to ask. It did make him think picking her up and shaking her might be like going on a treasure hunt, though.

"He is. He's with the cart, probably protecting his possessions from tiger attack."

Clay'd learned to code switch when talking about Doc in her disguise. It was something he and Doc had talked about a few times over the years, and always to the same ends.

"You're sure you want me to talk 'bout you like a boy when you're in your britches?" Clay asked during one very explicit, gin-laden conversation. "I know it upsets you when folks assume wrong 'bout you."

"'Want,' no, not really, but 'he' is appropriate in that case, yes," Doc said. "It's necessary for safety. As long as you're clear it's a false pretense."

"You're always a gal to me, Doc," Clay had said. "Just don't want to do you dirty."

Doc had smiled. "You're not nearly the twat I thought you were on initial meeting, Clayton. Thank you. "

Doc was wrong about that. Clay was most definitely all twat, but at least he faked it good enough to trick his best friend.

Gemma rolled her eyes at the mention of the tiger and pointed down the hall at a pair of rooms. "Well, you can have those two near the kitchen. I think I'll have the doctor look at my youngest son while he's here. Sammy's got a couple'a spots that make me nervous."

"Lucky Doc. Spots are his favorite."

Gemma's cackles followed Clay out the front door of the farm. Doc was assessing her baggage situation in the cart, and Clay waved at one of the smaller trunks. "Just bring something light. We ain't staying long enough for you to haul all of it inside."

"What about Irene's things? What if someone takes them?" She asked, talking about herself in the third person.

Clay followed her lead.

"Someone takes Irene's things, I'll buy her a whole new wardrobe, a'right? Just get your ass inside. I'm starving." Clay's tone didn't brook much in the way of argument. Under normal circumstances, Doc would tell Clayton where and when to stuff it for ordering her around, but this time—because of depression, fatigue, or a combination of the two—she was as docile as a fawn. She picked one leather satchel from the pile and hauled it over her shoulder. She'd abandoned her ruined dress in favor of a shirt and a pair of britches and was back to looking like ol' Seamus Miller now, complete with spectacles and a maroon bowler hat. Being so plain made her unhappy, but at least Clay wouldn't have to worry about her safety tonight. Silver lining to every rain cloud and all.

"Where's Adelaide?" Doc fell into step beside him.

"In the barn with her tiger. She's protesting, I think. She comes begging for a bed, it's gotta be with you. Cora wouldn't take kindly to me sharing mattress space with her sister."

Doc gritted her teeth, her eyes sweeping over Clay's profile. "Cora tried to kill you. She may have succeeded. She doesn't get a say in what you do and do not do anymore, Clayton. If you wanted to bugger Adelaide to the end of time, that's your right."

"Oh, Gemma's youngest son has the spots. She wants you to look at him," Clay said in response. His less-than-subtle topic switch scored him an elbow in the side, but the rest of him was too stiff and sore to register further discomfort. It was just one more ache in a sea of throbbing aches.

"You're an impossible idiot, and I… well. I worry for you," Doc said on a sigh, her nose crinkling like she smelled something foul. "I'll look at the boy. I simply love spots, don't you know. They're my favorite."

"Exactly what I told Gemma."

They crossed into the boarding house's common room, choosing a table by the open windows in case a breeze decided to grace their presence. Gemma's oldest child, a thirteen-year-old girl with the same pear-shaped, wobbling assets as her mother, came to deliver two plates of food. Clay would have felt guilty about eating such delicious fare while Addy sulked in the barn with her tiger, but it was her choice to be antisocial. If oats in a feedbag appealed to her more than the thickest, most savory gravy in all the South, so be it.

She was an idiot, but so be it.

Clay filled his belly and sprawled in his seat, his body and mind suffering equal amounts of exhaustion. Most nights, he'd swill some whiskey and scare himself up a card game before bed, but not tonight. Tonight was for the sleep of the dead. It occurred to him that a day in the saddle shouldn't bother him quite this much—that as much as he'd like to say it was a bumpier trail than usual or that he'd overworked himself saving Doc that morning, those things weren't true. Something wasn't quite right, and if he had to venture a guess as to what that something was, he would have to say the curse.

They said Bad Blood started small. Maybe needing to be tucked in between the sheets like a knee-high kid was the first sign.

"Thinkin' I'm gonna hit bed," he murmured. Doc waved him off, still picking at her food, and Clay clapped a hand on her shoulder as he passed her by. "Feel better. Tomorrow's a new day. Less dumb fucks to deal with."

"Oh, good. My life will be much better served with less dumb fucks. Sleep well, Clayton." Doc still sounded down about the day, and though Clay paused in his tracks and thought about trying to help his friend, a yawn spurred him toward his room. Tomorrow was soon enough to fix Doc. Nothing Clay could say would do Doc any better'n a good night's sleep anyway.

Clayton passed out before it was even dark outside. The crickets screamed, a million of them hollering their heads off at the setting sun, but after a minute or two, even they didn't matter. He was gone. He wasn't one to laze about in the mornings, but when dawn came a-knockin', he was still a-snorin'. It took a double tap of a fist on the door to break him from his slack-jawed, drooling stupor.

"Breakfast, Marshal," came Gemma's voice, and he rolled out of bed with a groan. He didn't bother with proper clothes, pulling on some pants and a holster before stumbling out his door to greet the day. He didn't give one damn if people saw his hairy chest or the burn scars along his shoulders and arms. All he cared about was filling his grumbling stomach and getting back on the road as quickly as possible. He glanced down the hall to Doc's door to see if she was awake yet. As if on cue, the knob turned and out walked…

Adelaide, lacing up the front of her dress and patting at her mussed, red hair.

He knew last night there was the possibility she'd come crawling inside looking for a bed. Saying you were sleeping in a barn was far different from doing it—hay stuck in your ears, back, and ass. There were spiders and itcher bugs and the floor smelled like horse urine. Addy may have gotten her Irish up over Montague's banishment, but she was too used to her comforts to last outside for any length of time. Her whining to sleep with one of them was as inevitable as the sunrise, really. So why was he so pissed that Addy had spent the night with Doc? Seeing her all bed-headed and looking so… so… post-coital irritated the hell out of him.

"Addy," he hissed, motioning her over. She lifted her head and smiled, her eyes drooping from a noticeable lack of sleep.

"Good morning, Marshal."

"Don't 'Good morning, Marshal' me. What the hell do you think you're doing? It's one thing to sleep in there. It's another to take advantage when Irene's down. Doc was lower than dog shit last night. You can't jump all over her like that! I don't want you using your cooter magic on my best friend."

"Take advantage? I didn't do anything Doc didn't want," she said, her left brow arching. She looked so amused by his upset that he wanted to biff her upside the head. He wouldn't because he'd never touch a hair on her fine, red head, but both of the sisters had a remarkable talent for getting under his skin.

"But Doc don't even like gals!"

"I'm aware."

When she didn't say anything else, he advanced, a finger pointed at her face. Addy had the audacity to tilt her head back and laugh. "I'm a fairy, Clayton. My personal specialty is glamour. I know Doc likes men." When Clay stopped short, probably looking as confused as he felt, Addy tossed her hands in the air and rolled her eyes to the ceiling. "How did Cora find such an innocent? Really, Clay. After all this time. Not that it's any of your business, but last night I was a six-foot tall Nubian gentleman with rippling muscles. I was delicious, really, and you should have seen the *size* of my—"

"A'RIGHT. I GET IT. I GET IT NOW," Clay said, cutting her off before she could tell him length, thickness, angle, or any other detail that would horrify him forever. It was clear he wasn't awake enough to handle Adelaide yet. He jammed his fists into his eyes and rubbed, in part to get the grit out and in part to maim himself in case any mental pictures traipsed their way into his brain. "I hate y'all sometimes, you know that?"

"No, you don't. You adore us." Addy's tinkling laughter brushed past him before disappearing into the common room. Breakfast smelled amazing—hot cakes and eggs and burnt coffee—and Clay stumbled along after her, craving sustenance and the day's first cigarette and maybe a good lye wash for his brain.

It took him a good dozen steps to hone in on the smell of burning hair. It took him a half dozen more to feel the scorching heat of a fire witch in her prime. His hand flew to his holster, his fingers gripping Gayle tight as he lifted his gaze to Gemma Sanderson's hearth. Standing there, all tall and pointy with her loathsome reptile perched on her shoulder, stood Elmira Lynch.

CHAPTER EIGHT

FIVE YEARS AGO

Sterling's injuries were healed overnight. Clayton was stuck in recovery for the better part of four months. Doc Irene feared infection, which meant day in and day out, she meticulously changed Clay's bandages and slathered him in ointment to mitigate the damage. After a week, she couldn't keep him in bed any longer, so to stop him from wandering outside and getting killed, she read him boring science books and regaled him with even more boring stories about the England she left behind.

In return, once Clay could use his hands well enough to hold cards, he taught her how to play poker like a proper American. "It's all in the eyes, Doc," he'd say, which made no sense to her at all. She insisted it was in the cards and the pairs and flushes therein, thereby making statistics a far more important factor in poker success than facial expressions. Clay did his damndest to explain the art of the bluff to her, but Doc never quite caught on. As such, she was a terrible card player. That was alright though; she made up for it with the quality of her doctoring and those little shortbread cookies she served at tea every day.

Clay only thought of Doc now because a couple of years after seeing her last, he'd swear he was looking at her again. Well, not her *per se*, but a variation of her. The scrawny human in a bowler hat and glasses sitting at the end of the bar bore a striking resemblance to Irene. The face was similarly shaped with smallish features and a square jaw. There were even cocoa brown eyes and too-delicate hands—when they picked up their glass, their pinky poked up like a little flag. Not too many men would have the testicular fortitude to drink that way in public. It made people think you were sly or French, neither of which were well-received in these parts.

But what was the likelihood that Doc Irene, dressed in boy clothes, would wander into a fly-ridden saloon in rural Mississippi? No one came here without reason. Hell, Clay and Sterling were only in town because Washington ordered them to be. The telegram hadn't told them why they had to visit, just to get here fast, so imagine their surprise to ride into a Salem-scale witch epidemic in Brookhaven. A half-dozen gals had already gone to the gallows thanks to a lynch-happy judge who listened a little too well to his fire-and-brimstone preacher. Another five rotted in jail awaiting their trials.

It took Marshal Cole shooting the judge in the ass and threatening to call in the army for the town to see things his way. The girls were loosed at suppertime, and not a single one set off Clay's sniffer—they were normal gals whose only sin was some good, old-fashioned harlotry. And that harlotry was precisely why Clay drank alone tonight. A couple of the ladies wanted to show Sterling how much they appreciated his intervention. The slick old coot was likely suffocating to death under the most grateful bosoms in all the South. A pair of gals had offered to keep Clay company, too, but none of the fare tickled his fancy. Poker and a bed where he didn't have to share his blankets were far more to his liking.

Sadly, not many locals were willing to sling cards with one of the lawman who'd ruined their string 'em up parties. Every table Clay sat at was quickly abandoned, gents making excuses about where they had to be and why they had to get there. Clay caught on quick and decided to nurse some whiskey to pass the time instead. Well, the Brookhaven, Mississippi version of whiskey anyway. The booze on the back wall of the saloon was labeled proper, but he was fairly sure the swill boiling inside his guts was homegrown moonshine. He nearly spit out his first sip, but then the barkeep smirked at him, and Clay felt obligated to empty his glass. He didn't want to give the native the satisfaction of chasing him off with his fiery backyard hooch. Clay was no dandy. No sirree.

He sipped his second glass of amber fire and peered down the bar at the Irene look-alike. The person peered right back. So began the awkward dance where they made all the motions of wanting to talk to the other but neither said a word. Clay, ever the patient one, broke within a minute. He lifted his glass in a salute, his drink ginger against the flickering overhead lanterns. "That you, Doc?" he called out. The bar was so empty his voice boomed, and something in the overhead rafters—bats or birds or maybe both—fluttered out the loft windows.

The person beneath the bowler hat nodded, vacating their seat to slide into the teetering barstool beside Clay. "Deputy. How are you?"

"Damn, you know, I thought that was you over there, but I couldn't be sure. I'm as fine as I can be in a dump like this. Mississippi and I don't agree. How've you been, Irene?" Clay slapped her on the shoulder a little too roughly, and Doc brushed at the spot like she was removing lint.

"It's Seamus when I'm dressed like this, if you don't mind. And I'm alive, which is better than the alternative. Rather glad to be so. I don't care for Mississippi much myself."

Clay tilted his hat up so he could peer at the woman who'd kept him alive years ago. "A'right, Seamus. You had trouble?"

Doc's answer was to roll down the crisp white collar of her shirt, exposing an ugly red ring circling her neck. It was rubbed raw along the sides, a series of purple and yellow bruises forming just below her jawline. Clay'd seen something like this before, at a lynching gone wrong where the swinger didn't swing right thanks to a faulty noose. He'd bucked and jerked on the string for a good minute before Clay'd done the merciful thing and shot him. When they'd cut down the body, his neck had looked like a piece of mangled beef. Doc wasn't quite that bad, but close enough that Clay flinched. "One of them decided to drag me behind his horse awhile."

Clay almost asked why someone would do that, but watching Doc sip her drink all ladylike, he was pretty sure he knew the answer. And it made him mad. Doc was a damned good person. Someone trying to kill her over her gender was not only unethical, it was illegal. "Who?" he demanded. He already felt ornery because of the spitting preacher and lack of poker. Throwing a pair of would-be murderous jackasses into the clink suited his disposition fine. He almost hoped they resisted arrest, too, so he could slap them around awhile.

Thinking that probably made him a terrible person, but he was all right with it.

"The matter's already been attended to, but thank you for your concern."

"Oh? By who?"

"By whom, you mean. And Cora."

Hearing the name made Clay go stock still. Despite not seeing her since N'Orleans, he thought about her all the time. Whenever a lady with sun-kissed locks walked by him, his stomach would drop and his toes would curl. He liked to pretend it was fury over the bogey attack. She'd put it in that box after all, and by association, she was responsible for the scars on his hands, arms, and chest. He must have told Sterling a dozen times that he couldn't wait to arrest her the next time he saw her. But then the blond on the street would turn out to be a stranger—no blue-tipped hair or stormy gray eyes, no sizzling magic anything—and his heart would sink to his boots. Sterling would mock him relentlessly for being such a limp dishrag over a con artist, and Clay would slink under his hat to hide from the unfortunate truth.

By the way his stomach swung down near his knees after hearing her name, he wasn't bothering to lie to himself tonight. He wanted to see her, and it wasn't to arrest her. If Clay's guess was right, Doc's injuries were fresh. The flesh was too ragged for the dragging to have happened much more than a couple days ago. That meant Cora was nearby—or she had been if she'd saved Doc. She couldn't have gotten far. Maybe if he left right now, he could catch her. Of course, he'd chase after her once he'd made sure Doc was all right. He couldn't just abandon her because the fae troublemaker had poked up her fine, gilded head.

Even if he sort of wanted to.

Damn it. I really am a bad person.

"There are two reasons I'm in this bar tonight, Clayton—if I can call you that," Doc said, pulling Clay from his Cora-centric reverie. Her voice startled Clay enough that he jumped in his seat and nearly pushed his drink over. The damned woman wasn't even here and she was making him stupid.

The solution to that was more whiskey. He topped off his glass and drained it. Twice. "'Course you can. It's my name, ain't it? What did you need?"

"The first is a personal favor. A rather big personal favor at that. Certain forward-thinking persons don't mind my eccentricities, but others would see me dead for them. I've been following Cora and Adelaide for some time, but they've been back and forth to the Fairy lands frequently lately, and when I'm alone... well." She motioned at her neck. "So what I'm asking—and offering, really—is to accompany you and Sterling as you travel. You are in a dangerous profession, and I'm sure accidents happen. I'd doctor you, and you'd... do nothing, really. Your presence would be enough to deter anyone intent on harming me, I think."

Clay was as surprised to learn that the girls went back and forth to the Fairy lands as he was to hear Doc's offer. The Unseelie mounds were located in Vermont, so did that mean they traveled from north to south and back again? He wanted to ask, but he was already destined to spend time spit-roasting in Hell for being so eager to abandon the doctor right after he'd found her again. "I can't really make that decision, Doc. I mean, far as I'm concerned, the more the merrier, but the marshal is the one who'd have to agree. I can run it by him—plead your case, if you'd like."

Doc smiled and nodded. "Cora said you'd say that, and I appreciate it."

"Did she? She thinks she knows me so well?"

"She claims she does, which segues nicely into the second reason I'm here tonight. Cora sent me to find you when she heard you were in town." Doc reached into the pocket of her shirt and pulled out a folded piece of paper. She used a single finger to slide it Clay's way, though when Clayton went to snatch it from her, she jerked it out of reach. "A moment. A promise before I give this to you. I need you to swear that you won't arrest her—not tonight or tomorrow. I understand that Cora's morally ambiguous. I know she's done some unlawful things in her past, but I would not be sitting here to offer this to you had it not been for her interference. I will not repay her kindness and friendship with betrayal. If I am to give this to you—and believe you-me, she wants you to have it—you must go with the intent of pleasure over business. There must be *no* business."

Clay nodded without hesitation. He talked a good talk when he was yammering at Sterling, but both he and the marshal knew he'd never have the stones to go through with arresting Cora. If she was going to jail, Sterling would be the one to send her, and as Sterling was busy wading through an ocean of grateful lady juices at the moment, Clay could safely agree to Doc's conditions. "You got my word. Think she knows I wouldn't hurt her."

Doc relinquished her hold on the paper with a nod. "She does, but I had to be sure. Enjoy yourself this evening, Deputy. And once you have the talk with Marshal Cole, let me know if I'm welcome. I'm staying at a rather ugly inn called the Mud Skunk, and the sooner I can abandon it for good, the happier I will be."

Clay opened the paper. Written in a feminine scrawl were the strangest directions he'd ever seen. "Take a left at the willow tree near the red barn—there's a path four pine trees down on the right" told him almost nothing about where he was going, but he was stupid enough to make the attempt anyway. He wanted to see her that bad. He'd probably end up in some swamp jungle that didn't exist on any map anywhere, but he'd been in worse places before—troll caves came immediately to mind. "Mud Skunk. I'll remember. Do you travel light? Mean, if we're gone tomorrow, can you be gone with us? We ain't always bunny fast, but there are times."

Doc blinked and cleared her throat, faint strain lines furrowing her brow. "Irene tends to travel heavy, but I'll pack her tonight on the eventuality you let me come along."

"A'right. I'll yap at Sterling in the morning." Clay rapped his knuckles on the bar and pulled a dollar from his billfold. "Drinks are on me tonight, Doc. Keep yourself safe while I'm gone, yeah?"

"I'll be fine for a single evening." Clay was almost to the swinging double doors of the saloon when Doc called his name again. Clay stopped and spun, his heel balanced on the tip of his spur. Doc gave him a long, heavy look that lacked the levity of before.

"Thank you for considering this," she said before taking a long swill of her liquor. She dropped it onto the bar and cleared her throat, not looking up at Clay. "You may be saving my life. So, yes. Thank you. I'll see you in the morning."

—

Clay didn't want to overthink Doc's parting words. Down that path lay madness. Did Doc mean "I'll see you in the morning" because Clay had to find her at Mud Skunk to give her Sterling's answer? Or did she mean that Clay would be spending the night with Cora? If it was the former, it was a nothing comment. The doctor was a polite person by nature and that was a kind thing to say.

If it was the latter…

Yep. Madness. Utter fucking madness. He couldn't think about it.

The directions he dismissed as stupid and confusing proved quite helpful. Cora's markers were difficult to see thanks to the late hour, but a good overhead moon showed him red barns, pine trees, strawberry patches, and a rotted stump. Fifteen minutes later, he was surrounded by forest he'd never traveled before. No road existed to lead his horse, but no road was necessary; dense brush formed natural barriers to either side of him, creating a grass pathway that eventually guided him to a curling trail of flat slate stones. He had no idea how far into the woods he was, only that it'd taken him a half hour to get there, and he sincerely hoped it'd be easy to find his way back.

It didn't take long for Cora's fairy-ness to slap him across the face. Electricity shivered up his spine and over his skin, bouncing from nerve to nerve and sending his pulse racing. His heart beat thick in his ears. The tips of his fingers throbbed. He kept riding. Every time he neared the woman, it was the same squirming discomfort followed immediately by a soothing thrum. The itchiness of it—that momentary wince—was nothing compared to the calm that settled into his bones right after. He felt more alive around her than anyone else, and maybe that was part of her charm.

Her cottage emerged from the woods like something drawn from a dream. Clay peered at its smoking chimney, swinging front lantern, and green door with equal parts excitement and dread. His teeth had ground down on his cigarette paper so much that flakes of tobacco littered his tongue. It all looked like it had been plucked from a fairytale—the rose bushes growing beneath the windows were wild and vibrant, their blooms red, peach, and white and kissed by the glow of lamplight. The gardens had pumpkins ripe for picking and herbs planted in tidy lines. A half-wall made of moss-covered stones and hard-packed mud surrounded the property. On the left side, there was a small well with a bucket hanging from a rusted hook. On the right, there was an enormous ring of blue-speckled mushrooms, the grass inside noticeably lusher than the grass outside.

A figure flashed by the front window. Clay's breath hitched. He spit out the cigarette, forgetting that he hadn't yet lit it. *Her.* She passed again, and he slipped off his horse, slicking his fingers through the hair at his temples and nearly knocking his hat askew. It wasn't greasy—he'd gotten a bath earlier—but it was flat and ugly, and he worried what she'd think. He wasn't usually jittery with women, but Cora was special. She wasn't like the gals who threw themselves at him and said they got lost in his blue eyes. She ran out on him and called him an idiot. She put bogeys that melted off his skin in boxes. She built illogical wind machines and more-illogical squirrels. She lied and stole with nary a second thought.

To his addled mind, the goddamned woman was perfect.

She must have sensed him hesitating on her front lawn because she came to the window and unlatched it, leaning over the box of flowers. The moonlight made her hair gleam like spun silver. It also made the white teeth inside her smile resemble horrible, gnashing fangs. Clay didn't know if he should run at her or away from her.

By the tilt of her head and the come-hither motion of her hand, probably far, far away.

Dang, she's pretty.

"Aren't you looking dapper, Deputy? Hobble your horse away from the mushrooms so you still have a horse tomorrow."

Such a nothing suggestion, and yet it forced him to ponder the morning thing again. Would he see it from Cora's window or from his rented room outside of Brookhaven? The possibility of staying with her made his pants shrink. That was surely the only explanation for the lack of room there; it had nothing at all to do with his twitching pants-pillager. He pulled his leather duster tight to his body to hide his ill-timed ardor. He was no twelve-year-old boy, damn it. Cora might be a fairy, but she was still a gal, and he'd put far too many notches on his belt for one gal to matter so much.

"Deputy?" she said again. "Are you coming?"

Not in the way you mean, but almost. He'd go to her in a minute, after he'd vanquished the rutting beast screeching for a thigh dive in the recesses of his brain. He wouldn't admit that to her, though, so instead he half-growled the one word racing through his brain on repeat: *hell.*

"Oh, that's a lovely greeting after so much time. Tie off your horse and get in here, you dolt."

Right, his horse. Focusing on her was easy—cathartic. Squirt was a gift from his father last spring—one of Old Gus's progeny. She was a sweet little sorrel with a star on her forehead, though Harland warned she was dim and not to expect too much of her. It was a bit of an understatement. Clay'd worn socks smarter than Squirt, but she was fast and strong, and that went further than brains any day of the week. If only he had the same attitude towards women, he wouldn't be fumbling in the dark in the middle of the Mississippi woods with a hard-on.

He left her near the well and trudged toward the house. He was as nervous as a wedding night bride as he removed his hat, his fingers clutching the brim hard enough to bend the lip. Cora's front door was a good half-foot shorter than he was, and he had to duck. She waited for him at one end of a two-person table, one hand holding up her chin, the other twisting a spoon around. It was the first time he'd seen her in the light without gloves, and he was surprised to find that the tips of her fingers were the same pale blue as the ends of her hair.

"You conquered the mighty front lawn, I see. Congratulations! I hope such an epic journey worked up an appetite. I made stew."

As the only thing Clay'd put in his stomach all night was two glasses of whatever the barkeep had passed off as whiskey, he nodded and sat at the table. He tried to figure out what to say to her after so much time. Her hair was down and flowing past her shoulders, her smile crooked in that mischievous way that suggested she'd done something awful. She wore a simple white blouse and a gray skirt that lacked the fancy buckles and ruffles he'd seen her in before. Her only accessory was a necklace—a plain brass key on a plainer brass chain. He was curious what it opened, but it was probably presumptuous to ask. Besides, he should start a conversation with something proper, like, "Hello" or "How are you?"

"Everything all right?" she asked.

"Yeah. It's fine. Thank you for the invitation," Clay managed. He picked up his spoon and stabbed it into the stew in front of him. She'd done something different with bread, scooping out the middle and using the crusty edges as a bowl, and it looked and smelled amazing.

"Excellent. Eat up. It's not poisonous."

Clay peered at her from beneath his brows, his spoon hovering just outside his mouth. Her saying something wasn't poisonous when he didn't expect it to be poisonous in the first place wasn't reassuring. Could he really put it past her to poison him? She'd nearly burned him alive with bogey goo once. Liquefying his insides wasn't completely out of character. "You put one of them blue mushrooms in here or something?"

"No! Those would those kill you, plus they're part of my fairy ring. I'd be sabotaging myself."

"A fairy what now?"

She rolled her eyes. "My goodness, Clayton. Didn't your mother teach you anything? Fairy ring. They're gateways between the fairy world and here?"

"Oh. Right. Just didn't know that particular term for it." His mother explained to him long ago that to pass from one world to the other, fairies had to visit places of power where the veil between the waking world and the dream world was thinnest. That unassuming looking mushroom ring must have been one of Cora's crossover places.

No wonder she didn't want Squirt eating the toadstools.

Cora smirked and shook her head. "You realize if I wanted to kill you, you'd be dead. A lightning strike and there'd be nothing left of you except a belt buckle and a pair of spurs. So eat up before it gets cold. Or don't, if you really think I'm a poisoner, but I think we both know better."

She had a point about the lightning, and he tucked into his stew with muttered thanks. He should have known she was ribbing him, but being near her turned his brains to jelly. For a man who prided himself on his glib confidence, it was humbling to be so awkward. He didn't relish it, but if the choice was to flail with her or to dazzle strangers with wit and charm—well, there was really no choice at all.

The stew was good, and he made appreciative tuts to let her know he liked it. He tried making conversation a few times, but the words twisted around his tongue before he could get them out. He'd traveled extensively since he'd seen her last—from New York to Charleston to Jacksonville—so there was plenty to talk about, but nothing felt adequate. Everything was too commonplace or predictable. He had one of the wildest jobs in the South, and yet he couldn't come up with a single good story to entertain a pretty fairy girl at dinnertime.

Lucky for him, she didn't mind the quiet; she smiled at him between bites of food while offering red wine and buttered bread. It wasn't until the little bastard squirrel scampered up to perch on her shoulder that he found his voice again. The critter peered at him with its gem-green eyes and chittered, the sound tinny thanks to its hollow body. "How the hell did you make that thing anyway?"

"Frederick? Oh, gears mostly. Mechanisms. A little fairy magic for the finer details. Are you interested in science?"

"Not particularly."

"Then I won't bore you with the schematics, but a majority of it is clockwork—like what you'd find inside of a pocket watch."

That made some sense to him, but not enough. Sure, the gears would power it, but how did it have its own intelligence? It acted like a squirrel ought to act, but as far as he could reason, gears wouldn't dictate behavior. There was clearly something else making Frederick all Frederick-like. "So how's it think, then? It has some kinda smarts."

"Oh, well—that's a little more complex, but there's an actual squirrel brain inside. Frederick was a flesh and blood squirrel. When his little body gave out, I gave him a new one so we could stay friends forever."

He flinched.

"What now? It was *alive?*"

She tilted her head. "Is there a problem with that? You knew I tinkered."

"Well, yeah, I knew, but… "

He frowned. Tinkering was one thing. This was something else. The notion of a creature, even a simple creature like a squirrel, being denied its death by her science-ing hands—well, would she do that to a person? Like, if he romanced her, would she rebuild him as some mechanical creature when he keeled over? He didn't want to be no metal cowboy. "Did it hurt him? There's something unnatural about it. I wouldn't want to be stuck in a metal body like that is what I'm saying. Dead's dead."

Cora smiled again, but in a softer way now—less like she'd eaten a canary. She reached into a bowl in the center of the table to produce a nut, and Frederick bounced down her arm to take it from her fingers. He held it between his metal paws to nibble, turning it this way and that just like any flesh and bone creature would. "It's sweet that you think like that, but his nerves were dead when I took his brain, so no pain at all. And he's a squirrel—there is no awareness of self in Rodentia. All he knows is he likes to climb trees and eat nuts. He has no inkling that the nuts don't do anything except fall into his empty belly. I'd never do this to a being who'd understand what happened to them—that understanding would be cruel."

Clay nodded and went back to his dinner. Dealing with it was much simpler than dealing with her and her weird death philosophies. His eyes skipped around the cottage. It was small inside, but she'd used the space efficiently. The main room had a fireplace at one end, the hearth and chimney constructed of colorful round stones packed into brown cement. The dinner table was off to the side, centered under the front windows so she could look out at her garden. A high-backed chair with a basket of spun yarn occupied the corner, the seat cushion hidden by a colorful, knitted afghan and an open, upside-down book. At the opposite end of the room was a closed doorway leading to what he guessed was her bedroom, and beside it was a long workbench with tools. She was assembling something involving long, hammered blades of metal, but what it was, he couldn't say. He wouldn't ask, either, out of fear of it being a con in its larvae stage. Not arresting her tonight, like he'd promised Doc, sure. Keeping her intention to commit a felony away from Sterling was different.

"I'm traveling again soon, and I wanted to see you before I left. I suppose I've missed you in my own fashion," she said, pulling his attention.

Clay swung his eyes back to her and snorted. "Have you? We haven't done anything proper to warrant missing. Outside of you running circles around me and Sterling."

"I suppose that's true, but that doesn't change the sentiment. I think about you a lot, I want to see you again after we part ways, and I have to assume you're in a similar position otherwise you wouldn't be here."

Hearing that made him feel… things. Things he didn't like to think about or acknowledge and wouldn't put into words. He put down his fork, taking an inordinate amount of time wiping the corners of his mouth with his napkin. He had no idea how to react, how to address the thickness growing in his chest, but she took that decision away from him by pushing away from the table and coming to stand beside him, her blue-tipped fingers gliding over his shoulder. The contact spark made him flinch, and when she shoved the table back with her rump to perch herself in his lap, sitting astride him and staring him in the eyes, he actually trembled. His hands dared to settle on her waist, feeling the softness there and the lovely curved flare of her hips. More sparks and sizzles. He breathed heavy through his nose. She wasn't too bony, and he liked that. He liked that he could press his fingers into her flesh and actually hold onto her. He lifted his face to hers and peered back at her, his blood rushing hard, his stomach fluttering in a way that made him wish he hadn't been so stubborn as to drink shit whiskey because a barkeep eyed him funny.

"You're ripe, Deputy."

They'd been building a mood up to that point—a mood that should have been a kiss. It *ought* to have been a kiss, dammit, and he wanted it more than anything he'd ever wanted in his life before, but then she'd gone and ruined it. He angled his face down to take a long sniff, mortified that he stank of sweat or horse or goddamned Mississippi hooch. He should have taken a second bath before he'd come out, because for all that he was pissed that she'd taken back the kiss before he even got it, he couldn't really blame her for not wanting it if he reeked.

"No. No, Clayton, not like that!" She tilted back her head and cackled to the roof of the cottage, the pale expanse of her throat right in front of his face. He wanted to press his lips to the skin. He wanted to taste her pulse and inhale her scent, but he couldn't. Even if his hands flexed and his mouth was dry from wanting her, he couldn't. Not yet.

"Like what then?" He demanded.

She tittered and peered at him, her fingers moving around the back of his head to thread through his hair. The first contact of her skin against his was the biggest jolt of all, one that made him dig his heels into the floor so hard he probably left crescent-shaped dents in the wood. He bit the sides of his tongue to endure her electric fire, his pupils dilating and his nostrils flaring with the strain. It died down quick, the sensation tapering off to an easy, undulating current that coated his body in a second skin, but it'd been fierce for a moment. He was grateful for the wad of skirt between her legs and his lap, not because of any arousal problem, but because he didn't want her to clue in to how badly his legs shook.

"Because when I met you, I said you weren't ripe yet. Like a green banana. But now you're a yellow banana, and as such, I'm rather pleased to be sitting here with you. You smell just fine, Deputy. Like leather, gun oil, and sweet tobacco. I like it. It's very you."

That was all the encouragement he needed. She liked him, he liked her, and he didn't stink. The kiss was back on, and he wouldn't be denied. He was a yellow banana, damn it, and being a yellow banana had certain benefits, like kissing the girl you've been dreaming about for more than five years. His lifted his hand, hesitant to touch her because he didn't want another explosive shock, but he'd risk it. She was worth it. His fingers slid into the golden silk of her hair, but this time, nothing stopped his heart. The initial blast was over and all that remained was gentle, pulsing air. He grinned like a fiend as he pulled her down to him, his mouth searching for hers. She met him halfway, her hands gliding over his chest and then ducking under his coat to hold him. Their lips fit together perfectly, like adjoining jigsaw puzzle pieces. He expected her to be cool like her magic, but her flesh was as warm as his own, and he took his time exploring her mouth, getting to know the hills and valleys of her lips like he had all the time in the world. He found he couldn't get enough of that bow in her upper lip, where all of those horrid little smiles came from.

It was Cora that pulled away first, before the kiss went from sweet heat to something more fiery. He couldn't even muster a protest. He clung to her, one hand resting on her side, one stroking along her smooth curls. His fingers twisted inside the blue loops of hair, stretching them out and then watching them bounce back around her elbows. Not only was it soothing, but it gave him a way to ogle her bosom without feeling like too much of a letch. It was fine to look, but less fine to get *caught* looking.

"Thank you for coming to dinner," she whispered. "I won't be back this way for some time, but when I am… well. I'll find you."

"That mean you been making our paths cross on purpose?" His voice was a little gruffer than he would have liked, and he stopped petting her hair so he could grab his mug of wine, taking a last, long haul to quench one of his two thirsts. It seemed the other one would have to wait, but he was fine with that. He'd waited five years for the kiss. Anything else had to be worth more. He felt too good—too content—to believe otherwise.

"Perhaps." She slithered off his lap to retrieve his Stetson, her fingers toying with the brim where he'd bent it. She fidgeted with it awhile, and then she put it on his head, adjusting the angle three times before she was satisfied with how it looked. "There. Now, the easiest way back is to follow the stone path out of the woods."

"But the stone path didn't go all the way to the edge of the woods."

"It does now."

He knew enough about fairy magic to not question it. He stood before her, his eyes sweeping over her pale, pretty face so he could burn her features to memory until the next time they met. She did one better and brushed her mouth over his—a tease of soft, smooth lips that was gone far too fast. She stepped away to clasp her hands together in front of her skirts. There were no goodbyes said, just a tilt of his hat and a nod of her head, and then he was walking out of the cottage and navigating the Mississippi night to find his bed.

He was three miles out before he realized she'd lifted his wallet.

CHAPTER NINE

NOW

Elmira Lynch and her lizard shared the common feature of large, bulging eyes, which was fine on the lizard but less fine on the woman. She looked like she was in a perpetual state of shock or—as Cora once unkindly put it—"like something big squeezed her middle too hard." With her narrow face, razor-edge cheekbones, and pointed chin, Elmira was about as attractive as the ass end of a dead heifer. And she wasn't even the ugliest Lynch. That'd been Betsy with her warts, but Betsy had at least been personable before the whole curse thing. Elmira was direct and abrupt and about as pleasant as getting your nose hairs plucked out one by one.

"Elmira," Clay said, trying for some semblance of dignity.

Addy was not so eloquent. "Cock."

Elmira's eyes skipped between them, her nostrils flaring so wide, she looked like a bull readying its charge. "My business is with the marshal responsible for my sister's murder, not your lot," she said to Addy.

"My lot? What is *that* supposed to mean?"

"Exactly how it sounds. We have no quarrel, woodkin. Stay out of this."

Addy scowled. "We'll see about that."

"Play nice, gals," Clay said, and both women turned their heads to frown at him. Admittedly, he'd been patronizing, but now they were pissed at him instead of each other. That had to count for something somewhere.

His fingers squeezed around Gayle's grip, but he didn't pull the trigger. There was still the possibility Elmira could be talked out of whatever fiery torture she had planned for him. Betsy had sprung her curse before a dialogue could occur, but Elmira seemed content to stare at him and run her bony, grime-crusted fingers over the bumps and ridges of her lizard's side. She was taking her time assessing the situation, which could work to his advantage. If he could just keep everyone calm...

"She started it," Addy said, her brows dipping into a sullen V. "And I'd argue that it's very much my business considering it was my sister that hired Betsy."

"You're Cora's sister?" Elmira's hand grew still on her pet. The lizard whipped its head around to hiss at Addy, its tail looping around Elmira's too-thin waist like a thick, scaly belt.

Addy eyeballed it and snorted. "I am. Is that a problem?"

Or not calm. That worked, too.

Clay rubbed his hand down his face, in part to clear the last vestiges of sleep from his eyes and in part to stop himself from strangling Adelaide. "DOC. GET YOUR BONY ASS OUT HERE," he hollered. If anyone could right this mess, it'd be the doctor. Doc'd been friends with Maybell for years now, even going so far as to drag Clay to a Lynch ranch social once. Irene, Cora, and the Lynch sisters spent far too much time discussing the influence of French fashion on southern debutantes. By the second hour, Clay was trying to slit his wrists with a butter knife, but Doc kept plucking it from his fingers before he could break the skin.

The prick.

Elmira's lizard cocked its head to the side to peer at him. Clay didn't even know what species it was except it had a crest on its head where the green scales turned red and spikes sprouting from its back. It was certainly bigger than any lizard he'd seen before—its front feet dug into Elmira's black frock on her left shoulder while its back feet clung to her right. Between the creature's size and the length of its claws, Clay was amazed she wasn't writhing in agony under its weight. "Doctor Miller is here?" Elmira said.

"Yeah."

"That's a pity."

"Why's that?"

"Potential collateral."

Clayton cringed, not only for Doc, but for the destruction those two words implied. Elmira Lynch had a proclivity for fire magic. She could do a number of other terrifying things, too, but fire was her favorite. In her younger days, she had a string of arrests for minor to mid-scale arson, and after an incident involving her estranged boyfriend and the cindering remains of the whorehouse he attended in lieu of her piano recital, she spent some weeks incarcerated. Lucky for Elmira, the town judge was sweet on Maybell, and he let the younger sister out of jail in hopes of poking the older. Elmira retired her fire fingers after that, but that didn't mean she wouldn't unleash them again given proper provocation.

As shooting her younger sister likely constituted proper provocation, Gemma Sanderson's boarding house was fucked.

"No need for that. Let's discuss this like civilized folk," Clay said.

"Will discussion bring my sister back?"

"No, but neither will harming Clayton. Good morning, everyone." Doc walked around the corner of the common room in her Seamus guise, looking for all intents and purposes like she didn't have a care in the world. Her fingers fidgeted with the cuffs of her shirt, rolling them up to her elbows in preparation for a long, hot Texas day. Her hair was slicked away from her face and her glasses sat crooked on her nose. Evidently, her evening with Addy had greatly improved her disposition. There was a spring in her step and a faint smile on her lips. There was also a series of thin, red furrows sprouting from her neckline and disappearing under the fabric of her shirt, which led Clay to believe that Addy's Nubian liked to scratch.

He really wished he hadn't thought of that, but damn his brain, it went there.

"Doctor Miller, out of respect for your friendship with my sister, I'd ask that you vacate the premises."

"No. This is asinine, Elmira. This house is filled with innocent people. You'll be tried and hanged for murder."

"Clayton Jenson killed my baby sister. She was barely eighteen years old. He is no innocent!" Elmira shouted the last, her face flushing pink, her narrow shoulders heaving. The lizard rose and fell with each of her breaths, but it never shifted position or clawed to maintain its grip. Instead, the crest on the top of its head stretched into a fan, making it appear taller and more menacing than it had moments ago.

Looking between the witch and her cold-blooded mantle, Clay came to the unfortunate conclusion that it was a familiar, and familiars were *annoying*. Most of them did something magical to announce their presence, like disappear from sight or fly or puke rainbows, but this one behaved itself. Familiars bonded to a witch would fight to the death to protect their masters. He couldn't count on it fighting polite.

Hell.

He had a real hankering to shoot Elmira in the face.

"Eighteen," Elmira reiterated, in case Clay missed it the first time. "You had choices."

"So did she, and last I checked, eighteen was an adult. I'm sorry for your hurt, but I acted within the law, Elmira. Your sister attacked me. I defended myself."

Elmira advanced on him, her bony hip striking one of Gemma's long dining tables. Her arm slashed through the air, and the table careened out of her way to smash into the wall, the wood blasting apart in a spray of splinters. The lizard inflated on her shoulders, every spike on its back standing erect, the tips changing from dusky orange to blazing red. "There were options! You could have held Betsy until we returned. You could have asked for our help in exchange for her life. Cora's threats don't scare the likes of us. Woodkin sluagh or no, we are the Lynches. THE Lynches!"

Clay'd never heard of a sluagh before, and he glanced at Addy for an explanation, but the red-haired fairy was too busy smashing her head into her hands to pay him any mind. That boded poor for all of them—she was about as sensitive as a brick. "Do I even wanna know what a sluagh is?"

She peeked at him through splayed fingers. "The spirits of dead sinners. They come like a flock of birds and consume anything in their path. Cora must have made a bargain with their queen. I don't even... she's an idiot. My sister is an idiot. No one bargains with Nichnevin, but Cora..." Addy's sentence disintegrated into a mess of stuttering, stammering Irish, frustration and panic written all over her face.

Clay wanted to ask more about this Nichnevin and what trouble she meant for Cora, but Elmira's hands splayed in front of her body, her palms facing the ceiling. Fire rushed to her elbows and then her shoulders, slithering over both black dress and lizard familiar to blaze around her neck like a lion's mane. "Enough chatter. You owe me blood, Jenson, and I am here to collect."

"Elmira! Not here. Not inside. Clayton, go. Outside. Out now," Doc demanded, her thin arms gesturing at the door. "She might kill us, but don't take the Sanderson house with us. Go. GO!"

Doc was right. For all that Clay wanted to start shooting, he had to keep the safety of the innocents in mind. Gemma Sanderson was probably in front of her cook stove assembling his breakfast. Her kids would be busy with chores or lessons while the other boarders would be climbing from their beds, stumbling blindly to the pots to take their morning pisses. They shouldn't go to their graves with their cocks in their hands because Clayton couldn't control one spindly Lynch.

He swung his back to the door and edged outside, Gayle pointed at Elmira's chest. By the look on her face, he wasn't sure he'd make it off the porch, but then Doc stepped in front of him like a human shield, Gayle's barrel jammed into the small of her back.

"If you want the marshal, you have to take me first, and I sincerely believe Maybell would be cross with you for that. Outside. All of you—outside. Your troubles have no place here."

Addy fell into step beside Doc, the two of them wide enough that all Elmira could see was Clay's cowboy hat poking up between their shoulders. The lizard lifted its head to hiss at Addy again, and she hissed right back, only louder and with more flying spittle. When it growled at her and whipped its head around to issue challenge, she responded in kind, going one further to stomp her feet in its direction.

"I appreciate that Elmira probably can't kill you proper, Addy, but she can definitely leave us humans a pile of shit and brimstone. Stop provoking the pet until we're outside, please?" Clay hissed.

"I don't like that thing. It's evil."

"So are you, but we keep you around."

"I loathe you sometimes. I hope you know that." Addy punctuated her statement with a hard whack to his leg. Two inches to the left, she'd have gotten him in his sweet-and-nasties, but lucky for him, she had piss-poor aim. Her fist barely grazed his hip.

The three of them waddled down the porch steps as a single unit, luring Elmira from the house by denying her a clear, bystander-free shot at Clayton. She followed them with slow, precise steps, her body encased in flame, her hands extended to either side and coming precariously close to igniting the whiskey barrels of flowers Gemma had planted beside the door. Clay searched the yard for cover, but there was nothing. It was a vast expanse of dusty flatland. There was a hitching post, a stack of crates, and the haul cart, which was parked near the stables twenty yards away. Everything big was wooden, and in their current predicament, wood was as useful as tits on a bull.

Elmira's boots hit the dust, and she circled, her hands crackling and snapping with hungry-looking flame. Doc glanced over at the cart and back to the witch, her hands going up in the air as if surrendering. "Clayton, if you can finish this without getting Irene's clothing destroyed, that would be appreciated."

"Do what I can," Clay said. Typical Irene being more concerned about her wardrobe than Clay's well-being, but he'd rib Doc about that later when there wasn't a woman hell-bent on murder coming their way.

"Excellent. Elmira, I'm going into the house now. I'm stepping away from Clayton so you two can have your brawl. I require my medicine bag." The only indication Elmira heard her was the tiny nod of her head. That was enough for Doc to dart away from Addy and Clay and run for the house. Clay had no idea why she needed a medicine bag, but Doc had her reasons.

"Elmira, we don't hafta do this," Clay said, one last attempt at diplomacy, but she dismissed him with a toss of her head, her hair escaping its pins to hang by her face like limp, black drapery.

"Yes, we do. Move, Fairy. Move, or so help me, I'll light you up with him."

Addy's answer was to let her glamour drop, her power surging around her in a blast of cold, wintry air. She couldn't call lightning or throw a tornado at an attacker like her sister, but what she could do no one did better. Glamour.

Addy's skin shimmered with her magic, her light so white and bright, he had to look away. It faded as fast as it'd come, and when he dared to look at her again, she no longer stood in front of him but to his left. Also, she was no longer a she but a he. She was him. Clayton found himself in the odd position of looking at himself. Addy'd given Elmira not one target, but two. It was probably the only advantage he could claim.

"Last chance to talk this through like normal folk, Elmira," Addy said, only in his voice and with his meter. It was unnerving to listen to, but he couldn't show that for fear of outing himself as the real Clay. Instead he lifted Gayle and pointed it at Elmira's head, his arm extended long. He felt more than saw the wobble there, the barrel wagging a little to the left before he overcompensated and swung it too far right. It could have been the aforementioned concerns making his gun feel heavier than usual. Or it could have been something else—something that sent him to bed before his proper bedtime last night.

Fucking curse.

"No more games, Fairy!" Elmira shrieked. The fire from her shoulders ran down her arms to condense between her hands, forming a blazing orb of spitting magic. It was the size of a dinner plate and the color of a setting sun, and within seconds, it was flying at the twin Clays. Addy and Clay dove left and right respectively, the fireball landing somewhere between their boots. Clay felt the burn on his heels, and he scampered away before it could do any real damage. He swung Gayle around and fired off a pair of shots. The first went wide, hitting one of the Sanderson porch posts. The other ripped a path through Elmira's right biceps. She screeched and clapped her hand on the injury, blood seeping between her fingers to run rivers down her arm.

Sensing its mistress's distress, the lizard flew off her shoulders, soaring at Addy with a high-pitched, angry squeal. Clay wasn't sure if the animal made a lucky guess as to which one antagonized it earlier or if it could see through her glamour, but it landed claws down in the dirt and charged, wisps of dust kicking up behind its heels and tail. There was a masculine grunt and a yelp as the horrible critter attacked, its two-inch-long claws lashing out in a flurry. Clay whipped Gayle around to try to help, but the lizard had latched onto Addy's torso. Shooting it meant shooting precariously close to Adelaide's person, and with his arm shaking as bad as it was, he couldn't risk it. She'd survive the initial blast, but her recovery would be contingent on finding the nearest crossover point to Fairy, and he didn't know where that was, nor did he know any local mediums who could track down the power places in a fairy's stead.

Elmira's hand pulled away from her wound, her fingers slick with blood. She advanced on Clay with a snarl, content to let her lizard dismantle the other Clayton rolling around on the ground. Clay scrambled to his feet and shot at her again. At the same time, Elmira screeched like a banshee. She screamed and screamed, the sound blasting across the Texas landscape with the fury of a dust storm. When she abruptly stopped, he thought maybe she'd done him a favor and gone and died, but then her chin dropped to her chest, and she grinned at him. Her thin lips receded to reveal two thick expanses of gum. With her brows dipping low over her dark eyes and a mouthful of crooked, pointed teeth, she looked every bit the storybook witch, the kind who lured children into her gingerbread house to eat them.

Good thing for him, he was no Hansel. Bad thing for him, she could cook him alive all the same.

She waved her hand again and he ducked low, thinking another fireball was about to singe off his eyebrows, but the only thing to come his way was his own bullet. It rolled across the ground and struck the toe of his boot, whole and unmarred despite Gayle's discharge. Elmira's shout had stopped the bullet. He would have been impressed with her witch technique, but it was difficult to admire something that left you dizzier than a drunk on a carousel.

At least the buzzing in his ears worked to his advantage. She was cackling, her eyes red-rimmed and wide with frenzy. Whatever filth spewed from the mad Lynch's maw was surely murder on the eardrums, but he couldn't hear a damned bit of it. He cocked Gayle, about to fire, but he paused when Doc burst out of Gemma's front door. Doc wasn't paying attention to her surroundings, too busy rummaging through her medical bag for something amongst the glass bottles and metal torture devices. Again, Clay couldn't take a shot for fear of hitting a friend. Doc stood almost directly behind Elmira.

Clay scampered left to fire, doing his best to avoid the squirming pile of Addy cowboy and lizard. Addy'd managed to reverse positions with the familiar, and she was now on top, the creature bucking and hissing with reptilian rage beneath her. She wasn't doing much to it other than using her body mass to squash it into the dirt, but as long as its claws were pointed away from her soft, meaty middle, Clay was confident he could concentrate on the bigger, meaner problem coming his way.

Clay braced his legs and readied his next shot. Gayle's barrel wavered worse than before, every muscle in his arm trembling. He locked the fingers of his free hand around his wrist to steady himself, but it was taking too long to get righted. Elmira pressed her advantage. Her fingers curled over into menacing talons, a spray of sanguine droplets flying from the tips. They spiraled through the air in Clay's direction, all haphazard and whirly like a Chinese firework.

On its own, flying blood wasn't scary, but when that flying blood transformed into flares of pulsing orange fire, he had good reason to worry. They looked volcano-hot. He had to run, but to where? There was the farm and the stack of crates to choose from, but neither appealed. Pale faces peered out at him through the dusty window panes of the boarding house. A single touch of fire to that dry-as-desert porch and the whole place would go up like a tinderbox. That left him only with the crates for cover, but those were almost useless. Not only was the wood thin and easy to destroy, but there were gaps between the slats.

The crates then, and with them, the likelihood of a fiery death. He let out a frustrated roar as he dove behind the stacked boxes, Gayle skittering from his hand upon impact. He huddled into a ball, his legs pulled to his chest to make himself as small as possible. His hat fell off and rolled away, the Stetson ambling across the ground like a lazy tumbleweed. Two orbs of fire struck the crates beside him, the blaze immediate, tall, and hungry. The black smoke that didn't billow towards the clouds filled his lungs, and he coughed so hard that he felt light-headed and starved for air. A third flare struck near his leg, but with nothing to feed the flame, it puffed out in a spray of charcoal ash.

Two more fire orbs sailed his way.

One angled for his face.

He lunged out of the way, yelping when he felt the heat whiz past his cheek. It was terrifying, yes, but also a relief—somehow, he'd avoided Elmira's Melted Face Surprise. What he didn't avoid was the second orb. It whipped around the blazing crates, not in a straight line trajectory but in an arc, like it was hunting him. It struck him in the shoulder, eating through shirt and skin with equal fervor. Pain ricocheted through every nerve in his body, his legs spasming as he slapped at the hurt, trying to extinguish it with the palms of his hands. But this was witch fire, and witch fire didn't die so easily. He screamed and rolled in the dust, back and forth to kill the embers needling at his bubbling flesh. It stopped the burn from spreading, but did nothing for the damage already done.

Elmira walked his way, the tips of her black boots kicking dirt into his face when she neared. She was talking, but he couldn't understand her. She was noise. Looming death and noise. He shook his head, wheezing thanks to the pain in his shoulder.

Her booted foot stomped down to grind his wound, his palm mashed into the ruined flesh beneath. The blistered skin burst, a flood of hot, sticky seepage running out between his fingers. His mouth opened in a soundless scream. Elmira didn't care; she crouched beside him, giving him a clear, unadulterated view of her thin, bony face. She looked so damned smug, so satisfied with what she'd wrought. Her eyes danced, her grin stretched wide so he had to stare at her hideous horse teeth.

It was one thing to die. It was another thing entirely to die looking at an ugly woman.

Gayle was close, a scant two feet away from where he lay. He wanted to grab for her, but his arm wouldn't *go*. He willed it to! It simply refused to cooperate, remaining a limp piece of meat at his side. Either the fire had done more harm than he realized or there was something noxious in Elmira's spell. He tested the left to see if it was similarly afflicted, but no. Right side only.

She'd ruined his shooting side.

Wasn't that just the crust on a shit sandwich?

Guess I'll have to improvise.

He flopped onto his hip to reach for his weapon, but those few seconds cost him. Elmira clued in that he was up to something and swatted Gayle away. Two feet became six and an impossible distance to crawl with a witch straddling him. He flopped onto his back and glared at her. She just smiled and started babbling again. He could make out words like "murderer" and "Betsy," but none of them mattered. What mattered was someone taking so much pleasure in his dying.

Hell with that. If she was going to kill him, he would damn well ruin her day first.

"Elmira," Clay rasped, his mouth so dry he probably spit grit every time he exhaled. "Just thought you should know I've seen sow nipples prettier'n you."

Antagonizing his murderer wasn't any smarter than shooting her sister had been, but seeing her good cheer dissolve was worth it. Sort of. She kicked his burn again, making him gag and shudder as another stream of foul-smelling fluid spilled forth, a bubble of it floating up toward the sky. Her hand moved up over his face, rusty flakes of dried blood raining into his eyes and mouth. Her nails were untidy and sharp and curved like her lizard's, though whether that was a side effect of their bond or quaint coincidence, he couldn't say.

She muttered something beneath her breath, and her poised hand erupted into flame, squiggling tentacles of fire extending from her fingertips to lash at his cheeks. Scorching heat emanated from their tips. He could hear the promise of his annihilation with every hiss and fizzle of the crackling magic, and he lifted his good arm to give her a shove, knowing how feeble a gesture it was. All he managed was to tangle a fist in her gown.

"Enough of you," she sneered, her squid-like appendages frenzying for his flesh. Her fingers pulsed bright. She readied her thrust. Then something went awry. A small, silver flash plunged into her neck. Clay's eyes—so dry from the fire, so greedy for tears—swung up to see Doc Miller stabbing Elmira with a syringe, a yellow fluid injected into the fat vein of her throat with brutal efficiency. Elmira gave a small shudder before her hand dropped, and then her chin dropped, and then her muscles went slack. She let out a single, pathetic mewl before falling forward, her body sprawling over Clay's prone form.

Somehow, he was in the odd and totally unenviable position of drowning in Lynch bubbies.

"Enough opiate to drop a bull elephant," Doc murmured. She grunted as she tugged Elmira off Clay, rolling her blank wide-eyed stare toward the morning sun. Clay cringed as some knobby, pointy witch part raked over his wound. It hurt, dang it, as bad as bogey fire hurt, and he breathed heavy through his nose to get past the toe-curling pain. When he felt less inclined to weep, he rocked himself into a sitting position, his face red and sweaty.

"She dead?" he managed.

"Not yet, but she will be. Her lungs will shut down any time now. Now Maybell can't blame you for killing two of her sisters."

"She will anyway, but you're a gentleperson and scholar for saying so. Don't let nobody tell you different. Addy all right?"

"I believe so."

Clay glanced over to see Addy beating the familiar into the ground with a broken slat of smoldering crate. She struck it a half a dozen times, but by the way the bloodthirsty little monster was sprawled in the dirt, the blows long since ceased to be effective.

"It's done, Addy. You killed it," Clay called, and she shot him a look that wasn't altogether friendly. Her fingers loosed the board. As soon as it struck the ground, her cowboy glamour faded, revealing a bruised and battered body. Her clothes were tattered thanks to lizard claws, her blouse barely covering her pale pink corset. Her skirt clung to her hips by a few pathetic shreds of cotton, and her fine stockings were marred with blood.

"You're damned near nekkid, though I guess that ain't nothin' new for a gal like you," Clay said.

"I'm quite fine, thank you for asking," she snapped. She lifted her chin to glare at him, but one look at his pitiful condition and her expression went softer than butter in summer. "Oh, Clay. Are you all right?"

Clay pushed himself to his feet and grunted. He hadn't examined himself yet because over the course of many years and many accidents, he'd come to the conclusion that once you looked at an injury, it hurt worse. Doc called it superstitious nonsense, but Clay would swear an oath it was true. As this particular injury was bad enough to shrivel his balls to raisins, the notion of worsening it didn't appeal much.

He looked anyway.

It felt like Elmira'd scorched his whole torso with her magic, but in reality, the circular burn on his shoulder was only two inches across. The outside skin curled over like the corners of an old book, the edges as black and crispy as burnt bacon. The inside patch was raw skin and pus bubbles, the biggest blisters already popped thanks to Elmira's totally-loving boot grind. "Been better. I can't feel my arm."

"What do you mean you can't feel your arm?" Doc demanded. She'd been trying to force Elmira's bug eyes closed, but they were so big and so bulbous, the lids wouldn't cooperate. She abandoned the witch to her drugged stupor, jogging over to Clay to eyeball his wound. She knew enough not to touch the burn itself, though she did reach for Clay's wrist to bend it to and fro like she was checking for a break. Her fingers traveled up to his elbow, and then to his biceps, pinching along the way. "Can you feel any of that?"

"Nope." Nothing Doc did mattered, not poking, not squeezing, not even stabbing it with the tip of her syringe. The arm was a piece of dead, heavy meat swinging by Clay's side.

"It's not like Sterling," Doc insisted, seeing Clay's grave expression. "That burn isn't deep enough to do nerve damage, so the paralysis is magical. It will wear off in time, and if not, Marie will be able to..."

"I know. I know what Marie will do. She'll fix curses and arms and every other damned stupid thing that's wrong with me." Clay was suddenly mad, madder than he'd been in a good long while. He was sick and tired of being sick and tired, and it was only two weeks into his curse. What would it be like in two months, or worse, five months? There was only so much time left to find Cora, survive a coven of vengeful witches, and get a cure before his body gave out. Now, he had to do all those things without the benefit of a good trigger arm.

He growled like a rabid dog and spit, a tension headache blossoming behind his eyes when wads of his expectorate rose from the ground to soar into the air. He had to get out of here. He had to get to N'Orleans before something else went wrong, but before he could do that, he needed his gun, he needed his hat, and he needed a goddamned cigarette.

Two Lynches were down, but there were three left to go.

Ain't that just a big ol' pisser?

CHAPTER TEN

FOUR YEARS AGO

The trip started nice enough. The hotel was clean, the company was good, and the card tables were full of rich idiots. But once they started the real, actual work, everything went to shit quicker than beans through a baby. It was too bad, too, 'cause Clay had a soft spot for South Carolina. During a previous visit—when the war was fresh over and reconstruction was underway—he said he could see himself settling here, maybe get some land and a fat wife to squirt out some Clayton-flavored babies. Since then, Cora'd wormed her way into his heart and mucked up the dream, but that didn't change how he felt about the Palmetto State.

He made it a point to visit as often as his schedule allowed. Whenever there was a job nearby, Clay pushed Sterling to take it so he could treat himself to a Charleston sabbatical. Sterling was generally amenable unless they happened to be halfway across the country at the time. He never used to complain about long treks, but lately—well, Sterling wasn't a young man anymore. After a few hours in the saddle, his back was as stiff as morning wood and his legs bowed like a wishbone. Doc said it was the normal aches and pains associated with arthritis, but Sterling rejected the prognosis, claiming arthritis was an old man's disease.

Doc, ever the gentlewoman, would simply smile.

Doc Miller had been with them since Mississippi, and though she slowed their travel significantly thanks to her ridiculous luggage, she made up for it in other ways. Weird marshaling wasn't easy, the myriad of faded war wounds riddling Sterling's middle an attestation to the dangers of the lifestyle. Clay wasn't quite as beat up, but he was amassing quite a collection himself, the newest one being a wendigo bite just above his hip. If it hadn't been for Doc's adroit hands, he may have lost his spleen or whatever important body part that was. His gall-something. Kidney. Gilly liver.

She'd saved Sterling's hide more than a few times, too. The first week traveling with them, Sterling made the mistake of trying to shake a river sprite's hand. It was an etiquette breach among that type of fairy, essentially translating to a big ol' "fuck you," and the offended party nearly bit the marshal's finger off for the faux pas. Sterling rushed back to town with his fingertip wrapped in a handkerchief. When Doc sewed it back on good as new, Sterling was so grateful that he didn't mention the fact that the doctor he'd assumed was a man—who'd comported themselves like a man since Sterling met them—-was suddenly and actually a woman, as was evident by Irene's powder, rouge, and heeled slippers. He hadn't mentioned it in the two years since, neither. He either accepted it as a part of Doc's personage or he pretended it didn't exist.

Whatever the case, Sterling didn't give Doc any shit about it and used Doc's proper pronouns and rules about gender switching for safety so Clay had nothing to say on the matter.

He did, however, have something to say on the matter of banshees taking up residency in hospitals.

"THAT THING NEEDS TO SHUT ITS MAW. ALREADY WISH I WAS AT THE HOTEL WITH DOC," he yelled to Sterling.

They stood on the stone steps of the Charleston Infirmary, a whitewashed building two stories tall with Grecian-style pillars supporting a black slate roof. Ivy climbed the wooden shingles, coiling around the graying, dingy shutters of the north-facing windows. They hadn't even crossed the threshold yet, but every time the banshee opened her danged mouth, Clay had to clap his hands over his ears to hear himself think.

Sterling reached into the pouch on his belt to retrieve a few wads of cotton. "You know anything about these critters?" he asked, his volume rising and falling depending on the banshee's proximity.

"Not much."

"They're like ghosts. Come at war time with the Morrigan. You know who she is?"

Clay nodded. His mother had given him a working knowledge about the gods and goddesses of her—well, their—people. The old gods were the arch mothers and fathers of the fae, the entities responsible for Fairy's very existence. All things that lived under Fairy's umbrella were either born to the gods or created by them. The Morrigan was a fearsome war goddess who traveled in the form of a raven to baptize battlefields with blood.

"Death goddess."

"Yep. The banshees are hers. They keen when a soldier's about to die to tell the underworld a soul's inbound. Haven't seen any of them since Gettysburg really." Mentioning the war, Sterling's eyes went tense, deep grooves settling into his weathered brow. The memory held weight all these years later, which Clay understood. Harland looked much the same when he talked about his time at war. Proof positive not all scars showed on the outside.

"Never knew you served. What regiment?"

"None. Some things can't go unattended, no matter what shit shape the world's in. The weirds are one of those things. I got sent to Gettysburg after the dust settled. Was a deputy at the time. Fifty thousand dead and almost a hundred banshees. They wailed so loud, you could hear 'em three counties over. We managed to send most of 'em back, but a few got away. I'm guessing this is one of them—came during the Northern Aggression and fled before we could subdue her."

Sterling stuffed his ears with the cotton and indicated Clay do the same. They walked through the tall, black doors of the facility. The receiving room was abandoned, the chairs against the wall toppled over after people left them in a hurry. The check-in desk was equally vacant; no personnel in sight. Considering hospitals usually had folks clamoring for medical attention, the emptiness was disconcerting.

"HOW DO WE MAKE HER GO AWAY?" Clayton shouted. He had to repeat himself four times before Sterling understood him. The marshal reached into his pocket to pull out a hand mirror, holding it up so Clay could see his own warped, bumpy reflection in the glass.

"Gotta show 'em how ugly they are. They run back to Fairy then."

"WHAT?"

"I SAID YA GOTTA SHOW 'EM HOW UGLY THEY ARE. Damn, this is annoying."

They ventured into the belly of the hospital. Clay sensed the banshee upstairs, a cold, fetid flavor of magic that filled the hospital with bad perfume. He pointed ahead to indicate where they needed to go. They ascended the main staircase, their hands empty save for Sterling's mirror. The halls before them were dim thanks to floor-to-ceiling wood paneling, a handful of gas lanterns flickering by the doors their only light.

It'd been two weeks since they were wired about the banshee. She'd come in on the heels of a storm, quickly settling into the infirmary's surgery wing and bellowing her rotten li'l heart out. Two dozen nurses had quit; six doctors refused to return to work until she was gone. Sterling telegrammed the mirror trick to the hospital administrator so they wouldn't have to wait for the marshals to travel from Virginia, but the banshee was such a horrible thing to behold, no one had the stones to do the job. That proved problematic for the patients as she tended to haunt their sickbeds, and if a doctor was too afraid to approach, people didn't receive their proper care.

Gave the banshee plenty to holler about, though.

They rounded the corner to the eastern wing, vacillating between silences so still Clay's spurs echoed through the halls to minute-long episodes of ear-busting wailing. There were no people near, only empty beds and tables strewn with medical instruments. Sterling never told Clay exactly what banshees looked like, but Clay figured he'd know it when he saw it. Normally, he'd just witchsniff her out, pinpointing her location with his own weird, but her magical stink was *everywhere*—clinging to ceilings and walls and floorboards. He was reduced to using his eyes and ears like a normal person, which he didn't like very much. Made him feel ill-prepared. If a banshee was so horrific to look at that people abandoned good work to get away from her, Sterling should have given him a description at the very least.

The marshal probably figured Clay was seasoned enough to handle anything. He went face-to-face with a wendigo and didn't soil his drawers, so what was one little fairy ghost?

And then she floated around the corner to peer at him.

It looked like someone had sewn a bunch of badness into one ugly monster. She was only four feet tall, but that was because she stooped at the waist, her spine curved like a cat's, the tall hump on the back sprouting black, leathery wings so long they dragged on the floor behind her. Her skin was yellow and shriveled, dead flesh clinging to a distorted, lumpy skeleton. She had no lips or nose, both features empty black voids, her mouth sporting toothless gums and a thin, reptilian tongue. Her eyes were covered by milky skins that hid her pupils. Her hair was a few sparse tufts of gray down near the moldering stumps of her ears.

If all of that wasn't bad enough, she'd rotted through at her neck, giving Clay an unadulterated view of her spine and the stringy bits that connected her head to her shoulders. The rest of her was half-rotten, too, but at least she'd cloaked it beneath a shapeless, gray robe tied off at her middle.

Clay stared at her because he couldn't stop himself from staring. When she spun to look at them, he scuttled away, his hand sliding down to his gun out of survival instinct. He didn't realize he was holding his breath until Sterling whacked him in the middle and forced the air to hiss out from between his teeth.

"Whatever you do, don't let her touch you. Banshee touch rots," Sterling said.

"Right. No touching. Not that I was go—" He cut himself off because she opened her mouth to shriek at them. This close to her cries, the cotton offered no protection. He staggered farther back, but there was no escaping, and so he crouched on his haunches with his palms pressed to his ears to drown her out.

"SHUT THE FUCK UP!" he screamed back, expecting his brain to rupture and bleed out over his clasping fingers. Her cry tapered off to a snarl before she drifted away in search of a dying soul. Clay'd only passed empty hospital rooms since arriving, but a patient had to remain somewhere for her to stick around. A banshee was nothing without an accessible corpse factory.

He lifted from his squat, his fingers massaging his ears in a vain attempt to stanch the high-pitched whine ringing in his ears. The last time he felt so bad was after he'd spent a night pounding rum—and other things—with Bijoux, the daughter of a Caribbean trader he'd met in Savannah. Least *she*'d been kind enough to wet his whistle before the hangover clobbered him senseless.

Not that he wanted the like from the banshee. He'd poked some ugly gals in his day, but he wouldn't touch this one with Sterling's cock and Doc pushing.

"I'm getting too old for this," Sterling rasped. He was down on one knee, his hand clutching his chest above his heart. His skin was pale, streaks of sweat running rivers down his cheeks.

Clay extended a hand to help him up, but Sterling waved him off, groaning as he pushed himself to standing. "I'm fine," he insisted, but he wasn't fine. He wove back and forth like he'd go ass over head any second. "Forgot what they were like up close. A real pisser, aren't they?"

"Yeah, a pisser. You sure you're all right?"

"I'm fine, I said."

To prove it, he took a few steps and promptly fell onto his ass, hitting with a clatter as his guns shook free of their holsters. Clay rushed to his side to steady him, and this time, Sterling wasn't stupid enough to refuse. He clung to the younger man, his fingers wrapped around Clay's forearm as he wobbled his way vertical once more.

"You sure you're up for this?" Clay demanded.

"I'm fine, I'm fine. When she blasted us, I got dizzy is all."

"Then let me do this. Gimme the mirror."

"Nah. I got it. Just need a minute."

Clay wasn't so sure. The marshal could barely stand even with Clay supporting him, but there was no way he could say so without the stubborn old coot having a shitter fit. Sterling had gotten to be a real curmudgeon since Doc mentioned arthritis, like he had to prove he wasn't heading off into his sunset years. It wouldn't have been a problem except he kept taking responsibilities away from Clay—responsibilities Clay'd earned by learning his trade and being a good deputy. This banshee thing was well within his skill set, but there was no way in Hell Sterling would relinquish that mirror.

"I can handle it, Sterling," Clay insisted, keeping his voice even so Sterling couldn't accuse him of insubordination. "You look like two pounds in a one pound bag."

"I know you can handle it. I wouldn't hire a stupid deputy, but I got this. Don't you worry."

Clay worried plenty, especially watching Sterling's stiff gait. He tried so hard to walk normal, it looked like he had an iron rod rammed up his ass. His steps were short and forced, and though he kept the mirror gripped in his left hand, he ran his right along the wall for balance. Clay followed behind him because he had to, but he didn't like it. If this went bad, what could Clay do to help? What worked against a hag that could bubble his brains inside of his skull with her voice? A mirror, yes, but anything else? Bullets were fair useless against fae folk.

He guessed he'd find out the hard way.

He loved finding shit out the hard way.

Only, no, he didn't at all.

This is so stupid.

He gritted his teeth and followed both boss and banshee down the hall to the very last door of the corridor. It was the post-surgical ward, the room thirty feet long with a single overhead lantern to light the expanse. A window on the far end allowed measly shreds of sunlight in, but it wasn't enough to combat the tomblike darkness. A dozen beds lined the walls, six on each side, thin gray blankets pulled taut over sterile white sheets, their pillows fluffed for people who weren't here. Small tables with oil lamps separated each bed, creating narrow walkways for doctors and nurses to attend the patients. A tray with rolling wheels was pushed against the wall, medical equipment stacked into neat piles filling the shelves.

It took Clay a moment to see the lady tucked into the corner. She was a frail thing, all bones and sallow skin, her eyes closed and her white hair brushed back from her face. Clay wasn't sure if she was sleeping or comatose, but either way, he hoped she didn't wake. The banshee hovered beside her bed, her leathery wings flapping. If whatever brought the old woman into the hospital wasn't enough to kill her, seeing that thing up close and personal surely would. She was heart-stoppingly hideous.

"Hey. You there. Leave her alone," Sterling called. He could no longer use the wall for leverage thanks to the beds, so he gripped the footrests instead, still tottering like a baby taking its first steps. Clay's hand lingered around Sterling's mid-back in case he had to interrupt another fall. If Sterling saw him doing it, he'd squawk louder than a hen in a foxhole, but Clay didn't care. He was too worried the old man was going to get himself killed.

The banshee craned her neck to peer at them, one of her hands lifting up to stroke along her cheek. Clay'd seen cats do similar when they groomed themselves, running their paws along the sides of their heads. The cats made it look cute—endearing and sweet—but with the banshee, it dehumanized her. Made him think of her more like an animal than a person. The notion of a creature that size and with that much power operating on animal instinct instead of real, true intelligence gave him the willies. It was like giving a cocked, loaded gun to a monkey.

She drifted their way again, her black, shriveled fingertip still worrying at her face. A strange, wet sucking sound wheezed through the holes where her nose ought to be, like she was trying to breathe. Sterling braced his legs apart for the confrontation and immediately swayed, his balance compromised thanks to her earlier screams. Clay anchored his hands around his waist to keep him from tumbling down.

"Stop acting like a poof. I'm fine," Sterling said.

Clay didn't let go. "Do the mirror."

"Let me go, boy. I said I'm fine."

"DO THE MIRROR NOW!" Clay ordered. The banshee hadn't moved fast, but with a room only thirty feet long, she hadn't had a long distance to travel either. She was in arm's reach, and here was Sterling bitching that his deputy helped him stand instead of concentrating on the job. Best Clay could figure it, the blast to the ears had fucked with him so much, his reasoning got broke. The marshal wasn't normally an idiot—loquacious, drunk, and argumentative, yes, but never an idiot.

Sterling cast Clay one last withering look before turning back to the monster. He hadn't expected her to be so close. Seeing that hideous face so near his own, he gasped and swung up his arm, the mirror glinting in the gaslight. The banshee had been calm until then, content to advance on them and chitter like an oversized chipmunk, but the quick motion startled her. She let off a semi-shriek, not nearly as shrill and ear-busting as her last cry, but enough to make Clay cringe.

Though this yell was a fraction of the awfulness of its predecessor, it was enough to fell the marshal. He buckled and the mirror slipped through his fingers, the glass crackling to bits inside of its frame. Clay dropped with him, his arms wrapped around his middle and held tight. He managed to cushion Sterling's fall, but he could do nothing about the banshee from down here, and she moved fast for a corpselike thing. Her fingers manacled Sterling's wrist, giving it a hard squeeze.

Sterling shrieked at the contact, his body bucking and writhing in agony. His legs kicked, the pants around his groin stained wet with urine. Clay pulled his gun and shot the banshee between her filmy, ghoulish eyes—not so much to hurt her, but to startle her into relinquishing her hold. The bullet sliced through her brain, ripping through the back of her skull and spraying gray, rotten matter on the floor behind her. Dollops of it rained onto Clay's boots, landing in squishy pudding piles that oozed down the sides like sludge.

It wasn't pretty, but it was effective; the banshee dropped Sterling's arm before erupting with another bellow. Sterling screamed and rolled around on the floor, clearly in agony, though whether that was a reaction to the touch or the scream, Clay didn't know. He didn't care, neither; his own brains were damn near boiling because she *wouldn't shut up*. Seemed blowing holes in her head pissed her off, and her answer to her new cranial ventilation was to bitch about it. Loudly. Until Clay's eyes watered. He shuddered and lunged for the mirror pieces, hoping something could be salvaged, but no, the biggest piece was smaller than his thumbnail and as useless as tits on a bull.

He whipped his head around in search of something shiny, the wads of cotton falling from his ears. He didn't care—they hadn't done anything anyway. Clay looked from beds to floor to end tables, but all the basins were made of ceramic, and the lanterns were equipped with clear glass flutes. His only hope was the rolling table with its medical supplies. Maybe one of the implements gleamed. Maybe there was a silver tray or a metal bowl somewhere in the mess.

Or maybe there was a brass bedpan.

Ain't elegant, but in a pinch…

It was an odd looking contraption, round at the bottom and a foot across in diameter. Attached to the catching pot was a long handle so a nurse could wedge it under a patient's ass without touching anything unsavory. Clay wriggled out from Sterling's flailing weight to crawl for it, his fingers wrapping around the handle and yanking it from the tray. It was oddly heavy and clanged as it struck the floor. The banshee didn't notice, or if she did, she didn't care. She just kept screaming 'cause it seemed like it was the only thing banshees were good for.

Clay yanked the pisspot close. For some ludicrous reason, the top of it was decorated with intricate brass filigree, like squatters actually gave a damn what they shit into. The bottom, however, was flat brass and real shiny. He flipped it over and, seeing his own face wavering back at him, swung it up at the banshee's head from the floor, grateful the bedpan was empty. Last thing he needed was a face full of stranger piss on top of everything else.

There was a resounding clank as the bedpan struck the banshee's chin—he hadn't meant to hit her, but it *was* a job perk. Her voice broke, her cry tapering off as she lashed out at Clay with her decrepit fingers. Clay scrambled back as she lunged for him, barely avoiding her swiping fingers. At one point, he could feel the skim of her jagged fingernails raking over his knuckles, and it was enough to birth a prayer to Jesus or Titania or anyone else kind enough to listen to him spilling from his lips.

"Come on, Beauty. Give her a looksee," he croaked, swinging the bedpan up in front of her face instead of into it. She wrenched it from his grasp with freakish strength, pulling so hard, she hauled him off the floor with it. She gave both bedpan and Clayton a violent shake, and he slammed into a heap at her feet, striking hard enough that his ribcage rattled.

"LOOK AT YOURSELF," he shouted at her. She hissed in reply, spraying him with her rancid spittle. It didn't burn his skin or make his eyes fall out, just stank real bad, and so he yelled at her again, his hands waving wildly at the bedpan. "LOOK AT YOUR FACE."

She brought it up over her shoulder like she might just use it to bash in his brains, but then she caught a glimpse of her reflection in the brass. Immediately she stilled, her eyes widening, her gaping mouth falling open just that much more. A curious trill warbled from her throat as she wheezed in another breath, her focus fixed on that shiny metal surface.

"That a girl. Look real good. Ain't you a daisy?"

The banshee stroked the pan with her fingertips. Her face twitched in parts, first along her cheeks and then near her nose and along her jaw. Her dead eyes narrowed and her forehead crinkled. With no brows or nose or lips, it was hard to get a read on her expression, but it was clear enough she wasn't real happy when she burst into pathetic sobs, throwing the bedpan into the wall with so much force it dented the wood. Her fingernails raked over her bare scalp. Her neck meat billowed as she sucked in air she wasn't really breathing. Her cries grew louder, and louder, until she tore away from Clay with a series of yelps that reminded him of a kicked dog. She fled her ugliness, ignoring Clay, ignoring the pile of writhing Sterling in her desperate retreat.

Seemed reality was too much for her. Fairy was welcome to take her back.

It would have been nice to bask in victory awhile, but Sterling let out a piteous snivel, the arm the banshee touched cradled to his chest. Clay closed the distance between them and hauled his friend into his lap. The marshal's face was mottled red, his nose and eyes almost purple from crying. Clay'd seen this man get bitten, mauled, and maimed by everything from trolls to goblins to frenzied pixies. For him to be so destroyed, it had to be bad.

"Gonna give it a look, all right?"

Sterling couldn't speak. His pale eyes remained glued to Clay's face as Clay lifted the injured hand. Clay had to stop himself from dropping it in revulsion—Sterling's flesh had shriveled to a wrinkled sheaf of leather, open sores oozing a steady stream of blood-tinged pus over his graying skin. His fingers looked skeletal, his wrist so narrow Clay could circle it with his thumb and forefinger.

Panicked, Clay tore the marshal's shirt open. The skin around Sterling's forearm clung to the bones so tightly that Clay could see the hole between the bones—could probably poke a finger straight through it if he wanted to. His elbow fared no better, a patch of bone splitting the flesh, strings of dead muscle clinging to the ivory surface like a meaty spider web. The limb was rotting away to nothing before his eyes.

"Hey. Hey, someone! I need help in here!" Clay screamed to no one and everyone. His voice echoed through the cavernous halls, swallowed by the infirmary's vast emptiness.

There was no answer.

It took ten minutes of wandering the hospital to find the sole nurse on duty. When she recoiled from Sterling's arm, too horrified to tend it, he sent her running back to the hotel for Dr. Miller. A half hour later, Irene arrived in a ruffled red dress that looked like she'd stolen it from a dockside doxy. Her wig was pale green and her lips were the color of a poppy. She'd even drawn a little black mole on the top of her cheek to resemble one of those French can-can girls from the posters.

"What happened?" Irene demanded, stepping up beside the bed with her medical bag in one hand, parasol in the other. She took one look at the ruined arm and winced, her nostrils flaring at the smell of decay. The parasol dropped to the ground, kicked under the bed and promptly forgotten.

"Banshee touched him. Ain't spread, but... well. Want to make sure. You know." Clay rubbed a hand over the back of his neck. Sterling's eyes flitted between the two of them, his mouth set in a grim line. He hadn't said a word since the accident, nor did he look inclined to start talking anytime soon. Clay figured it was shock or something of the like, but Doc Irene would know for sure.

"Bloody hell," Irene murmured, pulling a stack of cloths from her bag. "I need hot water and towels. Go. Go, go, go!"

It took Doc a full day to purge the arm of all the rot. It took Doc a week to concede that Sterling would never recover. She'd managed to avoid hacking off the arm at the shoulder, but the banshee's touch had decayed the muscles and nerves so much that Sterling couldn't move his fingers anymore. As if that wasn't bad enough, Irene insisted

Sterling stay in one of the infirmary's private rooms until she could be sure that his condition didn't worsen.

The internment was indefinite. So was Sterling's salty disposition. Every time Clay visited his hospital room with books or cards or whiskey, Sterling pretended he wasn't there, but Clay could be a real annoying prick when he wanted to be. This time, when Sterling played aloof, Clay brought out a translated copy of a Marquis de Sade book he'd stumbled across in his mattress travels. He read choice selections aloud, making sure his voice got real big during the filthiest parts so the old man couldn't ignore him.

"Stop that," Sterling said, "it's indecent."

"Sure it is, but it's better than Darwin. Doc did that to me when I was laid up." Clay glanced over at his friend from his bedside chair, smirking when he saw the marshal sitting up tall for the first time in a week. He refused to look at anything below Sterling's chest, though—last thing he needed was to see him pitching a sheet tent thanks to choice French literature. "C'mon. You like it. Who wouldn't. Two gals loving on each other is a beautiful phenomenon. Nature has gifted us this thing to think about."

"You're lucky Irene's resting. You wouldn't read me smut if she was around."

"Sure I would. She'd hit me for it, but that ain't a thing. She hits like a girl."

Sterling smirked, craning his head to the side to steal a peek at the next page. Clay lifted the book to read again, but two sentences in he was zapped by a wave of cold, electric magic. He tensed all over, his mouth going dry right as the silhouette of a gal appeared on the threshold of their hospital room. She was just a shadow, but the closer she came, the more he made out the finer details—the gentle sway of round hips, the long icy hair, the heart shape of a pale, feline face.

She waltzed into their room in a bright red cloak, the silk dress underneath the same blue hue as the tips of her hair. Her neck was strung with rows of pearls, her gloved hands covered in jewels that would have made a queen faint with envy. It was the fanciest Clay had ever seen her and, if he was being honest with himself, the most beautiful she'd ever looked to him. But seeing all that finery, he had to wonder who she was dressing for.

Worse, he had to wonder who'd given her all those sparkly things.

His stomach knotted, and his face went hot. He wanted to shoot someone. He didn't even have a good reason for it, but putting a hole in and through something would make him feel better about the jealousy worming its way through his thoughts. As that wasn't really a possibility right now, he rolled himself a cigarette instead, slicking his tongue over the tacky paper and stuffing it between his lips.

Smoke would help. Smoke always helped.

"Didn't feel you coming," Sterling said, watching Cora swing a heavy suitcase onto a table in the corner. He lifted his good hand and eyed the hemp ring, giving it a twist with his thumb. "Must be falling apart all over."

Clay stooped to wedge the book between Sterling's mattress and bed frame, hoping she didn't catch him stashing a dirty book. "Cora. How you been?"

Cora unsnapped a series of metal buckles along the case, her fingers fussing with a combination lock. "Fine, thank you. I'm playing diplomat today, which is why this must be quick. As it stands, I shouldn't have left Fairy—Adelaide's gotten herself into a pickle again. Maybe if she knew how to keep her goddess-damned legs shut, I wouldn't find myself in this position *again*."

Clay relaxed hearing that, stupid as it was to admit. Maybe she wasn't dressing pretty for another man after all. It shouldn't matter if she was—hell, he hadn't been living the monastic lifestyle since their last meeting—but the idea of someone else's hands traveling those fine curves made him all kinds of miserable. Hypocritical? Hell yes, but that didn't change how he felt.

She lifted the lid of her suitcase and leaned over something shiny and silver. Clay couldn't see what it was, and by the way her body was positioned, he wouldn't until she lifted it out, but his curiosity was piqued.

"Then why are you here?" Sterling asked. "Not like I wrote you a love letter begging you to come."

"Because Doctor Miller sent word that you were hurt and requested assistance. And you and I, we have… "She stopped fidgeting with her case to turn around and smile at Sterling, though her eyes strayed to Clay for a long moment. "We have an unusual understanding. I wouldn't go so far as to call it friendship, but you've been chasing me for twenty years, Marshal. If nothing else, we've enriched each other's lives. Maybe the word I ought to use is enlivened. I want to help."

"S'at so? You can undo banshee rot?"

"No, but I can restore you to a point. I simply must do it quickly." She hauled out the strangest looking invention Clay'd ever seen. It was two-and-a-half feet long and hinged with a silver knob at the middle, the top part sporting three black leather straps, the bottom sporting two. The lower portion had something resembling a glove attached to it, five metal prongs sticking out where a person's fingers might be. There were more joints and gears above the glove and a cap up top that looked like it'd fit over a shoulder.

Cora's gone and made Sterling a new arm.

Fancy that.

Sterling stared at it awhile before shrinking into his bed, his fingers tugging up the blanket past his chin to hide his mouth. The half of the face Clay could see looked plenty petulant, though—those silver brows knitted together so tight you couldn't tell left from right. "Y'ain't puttin' that on me, Girlie."

"I am, and you'll sit there while I strap you onto it. If you don't, Clayton will hold you down."

"I will?" Clay asked. By the look she gave him, he realized, yeah, he would, only so she wouldn't melt him into a puddle on the floor.

She approached Sterling with her contraption in hand. He looked like he might roll out of bed to bolt, but she tisked and motioned Clay to the other side of the mattress to block his escape. "I don't have time for this, Sterling. I have four hours to convince a goblin king that Adelaide is an unfit queen. If you keep me, she'll end up married to the ugliest, meanest thing in Fairy, and it'll be your fault." When he wriggled further under the blankets, she reached under and yanked out his arm with surprising strength. Much harder and she would have torn it off clean off, frail as it was.

"Damn it, Woman. Leave me alone!"

She ignored him and fit the sleeve over his shoulder, adjusting it so it sat flush to his skin. Sterling jerked to dislodge it, but she reached up to pinch his ear, giving it a hard squeeze with her sharp little fingernails. Clay's mother used to do that to him after he sassed her or ignored his chores. Hurt like the dickens then. Looked like it did now, too. Sterling yelped and went as still as a corpse, his eyes blazing fire.

"You're being silly. There's nothing to be afraid of. It's metal," Cora chided.

"I ain't afraid of anything."

"Then prove it and sit still, fussy pants."

That took the wind from his sails, and Cora was able to pull the straps on the device taut, adjusting the sleeve over Sterling's withered arm. When she was finished with the buckles, she took out a small screwdriver and tinkered with the hinges at the joints, tightening and loosening them so they fit the curvature of his limb. It took her ten minutes to finish, but when she stepped back, she had a big smile on her face, clearly satisfied with her work. "There. How does it feel?"

"Don't feel anything. Haven't since that rotter touched me," he said, sounding glum. He reached over to pluck at the metal, the plates on it so thin they looked like paper. "This thing is light."

"It's light because it's mithril, which is not easy to get out of Fairy these days. Oberon's a miserly… mmmf. Never mind! I don't have the time." Her expression turned dark, and she gave the contraption one last adjustment, her cheeks flushing so pink that Clay wanted to touch them to see if she ran hot. Well, he wanted to touch her, period, but this was as good a reason as any. "It's probably best you don't feel much, all things considered."

"What things considered?"

Before he could flinch away, she flipped a tiny switch on the inside elbow of the device. The metal arm gave a subtle shake, and Sterling jolted up in his bed, his jaw clenched, his eyes so wide Clay thought they'd pop out of his skull. "I feel—something. The hell is that?! I'm going to piss my pants!"

"Needles. And a current I supplied, but that will die down in a moment. My apologies to your bladder. When the brain orders a body part to move, electricity passes through you to make it happen. The banshee's touch destroyed that, but this will restore it. I'm afraid I can't give you your feeling back, but I can give you a functioning arm, and the only maintenance it requires is a little oil at the hinges now and again."

Clay watched Sterling settle back into bed, the wild expression fading from his face as the electrical discharge evened out to a steady thrum. The silver arm lay limp at his side, just a hunk of metal attached to a dead limb, but then two of his fingers twitched. They lifted off of the bed to wave for a moment before sinking down again. Sterling swallowed hard, his brow crinkling in so many lines it looked like a river map.

"It's… you did that. Thank you. I didn't… "He cut off when his voice grew thick, his gratitude evident in the glossiness of his eyes. He moved the fingers again, this time stretching them apart and curling them over into hooks. "It works. My good God, it works."

"Damn. You're gonna make him cry," Clay teased, though Clay himself was feeling soppy at the display. They'd all but written that arm off, but in walked Cora with a miracle of science and magic and everything was rainbows and unicorn shit again. He'd kiss her if he could. He would have kissed her even without the arm, but it was a double bonus reason to kiss her.

"Eat your hat, you piss stain," Sterling grumbled, but he smiled while he said it, utterly fascinated by the marvels of the restored limb. "Can't believe this."

"I'm glad to be of service. Do me a favor and give Irene my regards? I'm sorry I can't stay, but… well, Adelaide took the goblin king to her bed and now acts surprised that he kidnapped her into the lower caves. Idiot girl." She closed her suitcase and swooped down to brush her lips across Sterling's temple. "Good recoveries."

He flinched at the contact. "Yeah, thanks again. I'm in your debt, Gal."

For a heart-stopping moment, Clay thought she'd leave like that, without taking a moment to acknowledge him and the magical thing that'd happened between them a couple years ago. Maybe it hadn't meant a lick to her, but he thought about it every day, wishing she'd come back around, wishing he could have her in his arms again. But then she walked around the bed and pressed against him, her gloved hand splaying on the top of his hat to drag him down. Her upper lip tucked between his and demanded he give her the propers. He heartily obliged, his nose nudging at her nose, his tongue slicking out to tease at hers.

Right there in that hospital room, with Sterling and the rest of the world watching, he kissed her like he wanted to steal her last breath. And because it was Cora and nothing with her was ever easy, the entire time he tasted her, she electrocuted the shit out of him. Her magic pounded through his body; his skin itched to crawl off his bones. He clung to her and kept right on going. Even if his hair turned white, even if his heart stopped, he'd go to his maker squished up against the softest pointy-eared thief in the world.

Much to his disappointment, she pulled back, her rosebud lips swollen from too many kisses. It made him want to grab her and haul her to the closest empty bed to see if her other parts would zap him straight to Hell, too, but she tapped him on the nose with a fingertip and stepped away, a small curl of paper appearing in her hand. "One year from today, this address. Plan on not working a few days, Deputy."

"Marshal," Sterling called out from the bed. "You can call him Marshal."

Clay peered at the old man, doing his best to concentrate on the words rather than the blood rushing to his nether anatomy. "What's that now?"

"You're taking my star. I'm done with it."

Clay was too stunned to speak, so Cora did it for him. "Let me amend my statement then. I will see you in one year, and plan on taking a few days off, *Marshal*." When Clay turned his befuddled gaze her way, she stuffed the paper into his palm and blew him another kiss. "I really can't stay. Adelaide and all. Ta, gentlemen. Until we meet again."

"Bye," was all he could manage, too stupefied by the last two minutes to think straight. He watched her stride from the room with the empty suitcase swinging by her side. He could see her shape shrinking for a good half a minute before the rushing doctors and nurses crossed behind her path to block her from his view.

"She's got you wrapped around her finger so hard it's liable to fall off," Sterling snorted. "You damned fool."

"Yeah, she does. But that ain't—" Clay cleared his throat and threw himself in the visitor's chair, his fist closing around the address and squeezing it. He had to wait a year, but it sounded like she'd just made him a promise, and considering he didn't have the first clue how she really felt about him, he had to cling to whatever scrap she threw his way. He harbored no illusions about who had the power in their relationship—if it could even be called a relationship. "What do you mean you're done with your star? You just got your arm back."

"Because I'm lucky, and we both know it. It's time, boy. I been doing this for thirty years." Sterling peered at his metal arm, his fingers stretching and tapping thanks to Cora's invention. "Never made time for the softer things, and watching you two, I wish I had. Only advice I can give you—take the job, but don't let the job take you. That and—I know this'll be harder—but if Cora goes too far, do the right thing. She can be sweeter than peach pie at harvest time, but she also makes a living out of robbing folks. When she crosses the line, do what you have to do. If you can't, take off the star 'cause you ain't no good to the rest of the marshals when you side with the criminals."

"Yeah, I—"

"Hold on a damned minute," Sterling interrupted, his face breaking into a scowl. "Don't 'yes' me to death on this. I took it easy on you the last few years, letting her wander off without a tail, but I did that because she's got your nuts in her palm. It ain't always going to be easy. If you're shacking up with her, you'll see the ugly side sooner or later, and I gotta know you won't lose sight of right and wrong. If you promise me you can do right, you better mean it."

Clay considered the address in his fist like it was an extension of the woman herself. Sterling's question held weight, and, as such, it deserved due consideration. He was pretty sure he was in love with her, but did he love her so much he could overlook the uglier aspects of her personality? A little thieving wasn't such a big thing—even Sterling hadn't hauled her in for that—but if she went badder, would he turn away? He liked to think not, but maybe that was his arrogance talking. Folks did strange things when the heart was involved. So the question became did he have a way to keep his moral compass pointing north regardless of his feelings?

As if on cue, he saw Doc Irene coming down the hall to check on Sterling, her medical bag clutched to her chest, her skirts swishing over layers and layers of petticoats.

Yeah, he had a way to keep north. And it was a hundred and fifty pounds of gold-hearted girl. Doc Irene was the best person he knew. She wouldn't steer him wrong.

"I can do it," he said.

"Good." Sterling smiled and sprawled in his bed, his metal hand furling and unfurling as he worked his newly minted muscles. "Now then, I'm thinking it's gonna be a few hours before I'm strong enough to write Washington and tell them 'bout your promotion. So how about you read me more of that girl-lovin' book while we wait? Not that I like it, but you know… does pass the time. Be nice to see Irene whack you one, too."

Clay snickered and retrieved the book, thumbing through the pages to find exactly where they'd left off. "Sure thing, Marshal."

"None of that. It's Mr. Cole now, and I'll be honest, I'm feeling pretty good about it."

CHAPTER ELEVEN

NOW

Doc asked for an extra day to ship Elmira's remains back to her sisters—something about respecting the dead. Clay wasn't so sure Elmira deserved it, but he wasn't going to interfere. He had better things to do, like piss and moan about the burn on his shoulder and be grumpy about N'Orleans. Doc wasn't all that sympathetic. She sniped something about manning up before heading off to the local mortician to get the bones stripped; the body wouldn't travel well in the Texas heat.

When she came back, she crafted a letter to Maybell explaining Elmira's demise, paying particular attention to her role in the unfortunate debacle and taking full credit for the kill. The witch sisters would still blame Clayton, of course, but Doc was too optimistic for her own good sometimes.

Meanwhile, Clay and Addy had the unfortunate job of placating Gemma Sanderson. Clay tried buying her off, offering her twenty dollars and a passel of apologies for Elmira's antics, but she kept right on screaming that he'd endangered her babies and that he should rot in the Special Hell. Clay didn't know what the Special Hell was, but by the purple hue of Gemma's face, he assumed it was where the kid touchers went, and kid touchers were the worst.

Gemma berated him for a good ten minutes before Addy decided to take things into her own hands. Literal-like. Mid-tirade, she leaned over to whisper into the rotund woman's ear. Whatever she said stopped Gemma cold, and she peered at the red-haired fairy with a confused frown, her eyebrows lifting so high, they near touched her sandy brown widow's peak.

"What now?"

Addy whispered again. Clay had no idea what was said, but Gemma's expression softened and she twitched like she had ants in her bloomers. She looked from Addy to Clay and back again, like he was supposed to confirm or deny whatever it was Addy said, but he just shrugged. Sometimes, ignorance was bliss.

"That ain't even possible," Gemma murmured.

"It is," Addy said. "Would you like to see?"

"I... well, now I don't..." Addy offered Gemma a hand, and

Gemma went quiet. She was still flushed, but it was for a totally different reason than before. Had Addy been manipulating the situation with her fairy hijinks, Clay would have felt obligated to intervene on Gemma's behalf, but this wasn't that type of seduction. It was pure silver-tongued skill. Which, in the end, was what got them out of the Sanderson mess—Addy's silver tongue. Gemma took Addy's hand, Addy led her up the stairs, and the two women disappeared for some spring-squealing acrobatics.

When Addy resurfaced later, she looked pretty damned pleased with herself, like she'd climbed a mountain or—well, she had climbed a mountain, really. Gemma was a big, big gal. "Sprawled out like a purring pussycat, *with* her purring pussycat, if you get what I mean," she said.

Clay shook his head and moseyed toward the waiting wagon. He couldn't roll his cigarettes himself anymore, but Doc had been kind enough to pre-roll a dozen or so, and he stuffed one between his lips before striking a match. "That's a near Montague-sized pussycat, Adelaide."

"Yes, well, the softer the cushion, the better the pushing."

Using my own damned lines on me.

Cold.

Clay kept hoping the trip would improve once they left the Sanderson place, but it was stuck in a holding pattern of unpleasantness. Day by day, the blood curse chiseled away at his strength. His appetite waned, and his muscles ached. His arm flopped by his side, useless. He could barely keep his eyes open after dinner and—much to his dismay—sometimes required a midday nap. At first, those naps were done while on Squirt's back, but after he leaned to the side too much and ended up on his ass in a tumbleweed, Doc insisted he pass out in the wagon between the trunks.

"Ain't sleepin' in the back with that tiger," Clay said.

"Yes, you are. You're sick, Clayton, and if you're too ignorant to take care of yourself, I have no qualms about drugging you," Doc returned.

"Did you just *threaten* me?"

"Yes, I think I did."

Clay could tell by the gleam in Doc's eye that the little shit meant every word. In any other situation, he'd have appreciated this emboldened approach to doctoring. But being on the receiving end, not so much. Clay was pissier than an old man's drawers. He complained the entire time he wedged himself behind the tallest trunks, creating a wall of Irene luggage between him and the cat. Every time he shifted or rolled over to get comfortable, he caught a glimpse of orange and black fur or peering amber eyes. He clutched Gayle to his chest in case Montague decided to make a snack of him.

"I might have shit aim right with my left arm, but so help me, Addy, that thing comes at me..."

"Shut up and sleep, Clayton," Doc said.

Clay shut up and slept.

By the second week, Clayton's poor health translated to a poorer disposition—everything spit from his mouth was pure venom. It was safer for him to ride silent than to inflict his mood on his friends. Addy and Doc had enough sense to leave him alone, but most of that was that they were too busy basking in their *own* miseries. The ride was long, hot, and, by the time they crossed into Louisiana, moist. Good God in heaven, it was moist.

Clay hated that word.

Moist.

Just... ugh.

Sixteen days later, they rolled into N'Orleans. It should have made him happier than a pig in shit to be back. Mama's in the French Quarter made jambalaya so tasty he wouldn't order it anywhere else. The crawdads from Philipe's melted on his tongue, and the beignets on the corner of Rue de la Levee were served with extra powdered sugar. The Spanish architecture was astounding to behold, especially near the Garden District. No city could party quite like N'Orleans; Clay'd once attended a Mardi Gras fete so debauched, he didn't dare discuss it in polite company.

If a man wanted to lose himself in grandeur and excess, N'Orleans was the place to be, but Clay wasn't that man anymore. He climbed off of Squirt's back to check them into the Rue Bourbon Hotel knowing the stay would be short—four days, maybe five if Marie needed extra time. For all its charm and personality, the Crescent City had a way of wearing a man down. The downtown buildings were crammed in, and the streets were narrow. The carriages lumbering along the main routes came perilously close to striking pedestrians and shop-fronts alike, especially when they had to turn a tight, unforgiving corner. And then there was the smell. Something Sterling called "Bayou Cologne." Unwashed bodies, horse waste, and the polluted tang of the Mississippi rode the air, the stench only worsened by the sweltering humidity. There was no breeze to speak of during the day, not even along the river, which left the local population sequestered in shuttered, dark rooms until sundown.

Plus, there were the memories to contend with. The ghost of better days haunted the Beaumont Bed and Breakfast. Every time he passed it, Clay's gut clenched remembering that first week he'd spent with Cora. He'd never known happiness like that, and he doubted he ever would again.

Goddamn that woman for ruining something so special. Goddamn her for killing what could have been the closest thing to a happily-ever-after either one of us will get.

The hotel manager took Clay's money and asked if they had any accommodation requests. Clay didn't have the energy to explain Montague, so he let Addy glamour the manager into an agreeable mindset. It wasn't the most ethical approach to the situation, but it made life easier for everyone involved. Besides, Addy kept insisting the striped monstrosity was harmless. Now was good a time as any to test the theory. He just had to hope he wasn't testing it at the expense of a bellhop's face, but he was tired enough that he was willing to risk it this one time.

Doc snagged a couple of staff to haul her baggage while Addy wrestled her cat upstairs. Clay collected his things and carried them to his room with his one good arm. When a staff boy offered to assist him with his bags, he gave him the nastiest stink-eye he could muster before guilt got the better of him. He tipped the kid a nickel. Wasn't the youngin's fault Clay was an angry pile of mess. He was only trying to do his job.

He'd just slung his bags onto his bed when there was a rap on his door. Clay glanced over to see Doc filling his doorway, a pen and a piece of paper poised in her hand. "I'm sending word to Marie that we've arrived. Perhaps tomorrow will be a better day. Milton's cloud and all that."

Clay had no idea who Milton was, but he nodded all the same. "See if she can see us tonight or tomorrow. Sooner the better."

"Of course. And now, I bathe. I feel like I've been rolling in a swine pit."

Doc practically skipped back to her room. The woman loved her some Marie. The first time Clay introduced them, Doc was in her boy clothes, but Marie took one look at her and told her she didn't need to put on pretenses for her sake. Doc was stunned, but she was elated, too, unleashing Irene upon the Voodoo Queen in an explosion of silver ruffles, a silver wig done in a Louis XIV style, and her face adorned with period appropriate makeup. The enthusiasm was a little cloying, but Clay never said so aloud. When the whole world peered at you through prejudiced eyes, you cleaved to the ones who treated you with respect. Marie Laveau treated Doc like a real gentlewoman, and that was a rare treasure.

Clay wasn't quite so excited to see Marie this time around, but only because his mood was stained with bullpucky. On a good day,

Marie's company was an exceptional treat. Sterling introduced them about six or seven years ago, just after Marie's eightieth birthday. When Clay sat at her table for the first time, he hadn't felt a single flicker of magic, but then she'd cupped his cheeks in her warm hands, and he'd nearly crumpled beneath the force of it. She was spice smell and dirt taste—a strange combination—but the more he got to know her, the more he understood it. Her powers ran deep. She was the warm promise of everything that grew and flourished just below the earth's surface.

If she hadn't been so friendly, she would have been the scariest woman he'd ever met. Fortunately, her fondness for Sterling extended to his deputy, too, so there was nothing to fear.

Clay glanced at himself in the mirror before ringing the bell for service. His beard was too thick, his brow was streaked with dust, and his hair hung long around his neck. He'd thinned out some, too, the curse making the grooves beneath his cheeks too pronounced. He couldn't do anything about that, but he could fix the rest of it with a bath and a barber so Marie wouldn't mistake him for some street corner tramp.

It took him two hours to get pretty, or as pretty as a dying man could get. It took Marie the same amount of time to send her grandson to welcome them to N'Orleans. He'd never met this particular Laveau before, but Marie had something like fifteen children, and they'd all produced their own broods. The twenty-something gentleman standing in the foyer was six feet tall, his skin brown, his custom-tailored suit a soft dove gray. As soon as Clay walked downstairs to greet him, the man dipped into a low bow, his hand waving a gold walking stick to the side.

"Jacque Laveau at your service, Marshal Jenson. Grand'Mere extends her hospitality and has sent a carriage for you." His voice was thick with the Creole drawl, and Clay found himself smiling in spite of his mood.

"Your Grand'Mere works fast, but it's one of the reasons I like her best. Nice to meet you, Jacque." Clay normally shook with his right hand, but with his infirmity, he offered the left instead. Jacque closed his fingers around it and gave it a gentlemanly squeeze.

Any other pleasantries were lost to Addy's arrival. She appeared in a new yellow dress, her hair pinned to her head in crimson ringlets. She looked fresh-faced and lovely and—with the healthy amount of cleavage bobbing under her chin—ready to stake her claim on the city. When her green eyes settled on the perfectly-coifed Laveau, she let out an appreciative whistle, her skin adopting an alluring glow at the sight of such a virile gent. Clay rolled his eyes as she sauntered over to the stranger, her tongue skimming over her teeth in invitation.

"Well, look at what we have here," she whispered.

"Mademoiselle." Jacque smiled pleasantly and kissed the back of her fingers. And then he looked away.

It wasn't what she was expecting. Normally, she'd bat her eyes, give a little wiggle, and every man in the room had his pecker in hand before she could take another breath. Not this one. It took her a moment to figure it out, but when she did, her expression changed from heavy-lidded enticing to absolute delight. Clay didn't follow, but then Irene appeared at the top of the stairs in a powder puff dress of pink and strings of tinted pearls, and Jacque couldn't look away. He was utterly enchanted by the enormous wig, the heavy kohl around Irene's eyes, and the ruffled pink fan beating near her jaw.

"Monsieur Jacque, may I introduce the lovely Doctor Irene. Doc, Marie's grandson, Jacque." Addy gave an exaggerated bow as she stepped aside, allowing the two to make their introductions. Irene peered at the suave stranger leaning over his cane, her cheeks flushing enough she didn't need her circles of fuchsia rouge anymore. Much as Clay hated that he knew this, Jacque was just Doc's type—dark and handsome, tall and clean-cut. He suspected Marie knew it, too, and had served up her grandson as a fleshy welcoming gift.

Irene swished down the stairs, her gloved hand skimming over the polished mahogany banister. "A pleasure to meet you." The moment she took the last step, Jacque was at her elbow, offering his arm like he was escorting the Queen of England to afternoon tea.

"Welcome to N'Orleans, belle. You are lovelier than a magnolia blossom, aren't you?"

Irene glanced at Clayton, smiled, and then burst into the oddest giggles he'd ever heard. Rich baritones that didn't lend themselves to girlish squeals, and yet there he was making noises like one of them cat-sized dogs fancy ladies kept in their purses.

"Enchanté, Monsieur Jacque. Enchanté."

"Likewise."

They shared a smoldering glance before Jacque guided them to the carriage on the curbside. It was big and black and gilded with a teal brocade interior. The four horses hauling the rig were as glossy as the coach's lacquered exterior, and the driver wore proper black attire including a top hat and cloak. It was an elaborate set-up, probably more typical of N'Orleans' moneyed gentry than a freeborn octoroon woman, but Marie'd been selling her magic for more than fifty years, and she didn't come cheap. If anyone had disposable income to throw at something so ostentatious, it was her.

The moment the driver whipped the horses into motion, Clay stopped looking out the window. He didn't want to see how close they came to hitting other carriages, nor did he want to see how many pedestrians they flattened along the way. Addy was considerably less concerned about their safety, her face pressed against the glass to watch the scenery. Every time they passed a French Quarter landmark, she pointed it out and grinned. She also grinned at every giggle erupting from Irene's painted lips. Jacque kept whispering into Irene's ear, and she kept batting at him with her fan.

After twenty or thirty hard, jarring turns, the carriage rolled to a stop. Clay dared to peek out the window. Marie's house was two stories tall with tall green shutters and a wrought-iron terrace on the second floor. A veritable jungle grew there, potted plants, flowers, and herbs occupying every corner and shelf. She'd left room for a pair of chairs with a table wedged between them, on top of which an empty pitcher lying in wait to offer evening refreshment, but the majority of the space was dedicated to flora. Most of Marie's spells required gris-gris bags, which were stuffed with animal bones, hand-crafted wooden trinkets, and cuttings of her home-grown herbs.

Jacque helped Irene from the carriage and led them to the front door. It smelled like greenery inside, and Clay followed a long, candle-lit hallway with plush carpets and fabric-covered walls. Halfway through, a shiver of strange energy stopped him dead. Oily and cold, it was at odds with the warm, inviting atmosphere inside Marie's house. Clay crouched to get a better line on it, and he felt it shimmy down the wall to escape under the floorboards, the presence preferring the dark, secret places over ones in the light.

It wasn't Marie's magic.

"Everything all right?" Addy asked from behind him.

"Don't know. Something's here and I don't know what it is," he said.

"Clayton, cher. Get your fine flanks back here!" Marie's voice echoed from the back of her house, her tone as deep and as musical as he remembered. "I want to lay my eyes on ya!"

Clay glanced around the hall, the flames bending on the candle wicks. There was no breeze, and no one moved, which meant the unearthly Other was responsible for the disturbance. His left hand swept to his holster, his palm settling on Gayle's grip. "Marie? You got something new in the house? Something cold and deadish?"

"Oui, but I'll explain. Get back here!"

She didn't sound all that concerned about it, which probably meant he shouldn't be all that concerned about it either. He abandoned the hall to follow her voice to a friendly, shaded porch on the back end of the kitchen. There on an upholstered bench overlooking the courtyard sat Marie Laveau. Her liver-spotted hands rested in her lap over a jewel-toned knitted afghan. Her hair was hidden beneath a red headscarf, and her shoulders were draped in a colorful purple and gold shawl adorned with tiny, dangling beads. She had a strong profile, her cheekbones high and her nose narrow with a small hook at the end, her golden skin mostly smooth save for a few shallow lines around her eyes and mouth.

"As I live and breathe, if it isn't Marshal Jenson. Come. Sit," she said, patting the seat beside her.

"Good to see you, Marie. You sure about that thing in the hall?"

"In a minute, cher. You're so pushy."

He tried to take one of the chairs flanking the couch, but she reached for his dead hand and reeled him over by it. It was strange—he felt nothing in the limb, but because his magical senses were still functioning, the normal sizzle passed through his arm unnoticed before exploding in his shoulder. He nearly jumped out of his boots at the surprise of it, unable to suppress his startled suck of breath.

Addy smirked at him as she sank into one of the chairs, her hands smoothing the wrinkles from her yellow skirts. "Madame Laveau. Your reputation precedes you. I'm honored to meet you. I'm Adelaide WhisperWind."

Marie nodded and guided Clayton down beside her. "A pleasure, Woodkin Child. I'm surprised we haven't met before. I've heard your name. Sometimes it's the moneyed men of the Plantations praising your beauty. Sometimes it's the dock workers calling you the red siren of the seas. You're admirably indiscriminate."

Clayton coughed to cover his laugh. Marie'd just called Addy a world-class harlot, but she'd done it in such a way that Addy really couldn't complain about it. Not that she would—she wore her conquests like badges of pride, and if she'd slutted her way around N'Orleans before, she had to know Marie would find out about it. The Laveau was an extension of the city itself. She was its eyes and ears and heart.

Nothing got past her. Nothing.

"No one's called you a whore quite like that before, now have they, Addy?" Clayton asked, unable to resist needling her, even in his pitiful state.

Marie tutted at him and batted him on the nose. "I never said such a crass thing. I more suggested our woodkin friend is a diplomat of the sheets."

Addy giggled and turned her palms to the ceiling, her smile so wide she reminded him of Cora for a moment. Cora grinned like that when she'd been caught doing something bad, which was most days, really, because Cora didn't know how to behave herself, nor did she care enough about being caught to cover her tracks. "We all have our skills, Madame Marie."

"And I may need some of your *other* skills in a moment, Woodkin Child, but before we get to that—Clayton, make sure Irene visits me before y'all leave? I enjoy her company too much to let Jacque keep her for himself." It wasn't until she mentioned Doc that Clay realized she wasn't there. Jacque had swept Irene off somewhere private. God only knew what they were doing, and God could keep the information to His damned self, too. The whole thing made Clay sour; everyone around him was getting their fun bits funned on while he rotted inside his own skin.

Isn't fair.

"I can do that."

"You're a good boy, Clayton Jenson, no matter what that nasty gal did to ya." He wanted to ask which gal he meant—Elmira or Cora—but then she distracted him by lifting his bad hand to her mouth and flicking her tongue over his skin. Whatever she tasted there made her cringe, and she dropped the limb back into his lap with a dismissive wave. "Amateur work. Woodkin Child, hand me that over yonder? We need to bust some bad magic." She pointed into the kitchen at a deep brown satchel with leather handles sitting atop the table.

Addy did as she was asked, but when she foisted the bag, she hesitated, blinking down at it and shaking her head. "Is this supposed to move?"

"Oh, that's just Li Grande Zombi. Don't fret him."

"Li Grande what—" Addy's question cut off because she screeched. A huge black snake head poked its way from the top of the bag, the underscales of the reptile a bright, flaming red. Clay snickered. He knew about Marie's strange pet, a rather common Louisiana mud snake that extended a very uncommon six feet from head to tail, but he hadn't thought to warn Addy because he hadn't expected Zombi to be in the bag. Marie tended to wear him draped over her shoulders or keep him in a basket by her feet.

"Bring him here, cherie." Addy swallowed past her surprise and lugged him over, wincing every time Zombi's tongue flicked out to graze the back of her wrist. The way she practically threw him at Marie made Clayton wonder if Addy had a bit of a phobia where serpents were concerned, which was funny considering her talents with the domestic trouser variety.

"Zombi, my loves, is a servant of Ouncongo—the trickster god. We have something of an accord, don't we, Ouncongo?" She hefted the snake out of the bag and piled him in her lap in thick black loops. He didn't slither away, content to weigh down her skirts and peer at

Clayton with impassive eyes. Marie guided a foot of him around her wrist, his head cradled in the cup of her palm. "He knows the bad magic when he smells it. Take it. Take the magic, Ouncongo."

Clay had no idea what the hell was going on, especially when Marie began humming a strange, growling song beneath her breath. The snake wasn't doing much of anything yet except hanging limp over her arm, its scales shimmering like black diamonds in the afternoon sun. Marie chanted louder in a tongue Clay didn't understand, her eyes rolling into her head as she swayed in her seat. It was odd and somewhat scary, and Clay's good hand clung to the bench like it could anchor him against this storm of weird.

The spice scent came in on a much-needed breeze, wafting through the courtyard like gentle perfume. As the wind picked up, so, too, did the smell, growing in intensity until it filled his nostrils. It was followed by the rich undercurrents of growing things, of cut grass and mud and root cellars. The snake lifted its head from Marie's hand to bob in Clay's direction, finally oozing onto Clay's dead limb, winding around it in layer upon layer of coils.

"OUNCONGO, MANGEZ LE MALEFICE!"

That sounded a lot like French to Clay, but because he'd never been taught anything other than English and a handful of Spanish swears that were variations on the word fuck, he had no idea what she was saying. Zombi knew, though, as he went taut, clinging to the arm in a way that probably would have hurt if Clay could feel anything. The scales rippled, a flash of light traveling from one end of the snake to the other, white and then yellow and finally pearlescent gray. A viscous liquid of the same hue seeped from Zombi's body, and Marie jerked herself out of her entranced state to paw through her bag, retrieving a small glass jar and a simple piece of stripped wood.

"You should get feeling back very soon, mon cher. It may take some time, but the arm is saved," she said, running the stick down the snake's body to collect the mysterious goo. Clay didn't know what it was, but by the way it twitched inside of the jar, he wasn't sure he wanted to know neither. He just hoped none of the evil gunk had stained his leather coat. He liked his coat. It was his favorite—all soft kid leather and brass buttons. Made him feel pretty.

"Thank you, Marie. 'preciate it." He tried flexing his hand to test his strength, but nothing happened yet—he still felt numb from the shoulder down. Time, she'd said. He had a little bit of that to spare still. Not much, but a little.

Addy eyed him, and then Marie, sitting up straighter in her chair and tapping her fingers on the armrests by her sides. "That was wonderful, but what about the curse? The arm he could live without. The curse he can't live with," she said.

Marie frowned and nodded, her tongue slicking over her lips to wet them. She gathered the last of the spell refuse into the jar and capped it off before returning it to her bag. When she dropped it to the floor by her feet, Zombi returned to her, slithering across her shoulders to curl around her neck like the world's most unnatural-looking scarf. "That is a bigger problem. Your sister came here to warn me..."

"When? How long ago?" Clay interrupted. He cringed and murmured an apology, his eyes dropping to his coat. He pretended to adjust the sleeve, inspecting the camel-colored leather for signs of the viscous liquid, but there was none. Marie'd taken all of it so she could do whatever with it later on. He didn't want to think about it. Or maybe he did, so he didn't have to think about Cora being there, the woman he still loved but now was obligated to hate in equal measure.

Yeah. Goop. Think about the goop. Gray goop. Slithering in a jar. Intriguing.

Fucking Cora.

"Three weeks, maybe four." Marie reached out to squeeze Clay's good hand, though whether that was support or censure, he didn't know. "I said earlier I could use your other skills, Woodkin Child, and I meant it. Your sister knew Clayton would come to me. She warned me of the sluagh like she warned the other practitioners, but I am an old woman. The death flock—how do they threaten me any more than the sands of time? I waltz with Samedi every morning that I rise. Every night I lay my head down to sleep. She knows this."

"What'd she do?" Addy's voice lacked inflection. Her expression was flat, too, and Clay glanced between the women, suddenly very, very uncomfortable. Marie'd been good to him. If Cora'd hurt her in some way...

Marie pointed behind them, vaguely in the direction of the hall where that unknown entity lurked in the shadows. "She did that. It watches me always. I don't know what it does or what type of threat it poses. I assume it's a Fairy creature if it's under Cora's sway. I was hoping you could help me with it, Woodkin Child, because until I know what the threat is, I can't do a lick about it."

Addy nodded and eyed Clay, the heels of her palms pressed to her flushed cheeks, her good humor a distant memory. She was angry with her sister. For that matter, so was Clayton. You didn't just sic a monster on someone because you were in a snit with a mutual acquaintance, especially not someone who'd made you tea and cookies six months ago. Clay'd brought Cora by for a visit in the spring. She and Marie got on famously then, chatting and laughing and having a merry old time of it. A fairy monster in the house was a hell of a way to repay good hospitality.

"You have any ideas what it might be? I can talk to it, but I'd like to be prepared," Addy said to him.

"Doesn't really work like that. I sense the magic, but it's not like it tells me what I'm dealing with. Only reason I sometimes know is certain weirds feel similar and I can take an educated guess. This one's cold. Dead for sure, but that's all I know."

Addy grimaced and headed for the hallway, Clay close enough behind her that he tromped on her shadow. Marie remained on the bench with Zombi, smiling and waving at them as they turned the corner. Her fingers stroked over her pet's head, gently tracing the contours of his shiny scales. "I'll stay here, my loves. I get cold outside of the sunlight."

Clay peered at the bit of floor where the magical intruder had hidden. It was gone, no longer beneath the boards but somewhere higher. His left shoulder felt chillier than his right, and he laid his palm flat against the wall to pinpoint the source. His fingertips moved past a portrait of a younger Marie and over the curve of a sconce. The moment he touched the polished brass, he felt a thrum all the way to his elbow, the oily resonance making him want to find the closest basin and wash. He felt like he'd dunked his arm in a vat of chilled grease.

"Here," he said. "It's here."

Addy placed her hand next to his, and the shadows exploded, expanding in a blob of hissing, convulsing blackness that roiled across the wall, a dozen or more veiny, yellow eyes popping open to stare her down. Whatever the amorphous creature was, it had been hiding behind the light fixture, but something about Addy's touch scared it enough that it was willing to risk the open.

"What are you?" Addy demanded, chasing it as it skittered and flailed across the ceiling. It kept trying to sink low, to find its way back under the floor, but she was smart enough to use her hands as a deterrent, keeping it trapped in the upper portion of the wall. "Trobhad!" she snapped, slapping her splayed fingers just below the mass. She had it wedged in the corner now, the monster incapable of moving without making contact with her hands. A few snakelike tendrils eased out to test their limits, but the moment they came close to her skin, they shriveled away.

"Leaaaaaave me," it hissed, its voice the rasping rattle of something gone to grave long ago. Clay pulled his gun in case things went awry. Shooting it would probably be useless, but it made him feel better to have it handy anyway. Sterling had long ago told him it's better to have it and not need it than to need it and not have it.

Sound life advice, that.

"What are you, and what do you want with Marie Laveau?"

The thing wedged itself further into the corner, compacting in a ball of blackness a fraction of its original size. The position made the multiple eyeballs squish together into one hideous, bulging mass. "Nichnevan sends ussss to watch the queen. If she helpssss the half-born, Nichnevan will know, and she will come to feast on all who walk here. Leave ussss, Light Born. Leave usss to our darknesssss."

Addy grunted, her shoulders sagging. "Draugr?"

"Yesssss."

Clay stared at the back of Addy's head, awaiting her explanation. He'd heard of draugr before, but more in the context of mariners lost at sea who haunted the shores after their deaths. He hadn't had the displeasure of meeting one in person, but Sterling had told him stories about shapeshifting ghoul creatures that could grow their size to mammoth proportions and squash a man beneath their palms. This didn't look much like it could do that, but with Fairy kin, appearances were often deceiving.

"I could command you to leave, you know," Addy said instead, her chin tilted back to regard the repulsive thing. "You must honor the order. Even Nichnevan knows that."

"Yessss, but to do thisss you must renounce your affiliation, Light Born. Thisss meanssss you embrace your birthright. We would be happy to deliver the good newssss to your father if you are sooo inclined."

Addy's hands flew back from the wall like it'd burned her. Clay reached out to steady her, afraid she'd fall or flee in panic, but she did neither. She stared at the thing in the corner with fury on her face. The draugr let out another sibilant hiss before warbling with laughter, its body unfurling to stretch across the ceiling in a swath of inky, undulating darkness.

"What's going on?" Clay demanded, unsure if he should shoot or shit or run the hell away.

"I'm sorry," Addy said, so quiet he barely heard her. She turned to look at Clay with big, tear-rimmed eyes, her hands coming to settle on his shoulders and squeeze. "I can't help you, and that means Marie can't help you. I am so sorry."

CHAPTER TWELVE

THREE YEARS AGO

Clay'd never been happier for Doc's company than he was those first months after Sterling's retirement. He felt uncomfortable in the badge, ill-prepared despite years of Sterling's tutelage, and though Doc didn't really have any insight on the weirds to offer, she was more than happy to listen when Clay needed to talk or to help research when Clay was faced with a new and freakishly interesting flavor of monster.

What had started as an association of mutual benefit—safety for doctoring—had turned into a full-scale partnership and, finally, a friendship. Doc made Clay laugh. Clay made Doc crazy.

Lately, the crazy-making was because the hospital's year anniversary was upon them, and Clay suffered from the jitters. He knew his way around ladies and their parts, he knew how to dress nice and talk good to make a favorable impression, but the closer it got to the actual rendezvous, the more convinced he became that he'd forget everything about pleasing gals and instead would sit around staring at his turgid lap wiggler all night. It was *Cora.* She did things to him. Funny things. Terrible things. Wonderful things. If anyone could rob him of years of poking prowess, it was her.

"You'll be fine," Doc insisted as they rolled to a stop in front of the bed and breakfast. "If you feel yourself panicking, simply take a breath before you speak. Smile a lot, compliment her, listen when she talks, and whatever you do, don't offer to teach her poker because you're horribly competitive and will ruin everything. It's quite simple, really."

"I am not competitive. I just like winning. And simple ain't a word I'd use to describe women, Doc. Women have it easy because men are easy. Feed us, don't ask us to talk about feelings, let us poke you every once in a while, done. Perfect life."

Doc cast him a wry look from beneath the rim of her bowler hat. "Yes. I have it so easy. I'd envy me as well."

"Exactly."

Clay eased off of Squirt's back to retrieve the paper Cora'd handed him at the infirmary. It'd traveled across six states with him, the tears and stains indicative of the type of year it'd been. It was ridiculous that he even kept the thing; he'd long ago memorized the address, but silly sentimentality told him to hold onto it. It meant something. He didn't know what, but something, and he'd be damned if he threw that away.

Beaumont's on Canal Street—this was the place. It wasn't big, and in comparison to some of the other hotels around, it lacked a lot of the dramatic gothic architecture, but that in itself was endearing. It was a pinkish peach color with white shutters and window boxes full of colorful flowers. The front doors were propped open in invitation, giving him a good view of a spacious receiving room and a courtyard with a tall fountain. He saw people seated around a table eating finger sandwiches, and he craned his neck hoping to spot a pale blond head among the throng, but no such luck.

He would have felt her anyway, but he was zap-free, which birthed the worry that she wouldn't show. She was a conwoman, someone who made a living pinching purses and selling lies. It wasn't outside the realm of possibility that she wouldn't honor her promise. Doc assured him a dozen times that she would, that she knew Cora well enough to say she'd keep her word on something like this, but Clay had a hard time believing it.

"Hell," he muttered, guiding Squirt around back to hand her off to the stable boy. He paused to rub her forelock and snout, pressing his palm to her soft, velvet nose. She curled her lip to look for treats, and he flicked at her big ugly teeth with his fingertip. "Be a good gal," he said. "No biting." Squirt's ears tilted forward, and she stomped her hoof, her tail giving a saucy little swish to let him know what she thought of that.

Welp. Kid was going to get bit. Hazard of the job, Clay supposed.

Clay returned to the cart to help Doc with the luggage. Doc's glasses were lopsided on her face, her suspenders holding up a pair of brown, too-big pants. Clay took one of the heavier trunks from her and headed into the Beaumont, his own saddlebags draped over his arm. "When Irene's around, there're no glasses. That mean she can't see?"

"... effectively, yes," Doc said.

Clay grinned at her before dropping the trunk on the floor, the contents crunching in a way that suggested something glass had broken apart into a thousand pieces. He cringed, about to apologize, but Doc shoved past him to check on her cargo, her elbow jamming into Clay's side on the way by.

"Ow, damn it. Didn't mean no harm. Thought it was Irene's dresses. Sorry," Clay said.

"Even if they were dresses, you'd just drop them like that?"

"Well, yeah. They're dresses."

"Heathen."

Their banter was interrupted by a bald gentleman in a faded blue suit coat trudging down the stairs. He was oddly shaped, with long, thin legs and a bulbous gut that suggested an appreciation of malted beverages. The swollen red nose and flushed cheeks were another indicator that this particular sir liked himself some liquor when he wasn't playing innkeeper. "Gentlemen. Welcome to the Beaumont. How can I help you today?'

Clay rubbed his aching hip and forced a smile. "Name's Marshal Jenson. Hoping for a pair of rooms."

"Welcome, Marshal. We've been expecting you. You're on the second floor on the right, and Doctor Miller, I presume?" He glanced at Doc, who managed a nod despite gingerly retrieving broken shards of beaker from her case. "You're down here on the left. Miss Cora paid y'all up for the week, so I hope everything's to your liking."

Clay felt like a twelve-ton weight had been lifted from his shoulders. She was here, and she hadn't left him on the hook like he feared. Course, that meant he had to remember how to woo a lady proper-like, but that shouldn't be so hard. Like Doc said, just breathe. Breathe and no poker, apparently. "Thank you kindly, Mister…"

"Robinau. Joshua Robinau," he said, handing them their keys. "And thank you, Marshal. Doctor."

Clay pocketed the key and went back to the cart to haul trunks, making sure not to drop, ding, or otherwise damage any more of Doc's precious commodities. Doc stayed at his heels like a yappy puppy, carrying the lighter parcels and barking whenever Clay got too close to a wall or doorframe. It took a dozen trips, but eventually, Doc's wardrobe was stacked inside the way Doc liked it, which had no particular rhyme or reason as far as Clay could tell. Little trunks were on top of big trunks which were stacked on littler trunks, but Doc seemed pleased with it, and that was all that mattered. Plus, Clay was sick of carrying shit. If Doc wanted everything rearranged, she could do it her own self.

"Thank you, Clayton."

Clay grunted and climbed the stairs to his room, swinging to the right as the innkeeper instructed. There was only the one door, and he fitted his key into the lock, still not feeling any weirds nearby. That probably meant Cora was off robbing from the good people of N'Orleans, but there wasn't much he could do about it at the moment. He pushed the door open and stopped, surprised to see a pair of dresses hung by the window and a few bags leaning against the side of the bed. Perfume bottles, jewelry, and lady hats were strewn over the top of the bureau, while wrenches, sheets of metal, and other tinkering materials covered the top of the writing desk.

She was staying there. With him. Sharing a bed.

He swallowed a groan and swung his eyes to the ceiling, his heart thudding hard in his chest, his ears, and lower still. Ten years' worth of fantasies vied for purchase in his head, every one of them sweaty, loud, wet, and soft. He took off his hat to fan his face. It was too early for this. It was just a dress on a hook for Christ's sake, but there was no telling that to his treacherous body. He felt warm all over—well, warmer, which was saying something considering the bayou heat.

A bath. He needed a cold bath before he made a danged fool of himself.

He poked his head into the hall to call for Mr. Robinau, but a tinny chittering drew his attention. He dropped his gaze only to find himself looking at the purse-snatching silver squirrel. Frederick peered up at him from the bed, his metal ears rising in curiosity just like a real squirrel's would. Between his metal paws was an envelope with Clay's name scrawled on it, which Clay couldn't help but notice had a series of tiny chew marks along the top.

"Gimme that," he said, snatching it from the squirrel's paws. Frederick eyed him for a moment before bouncing off the bed to scale his pants. Clay kicked out his leg to shoo him off, but that just made Frederick leap to his duster coat, swinging back and forth and playing in the folds.

"Damn it, Squirrel."

Frederick ignored him to continue frolicking. Defeated, Clay shook his head and unfolded the note, looking once again upon Cora's precise scrawl.

Bring Doc to the Delta Star at five. Dinner on the Mississippi. —C

Having a plan helped; it gave him something to think about other than the promise of that big, empty bed. He went to the top of the stairs to holler for Robinau, Frederick squealing as he ran up inside of Clay's coat to roam around his back, down his slacks, and inside of his pockets. When he careened around front, his paws fidgeting with Clay's holster, Clay plucked him from the leather and dropped him onto his shoulder.

"Behave," he said.

The squirrel thwacked him in the side of his face with his leathery tail.

Come to find out, The Beaumont's bath was in a private room next to the kitchen so the staff wouldn't have to lug buckets of hot water up the stairs. Clay made his way there with fresh clothes in hand, but he had to wait his turn—Doc had already claimed the tub. Clay settled on a chair in the hall, Frederick sitting on top of his hat and making strange, mechanical whistling noises as he toyed with the brim.

"Dinner at five. Some place called the Delta Star," Clay said, loud enough so that his voice penetrated the door.

"Five? That's only two hours… oh, dear. Irene may have to miss it."

"Nah. If you hurry, plenty of time for paints. Still got an hour before we gotta go."

"Yes, quite right." There was a heartbeat of a pause before Doc added, "You wouldn't be encouraging Irene to make an appearance so you can get in the bath faster, would you?"

"'Course not. That'd make me selfish."

"Mmm. It would, wouldn't it?"

Clay grinned and tilted his head back, hearing the *sploosh* of displaced water as Doc scrambled from the tub. Irene's assembly usually took Doc hours, but Clay'd seen some impressively hasty transformations in the past. Sure, he'd encouraged this one so he could claim the bath for himself, but this was a special occasion. For once in his life, going out on the town required more than a shitty smile, a witty comment, and clean britches.

An hour later, Clay was bathed and ready to go—nervous, but ready to go. His face was shaved to a faint stubble, his dark hair slicked back straight to curl under his ears. He abandoned the hat and kept the coat, his hands skimming down his blue vest to smooth the wrinkles. His star shined on his lapel, a reminder to himself that he made a promise to Sterling last year that he intended to keep. He'd left the squirrel back in the room, which made him feel guilty—Frederick was clearly eager to come along, but the last thing Clay wanted or needed was another distraction from the matter at hand, which was wooing the woman of his dreams. Squirrels were not appropriate wooing tools.

He walked to Doc's room and knocked, expecting to have to badger Irene out the door, but she surprised him by hustling into the hall in a teal and pink dress, a strange, miniature top hat stuck to the side of her wig.

"I'm a wreck," she said, patting her headgear into place. "I hope you're happy. I rushed for you."

"Thank you kindly, Doc. You look just fine to me."

"*Fine?!* Do you know how awful a word that is?" Doc demanded, swishing her way out to the street to flag a driver. "Don't tell Cora she looks fine. Tell her she looks beautiful. Or enchanting. Or… don't use fine. Ever. It's a hideous compliment. Complacent and lazy." Clay eyed Doc and frowned, not because he was angry with her, but because she was probably right. Fine was a bad idea. Fine was stricken from the vocabulary for the foreseeable future.

No fine. No need to panic. Everything was fine. He'd be fine.

Ah, hell.

—

The Delta Star was a docked riverboat on the Mississippi that never went anywhere, staying anchored in port as a floating restaurant. It was probably supposed to be a quirky bit of N'Orleans ambiance, but Clay already felt queasy thanks to his nerves. His imagination adding a sway to the vessel didn't endear him to the place. He stopped just inside the door to guzzle water, swiping the glass right off the tray of a passing waiter in hopes that it'd stifle his nausea.

"Use your manners," Doc hissed, tugging Clay along behind her. Clay drained the glass and abandoned it on the table of a pair of dining guests, who peered at it, then him, and finally Doc with confused stares.

"Obliged," Clay said, and Doc groaned, gesturing with her fan at the open deck.

"There. Let's seat ourselves before you do something else horrid."

Clay didn't need to look where Doc pointed because he felt it. *Her*. Her magic was in his bones and in his stomach, that familiar thrum that both called and repelled him, and he lifted his face to peer through the French doors leading outside. Cora sat at a round table with a pink tablecloth and a vase of daisies, her hair pinned to her head with ribbons, her dress white and lacy and as delicate as spun silk. He would have been content to stare at her forever, at the pale blue tinge in her hair and her elbow-length white gloves, but then a second power rudely introduced itself, slapping him in the face with a blast of cold air. His eyes swung left of Cora to settle on Atlanta's own Sultan's Jewel, or as he'd come to know her since, Adelaide, the flirty redhead with the healthy bosom.

"Lovely. Addy's here. She's so much fun," Irene said, looping her arm through Clay's to walk him to their table. His eyes fixed on Cora the whole walk. She looked like a spring bride, all virginal and sweet. And didn't that line of thinking slick his palms with sweat?

"Irene!" Cora practically vaulted the table to get to Doc, her arms wrapping around the other woman so tightly a puff of powder exploded from Irene's neckline to pepper the air. There were happy reunion tears and peals of laughter, the latter mostly drowned thanks to the rustling of colliding petticoats. "I am so sorry I missed you in Charleston. Addy nearly married a goblin. It was terrible."

"It's quite fine, Lamb. Clayton explained everything. So good to see both of you." Irene swooped down to brush her lips across Addy's temple, leaving a spot of rouge in her wake. Addy rubbed at it with the back of her wrist, not really wiping it off so much as smearing it across her forehead.

"Good to see you Doc," Addy said, winking at Clayton and lifting her wineglass high. By the empty bottles lined up before her, she'd been drinking awhile now, and he quirked a brow at what looked like hours of liver torture. She took that as an invitation to lean toward him, her chin cradled in her palm, her mountainous cleavage squished together. "Fae are notoriously hard to intoxicate. Good to see you, Marshal Jenson. Congratulations on your promotion."

"Thank you kindly. And I didn't know y'all could drink so much. Not sure what I can do with the information outside of adjust my Christmas list."

"I'm sure there are plenty of things you don't know about fairy kind that I could teach you. Later, if you'd like."

"Find your own marshal," Cora snapped, extricating herself from Irene's embrace to flick her sister's ear. Addy batted her hand aside, her smile not-so-hidden behind her glass. "Hello. Pardon my sister. She's a slattern, through and through." Cora turned back his way, her hands clasped over her stomach. A flush stained her from cheeks to neck, a gentle peach shade that reminded him of the roses his mother grew on the farm, and for the first time since he'd met her, he wondered if he made her as dizzy as she made him. "It's good to see you again."

He would have been content to gaze at her stupidly for the rest of the evening, but then Irene cleared her throat, and he remembered he was supposed to be a debonair romancer. He took her fingers in his own and pressed a series of gentle kisses to the backs of her knuckles, catching a hint of vanilla on her glove. "You smell nice. Like—" He stopped himself because he almost said five-dollar-whore, which was good in one way 'cause gals that charged five dollars spent a lot of time and money on how they smelled. But as no *proper* lady wanted to be compared to a harlot, he opted for something a little more refined. "You smell as pretty as you look, and that's saying somethin', darlin'."

He glanced up expecting to see one of those mocking grins curling her upper lip, but her expression was soft, her lips gently parted and her breath coming thick. He knew that look, had seen it on women's faces before. It meant that his ears would be boxed in by lady ankles later. But unlike all those other times and all those other gals, this was *Cora*.

"I can clear the table and let you two fuck right here if you'd like. It won't ruin my appetite," Adelaide said. Clay's cheeks went hot, and he slid into his seat with a soft murmur. He hadn't meant to be so obvious, but Cora was so damned beautiful it was hard to think straight with her in arm's reach. He couldn't say that without sounding unseasoned, though, and so he concentrated on unfolding his napkin and tucking it around his legs, laying it two and three times to keep it straight.

"You're so crass," Cora said to her sister.

"Oh, and you're not? You just talked about my accommodating parts at the dinner table," Addy returned. By the twinkle in her eye, that clearly didn't bother her, but Cora snorted all the same.

"Act like a lady, and I'll treat you like a lady."

"No you won't, striapach."

"Tell me about this goblin king," Doc said, the subject change obvious but also appreciated. The sisters' expressions suggested they'd be content slinging insults all night long. Clay was fine with that in general, but if he wanted himself some Cora time, well, someone had to do something. Doc was that someone. "Cora mentioned you were nearly married?"

Addy whirled the wine around inside of her glass, some of it climbing so high it dribbled over the rim to splash her hand. She lifted it to her mouth and lapped at it much like a cat would lap at cream. "It was nonsense, really. He was so enamored with my Parisian Twist he kidnapped me to the caves, but Cora convinced him I'd make a terrible queen, so he freed me."

"Oh? How did she manage that?"

"Mostly by telling him the truth," Cora replied, slipping back into her chair. "Addy would have grown bored in captivity and fucked every goblin in the caves. The king would have been the laughing stock of the Unseelie Court."

"Such a gross exaggeration of my appetites, but in my defense, goblins can be quite fun if you can get past the fur and the occasional extra eye. Some of them have as many as six arms. That's useful! Just think what Clayton could do with six arms, Cora."

"No, please don't," Clay said, doing his best to ward off the visual worming its way into his mind. "Rather happy with my two arms, thanks." The idea of a woman as gorgeous as Adelaide giving herself over to a horde of furry, overly-eyeballed monsters nauseated him. Or maybe that was from being on the stupid boat. He picked up his water and peered at Cora. When he caught her looking back at him, he winked, but she one-upped him by pursing her lips together in an air kiss. It took every bit of willpower he had not to scoop her over his shoulder and carry her back to the Beaumont right then and there.

"What's the Parisian Twist?" He hoped a friendly discussion would keep him focused on things that weren't beautiful blonds who kept wetting their lips and—damn it, her fingers were tracing over the bare skin of her chest now. Goddamn her, she was making this—him, everything—hard. They needed to eat soon before any important parts of his anatomy ruptured.

"A delightful maneuver I picked up in France some years ago," Addy said. "It's when you're sitting astride a person and you reach under their cock to get a good, solid grip on the bol—"

"No!" Doc's cry sounded like a cross between a goose honk and a sneeze. Clay glanced her way, doing his damndest not to laugh when he saw the horrified expression on her face. She practically vibrated in her seat, her fan waving around so much it spit feathers all over the table. Normally, Doc could stand a blue joke or two, so Clay wasn't quite sure what her problem was, but then a waiter approached their table from the dining room with a basket of fresh bread between his hands.

Oh.

That.

Doc hated to be embarrassed. A stranger overhearing Addy's testicle torture story probably would have been embarrassing.

"Thank goodness you're here," Irene said to the mustached young man, the tattered remnants of her fan wagging at her face. "You're just in time. I am positively famished."

Clay was, too, but not for a single damned thing on the Delta's menu.

"Heaven forbid you'd come over a moment earlier while Adelaide was discussing balls," Cora said. The waiter was just about to hand them their menus, but he stopped short to stare at her, his mouth falling open wide enough for a fly to shoot down his throat. He choked, sputtered, and bent at the waist, and Cora stood from her seat to whale at him between the shoulders. "Now, now. No choking. That's not—no dying. That'd ruin dinner. Stop it."

Clay started laughing, Addy followed suit, and Doc dropped her head into her hands and groaned.

—

It was Cora's idea for them to walk home together after dessert. They weren't too far from the Beaumont, she said, and it'd be nice to have some private time. Clay readily agreed, though his idea of private time differed from hers. His idea involved exploring the hills and valleys of an exciting new territory. Hers involved holding hands and leaning into his side as they navigated the streets under the gaslights. He liked how she fit against him, and he liked how her fingers laced just right with his.

"We should talk," Cora said, and Clay glanced down at her, braced for whatever was about to spill from those rosebud lips. Those words had never meant a single good thing for him in the past. In fact, whenever he heard them, he usually ended up parting ways with the female in question because she was trying to marry him after a three day association, extorting money from him, or claiming her six-year-old kid was a product of a liaison they had three years ago.

"About what?"

"Us. What this all means."

"All right." Damn it, she wanted him to talk about feelings. He was hoping to dodge that bullet mostly because his feelings on things were short and uncomplicated, and that could be misconstrued as apathy. Best way to get a girl's ire up was to come across like you didn't care about shit she cared about, and if she asked how he was and he said fine, would she have a Doc fit on him? Probably.

Cora took a moment to think about what she wanted to say, her fingers drumming against his forearm. "There's a story I heard a long time ago… "

"How long is long ago for a gal like you?" He interrupted.

"Hush. I'm not that old. Now then, there was a girl who was gifted by Bran with a perfect singing voice. She was plain of face, but every man who ever heard her sing described her as the loveliest woman in Wales. One day, a young king came upon her in a glen. He sat and listened to her songs awhile, tears streaming down his face at the beauty of her…"

"Patsy. Who cries over singing?" Cora reached up to grab his hair, giving it a hard enough yank that a few hairs tore from his scalp. He winced and cast her a sideward glance, his fingers worrying at the sore spot. She wasn't precisely angry with him, but she did have that exasperated look his teacher used to give him when he'd spit on Tommy Mayfair's chair before class in the morning. "Pardon me. I'll behave."

"No, I'll summarize, because you clearly have the attention span of a hamster. The king forced the girl back to his castle to be his bride, and she stopped singing because there was no joy in it anymore. Without her songs, he found he'd married a sad, ugly woman. Do you understand what I am saying?"

The metaphor was simple enough, but his concern was with the finer details. They might not seem like a lot to her, but they were everything to him. "Freedom, and I get that, darlin', I do, but I'm also a marshal and—not to be indelicate—you rob folks. I can give you freedom in almost every way possible except that one. You do somethin' real wrong—and I mean real wrong, not this petty thief bullpucky—we got an issue."

She nodded and led him off of the main road to a small side alley between two buildings. It was dark there, the colors gone gray thanks to a lack of street lamps. Box crates lined both walls, a scraggly-looking cat eyeing them from one of the higher perches. "I've considered that, but I understand that limitation, and I can work with it." She took both of his hands in hers and peered into his eyes, the playfulness of before replaced by warmth and worry. He swept his thumbs over the backs of her fingers to let her know he was still listening.

"You know that I am fond of you," she continued. "I keep thrusting myself in your path because I think about you all the time. And I realized after our dinner at my cottage that something was wrong—not you being there, but you leaving. It took a while for me to come to terms with that. I barely know you, but I'm drawn to you. And if you want me, I'll do everything in my power to make you happy. But what you must understand is I won't be there all the time. I have a life. I have obligations outside of you. This isn't a debatable point, so if you can't stand the thought of me leaving even though I will always come back, I will move my things out of Beaumont and never see you again, because frankly, seeing you again would hurt me."

In some ways, it was everything Clay's pounding heart wanted to hear, and in others, it terrified him. She was offering herself to him on the condition that he take her as he could get her, which wasn't so bad until he thought about his mother. Would Cora be gone for decades at a time, too? Would they spend years being happy together, and then she'd leave only to come back looking as beautiful as when she'd gone while time had tromped all over his face?

"I'm flattered, and I… Cora. I don't—" He paused because he was scared. Scared of saying the wrong thing and making her leave. Scared of asking too many questions and sounding controlling. It wasn't easy for him to show her that vulnerability, but if he didn't want her drawing the wrong conclusions and running off to pack her bags, he had to. "My ma missed half of my growing-up years. Was there 'til I was nine and then gone 'til I was nineteen. Never understood how my pa handled it. I lo… I lo—"

He took a deep breath and looked down at their clasping hands, his brow furrowing with strain. This was harder than he'd expected. Feelings were bullpucky—especially these feelings. Why did he care for her the way he did? He'd been attracted to plenty of women in his time, some pretty and dignified and disinterested in pilfering, even. So why did this one hold him so? The answer was because she was different. She was strong. They hadn't had many real conversations, but everything she did was so self-assured. Her confidence was the draw. So was her heart. Sure, she'd nearly killed him with the bogey, but he'd recovered because she'd gotten him to Doc. And when Sterling lost his arm, she'd been the one to give it back to him.

Impulsive? Yes. Willing and able to swindle to her heart's content? Yes. But she was flinty and brilliant and sometimes she even knew right from wrong. He'd never find another girl like her in the world, and so he wouldn't try. He'd keep this one and make her his own.

Or be her own, which was much more likely the case, but his pride didn't like that quite as much.

"I'm probably in love with you," he blurted. "Not probably. Am. Have been. And I don't mind you running around the world sometimes, but I don't know that I can be my father. Ten years ain't nothing to you, but it's a long damned time to me."

"No. No, Clay. It wouldn't be decades. That's ridiculous. Your mother must have made a bargain to have to split her time like that. Seelie Court, I imagine?"

"Yeah."

Cora smiled, reaching up to brush a lock of his hair behind his ear. She still hadn't touched him proper, not without gloves or clothes between them, but he shivered all the same. It was an oddly intimate gesture, and it made him want to kiss her. Well, everything made him want to kiss her, but this especially so. "They're petty, controlling people, but they're not my world any longer. I might be gone a month, two months, but no more than that. I just need to know that when I do go, there won't be a fuss. I cherish my freedom above everything. Even you. Not that I can tell you why I cherish you because you're vain and arrogant and… I suppose that's probably why I like you, actually. I like vain, arrogant men. Handsome, vain, arrogant men."

"Then I will be the handsomest, vainest, most arrogant son of a bitch in all the West." He leaned down to brush his lips across her forehead. The contact zapped him straight to his boots, and he cringed, the pleasure-pain of her electricity sizzling through his body. He breathed deep and clung to her so he could get through those first few minutes of discomfort, the sensation so intense that he contemplated diving headfirst into the Mississippi just to escape it.

Eventually, the pulses slowed and then faded, the energy abating to a soothing massage of wind that undulated over him. "There we go," he murmured, the muscles in his body unfurling one by one. She reached up to toy with the hair behind his neck, twisting it around her fingers, and that's all the invitation he needed to do what he'd been thinking about since he saw her on the Delta. He pulled her body tight to his and kissed her. And it wasn't no gentleman's kiss; he kissed her like he wanted to brand her soul. He kissed her with love and passion and every other goddamned feeling he'd been harboring for a decade.

She'd said she was his, and he was hers, and he wanted her to feel that in her blood.

Cora held nothing back. She squirmed against him, her tongue teasing at his, her whimpers echoing through the alley. Before he realized what he was doing, he'd backed her into a stack of crates, but she went with it—with him—her arms sliding around his chest to hold him tight. Her hands swept from his shoulders to his sides, her fingers digging in to keep him close even as she hopped up to perch herself onto the box behind her, her legs parting so he could step into the bell of her skirts. He ground against her, wanting to negate all space between them, but a petticoat did a lot to hamper a man's ardor.

He pulled back for air, his nose touching hers as he panted through the fire racing through his veins. She peered up at him, her face bathed by enough moonlight that he could see her flush and the swollen plumpness of her lips. She looked so enticing, so ready for him that they had to leave *now* before he made a fool of himself. It was bad enough he wasn't going to be able to walk to the inn without the entire city of N'Orleans seeing what she did to him. "We should go back if we... "

"No," she said. He blinked at her, and she tugged up her skirts, wedging the layers of fabric beneath her bottom. He didn't get any time to enjoy the view because she dragged his hand to the inside of her knee. Silk. She wore silk stockings, and he groaned for mercy as she slowly guided his fingers up the inside of her thigh. "Here. Now."

It vaguely occurred to him that the first woman he gave his heart to should probably be loved somewhere a little more dignified than on a box crate in an alley. He meant to say as much, to tell her that he wanted to take his time and do it right at the Beaumont, but Cora's free hand unlaced the top of that fine gown. It was all over then because she didn't wear a corset, and he got a heavenly eyeful of fat, squishy perfections. He dropped his face between them, inhaling more vanilla as his lips glided over her contours, skimming until he found a rosy, pebbled nub to tease and suckle.

She arched at him with a ragged moan.

He savored her taste and scent and feel, getting to know every fine detail of her fine form. She fidgeted beneath him, actually jerking his face into her chest at one point so that he nearly suffocated in her flesh. That was all right. He'd die there and be damned happy about it. She released her grip on his wrist, but his fingers continued their ascent anyway, climbing to that marvelous unknown with all its decadent, naughty promise. Stocking met skin, skin felt smooth and oh-so-warm. When he explored high enough to discover her wet and inviting already, he silently thanked God that she was enough of a strumpet to not wear proper bloomers.

He nuzzled at her neck, raining kisses along that sweaty, pale column. He was ready for her, his cock straining and insistent that he stop being so considerate and get on with it already, but she had to want him as much as he wanted her first. He didn't even know if that was possible, but he had to try. She deserved his best, and if he had to think about something unsexy, like elephants or Charles Darwin books, so be it.

Lucky for him *and* his erection, Cora was about as patient as he was, which meant she wasn't patient at all. When he flicked his tongue over her ear and slipped his finger inside of her, she dropped her hands to his shoulders and shoved him away. Hard. He didn't expect it, and he actually stumbled far enough back that he struck the crates behind him, scaring off the voyeuristic cat in the process. There was a momentary panic that he'd somehow offended her with his pawing, but no. She shivered in front of him, her tongue slicking over her lips with her legs splayed in wanton invitation.

"Come to me. Now. I don't... stop fucking around, Clayton."

Oh. Well, he could do *that*.

He closed the distance between them to kiss her again, his lips moving restlessly against hers as his fingers fumbled with his trousers. He never had this much trouble with them when he had to take a piss, but put his fantasy woman spread out before him, and it took a half a dozen tries to get unleashed. She wriggled closer to perch her behind on the edge of the crate, and he stepped into her, pushing inside with one fluid motion. Tight, silken heat. He wanted to sob his thanks that she was such a good person as to let him put his thing inside of her, but that probably would have ruined the mood, and so he concentrated on pulling half out of her and slowly sinking back in instead.

"Damn it, go. Go now," she hissed in his ear, her legs lifting up to lock around his waist. He heartily obliged, sinking his hand into her hair as he drove into her body with one passionate, wet slap after another. Their eyes locked, Cora mewling through every hard thrust, the crate beneath their weight thudding and slapping against the ground with their exertions. "Like that. Like that I n-need—" Her voice cut off on a low, throaty groan, her hands spreading out behind her to brace against the building side. He pressed his face into her throat, already wanting to explode, but he'd wait for her because that was gentlemanly. And for Cora, he'd be a gentleman, even if his lady took three years to reach her peak.

But please don't take three years. Three minutes, okay, sure.

Fortunately, Cora was not a lady afflicted with slow anything. She let out a scream that probably told everyone in a half-mile radius what was happening between those old, dirty buildings. Her body hugged him in its velvet embrace as she writhed in pleasure. She was loud, but he didn't care. Let her scream. Let the world know what they'd done. Hell, let them watch. He refused to feel shame about the most amazing moment of his twenty-seven years. This was the woman he loved, and she wanted him enough to have him, too. It was beautiful and glorious, and no one could take that away from them. No one.

"I love you. I love you," he rasped, slapping hard at her one last time before joining her in a knee-weakening orgasm that forced him to slump into the crates to keep upright. Her arms dropped from the wall to hold him through his blinding pulses, the experience so intense he squeezed his eyes shut so they didn't explode. He could feel her shuddering beneath him, tremors of nerve-tingling delight that echoed his own, and he softly panted her name, moaning when her lips pressed to the heavy pulse at the base of his throat.

"Thank you," she whispered into his skin. He found that endearing in an odd way, and he managed a dry laugh as he pulled away from her, reluctant to leave but knowing this wasn't the time or the place to tarry in a passionate embrace. Cora seemed to know it, too, as she quickly adjusted her dress, her hands retying the laces of her top before shaking out her petticoats. He stepped back to tuck himself away, and she wiggled off of the boxes, her hair half in her ribbons and half out, giving her a wild, just-loved look.

It was the most alluring thing he'd ever seen.

"We should go before—well." She cleared her throat, and he nodded, waiting for her to collect her hair at her nape. While she was righted, he scouted outside of the alley, fully expecting an appreciative audience, but there was no one but the cat he'd scared off, He gave it a pat in apology.

Cora returned to his side a moment later. They walked from the alley in much the same state they'd walked from the Delta, though this time, there was nothing said. It was afterglow and private thoughts, which was fine until something occurred to him that hadn't before. In all of her talking, Cora never once said she loved him. She claimed to be fond of him, to want him, to not want to leave his side, but the three words he ached to hear never left her lips.

They didn't leave her lips the rest of the night, either. Not the second time they'd come together or even the third. No matter how sweet he was, no matter what soft words he gave her when their limbs were entwined, she never professed to love him. It ate at him. He was too stubborn to say so, of course, afraid it would make him look weak or like he expected her to validate his feelings, but it stung more than he liked to admit.

As she settled into her fluffy pillow with a soft sigh, he stared at the darkened ceiling and brooded. What was wrong with him? What did he lack that she wanted or needed in her life? She had plenty of flaws, but he liked her fine anyway. And she'd said she liked vain, arrogant men. He was all that and a little more, but he treated her nice, and he definitely tickled her fancy. The ragged fingernail tracks in his shoulders told him he'd done his diddling well. Hell, by the time they were through the second time, he'd offered to build a raft so they could float on her sea of satisfaction. She'd laughed right along with him, but still no love words had come.

Why not? Did she need to know him better? She said she cherished him but...

Damn it. He was dwelling. She was there with him as opposed to being anywhere else, and that was what really mattered. He shouldn't worry about it so much. He would, of course, but he shouldn't. Instead, he should sleep, and maybe tomorrow, when he wasn't feeling so damned vulnerable, he could ask her about it—in a casual way-like, so as to not sound like a whiner.

As tangled as his thoughts were, it took him more than an hour to drift off, but when he finally slept, he slept well. It didn't hurt that Cora felt good against him, her head tucked beneath his chin, her rump curved into his front and fitting him just so. He held her with his hand under her breasts, his palm flat against her beating heart.

Somehow, he didn't hear her climbing out of bed in the middle of the night. She'd managed to wiggle away without disturbing him, but a muttered oath just after dawn pulled him from his dreams. It was dark in the room thanks to the drawn shades, but he could make out her shape near the window, her body hunched over the writing desk. Frederick sat on her shoulder like a silver star, his paws buried in her hair.

Clay yawned and rubbed his fists into his eyes before rolling onto his hip to watch her, a pillow propped beneath his head. He hadn't the faintest clue what she was doing over there, but whatever it was, it wasn't easy work. Her shoulders trembled, and she kept pulling back to shake her hands like they were cramping.

"Come back to bed," he grumbled. She ignored him, her attention fixed on the desk-turned-workbench. Every few minutes she'd reach into her tool chest for an implement, and there'd be a tapping noise or a grinding sound followed by the crank of adjusting gears. Her selections were deliberate, her concentration absolute. It seemed to be going as planned until she let out a high-pitched yelp and jerked away from the table. An acrid burning smell wafted his way, something that reminded him of smoldering charcoal or maybe burnt feathers.

"Everything all right over there?"

"Y-yes. I'll be f-f-fine." Except she wasn't fine because she was crying. He slid from the bed to pad over to the window, throwing the curtains aside to let the morning shine on his bare ass. It wasn't the first time he'd greeted the day nekkid as a jaybird, and he sincerely doubted it'd be the last. He turned to peer at her then, to see what had happened to make her cry. Cora didn't cross him as one of those delicate flowers who wept at every cat's fart, so he figured she had to have done something ugly to warrant the tears.

He figured right. Her pale blue fingertips were black, the pads smoking like they were on fire.

He didn't understand how she'd managed it until he looked over at the desk. There, gleaming and golden and full of fairy-scorching iron, was the most beautiful gun he'd ever laid eyes on. It was bigger than a pistol but smaller than a rifle, the grip covered in delicate filigree that extended up to a pair of gears near the sight. The barrel looked like it was made of walnut, the wood polished so fine he could see the reflection of his dangle on the surface.

"What'd you do, darlin'?" He glanced back at her ruined fingers. She sniveled, and he peered at her beautiful face, at the tears raining down her cheeks. He leaned in to kiss them all away, his lips skimming up her face to press to her forehead. It didn't spark as much as usual, or maybe he was just growing accustomed to having a lady friend that could regularly electrocute him. Either way, the discomfort was minimal. "Why?"

"Because I wanted to. I wanted to show you..." The sentence faded, and he crouched down to pull her into his embrace, holding her as her fingertips smoldered behind his back. Frederick jumped away from them to scamper over the desk and to the window. Clay understood then what he hadn't understood before sleep: love wasn't always about three words. Words were easy and empty and too-often unmemorable.

Love was about actions.

And some actions spoke volumes.

CHAPTER THIRTEEN

NOW

The only things Addy could—or would—tell Marie about her hall haunter was that it was a draugr in the service of Nichnevan, and while Nichnevan may be the queen of the sluagh, she had other terrible things at her disposal. Some of those things were actually worse than being eaten alive by dead birds. As Clay had no idea how to evict it without complicating all of their lives, he told Marie he'd research it and get back to her, which really meant he'd write Sterling and ask him. Sterling's library of weird material was second only to the capital's. Too bad both were too far away to access with regularity.

Marie was surprisingly fine with having to wait. "It's been here three weeks, cher. It doesn't much bother me. Take your time." He didn't particularly *want* to take his time; this curse had to go before he was reduced to the bedsores and bedpans type, and really, he'd shoot himself before he let it get that far. Wasn't anything glorious about suicide, but it was a fair bit more dignified than making Doc clean his piss for the rest of his limited days.

They spent the afternoon sharing tea and biscuits in the sunshine of Marie's courtyard. After a couple of hours, Clay dragged a sweaty Irene out of Jacque's embrace and forced her to be social. Once Doc recovered from her post-Jacque stupor, she gushed to Marie about her grandson, talking like they'd known each other for eons instead of their actual five-hour association. Marie smiled at every stammered compliment, even going so far as to spare a wink at Clay when Irene flopped into her seat to fan her face from exhaustion.

"I'm glad you two are getting on, cherie," was all Marie said.

Clay grunted. He was already sick of Jacque's name, and it'd only been a half a day.

Addy kept to herself throughout most of it, which Clay attributed to the draugr's threat. He didn't know much about the sisters' past as it pertained to the Seelie Court, only that something had happened years ago that landed them in the embrace of the Unseelies. He pressed Cora for details once, but she refused to discuss it. The one thing Clay was able to glean was that Addy and Cora hadn't been kicked out as Sterling once suggested but had willingly transferred their allegiance.

Witnessing the exchange between draugr and Addy, it seemed they'd done it because there were issues with their pa. He was intrigued. He didn't ask about it because he didn't want to piss off Addy, but he was intrigued.

When suppertime came, Clay made a motion to head back to the hotel, but Marie insisted they stay. The torches and candles were lit to welcome the twilight, a small army of glow bugs moving in to twinkle over the flowering bushes. Marie's eldest daughter and namesake arrived to cook for them, throwing together a meal so tasty Clay was able to finish it even with his foundering appetite. The only thing that made it unpalatable was the looks Doc and Jacque shared over their plates. They were so sugary sweet he thought his teeth would rot right out of his head.

I'm jealous.

Ain't that the pits.

As Marie Junior's four-layer chocolate cake gurgled inside his bloated stomach, the elder Marie began to yawn. Clay was almost thankful for it; his cursed body gave out hours earlier than he would have liked, and his ass was already dragging. He got headaches a lot lately, too, which left him cranky and antisocial. He'd tried harder with Marie because she just flat-out deserved his best behavior.

Addy bowed politely and thanked them for the lovely time while Irene rushed off with Jacque to exchange goodbyes. Watching them, Clay had one of those uncomfortable moments where he thought about the "what if" of his curse. He didn't like to do it—made him feel like he was burying himself prematurely, but from time to time his brain forced him to dance with his precarious mortality, and Doc clutching at Jacque's elbow made him wonder if this was Marie's way of ensuring Doc wouldn't be alone no matter the outcome.

"Clayton, non. It's too soon to think like that," Marie said, hearing things no human ought to be able to hear. She reached for his functioning hand to stroke over his fingers, the gesture full of warmth and affection and at odds with the earthquake her magic sent through his body. Clay swallowed hard, his eyes feeling tighter than they should.

"I wasn't sure if… well, you understand."

"I do, but that had no bearing on this. I simply thought two delightful souls deserved some delight. Love is a beautiful thing in all its guises, oui?"

He forced a smile. Love sure didn't feel so beautiful when you hated as much as you loved. The draugr was one more reason to be done with Cora. He wasn't quite there yet—she had her hooks into him too good—but he got closer all the time, and that scared the hell out of him. Once he lost his feelings for her, he lost another portion of his identity. It was taking off the star all over again, except on a bigger scale.

"Ya still wish to find her, and that speaks more to your feelings than anything," Marie said, still sampling his thoughts. "And I don't mean to intrude inside your head, but I hear everything, and at my age, it's hard to tell if it spilled from your lips or not. I can help you find her, you know, if you have something of hers—hair, nail clippings, teeth."

He should have known she'd offer, and in offering, ask for a piece of Cora. As he'd cleared out Cora's belongings when they'd parted ways, he was fresh out of workable material. "Seems I should have kept those toenails I hoarded. Didn't, but should have," he replied.

Marie tittered and pulled herself up, her hand twined with his as she hobbled toward the front door. "Afraid I can't help then, but I doubt Sterling threw that ring away. Doesn't seem like the type of thing he'd get rid of. I bet he'd let ya borrow it. Charm like that don't exactly lose power."

Clay hadn't considered that mostly because he hadn't considered the extra trip to see Sterling. Venturing out his way would put them behind target, but honestly, he wasn't sure what the target was anymore. He still had no clue where Cora was, and he guessed every witch along the delta had been warned not to help him. The powerful ones probably all had nightmare creatures babysitting them to ensure he rotted proper. What was the harm in swinging up to good ol' Arkansas?

"I'm thinking that's a fine plan. Need to read up on the draugr anyway."

"That ya do. You're a good boy. Now get down here and give me some sugar before hustling."

Clay brushed kisses over both of Marie's cheeks, the spice-and-dirt flavor filling his nose and mouth almost overwhelming. "I'll see you soon, Marie."

"Mmm hmm. Travel safe now. Give that ol' Silver Fox my best, and tell him to get down here to visit soon. I have no intention of living forever, so he better make the time."

"I will." Clay accompanied a silent Addy to the carriage to wait for Doc Irene. Fifteen minutes later, her cheeks covered in tracks of black tears, Irene climbed in across from them to slump in her seat, a handkerchief pressed to her mouth. Jacque stood in Marie's doorway with his pants undone, his suspenders crooked, and his hand raised in a parting wave. His expression wasn't quite as tragic as hers, but it was clear he wasn't happy to see his newfound lady fair go.

"Go," Doc said. "Go now before I tell you not to."

As Clay wasn't quite ready to relinquish Doc to Jacque yet, they went.

—

They decided they'd leave at dawn. Clay offered to stay for a couple of days to let Doc and Jacque get their love on, but Doc insisted they depart before she changed her mind about going at all, and Addy's ardor for a party had waned after the draugr's threats. She was twitchy and distracted on the carriage ride back to the hotel, which was not a state Clay'd ever seen her in before.

It did nothing for his nerves.

After he got himself packed—still a one-armed venture that took far longer than it should have—he made his way to Addy's room and knocked on her door. It swung open with a shrill creak, the hinge thirsty for oil. He poked his head in to ascertain Montague's whereabouts. The tiger was stretched out across Addy's pillows, his tail flicking like he'd contracted some of his mistress's agitation. Adelaide stood by the window looking out at the night, her fingers drumming on her bureau top.

"I'd offer to get you drunk, but that don't work with your type. What'll help?" He let himself inside. Addy glanced over her shoulder to eye him, but before she could get out a word, he raised a finger. "That ain't poking you. Not even sure I can right now. Arm don't work. Who knows if the pecker does?"

"Leaving, I suppose. Getting away from this place. I don't…" She muttered and sat on the edge of her bed, her fingers raking furrows in the blankets to either side of her wide hips. "I don't want to be found by my father."

"Mind if I ask why not?"

She frowned and stared at the floor, her bare feet squishing into the plush area rug, her toes playing with the fringe along the edge. "How much did Cora tell you about why we left the court?"

"She didn't."

"Of course she didn't because she's a pain in the arse." She sighed, her chin dropping to touch her chest, hair tumbling past her face to hide her away behind a curtain of red spirals. "She was trying to protect us, but I'll…shite." She mumbled beneath her breath, unintelligible half-thoughts more gibberish than not. He said nothing. He wouldn't push her for information she didn't want to give, but if she needed to talk, he'd listen. They'd never been more than casual friends before, but after she'd saved his hide at the Sanderson House, he felt closer to her, more like she was someone in his life beyond Cora's harlot sister and occasional traveling partner.

"I can't tell you too much for the same reason Cora wouldn't. Sometimes, the walls have ears. The wind can carry a name to the far end of this world and the next. It's why we don't talk about our before-lives much. It's why we move around. You never know who or what is nearby."

"All right." Clay leaned against the doorframe, letting his rotten arm support his weight. It spasmed in response, the muscles inside coiling so tight he let out a surprised squawk. Pain shot from his wrist all the way to his shoulder, a hard pulse that stabbed like the worst pins and needles. Both Addy and Montague lifted their heads to look at him, but he waved them off. He'd take the unpleasantness of a waking limb over the nothingness of a sleeping one. "Pardons. Arm's starting to work. Go on."

"Oh. Well, good. About the arm. The rest of it—" She sprawled back to rest against Montague's stomach, the tiger craning his head to lap at her hair. Being slathered in giant cat spit didn't seem to bother her none, as she reached around for his tail to stroke it between her fingers. "The Court's designed around the old world's model. They've progressed in some ways—women have as much say as the men in matters of court business—but one thing they haven't gotten over is arranged marriages. Sidhe children are traded back and forth for political gain, and we don't fight it because we're raised with the notion that this is how it's always been.

"The Unseelie Court used to operate the same way, but when they came to America, they adopted many of the country's more enlightened views. They realized marrying people without their consent created more problems than not." Addy took a moment to clear her throat, her eyes rising to the ceiling as she collected her thoughts. The last bit of explanation had come easy for her, but whatever she wanted to say next bogged her down, her hesitation manifesting in more grumbles and stammers.

"Let's just say that some of us would have done anything to escape what our parents had planned for us," she finally said.

Addy's information filled in a lot more gaps for him than she probably realized. It explained a lot of Cora's behavior. Cora always refused to talk about her past—said it was behind her, and she wanted to look ahead—but it was clear that her past influenced her present and future—in her lust for freedom and the way she made decisions. All of that was based on the rules and limitations of what she left behind. Had she shared even a fraction of it with him, he'd have understood why she made certain choices, and had he understood, he wouldn't have been so upset before they got to Little Rock. Maybe the whole situation wouldn't have gone to Hell so damned fast.

The woman is so damned stubborn sometimes.

But then, so am I.

But it wasn't about them right then. It was about Addy who'd all but confessed to being scared of her own people. There probably wasn't much he could do to help her, but he was willing to try if for no other reason than he felt like he owed her. "You're afraid the draugr will tell your father where you are," he said.

Addy nodded. "If my father finds me, he'd... the Unseelie Court is not the only one with its monsters. The Seelie Court simply dresses theirs in prettier clothes."

"But I thought you renounced it. You're done with them, so if..."

"That wouldn't matter to him. He takes what he wants."

Clay grunted and looked at his boots, unsure of what to say. No one had ever bullied him before, and as far as he could tell, that's what Addy and Cora's pa was—a powerful bully with powerful people at his disposal, which made the whole problem a lot more complex. It wouldn't be a matter of shooting someone and moving on. It would be a matter of shooting many someones and then combating the army of Fairy nightmare creatures in their wake.

"We'll leave just after dawn then. Get you out of here in case that deader talks foul," he said after a minute.

She cast him a grateful smile and pushed herself off of the bed to pack. There wasn't a lot to do—they hadn't been here long enough—but she kept rearranging things in her bags, likely trying to distract herself from her worries. Montague glanced at Clay one more time before letting his head *thwump* back into the pillows.

Addy smiled affectionately. "Thank you. Now, get out of here and sleep. You look terrible."

"I am. Tired, I mean. Too pretty to look terrible. Sleep good, Addy."

"I'll try."

Clay walked down the hall to his own room, pausing outside of Doc's door and listening to check on her. He could hear trunks being moved, and in between, Irene sniffling and hiccupping. She'd been doing that since they left Marie's—bursting into periodic weepy fits. He did feel sorry for her, but it was hard to take it too seriously; Doc had only known Jacque a day. Clay understood love at first sight better than most, but this was a little extreme.

Or is it? Irene was free with Jacque, and adored for her freedom.

That's not too hard to understand, is it?

"You all right in there?" he asked.

"I...yes. I will be. I'm just being silly," Doc replied.

A yawn crept up on him, and Clay stifled it into his shoulder. He knew he should press, should make Doc talk it out like he'd done

Addy, but he was too close to passing out. His eyes stung with tired and his body felt heavier than usual, like he was lugging around extra weight. "You sure?"

"Yes. I'll see you in the morning."

"Bright and early."

"Of course."

He stumbled to his room and into his bed, not bothering to strip himself fully, just removing his shirt and guns and tucking Gayle beneath his pillow. Trousers and boots still on, he tipped down his hat to cover his face. The muscles in his arm still pulsed but grew more tolerable as time wore on, the knotting reduced to an annoying, but ultimately ignorable, quivering.

For all his talk about dawn and bright and early, Addy had to drag him out of bed the next day. He heard a soft knocking, which he ignored awhile because she was silly enough to let him, and that turned to hard knocking that he blocked out with two pillows around his ears. After that, she jigged his lock and forced her way in to throw a glass of water at his bare chest. It wasn't cold, but it was shocking enough that he shouted and shot up in bed to whip a pillow at her. It struck her right in the chest, a burst of feathers exploding upon contact.

"Goddamn it, woman. What was that for?"

"You wouldn't wake up." Addy tossed the pillow back at him, giggling when it struck him in the face. "Coffee and toast downstairs. Doc's getting the cart ready. I already had them saddle Squirt."

"I coulda shot you, you know," he complained, rubbing his eyes with both fists. It was the first time he'd been able to do that in weeks; the right arm was weaker than the left, but it was functional without pain.

"You could have, but we both know it wouldn't have done a lot of good."

She sashayed her way out of his room. He dragged himself from the bed, scratching and peering at himself in the wall mirror. Something wasn't right. He didn't look any worse than when he'd gone to bed, but everything was shadowy. Dimmed. To most people, it wouldn't have been noteworthy, but Clay was a gunman, and gunmen relied on their sight, and he didn't have perfect sight any longer. He would have liked to attribute it to exhaustion—he'd gotten a good seven hours of sleep, but with the curse, he really could have used twelve—but he knew better. The curse was doing its curse thing. Over the past weeks, he'd lost stamina, weight, and control over his limbs. Why would his vision be any different?

"Christ." He forced himself to get dressed and join his friends despite the sick feeling swelling in his gut. Being piss-pants scared was a hell of a way to start the morning. Even with the weakness, he could function if he took care of himself. Naps and reserving his strength meant that for short durations, he could be the regular, usual Clayton with all his usual Clayton abilities. Sure, there was a little arm shake to contend with, but he was still a better shot than most in spite of the difficulties. But if his eyes went, there was no reserving anything for that. Blind gunman did no one any good.

I'm running out of time.

He shrugged into his duster and lit himself a smoke, grabbing the saddlebags off the bed and heading downstairs. Addy awaited him in the foyer. She'd commandeered a small table near the hotel doors, the tray before her covered by a fancy dome of silver with a handle. He flipped it away to grab his fare, ignoring the pot of coffee.

"We gotta go," was all he said.

He didn't wait for her to argue, just made his way out the front door to pack his gear into the cart. Montague lifted his head when he neared, the cat sandwiched up to the back ledge of the driver's bench, but for once, Clay didn't give a damn he was there. He had one interest, and that was to get to Arkansas to see Sterling. He could research how to banish the draugr and, if there was a way to get rid of it, get back to Marie. Or—if the old man lent him the ring—Clay could find Cora and plead for his life, which was what she'd probably wanted all along. It was possible she wanted him dead, but he'd never known her to be bloodthirsty before. It was far more likely that this was some big, stupid gesture to get him to apologize. The draugr and sluagh were her way of ensuring he had no alternatives other than falling on his knees.

Well, he'd do it. He'd beg because he wasn't so stupid as to let his pride rob him of an extra thirty or forty years, but he'd hate her for it. If this was about revenge and a scorned heart, fine, but anyone who'd go this far to see him suffer didn't deserve his love. He'd purge her from his system like the poison she'd become.

It took Addy and Doc a couple of minutes to realize he hadn't waited for them. By the time they climbed onto the cart bench, Clay was already halfway up the road, his knees squeezing around Squirt's middle to spur her onward. He wanted to be off, to ride as fast and as hard as he could to Arkansas, but he had to keep Addy and Doc close. It wasn't a solo venture with a body that insisted on falling apart piece by piece.

By the time Doc cracked the haul horses' flanks with her crop, Clay'd had enough time to stuff all of his cold toast into his mouth and light another cigarette. They cut a brisk pace through N'Orleans, sticking to the main roads that would eventually lead them to Baton Rouge. From there they'd head up to Shreveport before crossing over into Arkansas. By Clay's estimation, they were about four hundred and fifty miles away. Traveling by cart, he could plan on a conservative twenty miles a day. That meant a three-week trip, closer to two if they had a few good days, but that would depend on weather and horse exhaustion.

With the curse's acceleration, it seemed like too long, but there wasn't much he could do about that unless he wanted to stable the horses and boat up the Mississippi, and to hell with that. He already spent half his day feeling like shit. Adding seasickness to the mix was unnecessary.

They traveled hard that first week—quietly, too, each of them lost to the tangle of their own worries. Addy and Doc took turns driving the cart while Clay spent half his time on Squirt's back and the other half resting among the luggage and tigers. He got less and less worried about Montague as the days wore on, the cat seemingly ambivalent to his presence or the presence of anything other than Adelaide's scratching fingers or any deer unfortunate enough to wander nearby. The cat was a hell of a hunter, lounging lazily one moment and then flying through the air to chase some poor grass-eater the next. He did all right feeding himself, though, lugging back full carcasses at sundown for what Clay called "viscera and blood spray dinners."

Wasn't the most appetizing thing to behold, but he had to eat like everyone else. Clay just wished he'd do it somewhere Clay wouldn't accidentally step in animal brains. That stuff got stuck in his spurs.

The roads between N'Orleans and Baton Rouge and then Baton Rouge and Shreveport were established routes, which allowed them to skip from hotels to boarding houses to inns along the way. One night, they were reduced to bunking in a farmer's barn, but that wasn't so bad with the cart to keep them off the floor. The sleeping arrangements were tight, him jammed up close enough to Addy's flanks he might accidentally impregnate her, but they were safe and quasi-comfortable. And, if it came to the other bit, at least they'd make handsome nipple draggers.

The going didn't get rough until they neared the Arkansas border. They were past civilization, and at the point, they had to make camp outdoors during the night. Doc didn't like the wilderness—said man had evolved enough that sleeping outdoors was unnatural. Clay interpreted that as Doc being afraid of things like wind and grass and bugs, but Doc insisted it was more carnivorous fauna and bandits that concerned her.

"And snakes. The poisonous variety. I'm quite fond of the normal ones. They consume Rodentia, which are terrible disease carriers,"

Doc said, watching Clay assemble a makeshift shelter between a pair of trees. It wasn't glamorous, a piece of leather attached to two ropes and then stretched taut to posts in the ground, but it'd keep them dry if it rained and safe from the punishing sun in the morning. "We could remain in the cart all night, you know," she offered.

"We could, but with three folks and a tiger, it's a crunch," Clay said. "'Sides, don't poisonous snakes eat rats, too? They serve their purpose."

"Well, yes, but they also bite people, which is the problem. If they don't kill you immediately, and they probably will, they do irreparable nerve damage. And there are no less than four poisonous species in this area. Copperheads, cottonmouths, coral snakes, rattlesnakes… we're near a stream, which is prime cottonmouth territory." Doc glanced at the running water behind them and adjusted her glasses on her nose. "The alternative is to not water the horses, so we're gonna have to take a gamble." Clay stopped hammering the tent stakes to rub his eyes. They stung a little, partially from the sweat pouring into them and partially from his own failing vision. He hadn't mentioned anything to Addy and Doc, afraid to worry them, but the dimness that started at the hotel was worsening. He could see straight well enough, but his peripherals were going. The world closed in around him, a fog of encroaching darkness.

"I think I might sleep in the cart, if it's all right with you. The idea of something slithering on me—slugs. There are probably slugs, Clayton. Ew."

"Can do what you want. I'll be under here. Been touched by worse'n slugs in my life."

"Yes, you have. Like that strumpet in Nashville with the terrible teeth. What was her na—Ruby! Ruby Begonia."

Clayton grinned. "Ruby was a nice gal. You leave her alone."

"She looked like a boar, complete with bristles!"

"Boar gals with bristles need love, too."

Doc shook her head and climbed back into the cart to scribble in her book. It was probably another letter to Jacque. Every time they passed a post, she dropped a note to her fancy lad, giving updates on their trip and talking about whatever interesting or uninteresting things they did throughout the day. Clay wouldn't give her shit for it—he remembered what it was like when Cora took off and how much he missed her. He remembered wishing he had a way to write her, but her adventures usually took her not just off the map, but into another world.

No post rider with half a brain would venture past the veil and into Fairy's chaos.

Clay finished adjusting the tent and glanced around at their camp. They'd picked a nice spot near the creek, the cypress trees forming a semi-circle of looming monoliths over a flat patch of grass. Addy had just finished brushing the horses and was hobbling them near the banks. Doc had prepared a fire pit for dinner, a circle of stones set around a pair of iron forks with a spit bar between them. No game hung there yet, but would in a little while. Clay still had the wherewithal to shoot them some venison or rabbits. Even Montague was settled in, the cat sprawled in a sliver of sunlight with his paws pointed at the sky.

"I need to go for a walk," Addy announced, brushing her hands down her gray skirt before plucking a leaf from the ground. She carried it to the stream and dipped it inside, folding the sides up so it made a green bowl. Clay thought she'd drink from it, but then she scanned the ground along the banks, eventually selecting a single pine needle and dropping it into the water inside the leaf.

"The hell are you doing?"

"Finding a crossover point for Fairy." She squinted at him and then past him, her eyes fixing on the forest they'd traveled through over the course of the day. Montague oozed from the cart and into the tall grasses to follow her, the motion so fluid he looked like he had no bones. He loped past Addy and somehow managed to disappear into the surrounding brush despite his loud, orange coloring.

"He's very persistent," she added as an afterthought.

"Who is?" Clay asked.

She shook her head in response.

Clay chewed on the butt of his cigarette. The unspoken "he" could have been the tiger, he supposed, but her reluctance to talk about it suggested she meant her father. "Still? It's been more'n a week since we left Marie's. Wouldn't something have happened already?"

"Not while I was in an industrial place like a city. Too much iron. Too little whimsy for the old ones to risk," she said, forcing her way past the brush between the trees and toward the dense woods. "The veil is thick in settled areas, harder to get through, so I was safe there. Here, I'm out in the open."

Each of her footfalls was echoed by the snaps of breaking twigs and sticks. Clay got up to follow her, curious how the leaf compass worked. "Be back soon," he called to Doc. Doc raised a hand to let him know she'd heard. He jogged to catch up to Addy, falling into step by her elbow as she circumvented an oak tree and wandered to the left. "That leaf contraption—that'll lead you?"

"Yes"

"Huh. That work for everyone?"

"Everyone of fairy blood." Addy cast him a sideways grin. "It'd probably work for you if you ever wanted to brave the weird side, though I'd recommend a chaperone for your virgin trip."

He had zero inclination to go into the madhouse of Fairy, but it was nice to know he could if he ever got dumber than he already was. Cora'd told him all about her world—how things that appeared welcoming were often nightmare traps waiting to be sprung. He knew that nothing was as it seemed there, even the passage of time. What was three days in Fairy could be three weeks in the human world, which accounted for some of Cora's longer stints away. Distance worked funny, too; a day and a half of human travel would only take two hours there, which was probably why Addy wanted it as an option in case her pa came after her. It was a far quicker escape than on foot or on horseback here.

He watched the pine needle float around inside the leaf. Every few feet, it'd twitch before settling on a direction, which was west as far as Clay could tell.

"There," Addy said, pointing at a circle of grass in the midst of a cluster of pine trees. "It's not too far from camp. Good." It was a magical place where colors were more lush, the grass made of emerald, and the dandelions pure gold. The air was heavier and thicker and too still, no wind blowing despite distant trees rustling. Addy abandoned her leaf to cross into the clearing, her hands spread to either side, her fingers waggling like she was feeling around for something. Clay stayed back, expecting his witchsniffer to go crazy at any minute, but there was nothing. There hadn't been anything at the mushroom ring at Cora's house neither but this place felt different somehow—more magical.

"Where are… oh, there you are." Addy grinned, staring at what looked like a patch of nothing. Clay watched in a mix of fascination and horror as long, brown, stick-like things stretched out of that nothing, curling around a portion of the landscape and peeling it back like a page of a book to expose a kaleidoscope of colors beneath. They were fingers—eerily long fingers with far too many knobby joints—pushing and shoving at his reality to make a doorway where there ought not to be one.

"No, no. Not now," Addy said, patting the bizarre appendages. "I just needed to know you're here. I'll be back if I need you." The fingers twitched before receding back behind the nothing-at-all and righting the world.

The portal disappeared, but a pulse rode the air. Clay's witchsniffer thrummed, his skin throbbing and his teeth grinding as a foreign energy crashed into him. The power was tremendous, and he steadied himself against a tree, his eyes closing as he fought for equilibrium. It took him a good minute to figure out what was wrong with the onslaught. It came from the wrong direction. The Fairy portal was fifteen yards dead ahead of him, but the awful, foreign magic came from somewhere behind.

From camp.

The magic came from camp where he'd left Doc alone with a bunch of horses and a tent.

"Doc!" he shouted, turning tail and running for the cart. He shouldn't assume whatever weird had found them was out for blood, but with the various threats in their recent and not-so-recent histories, he couldn't be too careful. Addy followed along behind him, and then she caught him at a full sprint, freakishly fast thanks to her air fairy tricks. They hit the stream at the same time, bursting through the underbrush to stagger to a stop by the pit fire.

Of everything and everyone that could be there, he'd hoped it wouldn't be a Lynch sister. A visit from the draugr or maybe some fairy working for Addy's pa wouldn't be so terrible. But, as his luck was worse than a one-legged man in an alligator pit, it wasn't just *a* Lynch sister, but *two* Lynch sisters.

Standing shoulder to shoulder in front of the cart, their hands clasped politely in front of their matching skirts, were Augustine and Thomasine Lynch. They peered at him, peered at Addy, and then back at him again, Doc's crinkled letter clutched in Augustine's hand.

"Clayton," they said in unison.

Balls.

CHAPTER FOURTEEN

TWO YEARS AGO

It was Cora's fault, but then, most things were. How she'd managed to rope him into accompanying her to a tea-and-sandwich luncheon hosted by a bunch of Irene's gal friends, he couldn't say. No, wait, yes he could. She'd asked him to go when she had her hands wrapped around his... right. That's why he'd said yes. She'd struck during a weak moment, clever minx that she was.

If he had half a brain, he'd have held out for a few dozen repeat performances. Sitting in a carriage bound for some Texas ranch fifteen miles outside of civilization, he was pretty sure he got the short end of the stick. Addy was smart enough to bow out, though that had more to do with the three German gentlemen she'd befriended at the hotel. They'd been holed up in her room all weekend, and as far as Clay could tell, she'd been sampling their schnitzel so much that they'd walk bow-legged the rest of their days.

Poor Frederick was there, too, pouting that Cora'd left him in the room. She brought him everywhere, so the notion of her locking him away surprised both Clay and squirrel. When Clay asked her about it, all she'd say was, "Meet Betsy. You'll understand." It probably wasn't meant to be as ominous as it sounded, but it was yet another reason Clay wished he'd had the foresight to decline her invitation.

At least he had Cora nestled into his side now, her head perched on his shoulder as she napped. Her skirts were bunched around her knees, showing off her pale pink stockings and matching slippers. Her hair hung free, some of the thick tresses pinned between his back and the seat. He was afraid of moving for fear of hurting her, and thanks to it, his extremities alternated between numbness and pins and needles. He'd wrestle a greased pig for the privilege of stretching his legs.

"She's adorable," Irene said from the opposite bench.

"Is. Even when she snores."

"She snores?"

"Like a bear."

Irene tittered and waved her fan back and forth, sending strands of her red wig billowing around her shoulders. Clay shifted his boots back, partially to regain the feeling in his toes and partially to avoid mucking up Irene's skirts. She'd worn an enormous dress today, the belled bottom draped over two or three layers of thick petticoats that commandeered far more than her half of the carriage floor. Between the two gals, Clay could drown in lace and silk. Fortunately, he was taller than they were, so there was a small chance of survival if he kept his head held high.

"Who are these folks anyway?" Clay dropped his voice to a whisper so as to not wake Cora. Not only did she snore like a bear, she roared like one when anything disturbed her sleep.

"Well, my friend is Maybell Lynch, but her four sisters will be there, too. I don't know them as well, but they seem like lovely girls."

Clay'd heard of the Texas Lynches before. Sterling once told him the Lynch matriarch was the bad kind of crazy. Couple years back, she'd held the mayor hostage because he'd judged another blueberry pie finer than hers at the county fair. When lawmen fell on the ranch to recover him, every bullet fired turned into a pigeon that promptly flew back 'round and shat on their heads. She only let the terrified officiate go home after Mrs. Mayor begged for her husband's release. By then, word had spread near and far that Eloise Lynch was powerful, mean, and softer than a nappy full of baby crap.

No big surprise Cora "forgot" to name their hostesses. Clay didn't believe for a second that was coincidence neither. "Wait 'til he met Betsy" indeed.

"Cora didn't mention we were visitin' a nutter."

"Oh, no. Eloise passed a year ago. Maybell runs things now, and she's much kinder than her mother. A little less—" Doc paused to choose her words. "—reactionary."

"She a witch?"

"Well, yes. They're all witches. I hope that's not a problem?"

Clay shrugged and looked out the window at the vast Texas nothing. "Nah. Afternoon just got more interestin' is all."

All he could see was sand. A few cacti sprouted from the ground, specks of green to break up all the beige, but it did little to improve the depressing, monotonous view. Most parts of Texas were green and beautiful, especially along the Louisiana border. Not there. It was dry enough and ugly enough the devil himself wouldn't want it. Seemed odd that the witches would choose to live out past the city borders when Houston itself was so pretty, but he supposed it kept most folks at bay. Witch haters would have to trudge through nasty terrain to get to them.

"How'd you befriend a witch anyway?" Clay asked. "Ain't like you collect weirds like me and Sterling."

"In the simplest manner, a doctor would befriend anyone, I suppose. They had the chicken pox. Maybell came looking for a doctor willing to treat people of… well, different people. I happened to be in Houston with Cora and Adelaide at the time and volunteered my services. Over the course of treatment, we grew friendlier. I introduced them to the fae, and here we are."

"You signed up for witch healin' duties as easy as that?"

"Why wouldn't I?" Doc asked. "Most people would refuse to treat me because I was born in the wrong skin. I couldn't do the same to someone else simply because of magical affinity they didn't ask for."

There was a marked difference in Clay's mind, but he didn't say so. Doc'd tell him he had a prejudice, and maybe he did, but it'd developed over time as a result of too many strained encounters with broom jockeys. Sure, there were a few great ones like Marie Laveau and her daughter, but for every one of *them* there were five or six of the other type who'd kidnap a mayor because he didn't like her blueberry pie.

Trouble. All of 'em.

Cora snorted beside him, all sweet and quiet-like before letting loose with a sinus-clearing snore. It was loud enough to wake her from her stupor, and her eyes flew open, one of her hands squeezing his knee, the other flattening against the window pane. Irene let out a cough that sounded suspiciously like a strangled laugh from behind her fan. Seemed she was smart enough to hide from the startled ursine in their midst, too.

"How close are we?" Cora yawned, her maw opening so wide it nearly split her head in half.

Irene pointed at the window, and sure enough, there was a farm smack in the middle of all that sand. Clay's witchsniffer snapped to attention, magic buzzing in his bones and rippling over his skin. It wasn't one power but many, and he felt dizzy in the face of it, his system incapable of honing in on just one strand so it channeled a little bit of all of them. He wanted to run, to dance a jig, and to peel off his skin all at the same time. None of those things were possible, though, so he squirmed like he had ants in his drawers instead.

Such a strange feeling.

Such a strange place.

The property was two different worlds converging without any thought for logic or sanity. Grass stretched out in an enormous circle in the middle of the desert, fences holding sheep and horses inside so they didn't wander out to their dry and dusty deaths. There was a pond as well as looming oak trees to provide patches of shade. Oaks shouldn't thrive there, yet these were tall enough to touch the clouds. Breezes blew, but only around the farm. The rest of the desert was as still and punishing as ever.

There wasn't one main farmhouse so much as a smattering of smaller cottages forming a half-circle around the drive. Clay counted five separate structures—one for each Lynch, he presumed. He'd seen some remarkable magic in his lifetime, but gals with the power to make the arid Texas hellscape into a functioning, verdant ranch were pretty damn special. Scary, but special all the same.

The door to the middle cottage opened, and out walked a statuesque brunette in a blue frock, white apron, and a fawn-colored cowboy hat. She was a real looker, from her glossy chestnut hair to her high cheekbones, but there was something imposing about her that Clay found off-putting. Her expression said she was willing and able to pop his head off his shoulders like a dandelion blossom from the stem. Pretty or no, she wasn't the type of gal his survival instinct would let him appreciate too long.

Not that he was looking anyway. Cora had him hooked good.

He climbed from the carriage to help Cora down the steps, waiting while she adjusted her skirts and retrieved her parasol. There was a commanding throat clear from behind him, and Clay turned around to offer Irene the same courtesies, holding her gloved fingers while she exited far more demurely than Cora had, but then, she had to be more careful. Her dress was so big any fast movements would send her sprawling to the ground like a turtle upended onto its shell.

"Don't get used to this," Clay whispered. "One time favor."

"Shut up, Clayton. Be a gentleman for once." Irene jammed her elbow into his side before dropping into a curtsey at the tall woman's feet. "Maybell, so good to see you again, dear. May I introduce my friend, Marshal Clayton Jenson? You know Cora, of course."

Maybell spared a nod for Cora before swinging her attention to Clay. Pale gold eyes surveyed his face and the lapel of his duster, that severe countenance going to granite when she spotted the star glinting on his chest. "Sterling Cole's successor, yes?"

It wasn't a question so much as a demand, and Clay stiffened at the tone, now twice as convinced Cora could shove her tea-and-sandwich luncheon where the sun didn't shine. Next time she wanted him to act as her arm puppet, he'd ask which dragon would be hosting first. "The one and only. Nice to make your acquaintance, Miss Lynch."

He wasn't sure what to expect from her, but a warm smile with straight, white teeth was not it. That's what he got, though, and she stuck out a hand, not for kisses on the knuckles or anything ladylike, but for a good, hard shake. He accepted, impressed by the firmness of her grasp. "A pleasure. My mother adored Marshal Cole."

She did? That was news to Clayton. Everything Sterling ever said to him about Eloise Lynch focused on her batless belfry, but as he wasn't stupid enough to mention that in polite company, he smiled and looped his arm around Cora's waist instead. "Sterling's a fine man, but don't tell him I said so."

"I wouldn't dream of it. Cora, a pleasure to see you again. No Adelaide today?" Maybell offered that same shake to Cora, her hand engulfing Cora's fingers. It took Clay seeing that for him to clue in to how big Maybell was—huge across the shoulders and limbs, as tall as him, and thick. She wasn't fat, but solid, and he had to wonder what kind of man could hope to saddle a woman like her for wife. Hercules maybe, but that's about all he could think of.

"She's busy playing hide the schwanz with some Germans she met in the city. She sends her regards," Cora said, her grin practically sparkling. "Where are the other girls?"

Maybell lifted two fingers to her lips, giving off a whistle that would have done any cattle herder proud. Thinking along those lines wasn't all that kind considering she was beckoning gals not cows, but one glance at the first Lynch sister to appear and he figured he wasn't that far off the mark. How an Amazon like Maybell could have a sister so short, squat, and covered in warts, he couldn't say, but damn. Outside of the color of her hair, there wasn't a slight bit of resemblance between Maybell and Sister Two, though Clay scoured the girl's plain face for some hint that they shared blood. Wasn't there. A hooked nose, a guppy mouth, and pinched brown eyes made the new Lynch look... well. Uglier than a pile of puke came to mind.

"This is Betsy, the baby. She just turned sixteen a week ago. Betsy, love, this is Marshall Jenson, Miss Cora's gentleman friend."

Betsy waddled out of her cottage with a basket in her arms, three kittens mewling and crawling over one another inside a pile of blankets. They were cute little things, fluffy and fat with charcoal-colored fur and long white whiskers. "Oh, hi. Hello. I'm B... I'm B... " She hesitated a moment and took a long breath before trying again. "I'm Betsy."

"Good to make your acquaintance, Miss Betsy. Nice kittens you got there. They your pets?"

"No. I'm practicing on them."

Clay was about to ask what she was practicing, thinking maybe she'd say crocheting cat hats or some other kid thing, but Cora grabbed his hand and dug her fingernails in hard enough that he hissed through his teeth. He shot her a glance but she wasn't looking at him, instead staring straight ahead, the stretch of her lips more a grimace than a smile.

"Betsy's got a rare talent with curses," Maybell said, frowning. "But she doesn't quite understand that not everyone appreciates that.

Put those back, Betsy. It's not polite to... lots of folks don't want to see what you can do, all right? It's like playing with your food." Betsy smiled shyly and ducked back into her house, bringing the yowling pride right along with her. Maybell sighed and shook her head, her hands planting on her hips. "Pardons. She's young and awkward at times. Sweet, but a little unright if you know what I mean. We take it easy on her."

Clay didn't know what to say to that, and so he nodded. He now understood why Cora wouldn't bring Frederick along. Who knew what Betsy the Unright Curse Maker would do to him? Bad enough she was experimenting on kittens in the privacy of her cottage. Poor things. Cora was likely having a shitfit behind that pseudo-smile of hers. She loved animals, big and small. Always took the time to pat them whenever there was a moment to spare.

Visions of Cora running up and tackling the youngest Lynch ran through his head, but then his attention was pulled to the furthest cottage along the drive. The front door squealed and then clapped closed behind a fresh pair of women. Maybell motioned them forward with a smile, her hand drifting to the taller of the two sisters when they neared.

"These are the twins, Augustine and Thomasine,"

Twins? They didn't look much like twins to Clay. Maybe Eloise brewed them in her gut at the same time, but they were as different as night and day. The one named Augustine leaned into Maybell's side. Tall and willowy, she had pale skin and dark hair that hung in a straight black veil to her hips. She didn't have much in the way of curves, but she did have a face that could haunt a man's dreams. Her eyes were heavy-lidded and rimmed by dark shadows, which, against her milquetoast pallor, made her wraithlike. Her features were fine—golden eyes, an aquiline nose, an even mouth—but the otherworldly quality to her demeanor made her prettiness unsettling. It was like admiring a corpse—you could say the corpse was pretty, but that didn't mean you wanted to fuck it.

Well, some folks might, but that made them strange. Or real lonely. Whichever.

Thomasine, on the other hand, was short, round, and cute as a button with her bright smile and smooth, creamy skin. There was a spray of freckles on her nose the color of good honey and a flush in her cheeks that reminded him of strawberry wine. He winked at her in greeting, mostly 'cause he liked the wiggle in her waggle, and her ensuing giggles were charming—all bubbly and sweet. She must not get a lot of romantical attention in the middle of the desert, but then, that probably wasn't a bad thing. Any fella that ventured out so far was probably a criminal and didn't deserve a jewel like her.

"Don't mind the flirting. He thinks he's a charmer," Cora said, her hand sliding under his jacket to pinch his flank. It stung a bit, but he was so grateful she was out of that stone-jawed kitten stupor he didn't swat her off. Besides, he knew Cora well enough to recognize a warning when she presented one. The pinch was a reminder to watch himself. That the girls might be adorable, but they were dangerous, too.

"If he'd like to see real charms, I would be more than happy to show him," Maybell replied. The words were friendly, but her expression held an edge, her eyes and brow riddled with strain lines that hadn't been there before.

She's the mama bear in Eloise's stead.

I see.

"Pardons, Maybell. You just got a passel of lovely gals here, and I'm a simple man whose day can be made by a pretty face or—" He was going to say three, but not wanting to insult Betsy, he lied through his teeth. "—four. 'Sides, I'm standing next to a woman prettier than a spring morning. She's more than enough lady for me."

"I'd imagine so. The Woodkin are notorious troublemakers." Maybell softened the remark with a smile, and Clay tucked the term away for future use. Woodkin. He'd never heard it said that way before, but he liked it. It was a fancy way around saying "fucking fairy."

"I am sure I have no idea what you're talking about," Cora said.

Clay brushed his lips across her hair, flinching through the resulting zap. "Sure you don't, darlin'."

Their banter halted at the appearance of the final Lynch, who stomped out of her cottage like she was crushing ants. This gal bore a passing resemblance to Maybell, but in all the bad ways. Where Maybell's strong features were offset by her heart-shaped face, this sister was angles and juts. Her cheekbones were too pronounced. The hollows in her cheeks cut so deep she looked gaunt. Her nose was also long and hooked, reminding him of an eagle or a hawk.

"I'm Elmira," she snapped. She grunted at him, grunted at Doc and Cora, and then disappeared back into her cottage with a slam of the door, either figuring her social contract was fulfilled or deeming Clay and company not worthy of her time. He peered after her only to discover something in the window of her house peering *back*. It wasn't Elmira but an enormous reptile, its tongue darting out and its head cocked to the side.

"She's got a monster in there with her," Clay said, his hand slipping to Gayle's grip. "You need me to take care of it?"

"Monster? Oh, no. That's just her pet," Maybell said. "Elmira's eccentric. Don't mind her."

Eccentric was one way to put it, he supposed.

Maybell motioned them toward the middle cottage, which was bigger than the rest and sported the greenest garden. The shrubs around it bloomed with all manner of colors, reminding him some of Cora's Mississippi refuge. Cora clung to one of his elbows, and Irene stepped up to take the other one. He was squished between two ruffled dresses, every step toward the house a test to see if he could avoid killing himself or either of the gals flanking him.

"I was so sorry to hear about your mother," Irene said, brushing past Clay to shove her way into Maybell's abode. It was tidy inside and on the Spartan side, which didn't surprise Clay at all. Maybell crossed him as brutally efficient. There wasn't a speck of dust on her tables or a cobweb to be found in her rafters. Any spider stupid enough to take up residence in a Lynch household deserved whatever it got.

"She lived a good life," Maybell said. "Though I wish she'd been more careful. She could have lived another twenty or thirty years if she hadn't blown herself up. The best we can do is learn from her mistakes, I suppose. Tea?"

Morbid curiosity made him want to ask exactly how Eloise Lynch expired, but one look at Cora and he knew to keep his mouth shut. He'd already gotten Maybell's evil eye for looking too long on Thomasine. He didn't need to court her undying disdain by prying, too.

"Tea would be lovely. Cora?"

"Yes, please."

The ladies sat at a large, circular table with a lavender tablecloth and a vase of pink flowers. The table settings were scalloped ivory china with hand-painted roses along the trim. Sandwiches, cakes, and sliced fruit occupied the rest of the free space. There were ten chairs in total, all mismatched styles and painted different colors, but it looked nice anyway—pastel and feminine. Clay'd never been more out of place. That didn't stop him from removing his hat and sliding in next to Cora, though, watching Maybell make the rounds with her teapot.

If Cora ever doubted that he loved her, she could look back on the day Clayton Jensen was surrounded by girls and not one of them was nekkid.

The twins seated themselves while Maybell poured, Thomasine claiming the seat opposite him, Augustine to her left. To stop himself from enjoying the view too much, his eyes strayed around the cottage, from the clusters of herbs lined up in neat rows on the walls to the portrait above the mantle of a young man with a bushy beard and a pale blue uniform.

Maybell leaned over his shoulder to drizzle tea into his cup. When she noticed his attention fixed on the picture, she paused. "That's my pa. Jebediah Arren Steacher. He served under Zachary Taylor in the Mexican-American War."

"Fancy that. I can see the resemblance." And he could. The man on the wall had the same face shape as Maybell. He also had that expression that suggested if you got too near him on a bad day, he'd snap your leg bone in half and use it for a toothpick.

"I wish we still had the portrait of *our* pa," Thomasine said, her teaspoon clinking against the edges of her saucer. "It'd be a nice keepsake."

So they had different fathers. The revelation piqued his curiosity, though if he was being honest with himself, everything about the Lynches was fascinating to some degree. Not the tea-and-sandwich parts, but the gals themselves. As it was possibly the only opportunity he'd get to inquire about their weird little family, Clay had to think of the best way to frame his questions so he didn't sound rude. Well, ruder—no way to really make the point he wanted to make without being a little insulting. "I noticed you gals don't look all that much alike. You've all got your own fair charms, of course. Your Mama married twice?"

"Four times, actually," Maybell said.

"Nearly five, but Sterling got away," Thomasine offered. "Or, should I say, they parted ways before the nuptials." She tittered and squished a biscuit into her mouth, her fingers dashing at the crumbles on her lower lip.

Clay'd been ready to take a sip of his tea, but hearing that Sterling had almost become Mr. Eloise Lynch the Fifth stopped him cold. "What now?"

Maybell grinned and slid into her chair, taking the time to unfold and refold her napkin before placing it in her lap. "Mama was married to my father first. He took an unfortunate tumble down the stairs on his thirtieth birthday and landed face first in his own birthday cake. His neck was broke so bad his head was turned around on his shoulders."

"But Mama married again in 1850, this time to Elmira's daddy, Daniel Wyrith. He choked on a meatball." The voice was raspy and unfamiliar, and Clay glanced over to see if it'd been the ghoulish twin, Augustine, who spoke. She hadn't touched her tea, nor had she put any food on her porcelain plate, probably because doing so would make her look too human, the creepy thing.

"Tragedy, really," Maybell said. "And then there was Thomasine and Augustine's father, Martin Bitterton."

Thomasine nodded. "Mama loved him best, but Elmira got into her firebug stage, and he burned up when she leveled the first ranch.

We weren't even one yet."

"Tragic," all three girls said at once, right as Betsy waddled through the cottage door. She graced them with a big, yellow smile before throwing herself into one of the empty chairs, her warty hand reaching for the plate of cookies. Clay watched her fingers slide over a good half dozen before she chose her confection. Unkind as it was to admit, he swore then and there he'd keep to the fruit and cakes. Warts had touched those cookies, and he wasn't gonna eat no goddamned warty cookie.

Clay cast Betsy a tepid smile before looking back at Maybell, dazed by their explanations. "Elmira lit him on fire?"

"Not on purpose, of course, she was only seven," she said. "We don't have much control over our abilities at that age, but we learn."

Thomasine nodded. "Mama was heartbroken, but then Father O'Connaugh came to offer spiritual guidance."

Clay didn't know what a priest had to do with anything and wasn't sure if it'd be rude to outright ask, but Cora didn't worry about such things. Maybe she felt more comfortable with the Lynches thanks to their longer association, because she trudged right on through that open door without a second's hesitation. "What does a priest have to do with anything?"

"Well, he was a priest when Mama met him."

"And?" Cora pressed.

"Then he became Betsy's daddy," the twins said in unison.

"Oh. Oh, I see," Cora said, her upper lip curling into a half smile. Seemed she was as transfixed by the dysfunctional tale as Clay was. "That's sordid."

"Well, it was, but—" Maybell paused to peer at her sisters, the Lynches sharing one of those wordless moments where people understood each other without having to say a single word. When they all nodded their accord, she continued. "—Mama drowned him in his pisspot."

Cora had the sugar jar in hand when Maybell said that, but she had to put it down, her eyes wide with delighted surprise. Clay wasn't sure what to do. The Lynches were admitting their mama was a murderer, and he felt like he should do something about that as a marshal, but it wasn't like he could go find Eloise's corpse and arrest it, so he looked to Irene for guidance. Doc was always the sensible one in situations like these. Unfortunately, Irene's mouth hung open in stunned silence, wide enough she'd catch flies sooner or later.

Well, shit. She was no use at all.

"But why?" Cora asked. "Why would she… what did he do?"

"He was drunk as a skunk all the time," Thomasine said.

"And when he was drunk, he sang," Augustine offered.

The sisters peered at their guests like this explained everything, but Clay was lost. What the hell did singing priests have to do with anything? Singing was bad?

Maybell tutted, her fingers waving impatiently like she was chiding a child. "He sang all the time. Morning, noon, night. Depressing Irish ballads. By then Mama had met Sterling and fancied him, so when Father O'Connaugh passed out in his own pisspot..."

"She put her foot on the back of his head and let nature do the good work," Thomasine finished.

There wasn't a single natural thing about any of what Clay had heard over the last few minutes. In fact, it was so convoluted that he couldn't muster a response, not even to ask what happened between Sterling and Eloise—and he *really* wanted to know that story. Sterling always loved the ladies, but not for more than a night or two. Eloise sounded like a much more involved situation.

"Well, that's really something!" Irene said, forcing a smile that rivaled Cora's teeth-gnashing kitten one. "Quite the story of... you are all remarkable women. Survivors, though I am sorry for your losses."

The Lynch sisters raised their cups in salute, and Clay and Cora did the same, figuring this was their ritual to honor the men who'd met odd, untimely demises at the hands of Eloise Lynch.

Birthday cakes and meatballs and fire and pisspots indeed.

Doc Irene fanned her face so hard her hand nearly snapped off.

"Not to change the subject," she said, though Clay knew that was exactly what she was doing. "What do you ladies think of my dress? I had it custom tailored with a French bodice, but I'm not sure if it suits me."

The room erupted. There were squeals and fits of overlapping chatter and talk about silk and linen and cotton. Clay didn't give two damns about such feminine nonsense, and so he muttered his excuses, intent on going outside to roll himself a smoke. As he dropped his Stetson back on his head, Cora's hand reached out to grab onto his coat, hauling him down hard enough he had to stoop lest he lose his sleeve.

"Steal the kittens," she whispered into his ear, close enough for her lips to brush over his lobe. It sent an electric shiver down his spine for more reasons than one.

"What now?"

"Steal them. Go on. Get them while she's distracted. We'll leave early. I'll fake sick. Just get them away from her." Cora's eyes strayed to Betsy, who was bouncing in her seat and clapping her hands in delight at whatever inane thing Irene just said. She looked as sweet as a warty, cookie-crumble covered gal could look, but if she was capable of afflicting little kittens with witch curses, appearances were deceiving.

“You think I should steal from a Lynch? A curse-making Lynch at that?” he demanded.

Cora eyed the witches and then eyed him. Outside, he could hear thunder rumbling in the distance, the desert about to get its first good dousing in who knew how long. “You better,” she said. “Please.”

CHAPTER FIFITEEN

NOW

Clay couldn't see Doc. She'd been perched in the cart scribbling her love letters before they'd wandered into the woods, but the bench was empty, and their camp was silent. Montague hadn't returned either, still off adventuring, which meant Doc had been well and truly alone when the witches arrived.

"Doc?!" Clay called, swinging around to search for his friend. The rapid movement made his vision swim, the blackness along the edges rising like liquid sloshing in a bucket. It was disorienting and not a little bit nauseating. He stilled, the darkness receding back where it belonged, but not before the world was cloaked by ink.

Temporary or not, it sucked.

"Here. Laying down. Have to," Doc squeaked from somewhere amidst the luggage. "Oh, dear God."

The sides of the cart were too tall for Clay to see over, so he dashed ahead to check on her. Augustine slashed her hand through the air, and he smashed into a solid, invisible nothing—a wall he couldn't see, something she constructed with magic—and his nose crunched into his face upon contact. It wasn't broken. There was no blood to indicate he'd done real harm, but it stung bad enough that he cupped it in his palm and staggered back, cringing.

"Gals," Clay said, one hand going to his gun, the other rubbing at the ache. "Was that really necessary?"

"Yes," they said, again in tandem, which made them creepier than they ought to be.

Fucking witches.

Augustine looked as fresh-dead as he remembered, with that toneless skin and too-dark hair. The flat white dress she wore did nothing to enliven her. She was a living ghost, a specter well before Death came calling. The fact that she refused to wear shoes only enhanced the illusion. He could see her bare feet peeking up over the blades of grass, her toes muddy from walking along the creek. He'd heard of Women in White before—beautiful ghosts who lured unsuspecting travelers to their deaths with their unearthly charms. Maybe Augustine rehearsing for her big hereafter.

Thomasine was unchanged as well, a vibrant vision of squishy curves and freckles in her pale blue dress. Except that vision was pissed at him. Her ballooned cheeks, flaring nostrils, and squinted eyes said she wanted to murder the shit out of him. Not slit his throat and be done with it, though—more like long, painful, torture death with stabbing and maiming and maybe fire ants in open wounds.

"What's wrong with Doc?" Clay demanded.

"Nothing yet, but she'll get her justice," Augustine said. She shifted away from the wagon to drift toward him. He got his first hint of her magic then. It manifested in his mouth of all places, lining his cheeks and coating his tongue. It wasn't a taste or a flavor but a weighted presence, like he was chewing cotton. He spit to get rid of it, but because it wasn't a regular solid, there was nothing there to expel. He was stuck with the sensation that he was choking on a mouthful of fuzzy clouds with no way to purge it. Well, other than killing Augustine, which he didn't want to leap to right away. There was still the possibility they could work something out. Unlikely, yes, but he didn't jump straight to murder all the time.

Just some of the time. Like with Betsy.

Doc let out a squeal from inside of the cart, sounding like a sow at slop time. "Snakes," she said, her voice high with fear. "Snakes on me."

Hadn't they just been discussing snakes? Clay frowned and glanced between the cart and the approaching witch. "You bit?" he called out.

"Not yet. But, oh, they're wriggling on me. I can feel them slithering."

Clay wanted to take another stab at saving her, but he heard movement from behind and swung around with Gayle in his grip. The barrels pressed right into Addy's guts. She didn't hesitate before batting at his wrist and stepping in beside him, her hands stretched in front of her to feel for the wall of magic responsible for shoving his nose through his face. It didn't appear to be there anymore, but that didn't mean Augustine wouldn't remake it at the drop of a hat. She'd been quick like a bunny with the last one.

"They must have overheard her earlier," Addy said. She looked up at the sky and then down at the grass, oddly calm considering their circumstances. "They're illusions or constructs of some kind. Not real snakes."

Thomasine lifted her chin so she could look down her nose at them, her arms folding across her chest. "Or you could be wrong and one of us has an affinity for snakes, like Elmira did with Happy before you killed her. You can gamble if you'd like."

"What the fuck's a Happy?" Clay asked.

"Her familiar."

Elmira named that hideous lizard thing with its spikes and hissing and gnashing teeth Happy?

There was more wrong with her than an arson fetish.

Addy must have thought similar, because her upper lip curled into a lopsided, shitty grin. "More appropriate to call it 'Squish' now, I'd think. I beat it to paste. I'd do it again if I could, too. That thing was mean."

Augustine didn't like hearing that, and her fingers curled over with another spell. Clay lifted Gayle and aimed it at her forehead, using his free arm to steady his wrist best he could. Dang, this gun was heavier every time he lifted it. "You're instigating, Addy. Can't blame you, but let's keep our heads if we can."

"Oh, please. We're all dead anyway." She motioned at the crumpled letter in Augustine's hand and then at the glowering Thomasine. "She has Doc's confession in hand. You killed Betsy. The only one they might not murder is me, and there's no way I'm going to stand idly by while they light you up."

Clay smirked despite his arm going to lead. He swallowed an untimely yawn, too, the adrenaline that went with fearing for his life not enough to topple the curse's fatigue.

This is going to shit faster than a monkey party.

"Much obliged, Adelaide. You might be a lady after all," he managed, but it sounded more like a croak than not.

"Hardly," Augustine said, her attention skipping from him to Addy, her eyes perusing Addy's person. Her blank mask slipped for just a moment, but it was long enough to see the derision lurking just beneath the surface. "Dr. Miller killed Elmira by her own admission. Were you involved, Woodkin?"

"Definitely."

"Then you're forfeit, too."

"I disagree."

The air pressure beside Clay dropped like an anvil. Addy's magic exploded in a frozen wash of power, sending goose pimples erupting all over his skin. She'd been waiting for the witch to look at her, had probably said what she'd said about Happy specifically to draw her attention, and now that she had it, she had no intention of letting it go. She shimmered and glowed from the inside, her eyes brightening to glimmering emeralds. Unlike the Elmira situation where she used her glamour to alter her appearance, this time, she tempted and tantalized with it. She loosed the cork on her bottled carnality, directing every ounce of hypnotic, toe-curling enticement at the woman a few feet in front of her.

At first, he wasn't sure Augustine was hooked. She wasn't the most expressive woman in the world. She vacillated between aloof and displeased, and he wasn't sure if she actually had the muscle control to smile, but then her mouth gaped open and the paper in her hand fluttered away on the wind. Her pupils dilated so much they swallowed her irises.

Addy had her all right, like a fish in a net, and she sauntered up with her hand raised, her fingers skimming down the soft planes of Augustine's face. "That's it, Lovely. We can all play nice now, can't we?" she crooned.

Augustine nodded stupidly. "Yes. Of course, we can."

"No need for hard words?"

"No."

"Good girl."

Thomasine disagreed. The plumper Lynch was not enthralled; either Addy assumed Clay would handle the other twin while she manipulated Augustine, or maybe she thought she'd snare them both with one spell and failed. Whatever the case, Thomasine saw what was happening with her sister and decided to intervene, her hand lifting and thrashing through the air.

It was one of those stupid things he never would have thought of but he should have—the spit over the fire. Another hour, it would have been fitted with game for supper. Thomasine found it first, though, and she used her magic to tear it from its holders and send it careening like a javelin. Clay saw nothing until it struck Addy between the shoulder blades and rammed all the way through the front of her chest. There was no stopping for things like bones or organs. It was a pin through a pincushion, splitting her squishy insides from one side to the other.

Addy gurgled as the sharp end ripped through her chest, a spray of blood bursting from her front to paint Augustine's face. Clay swung Gayle at Thomasine and pulled the trigger, his arm going numb when it blasted. Thomasine was so busy watching Addy crumple to the ground, she didn't try to outmaneuver him, and the bullet took the top of her head clean off, bits of skull, brain matter, and hair splattering the side of the cart. Her body sailed backward to strike the hard wood, a startled expression on her freckled face before she flopped to the ground, granting him an unadulterated view of the insides of her skull.

Fae thrall broken, Augustine let out a shrill scream and rushed to her sister's side, dropping to her knees to pull her twin to her blood-stained chest. Clay probably should have put a bullet in her right then, but he took the opportunity to check on Addy instead, and he didn't like what he saw. The spit had come through on her right side, so it missed her heart, but even a heart shot wouldn't have been enough to drop a fairy. They were startlingly resilient. It was the sizzling sound that scared him, like fatty bacon hitting a fry pan.

Iron. The spit was made of *iron*.

He'd never been unfortunate enough to see a fairy die from iron poisoning before, but the way Cora told it, it was ugly. One of the few stories she'd shared with him about her past came after she'd burned her fingertips making Gayle. Back in the worst days of the Fairy Wars, the youngins were kept beneath the fairy mounds for their protection, but every once in a while, Cora's nanny would sneak her and her cousin out to see the sun. Cora was a little spit, no more'n five or six, and she'd sat down in the grass to play with her dolls while her cousin ran for the trees. A minute or two out, he let out a hell of a scream. When she'd looked up, she saw him trapped in the fangs of an iron bear trap.

The way she described it, it was like watching a watercolor painting getting rained on. There was blood and all that other gruesome stuff, but the longer the iron was in his system, the more his colors melted. The peach of his skin and the blue of his eyes swirled. His features sagged and dribbled down onto the runny texture of his now-fused shirt and torso.

If he didn't help Addy, she would be reduced to a bubbling puddle of melted rainbow.

"Doc! Doc, Addy's hit!" he screamed, trying to keep Gayle leveled in Augustine's direction and crouch by Addy at the same time. It was awkward, requiring a lot of juggling and repositioning, the whole situation made all the more difficult by his wavering arm and inability to see anything unless he looked straight at it. He knew he could shoot Augustine and be done with it, but that didn't feel right. Her back was to him. Putting a bullet in someone when they were mourning their dead sibling was a craven thing to do. Yeah, she'd come all this way just to murder him, but if they were going to throw down, they'd do it with their respective dignities intact.

He heard thudding in the cart, scrambling, followed by a high-pitched shriek. He glanced up to see Doc clambering to her feet, a dozen snakelike ropes sailing through the air as she tore them from her chest. As each coil struck the ground, they exploded into wisps of soot. Constructs. They had a physical presence, and in the cases of golems or larger creatures, brute strength, but snakes that size wouldn't have done much harm. Doc'd been safe all along.

Adelaide wheezed. Clay peered down at her, his chest going tight. Her green eyes were enormous, the corners leaking tears over her graying cheeks. The puncture in her chest frothed with colorful foam, pink, green, and blue crusting the edges of the gaping wound. She was melting from the inside out, her colors running together like that kid Cora had described all those years ago.

"Hurry up, Doc. We ain't got a lot of time."

"Coming. I'm coming," Doc said, vaulting the side of the cart and running to Addy's side. One look at the spit and she sucked in a breath, her mouth flattening to a grimace. "We have to get it out of her. It's better to have the hole than to… good Christ." She dropped to her knees and grabbed it, her fingers wrapping around it to give it a hard tug. It didn't move more than a few inches. Addy screamed, her hand swiping out for Clay's wrist so she had something to hold onto. Doc cursed and tried again, but she couldn't get it to move more than an inch with each pull.

"I need help. Help me," Doc barked.

Clay nodded and forced a smile for Addy, doing his best to ignore how fast she breathed and how her eyelids fluttered like butterfly wings. Her pupils were dilated, a trickle of blood spilling over her bottom lip to stain her chin. "Stay with me, y'old slut. Don't you dare fuckin' die on me," he ordered, positioning his hands around Doc's. Getting a grip on the spit was hard. It was covered in blood and her iron melted insides, and every time he thought he had a hold, it slid from his fingers.

"On three," Doc said. "One, two, THREE!" Their combined effort jerked the spit from Addy's body, but not without consequences. A geyser of blood bubbled from the hole in her chest, her back arcing as the pain ransacked her body. She made no sound beyond her labored breathing, but that was enough for Doc to diagnose her. "It punctured her lung. We need to get her to Fairy. She'll heal there. If the damage inside isn't too great…" Doc clapped her hands over the injury and pushed down, arms drenched with blood. The whirling color was there, too, oily and thick where it wasn't foaming pastel pinks and blues.

"There's a gateway," Clay said, pointing at the brush behind them. "Over yonder. I followed her to it."

If Doc questioned why they'd been looking for a crossover point, she didn't waste time asking. "We have to bring her. Fairy takes care of its own."

Doc stuffed a handkerchief into the gaping hole in Addy's chest, but it soaked through within seconds. Nothing Irene did—not pressure, not tourniquets—made a lick of difference. Addy shuddered and went slack, her eyes rolling up into her head as she passed out. Doc slid her hands under Addy's armpits and waited for Clay to take her legs.

Clay stuffed Gayle back into the holster and hesitated, sparing a glance for the remaining witch in camp. "Augustine Lynch!"

She lifted her head oh-so-slowly, her miserable, red-rimmed eyes staring at him through a fringe of dark bangs. That pale face was pink from crying, her nose cherry red. Clay tilted his hat at her, forgetting that he was covered in Addy's blood. The Stetson bore a rusty brand along the brim. "You lost yours, we lost ours," he said. "Collect your dead and go home. Tell Maybell to go home. It's between me and Cora. Y'all got roped in, and I'm real sorry for that, but we can be the bigger people and walk away with our lives. End it."

Augustine looked back down at Thomasine, her bloody fingers traversing the curves of her sister's face. He thought he saw her nod, and that was good enough for him. It had to be—Addy needed help. He looped his hands under Addy's ankles and lifted. On a good day, a normal day, he'd have told Doc to stand off and he'd carry Addy to the glen by himself, but with the curse, he couldn't manage it alone. He wanted to, but he couldn't.

They set off into the woods, moving as quickly as their bloody burden would allow. Addy's head fell back when they crossed into the forest, her thick, red curls dragging over the debris-laden floor. Her eyes stared blankly at the sky. Her mouth opened and closed like a fish on a bank gasping for water.

All the while, her rainbow insides bubbled like a tarry brook.

"It ain't too far from here. North. Glen, so no trees around—you can't miss it. I dunno how to get 'em to open the fairy door, but maybe her being there's enough," Clay said. Doc nodded, and they pushed onward through hip-high shrubs, lifting Addy so her skirts wouldn't tangle in the briars below. If she could hold on for five more minutes, if Fairy took her home, it'd all be fine, but he wasn't so sure they'd get there in time. Her skin was turning charcoal. Her colors were fading.

His legs quaked beneath him, struggling under his own weight, never mind hers, too, but he clenched his jaw and forced himself to continue despite the sweat splashing in his eyes. Addy wasn't a small girl. When she sat in a man's lap, her ass oozed over his legs. At least, that's what happened with Clay. Admittedly, he was on the scrawny side, but he'd played chair for her enough times to know her plush intimately. She was a heavy load to haul.

His boots tromped over sticks and leaves. His heels tripped on the bigger branches as they made their last push for the glen. It was on an incline, something he hadn't noticed the first time they'd ventured out, but he certainly noticed then with his physical decline and Addy's extra weight. He couldn't see the doorway critter with the stick fingers yet, but maybe if they got closer…

Clay was so focused on getting Addy help he didn't hear Augustine coming up from behind. His only warning she'd come was

Doc's shout, which came a second too late. Clay's back exploded in agony, a burning sensation starting at his shoulder and curving around to his hip. He dropped Addy's legs, which made her shriek, to let out his own pained groan as another strike landed across his ass.

One time at the farm when Clay was real little, Harland snapped a whip at their sheep to move them out to pasture. It wasn't meant to hit anything, just make the noise to spur the animals, but Clay'd walked out of the barn at the wrong time and gotten the tail end of the lash across his shoulder. The scar faded over time, but he never quite forgot the bite of that searing heat. It was an extraordinary, individual pain.

He experienced it for a second time in the middle of the Arkansas woods, a minute from Addy's refuge.

Augustine let out a shrill scream before sending a third coil sizzling across his skin. He grunted and looked back, wincing and shuddering at the pulsing pain ravaging his body. The witch stood behind him, covered in her sister's blood. She slashed her hand through the air, and an invisible lash took him across the meat of his cheek, slicing him open before ripping across his upper chest and dropping him to his knees.

She'd nodded, though.

He'd seen her nod when he said it was over, so if she'd nodded, why would she come after him? He'd been good enough to not shoot her in the back of the head when he had the chance. She should have returned the damned favor.

"Augustine, d-don't," he implored. She ignored him, lashing him again, this time ripping his shirt open and leaving a welt around his neck. Whiplashes were one of those things that didn't have the good grace to go away quickly. They pulsed long after, throbbing as the blood pooled just below the skin's surface. He'd hurt for hours yet, days once the bruises set in, and with marks on both his front and back, there was no way to avoid the lingering aches.

Doc made a worried mewl, but Clay waved her off. "Go. Drag Addy if you have to. Just get her to the clearing to the north. Circle of trees and—" His instructions ended on a howl as Augustine shredded him again, his shirt splitting to expose his torso to future cruelties. Long tatters of cloth hung past his belt, the edges stained with splotches of blood.

Doc hauled Addy away. Clay pulled Gayle to fire off a shot. It went wide, so he fired another, which dinged the tree by Augustine's head. She never batted an eye. Her graceful arm slashed down in front of her face and again he was lashed, this time across the forearm and around the small of his back. He hissed and squeezed the trigger, but the third bullet embedded itself in the soil by her feet.

"Augustine, don't. We can work this through. Please," he implored, but there was no pity in the Lynch. She was a vengeful ghost of a woman intent on his death.

Which, if he was being honest with himself, he couldn't blame her for, not covered in her twin's blood the way she was. Not mourning her sisters the way she was.

He'd hurt her. It was her time to hurt him.

All's fair.

She lifted her hand, her fingers bursting apart like a violently blossoming flower. He was lifted off the ground and thrown into the trunk of a tree ten feet back. Raw skin on bark was agony. *Impact* was agony, and he slumped into the tall grass tangled 'round the roots, his hat blown away, his gun flown off to who-knew-where.

Her hand lifted again, readying another torment. He said a quiet prayer and braced. After N'Orleans, he hadn't harbored much hope he'd get through the curse. Marie'd been his best shot, and even her hands were tied. The Lynches were too much. Sure, he'd beat Elmira and Thomasine with the help of his friends, but even if he'd survived Augustine, the worst was yet to come. Maybell made her siblings look like amateurs. There wasn't much point to pretending the odds were ever in his favor.

He'd given it a good go, though, because he was an idiot, like Cora'd said after he got the bogey burns all those years ago. At least she'd have to live with his death for the rest of her life. When her temper finally simmered down and she had to wrestle with her conscience—or, you know, play with his rotten head after Augustine delivered it on a silver platter—she was going to feel lower than chicken crap.

Serves you right, you beautiful bitch.

"One moment 'fore you kill me. Dying man's wish, if you don't mind," Clay rasped. He didn't expect Augustine to honor the request, but her hand faltered all the same. He reached into his pants' pocket and pulled out his tobacco bag. His muscles screaming with the motions. He pawed through the loose leaf to find the remaining pre-rolled cigarette and tucked it between his lips.

Augustine was nice enough to light it for him with a flare of magical fire.

"Obliged," he said, taking a long suck. Going to his maker with a good draw in his lungs seemed an alright way to go out. He was about to nod to her to proceed with her murdering, had even lifted his fingers to his temple to salute her, but then Montague made his presence known.

His loud, teeth-gnashing, orange-stripes-of-death presence.

There was a roar, because that's what tigers did, and then a flying behemoth. Augustine craned her head in time to see the enormous cat sailing at her from a cluster of underbrush. A momentary expression of surprise crossed her face before the tiger propelled her into the grass. She lifted her hand to cast a spell, but before she could do much of anything, those powerful feline jaws closed around her neck and bit down. There was a wet snapping, a gurgle, and then there was nothing.

Augustine Lynch sprawled across the forest floor like a bloodied ragdoll, a tiger straddling her limp body.

Clay stared and smoked, not quite sure how to process it. It had taken less than four seconds for the tiger to maul the witch. He'd come out of nowhere, like he'd been waiting for the perfect moment, and when it presented itself, Montague snatched it up in his powerful jaws and... well, by the way he was dragging the corpse toward the tall grasses, he probably planned to eat it.

"None of that," Clay said, squinting to see through the wafting smoke. When Montague paused to eye him, the pale woman dangling from his jaws, Clay wagged a finger at him because that was the only part of his body not in agony. "It ain't nice to eat folk, dead or not." The criticism was half-hearted at best, but he had to make the effort. Some things weren't meant for human eyes; seeing someone you'd drunk tea with eaten by a tiger, post-mortem or not, was one such thing.

"We gotta get back to Addy, cat. C'mere." Clay'd always dismissed the tiger as a big, stupid beast, but he was smarter than he looked. He pranced to Clay's side, even going so far as to swipe at his hip with his paw when he neared. Clay rolled onto his knees to get up. He hurt in places he wasn't sure Doc could name, but he wouldn't let that stop him—Addy needed him. Wasn't going to let his favorite trollop die because some witch kicked his ass all over southern Arkansas.

He groaned and buried his fingers in Montague's coat, using the huge animal for purchase so he could wobble to his feet. The world spun around him, his back and chest pulsing with a burning pain that stole his breath. He tottered more than walked toward the clearing, spitting out his cigarette so he could take deep, hungry breaths along the way. Montague stayed with him, half-leaning into him as furry support.

They followed Addy's trail of blood and foam curving along the ground. Doc must have dragged her the rest of the way to the crossover point. Didn't seem right that a gal in Addy's shape had to be moved like that. Wasn't shit Clay could do about it with the Augustine situation, but it wasn't right.

Every step toward the glen was torture. At one point, he eyed a tree and thought about resting, but Montague head-butted him in the thigh to keep him going. A few steps later, he spotted Doc Irene. She sat in the tall grasses, a limp, dirty Adelaide clutched to her chest, one of Doc's thin arms looped around Addy's waist. Addy's hair cascaded over Doc's legs like a bloody river.

"They didn't open?" Clay hollered.

Doc glanced up, her spectacles fogged, her cheeks wet with tears. "She's not breathing. They won't open the doors, Clayton. I did try, but she's just..." Doc's voice trailed. "I'm glad to see you, though."

"No. No!" Clay stumbled ahead of the cat, falling along the way and not bothering to get back up again. He crawled to his friends, dragging Addy from Doc's lap to hold her to his chest, ignoring the screaming pain of her body striking his ruined skin. He ran his hand over her forehead to tuck a fat lock of hair behind her pointed ear. "Addy. Adelaide, cut the shit now." She was too still, and he looked up to where he'd seen those long, branch-like fingers peeling the world away. "COME ON, YOU. OPEN UP. I GOT ONE OF YOURS HERE. SHE'S IN A BAD WAY."

The only answer was a soft wind that sent the grasses swaying. It wasn't good enough. His panic gave way to anger, and he shook Addy's body, his fingers biting into the meat of her upper arms. "ADELAIDE. Y'AIN'T GONNA DIE ON ME HERE." He pressed her face against his neck and glowered at the emptiness of the glen, his eyes burning worse than the lashes marring his back.

His voice broke as he screamed at what he couldn't see but knew lingered so close by. "C'MON THEN. YOU GONNA LET HER DIE OUT HERE? I'M A HALF BLOOD. MY MOTHER'S SIDHE—ANABELLA JENSON. ANABELLA OF THE ROSES OF THE SEELIE COURT. OPEN UP, Y'HEAR?"

More wind, but no portal. Doc pressed her fingers to the base of Addy's neck, hiccupping her way through a sob at what she found—or didn't find—there. Clay stared not at her, but through her, something black and ugly squirming in his guts. Cora's revenge games had killed Addy. She'd killed her own sister because she wanted to punish him. It wasn't what she meant to do, but she never meant to hurt people with her antics. Not now, not in Little Rock with that poor kid, yet somehow everyone else suffered because she didn't give one good goddamn about consequences.

"I can't forgive her, can I?" He croaked.

"I don't know tha—what the bloody fuck is that?!" Doc lifted a finger and pointed. Clay swung his head around, his teeth gritting against the rising darkness at the edges of his vision. When it settled again, sediment still at the bottom of the pond, he was able to make out the twig-like appendages hovering midair. The first two joints of the fingers grabbed the landscape and curled them back, tearing reality in twain.

"Give her over. Give her to 'em," Clay said. He tried to stand, but the combination of curse, hurts, and associative fatigue left him pinned beneath Addy's weight. Doc pulled her away, was about to drag her to the mysterious hands, but Clay motioned at Montague. "On him. He'll take her. He's a good cat."

Doc nodded grimly, getting Addy situated best she could. Addy flopped and rolled, a collection of bones in a meat sack. Clay kept hoping she would bark at them for manhandling her or whine because they jostled her too much, but she was *gone*. He watched helplessly as Montague took her to the waiting hands. Even when they hoisted her like a piece of trash, she never uttered a word. She was wrenched behind the landscape, her body swallowed by the Fairy land's strange miasma of color.

Clay contemplated following to ensure they took care of her proper-like, but Montague beat him to it. The tiger glanced at him once, lashed its long tail, and then trotted into the swirling gateway like crossing over wasn't a terrifying prospect. As that hulking, striped body disappeared, Clay wanted to weep. He'd never really liked the damned cat, but it had earned its stripes by saving his life and maybe—if they all got real lucky—Addy's, too.

The stick hands reappeared to patch the hole it had torn in the glen. Reality rippled before being pulled taut, like a sheet being stretched across a lumpy mattress. There was a glittering shimmer, a blast of warm magic, and Fairy was once again hidden away, its strange guardians Addy's best hope for slutting her ass all over the South another day.

Too weak to stand, too miserable to do anything other than to wish for simpler days, Clayton sprawled back in the grass and closed his eyes, listening to the wind playing in the trees. When Doc reached out to hold his hand, he couldn't muster a single snide, shitty thing to say.

His witch-cursed world was falling to pieces, and he'd take any comfort he could get.

CHAPTER SIXTEEN

ONE YEAR AGO

Cora had a thing for pillows. She couldn't have just two for her bed, she had to have forty, and every night before falling asleep, Clay tossed a heaping pile of them onto the floor so he wouldn't suffocate in their fluffy depths. Both Frederick and the stolen kittens appreciated it; they played king of the mountain with fair, loud regularity as a result, keeping up both Clay and Cora with their antics.

"Pillows are stupid," he announced, eyeballing a kitten perched on the topmost pillow. He wondered if that was the little shit who'd yowled until midnight or if that was a littermate.

"No, you're stupid," came Cora's sleepy reply.

He craned his neck to peer at her. The cats were forgotten. She was snuggled up in the sunlight, a tired smile stretched across her mouth, her hair curling over her bare breasts. He liked her best like this—not nekkid, but at ease. The nekkid part didn't hurt, but there was something breathtaking about her first thing in the morning, with or without her clothes on. But since she didn't have her clothes on...

So many lecherous thoughts, so little time. He must have worn his intentions all over his face, because she dove beneath the blankets to escape him, her laughter loud. "I know what you're thinking, Clayton Jenson, and I need to get some work done today."

"Work can wait. Ain't like an hour will matter," he said, crawling toward her. She giggled and rolled away, attempting to wriggle out from the cocoon of blankets on his side of the bed, but he managed to grab her before she hit the floor and hauled her back by her ankles. He lay on top of her then, pressing himself against the soft squishiness of her flanks and burying his nose in her hair. She zapped him good through all of it, but he was practically immune to that now—after the fiftieth electrocution, a man grew conditioned.

"If you really don't wanna... " he murmured.

She squirmed and that felt real nice, so he nibbled along the side of her neck, his hands reaching under to cup and squeeze and pinch the fun, wobbly parts. She whacked him atop his head with another peal of laughter. "Later. If you can behave yourself. But I'm too close to finishing my machine to let you distract me."

"That thing again?"

She bucked him off and pulled on a pink gown, not bothering with proper unders. It did nothing to lessen his ardor; he was as randy as a goat in spring, and the idea of diving under her dress and making the best kind of trouble was terribly appealing. He couldn't yet, but that was his own fault for starting what she wasn't willing to finish. He hadn't been thinking that far ahead. When he saw a pretty, nekkid Cora smiling at him, he fondled and hoped for the best.

"Oh, hush. Nearly finished." She made her way out to the kitchen, the roll of her hips a siren's song that compelled him to follow. She jiggled with every step, and he groaned to let her know how badly he wanted to take her back to bed for the rest of the day. The week. Their lives.

"Fine, but I'm relenting under protest, darlin'."

They didn't get to spend a lot of time at her Mississippi cottage—it was the first opportunity they'd had to steal away since N'Orleans. The plan had been relaxation and enjoying each other's company before Clay had to return to the grind of plucking toddlers out of monsters' mouths. For the first time in a long time, his shoulders were blissfully weight-free. Unfortunately, Cora wasn't quite so good at putting her distractions aside. She still worked half the day, that danged bladed thing entertaining her almost as much as he did.

As stupid as it was to admit, he was jealous of the attention it got. Didn't it know there were pokes to be had? Apparently not. Or if it did, it didn't care that he suffered. Wasn't much he could do about it except distract himself with breakfast. Food was a poor substitute for sex, but it'd do in a pinch.

He paused at the table beneath the open window to spread honey on a couple slices of bread. Frederick seized the opportunity to use his pants leg as a personal ladder and launch himself into the yard. Between bites, Clay watched the squirrel bound for the trees, Frederick's silver body flashing in the sun. He'd adopted something of a routine since they'd arrived. He'd take off to steal himself some nuts and then drop them into Clay's boots. That was his newest little game, to shove all his treasures inside Clay's clothes when Clay wasn't looking. It'd been endearing for about ten minutes, but then Clay'd gotten a chunk of walnut shell jammed into his heel and it wasn't so cute no more.

When Frederick disappeared behind a wall of thick, forest underbrush, Clay abandoned the window to throw himself into the chair by the hearth, watching Cora flit around the room in preparation of tinker time. "You think you'll finish that thing today?" He crammed the last of the bread into his mouth.

"I think so. Look." She lifted her device with both of her hands, careful not to touch anything near the top, probably because the top looked like it'd lop off her fingers. The contraption resembled a parasol with a hooked handle and expandable umbrella, but instead of fabric, the umbrella portion was constructed of a dozen three-foot-long by three-inch-wide blades. She pushed a button to open them, and they stretched out in a fan of glinting, quivering cleavers. "Tin," she said, her voice gushing enthusiasm.

"That's significant why?"

Cora collapsed it with the push of a different button and returned it to the table. "Tin is light, and with flight, I wouldn't want to add any more weight than necessary."

"Flight? You mean like a bird?"

"Somewhat. It'll lift me off the ground anyway—straight up and down so far, but this is just the beginning. I have big plans for future advancements to go side to side. Isn't it marvelous?"

He wasn't sure marvelous was the word he'd use. Things that flew up inevitably came down, and if she made even the slightest miscalculation, he could be scooping her remains off the ground with a spatula. "Well, it's marvelous if it's safe. Other'n that, it's deadly."

"I'll be fine. Air's my element. I really can't fall to my death. I'd more float down, like a leaf from a branch."

He felt a little better hearing that, though he still didn't relish the idea of her floating all over the place with a test model. She was the inventor, though, and this was one area he didn't feel comfortable expressing his opinion. He knew nothing about science. Instead, he watched her choose her tools for the day and line them up along the edge of her work station. "That mean you're the only one that can use it?"

"So far, but imagine the possibilities! If I could find a way to power the blades without magic, it'd... oh. It'd be amazing. People everywhere would want one." Her eyes fixed on him, but he had the distinct impression she wasn't seeing him. Her mind was somewhere else, likely counting the dollars and cents of a burgeoning business venture.

Which birthed another worry. Cora'd been good with the whole conning thing over the last year. She was far more apt to help him with a job than she was to swindle regular folks of their hard-earned money, so he hadn't had to worry about the pesky conflict of interest their relationship presented. Until now. She talked about this invention differently than the others. There was something calculating in her expression that made him uncomfortable. He didn't like to be suspicious. But he wasn't born yesterday neither, and she was acting funny.

"Well, yeah. If you get 'em to work right, you could sell 'em. Make yourself a nice little profit," he said carefully. "Though you'd want to make sure it was safe for everyone before you went out with it."

"Hmm? Oh, yes. Profits. Absolutely."

"I said safe."

"That, too."

She turned back to her table and reached for her goggles. They were thick and ugly with a second set of lenses for magnification so she could work on finer details. She stooped, her adroit fingers adjusting a series of tiny mechanisms. He wanted not to care what she was doing, but the niggling suspicion that the umbrella was a problem in its larval stage plagued him. But how could he broach the subject? If he pressed her about it or played his hand that he worried about a con, would she accuse him of not trusting her?

Probably. But he had to say something or it'd eat at him, and that was a surefire way to ruin their vacation.

"Don't mean to be a prick, but you're gonna make it work *before* you start sellin' 'em, yeah?"

She didn't even have to turn around for him to know he'd pissed in her porridge. Her shoulders stiffened, her chin lifted, and she put down her screwdriver far too slowly. Her fingers drummed over the table, from pinky to thumb and back again.

She was furious, which probably meant he'd be fifty before he got to till her lady garden again.

Hell.

When she didn't say anything right away, he decided he'd try to make it better—also a terrible plan, but after one catastrophic mistake, a second didn't feel quite as daunting. "I don't mean to sound like I don't trust you. It's just… I guess I'm worried." He stopped and reached for his tobacco bag to roll himself a cigarette. Focusing on that instead of the small tornado ten feet away from him seemed like a good way to keep his head attached to his shoulders. "If you need money, I got money. What's mine is yours, is all."

She took her time speaking, probably so she didn't scream at him. Her face had flushed so pink that it reminded him of a flowering azalea, which would have been sorta pretty if it wasn't accompanied by a killing glare. "Even if this was something I'd profit on early, it's within my rights. I can make my own decisions."

"'Course you can. You can make any decision you want, darlin', but if you're making a profit at the expense of others with a faulty product, that *ain't* within your rights. That's the law. Like I said, I got money. It's yours." Yep, that only made it worse. She tore the goggles off of her face to slam them onto the table beside her. They both knew he'd never arrest her for thieving, but if he could say something that'd dissuade her from swindling consumers beforehand, he would. He'd be a shit marshal otherwise. "You know, when we talked about this a year ago, you said you wouldn't con. You gave your word. And if I misjudged the situation, then I am all sorts of sorry."

"Actually, *Clayton*, I didn't give my word. I said I'd try to work with you being a marshal. And I have tried, but that doesn't mean I won't... stop telling me what to do."

Something about that statement got his hackle up. No, not something—he knew exactly what it was. If she remembered that she said "try" a year later, that meant she'd been deliberate with her word choice back in that alley. That meant she'd shaped her commitment so there was a way to get out of it when the need arose.

"A'right. So lemme ask you this." He paused to slide the cigarette between his lips and take a drag, hoping the smoke would keep his temper in check. He couldn't recall being angry with her before, but it was bound to happen sooner or later. "You said you'd try not to break the law, and you have succeeded admirably so far. 'Preciate it. But you couldn't just say, 'No, I won't break the law.' Why not?"

"Is this an interrogation now?" she demanded.

"Nah. More a talk that's long overdue about commitment. Won't commit to not robbin' folks, won't say you love me. Won't even talk about what we do beyond tomorrow most days. I know you're fond of me, but when it comes to giving me your word, you won't do it. You're squirmy. Why?"

He hadn't meant to go that far with his observation, but her pointing out that loophole got under his skin. He was the type of person that'd stick his neck out for the folks he cared about. He'd make a promise and keep a promise because that's who he was and what he did. The fact that she twisted herself into knots to avoid doing the same made him question things like whether or not she had invested in their relationship the way he did.

That left him feeling vulnerable and, by association, surly.

"How..." She cut herself off with an irritated scream. He could hear a storm moving in outside, a rumbling thunder that echoed from the edge of the surrounding forest. The sky had been cornflower blue not five minutes ago, but one glance out the window and he could see dense gray clouds across the horizon. It seemed Cora's temper could manifest in the form of turbulent weather. Lovely.

"How have we jumped to this conversation?" she demanded. "It started with a con I haven't committed, and now we're onto me not saying whatever it is you think I should say?"

He peered at her through a cloud of blue smoke, his free hand gripping the arm of the chair. "Wording shit so you can wriggle out of it later on—whether that's cons or us or whatever the hell we're talking about—that's a game. I don't like games. So we're talking about games now."

"It's not a game. I simply don't like to make promises. Isn't it enough that I'm here now?! That I've invested a year in you?" Her voice grew louder with her anger, and he felt his tenuous grasp on his control slipping right along with it.

"No, it ain't, because a year is grand, but what about a month from now? A year? I want a life with you, Cora, and you refuse to commit to anything. Shit, if I asked you to promise you'd breathe in the next minute, you'd probably tell me you'd have to think about it!"

The skies boomed, lightning striking so close to the window the zap ghosted itself upon his vision. Rain pissed down around them like a hurricane, punishing the roof slats and pummeling the grass to a flat green mat. Frederick sailed in through the window to take shelter under the table, but one look at his mistress's cold gray eyes and he darted off to take cover in their bedroom.

"I picked you. I've never picked anyone before," she said. "That has to be enough, you stupid, stupid man!" Before he could think to move out of the way, she grabbed her goggles off her workstation and flung them at him. They struck his chin, and he roared, pain blossoming along his jaw as the edge of the lens ripped him open. Blood drizzled onto his bare chest in crimson trails.

"Cac," she muttered, scampering through the kitchen to snag a towel. She returned with one in hand, but he brushed past her to attend himself, using an old dishrag to mop at the blood. He didn't want her touching him. He was too mad. They'd gone from a morning of happy snuggling and flirty chatter to him saying something she didn't like to hear, shouting, hurt feelings, and stupid violence.

"Two things," he said quietly, his cigarette tucking into the corner of his lips. "The first is I will never raise a hand to you, but that goddamned well means you won't raise one to me. We need to fight, we'll fight, but not with hands or fists or teeth or anything else or I will pack my shit and go. Got no patience for tomfoolery. We clear on that?" He tore the cigarette from his lips and mashed it into a nearby saucer, the stub smoldering out in a smear of black ash and burnt paper.

She watched him and swallowed, her jaw set in a mutinous line despite the worry lines across her forehead. It was an odd combination, like she was sorry for what she did but she hated him for having to be sorry in the first place. He was fine with it. He hated her a little bit right then, too.

"Second thing." He walked into the bedroom they shared so he could root through his bags, moving the canteens, rope coils, bullets, and everything else aside to find a white box he'd been traveling with for almost six months. He held it in his palm, frowning at the rusty fingerprints marring the painted exterior. This wasn't one of those things that should be smeared in blood, but nothing quite went as planned with Cora.

He took it into the kitchen and slid it across the table, the box stopping at the edge and threatening to plummet to the ground. "No more half measures," he said. "Haven't been interested in half measures since I met you, not going to start now. I don't want any more half-assed commitments. If you're here, and you're planning on staying here, I'll be the happiest man in the world. If you're not and this is just a way to pass the time, let me know so I can figure out if that's enough for me."

Cora eyed the box and then him, but made no move to take it. It was never supposed to be a proposal, more his way of expressing the depth of his emotions, but seeing the color drain from her face, something had gone awry. Her anger had melted away to terror, like she'd opened a closet door and seen the boogeyman. "Is... is that an ultimatum?" she managed, her voice cracking halfway through.

"No. It's to show you how serious I am—have been. I'm not asking now, and maybe I won't ever ask after you tell me what's going through your head. Which... damn it. Maybe this is an ultimatum, but not in the way you're thinking." He paused to collect his thoughts, to better convey what he needed from her. It didn't have to be marriage and children. It didn't have to be traditional love with bouquets of flowers and a little farm. But whatever it was, it had to be honest and real. No more holding back. "I need transparency," he finally said. "I need to know where you stand, and maybe more important than that, where you want to stand down the road. Fucking's great, but it ain't the be-all and end-all. Mean, we get it real right and I'm glad for it, but there has to be more to it. To us. Least, for me there does."

Cora reached for the box, but her hand stopped just above it, fingers twitching. She glanced up at him and licked her lips before swiping it from the table and cradling it to her chest. She didn't seem to mind the blood stains, instead holding it to her bosom like she was afraid it'd get away.

He'd bought the ring back east, when they were in Savannah. There was an old man out that way named Abraham Ber who had the distinction of being a jeweler by day and a necromancer by night. Strange combination, but Abraham was one of the more colorful characters Clay'd met. A wonderful gentleman—jovial, smart, witty, and talented, but damned odd. He liked to reanimate famous dead folk. Thought it was interesting to interview them about their life experiences, and the fact that they were dead never seemed to bother him none. When Clay asked him about the ethics behind it once, Abraham shrugged and said, "I always put them back!"

If it was good enough for Abraham, it was good enough for Clay.

Usually, Clay contacted Abraham when he needed a corpse to tell him how it got corpsed in the first place, but on his last trip, it was for a ring. A big, expensive ring, to be exact. A diamond as big as a fingernail and surrounded by emeralds. Abraham had designed it special for him, charging him an arm and a leg and a piece of his soul for the end product, but the craftsmanship was so great that Clay was more than happy to pay it. It was a one-of-a-kind treasure for *his* one-of-a-kind-treasure.

Seeing Cora opening the box and staring at the contents, her eyes welling with tears, he wondered if this was yet another mistake. He was making all sorts of them today, but maybe the first one had been back in the fall when he'd had this crafted in the first place. She took it from the box and slid it onto her finger—not the finger it was designed for, but her pointer—her eyes caressing the shining jewels. She flashed it this way and that, her nose turning pink as she started to sniffle.

"It's beautiful," she said.

"Giving a beautiful girl an ugly ring would be a crime."

"I want it, Clayton," she whispered, jerking her head up to peer at him. "I want this more than you could know, but I can't… I can't right now. I can't—don't—commit because—" She dashed at her cheeks and returned the ring to the box before thrusting it back onto the table. He watched her step away from it like she was afraid it'd bite her. "You've heard the saying that wishes have power?"

"Sure." He hadn't, but he'd lie to get this over with faster. Now that she'd taken off the ring, now that she'd effectively told him no and that she wasn't going to be his wife anytime soon, he wanted to slough off the conversation like muck from a boot. He wanted to go back to that morning with the cuddling and the flirting, but life didn't work that way. Instead, he was left to hurt. The pain where she'd hit his chin was nothing compared to the dull ache in his chest.

"Wishes have power, and so do promises. A word given… there are things that bear witness to the promises we make. I can't have any witnesses. I don't do it to hurt you, and I'm sorry—I do enjoy you, enjoy staying with you if you can bear to keep me around despite my limitations."

Hearing that she had extenuating circumstances softened the blow of the rejection some, but her not explaining those circumstances harkened back to his whole problem about her vagaries and loopholes. It was all a big, ugly circle of her finding ways to not tell him things. "Transparency, Cora. Why can't you? If it affects me as much as you, don't you think I should understand what's happening?"

She stomped her foot and squatted down on the ground, the heels of her palms pressing into her eyes as she began to sob. Her dress pooled around her bare feet in faded pink puddles, the rain outside tapered off to a miserable drizzle. "I can't tell you. I'm sorry! I'm so sorry!"

Looking at her on the floor rocking back and forth like a whimpering child, so was he.

CHAPTER SEVENTEEN

NOW

It wasn't the clickety-clacking of the wagon wheels on the gritty roads that woke him, but the jostling of the cart. Every divot in the road shook it, which in turn shook Clay's abused body. Stabbing pains wracked him from head to toe, and he hissed, forcing himself out of his sleep-drenched stupor. The world around him spun in a hazy kaleidoscope of greens and blues and whites. He felt like he was looking at one of those artsy paintings where up close you couldn't make out the picture, but if you stepped back you saw how the colors blended to create the image.

"The hell's going on?" he yelled, immediately regretting the outburst. His cheek was on fire. He didn't remember *why* until he lifted his fingers to touch it and smeared himself in stinky yellow paste. His mind slotted the proper puzzle pieces into place. Augustine. Whip lashes. Doc must have tended to him sometime after he'd hit the ground. After Montague and Adelaide…

"Aww, shit. Addy," he groaned. "Is she all right?"

"Go back to sleep, Clayton," came Doc's tired reply. Clay craned his head to eye the driver's bench, the blackness in his vision rising and receding in turn. He could see Doc's profile, the way her shoulders slumped as if she carried burdens too great for her slight frame. Puffy, dark bags had formed under her eyes to bulge out from the bottom of her spectacles. Her shirt was grimy with dried sweat, and her suspenders hung loose around her waist.

To see her in such disrepair proved what Clay already suspected: life sucked.

"You need me to take the reins?" Clay offered. He tried to push himself up, but feeling the tight skin of his back straining and, in at least one place, cracking open like a fault line, he slumped back into his nest of blankets. Doc must have made up a bed for him at some point, tucking him in like a kid past his bedtime.

Hell.

"Rest, Clayton."

"You need rest."

"I'll get it."

Clay grumbled and peered up at the sky overhead. Everything looked fuzzy, like the world was bathed in fog. He blinked to clear it, but it didn't help—the clouds weren't shapes as much as smears across a blue canvas. It hadn't been so bad back at camp, but such a short time later, *everything* was wrong with his eyesight.

"How long I been out?" He attempted to keep his voice from belying his mounting panic; the realization that he was trapped in a failing body made him claustrophobic. What if his curse was to have a sound mind inside a rotting body? Would he die screaming on the inside with no way to get it out?

He wasn't ready for this yet. It was supposed to take more time. It was *too soon*.

"A few days. I've kept you sedated. It was the only way I could think to keep you still so your wounds would heal properly."

"You been driving all this time? To Sterling's?"

"Yes, with naps between. We ought to be there in the morning."

"A'right. Yeah, that's real good. Thank you, Doc." Originally, he'd planned to request Sterling's help with finding Cora, but his physical decline had changed all that. He wanted to see him again, or if not *see him*, then to hear his voice. Clay had a good relationship with his father and wrote home monthly, but he was closer to Sterling in most ways. Sterling had walked the marshal's path. He'd taught him everything he knew about weirds. He was his mentor and his friend and had talked more than his fair share of sense into a young Clayton's head.

Forced to choose between a trip to Arkansas to see Sterling and a trip to Atlanta to see his father, he'd pick Arkansas because he'd simply have more to say to Sterling.

Besides, Sterling could handle seeing Clay broken down. His parents and sister? Not so much. He'd rather his family remember a healthy Clayton in his prime over a deteriorating pile of meat. It was better to write a letter home telling them he loved them and then die without causing too much of a fuss.

And that's where his head was; he wasn't going to Sterling to solve anything.

He was going to say goodbye.

"Well, Doc, sorry to say I'm shitting the bed. If the curse don't kill me, Maybell will. It's just a matter of time." Admitting this wasn't nearly as profound as he expected it to be. There should have been peace in embracing his mortality, but instead, he felt like the same weak, achy Clayton he'd been before the words spilled.

"I know," Doc said.

That wasn't what Clay expected to hear. Maybe he thought Doc would rally for him or insist he not give up. Maybe he expected accusations of fatalism, but all he got was Doc's quiet acceptance and a long sigh. It made Clay feel dumb, like he was the last one cluing into something important.

"Wonder how Cora will feel when she finds out? Hope it's real bad," Clay said, forcing a chuckle so he didn't sound too melancholy. Gallows humor was only okay if you added the fake laugh.

Doc whipped the reins, spurring the horses into a trot. "You may yet see her. I expect she'll find you if Addy is dead, though to what end, I'm not sure."

"Probably to blame me."

"Perhaps, but with her sister gone and you following shortly thereafter, it'll quickly become evident where the fault lies. She'll be looking for her friends and realize there aren't any left. Not even me, and I…" Doc paused to take a breath, her expression darkening. "I've known her longer than I've known you, but that doesn't mean much anymore. If she can do this—to you, to Marie—and not care about the collateral damage she's wrought, she's not the person I followed to the States."

Despite his aches and pains, Clay forced himself upright. There was no way he was staying horizontal with vertical still an option. He hurt bad, and his vision swam, but he was a stubborn bastard, and he wriggled his way toward one of Irene's trunks to lean against it. He spotted his duster wadded up amongst the food supplies and yanked it over to fish out his tobacco bag.

Rolling himself a cigarette had been second nature since he was thirteen years old, but his fingers trembled so much, it'd become a herculean endeavor. He wasn't nimble anymore, and for a man who prided himself on straight shooting, it was a blow to his pride. But then, all of it had been, hadn't it? Wasn't that Cora's point?

"Think I'm gonna give Gayle to Sterling," he said. "Even if the old man don't want it, he'll know someone who will. It's a fine gun that shouldn't be buried with me."

"… can we talk about something else, please?"

"Sure." He finally got the cigarette righted and plunked it between his lips, having to strike the match four times before it took flame. The cart rambled on while he smoked, his eyes narrowing as the wind blew through his hair. He had no idea where his Stetson had gone, but it was probably time to let that go, too. He'd stained the hell out of it with Addy's blood.

Poor Addy.

"How'd you meet 'em anyway? The gals?" Clay asked, looking to distract himself from the memory of Adelaide's ruined chest and wilted body. "Don't think I ever asked you in all these years."

"No, you never have, but you are rather self-absorbed so it shouldn't be surprising." Doc softened the jab with a strained snicker. "Pardons, I had to. It was right there."

"Ain't an insult. I am self-absorbed, but you would be, too, if you were a perfect specimen in every way. 'Cept for the part where I'll be crappin' my pants soon, but we'll cross that bridge when we get there."

"I am going to pretend no fecal matter was invoked into our conversation and answer your earlier question if you don't mind." Doc hesitated long enough to be sure Clayton didn't have any *other* smart-ass commentary before continuing. "I wanted to travel after I finished my studies. It was something I'd always wanted to do, and upon graduation, I made my way across Britain. Wales, Scotland, Ireland. I'd meant to go to Paris and Italy, but I didn't get far because I met a man.

"A man, young like me, though he was still at university. He was brilliant. An artist with a pen, really, and we…" Doc took a deep breath to collect her thoughts, her tongue slicking over her lips. "I took an apartment near his college, and we spent a year together. He adored Irene—was the first man to fully embrace her. Me.

"To make a very long, terrible story short, he was too invested in his studies, and I was too invested in him. We parted ways, and I was devastated."

Clay nodded, not feeling like he had words good enough to offer in response. Despite however many years ago the separation must have been, heartache laced Doc's words. Not being the most demonstrative man in the world, Clay figured whatever retort he came up with would lack the proper emotional depth, and so he sat and he listened and smoked and hoped it was enough.

"I went through a bad spell after that," Doc said after a time. "I all but gave up on my doctoring. Irene spent her evenings at the roughest dockside bars in Ireland. It was a slow form of suicide. Eventually, one of those stinking sailors would have killed me for being different, but I didn't care. I felt like my heart had been torn to shreds.

"But then one night, in the spring of 1872, two girls wandered into my seedy tavern. Instead of avoiding me like the rest of the patrons, they sat at my table. They didn't care how or why I dressed the way I did. They simply wanted to sit with an unsavory. To put things in perspective, it was such an awful establishment Adelaide didn't go looking for a cohort for the evening."

"That is saying something," Clay said, grinning despite the stab to his chest at her name. "Not even sure a pulse is necessary for her to bed folk."

"She has standards. They're simply a little lower than most others."

"A little?"

"Hush, Clayton. Did you want to hear the story or not?"

"Well, yeah."

Irene frowned. "As I was saying, I didn't know they were fairies at the time, and honestly, I wouldn't have cared if they'd told me outright they were. When they asked why I'd frequent such a classless place, I had no better answer than, 'Why not?' And after two bottles of horrid wine, they asked me if I'd like to come to America and travel with them, and I found I had the same answer. 'Why not?' I was still half-sotted when I got on the ship, but a day out of port, I sobered up enough to know I might have been slightly impulsive."

"Slightly? You ended up on another fuckin' continent. More'n a little impulsive, don't ya think?" Clay stubbed out his cigarette on one of Irene's trunks, hoping she wouldn't find the round spot of char he'd left in the supple leather, or if she did, she'd find it when he was too dead to have to listen to her bitching. He promptly set about rolling another cigarette, making sure he took his time so he didn't spill tobacco leaf all over his pants like last time. If he was careful with his stash, it ought to last him right up until the moment he gave himself over to the Great Sheriff in the Sky.

"Yes, well. That's how I got here. Why I've remained is beyond me sometimes. It's really no better here than it was in England. I'm just as apt to lose my head to some ruffian or another."

"You stayed 'cause you got me. Like I said before, perfect specimen of a man. You took one look at me and said, 'I need to know that upstanding gentleman.'"

"Is that the reason?"

"Hell yes it is."

This time, when Doc smiled, it actually reached her tired, swollen eyes. "Perhaps that's so, Clayton, but you're not sick enough yet for me to admit it aloud."

—

They arrived on Sterling's doorstep by mid-morning.

The marshal had retired to a small house overlooking a pond, the exterior sporting weather-grayed shingles and blue shutters. There was a wrap-around porch with a big, ugly dog sleeping in a sliver of sunlight, the creature sprawled on its back with both its paws and its furry giblets pointed at the roof. A stone pathway curved down to the water, the new-looking dock a fisherman's dream with its reclining wooden chair and bobbing rowboat. A small barn was angled off in the back with a fenced-in paddock, a black mare grazing while her foal nursed for its breakfast.

"Nice place to retire," Clay said, oozing his way from the back of the cart. Doc lent him an arm when his legs went weak, and he leaned against her until he felt like he could walk on his own. The moment he got his steel back, he ambled over to pat Squirt. She'd been tied to the back of the cart for some days and was starved for human affection. At least, that's how he interpreted her eating his shirt sleeve. Otherwise she was just stupid.

Which, well—fine, it was both.

"I am horribly rank," Doc murmured, her attention skipping to the pond. "And that looks tempting."

"Let's see the old man first. Be a little strange for him to look out his back window and see your pale ass pointed his way. Might just shoot and put a second hole in it."

"Charming, Clayton. You are ever the gentleman."

"Ain't I just."

They walked up to Sterling's front door, the dog not doing much more than cracking an eye and thudding its tail against the porch when Clay knocked. Inside, there was the creaking of weight on floorboards before a grizzled-looking Sterling stepped outside. He wasn't wearing a shirt, his upper chest bare and tanned from too much time in the sun. A spray of white hair matted his chest and traveled down into his faded gray trousers. He'd grown a short beard, and his hair curled past his ears to tickle his neck, the silver strands desperately needing a barber.

Clay grinned at him, Sterling grinned back, and before Clay knew better, he was pulled into a bear hug, a loud, clanking metal arm patting him on his back.

"How the hell are you, son? Doc! Good to see you!"

"I'd be better if you weren't beating the shit out of me with a hunk of tin," Clay said.

Sterling shoved away from him, his hands going to Clay's upper arms so he could look him over. His eyes narrowed as they traveled Clay's face and body. Tailored clothes were loose and frumpy over Clay's bones, and his cheekbones were too high. "You smell worse than a French, whore and you're too skinny. S'going on?"

"Lots of things, but before I tell you, you mind if we take a dunk to get the stink off? Been a hell of a couple of months."

"Course, course. Y'all head down to the water and I'll take care of your horses."

Clay would have run toward the pond if he could have, but instead he sauntered, trying to keep his gait steady and his head held high. He nearly stumbled once when his boot heel got caught in a crater in the middle of Sterling's yard, but he righted himself before Doc could reach out to steady him. He collapsed into the chair by the rowboat, practically tearing off his clothes, letting them land in a grimy heap in the grass. They weren't any good anymore and would need to be thrown away.

Doc's weren't in much better condition, but that didn't stop her from folding each piece and making a tidy stack.

"M'sure the lice appreciate your hard work," Clay said, walking into the water with no concern for his nudity up until the point that he had to dunk his privates. The water was colder than a well-digger's ass, but after a shudder and the inevitable shrinkage, he settled in to wipe the dirt and sweat from his skin, doing his best not to notice how his ribs bulged. Doc paddled around nearby, and the two of them spent a good hour getting clean while Sterling untacked the horses and put them to pasture.

By the time Clay climbed out of the water and trudged toward the cart to get fresh clothes, Sterling was coming out of the barn rubbing his chest. "That horse of yours nearly took my nipple off, the bitch."

"Ain't like you're using it."

"True, but that don't mean I want a gash in my chest."

"Too bad. She's yours."

Sterling eyed him and then frowned, keeping his head up so he didn't see any wobbling Clayton parts when Clay did the one-legged hopping around thing to dress himself. "Why are you whipped? And why you giving me your horse? You dying?"

"Yep." And so the talk began, starting in the yard by the cart and ending inside Sterling's house. It took Clay almost an hour to get everything out, from Cora to the Lynches to Addy and now their trip to Arkansas. Sterling listened with an ugly ol' frown on his face, but he never interrupted, giving Clay and—when Doc finally joined them midway through the conversation—Doc plenty of time to explain everything that'd happened over the past few months. Clay was up to the part where he wanted Sterling to have Squirt and to find a proper home for Gayle when he finally expressed his opinion.

"Bullshit. There's time. You find Cora and she gets you back to Marie through Fairy. They'll let you pass with her." He paused to hand over a few glasses of whiskey, which Clay gratefully downed, but Doc eyed it like it'd give her the bloody flux. She slid her glass to Clayton with a shudder. "Would take you two days. Maybe three," Sterling said.

"But there's travel time to find Cora, too."

"So? I can help you track her down, but I'll put money on her waiting for you in Mississippi."

Clay was just about to down his second shot, but Sterling's words stopped him short. Why hadn't that occurred to him before? That she'd be at her cottage? Probably because she hadn't spent a lot of time out that way when they were together. They'd visited once for vacation, and the first time he'd kissed her, but it wasn't like they'd lingered there. She was always on the move. Still, it made him feel a little stupid that it never occurred to him she might be waiting for him at the only home she could really claim. "Well, maybe she is."

Sterling said nothing, pushing away from the kitchen table to root through a drawer in his living room. It was a nice room, comfortable, though it appeared to act more as a study than a relaxation haven. Books lined the walls, all magical research tomes focusing on one weird or another. Years ago, before Sterling officially retired, he said Clay'd inherit these one day—one of the best collections of its kind in the country. Now, who knew where they'd go? If Clay was right and he was toes-up and buried in a matter of months, where would Sterling bequeath them?

Clay wasn't given long to ponder it. Sterling retrieved a pair of items from his sideboard and brought them to the table. One was that woven ring Marie had made all those years ago—the one that helped him track Cora. It had seen better days, the threads and hairs gray from years of wear, but it was still intact despite fraying along one edge. The other was a plain old silver compass.

"Go on then," Sterling said.

Clay did as he was told, picking the ring up and letting out a grunt. The moment the pads of his fingers coursed over the ticklish hairs, power surged up his arm and shoulder. As a magical item—or, more accurately, as a magical item made by a powerful practitioner—the ring resonated like a weird would. It wasn't electric like Cora or earthy like Marie, but something altogether different. It had a raw, chaotic energy attached to no real flavor.

"Christ," he murmured, forcing it over the first knuckle of his finger. His hands must have been bigger than Sterling's because it wouldn't go any farther than that, but it was on enough for him to clue into the tug he felt coming from his right side. It was strange, almost like the hand of God was reaching down to right his direction.

"If I'm guessing right, it's pulling southeast. Check the compass?" Sterling said.

Clay did. It *was* pulling southeast, which meant Cora could very well be at her cottage. She could also be in Georgia or Florida, too, but he wouldn't point that out for fear of sounding argumentative. "S'pose it's possible."

"More than possible. It's likely. She's waiting for you, son. You're just taking your sweet time getting back to her. Y'all hungry?"

He wasn't, but he'd eat so neither of his friends would nag him about it. They settled at the dinner table in front of some gamey stew with crusty bread. Halfway through the meal, he glanced over at Doc, surprised to discover the annoyance on her face whenever she looked at Sterling.

Finally, it was too much for her.

"Pardon me," she said, tapping the bowl of her spoon against the tabletop. "But there's some logic lacking here. Why would Cora kill Clayton with a curse and then expect he'd *want* to see her? I think he's an idiot on insisting, to be blunt."

Sterling shrugged and took another bite. "There're a few reasons, I suppose. Maybe to gloat, but that doesn't seem her way. Well, it does, but she's not cruel at her core. Just impulsive. The reason I suspect? She didn't mean to hurt you this bad. I threw her in the clink after Little Rock, but even spitting fire, she said she couldn't believe she loved a man like you. She'll shit her drawers when she sees you this bad off. Guaranteed."

Clay couldn't say anything, so Sterling did in his stead.

Sterling rolled his wide shoulders and shook his shaggy head. "My opinion? She didn't sic a death curse on you, son. Something went wrong somewhere. Something went wrong with The Lynch."

CHAPTER EIGHTEEN

SIX MONTHS AGO

Clay'd heard a lot of good things about Little Rock, everything from it being one of the prettiest towns south of the Mason Dixon to one of the most welcoming, but when he, Cora, and Doc Seamus rode in on the heels of a murderous leprechaun—something Clay found far funnier than he ought—he was immediately put off. A man had been hanged from a tree on the outskirts, and by the holes pecked in his clothes and the burlap hood covering his head, he'd been there a few days.

Horrified, Cora jerked the reins to halt the horses, the abrupt stop waking Doc from her nap. They hadn't been allowed to take a boat out yonder thanks to an outbreak of yellow fever in Tennessee, so they'd come by road. Doc and Cora took turns driving, and Cora'd volunteered for this last haul, a stretch that had lasted nine hours by Clay's watch. The leprechaun was probably halfway around the world by that point, but Clay was obligated to investigate his last known whereabouts, which was a county directly north of here.

"Who is loathsome enough to leave a body like this?" Cora demanded, and Clay twisted in the saddle to see if anyone nearby could shed some light on the poor, strung-up son of a bitch. The road was empty save for their cart, though he could hear the din of a busy town not too far away. Someone there had to know about the hanged man. He was too rotten to go unnoticed.

"Dunno, but I'll ask around."

"Do. This is unacceptable. People drive by here—families. I can't even imagine explaining this to a child. It's vile. Goddess's tits, he smells." Cora shuddered and shrank back on the driver's bench, her arm pressed against her mouth to stifle the deader's ripe perfume. Behind her, her basket full of trouble stirred, the kittens-turned-cats waking when their mistress accidentally bumped them with her skirts. Cora snapped her fingers, and Frederick jumped from inside the cart to sit on the basket top. The poor little guy had been reduced to cat wrangler ever since the Lynch ranch; if he didn't contain the gray fury inside their wicker cage, the stupid things would be bear scat within a day. At least, that's what Cora said, and though Clay wouldn't have minded nature taking its due course, she'd have been devastated.

The last six months had solidified his stance that dogs were a sight more pleasing than cats. Smarter, too. And quieter.

"I'll get someone to cut him down. Y'all get us a room. And I—" Clay paused because the cats yowled so loudly he had to shout to be heard over them. "Dang it, Cora, I can't hear myself think. Never mind. I'll ride ahead and get it settled. Meet me in town."

Cora's fingers brushed over the basket almost like she was patting a furry spine instead of a reedy weave. "Hush. All of you. You're upsetting Clayton." As they were cats and cats gave dick-all about anything other than eating, sleeping, shitting, and fucking, they kept right on screeching. Cora cast him an impish grin because *weren't they so cute*, and he grunted, digging his heels into Squirt's side to get away from the cacophony of feline despair.

It didn't take long to find the main stretch of town. Buildings lined both sides, a saloon, a church, and a trading post the most prominent structures. By Clay's estimation, they were less than a mile away from the hanged gentleman, and he pulled open his duster to reveal his shiny star, jerking his thumb at it when he addressed the twenty or so people milling at the produce bins outside of the General Store.

"Ladies, gentlemen. I'm looking for the local sheriff?"

A woman glanced up from her bucket of corn and pointed down an adjacent street. She was older than the grit beneath her shoes and had more wrinkles than sun-dried jerky, but her voice was strong and her back was straight. Seemed they bred 'em hardy in Arkansas. "That way, Marshall. Lord bless you, and welcome to Little Rock!"

If the nice God words were any indication, she was a Christian lady, and they were generally a helpful bunch when you were a handsome white lawman. Not only would they answer your questions honest-like out of fear of rotting in Hell, but they sometimes fed you cornbread and hash if you looked tired and miserable enough. If he'd been traveling alone, he might have tried his starving marshal routine on her, but with Cora around—well, she ruined it by mocking him whenever he accepted charity. She said he was taking advantage of his privileges, which was true, but he'd never admit it.

"Strange question, ma'am, but you haven't by chance seen a small man about knee-high runnin' rampant? Red beard, green knickers. Might be—" he almost said, "Smashing folks to bits with a bloody bag of gold," but that's how rumors got started. "—surly with his money?"

She blinked at him and then frowned, her eyes going wide at his colorful description. "No, sir. Is it a child you seek? Or… or a demon?"

"Nah, never you mind. Heard a rumor is all. 'Bout a little green man. Just watch out if you see one, a'right?"

"Watch out for short, greedy men?"

"That's the gist of it, yeah." Before she could ask further questions and incite local panic, he tipped his hat and rode back to the cart. Doc held the basket of cats in her lap now, one of her hands plunged inside to stroke fuzzy ears so the little monsters wouldn't squawk. It helped some; they were no longer caterwauling but purring instead.

Stupid things.

"I think I spotted a hotel that way," Cora said, pointing at an intersection behind her. Frederick was perched on her shoulder, his metal hands fussing with her hair, but the moment she made a motion, he mimicked it and pointed, too. She snickered and reached up to tap her fingernail against the underside of his metal jaw. "Did you want to meet us?"

"Sure. I'm gonna take a ride to the jail to get that man cut down. See about a bath for me, darlin'?"

Cora nodded and clicked her tongue to push the tired horses along. Clay watched them disappear around the street corner before angling Squirt at the jail. It wasn't much of a building, two stories of unpainted clapboards and a small shaded porch, but it didn't need to hold criminals for long. Arkansas had a prison to the west, a place known for renting out its convicts for cheap labor. This little shanty didn't do much other than house 'em a few nights before they were shipped off to a back-breaking sentence of mining, farming, or construction.

Standing in the doorway with a pipe between his lips and a fine, black cowboy hat on his head was a man around Clay's age. He was clean-cut and well-dressed, faint lines creasing the skin at the corners of his eyes. His hair was kept short, wisps of blond-red poking out from around his pressed white collar. Like Clay, he wore a long coat over brown slacks and boots. A pair of pistols hung on his hips along with a pair of silvery handcuffs and a coiled whip.

Clay nodded at him. The man nodded back, and they exchanged smiles.

"Name's Jenson. Looking for the sheriff?"

The man flipped open his jacket to reveal his own shiny star. "You found him. Sheriff Alan Long. Welcome to Little Rock, Jenson." When the sheriff extended his hand, Clay swung off of Squirt to meet him halfway. The impact with the ground sent stabs of pain through his shins and thighs, and he swallowed a groan; he was accustomed to riding hard and long, but he was also accustomed to a soft bed and a soak in between.

Damn, he was going soft.

Their fingers clasped, and Clay pulled back to string his thumbs into the loops of his holster. "You got a man strung outside of town.

Birds been at him. You taking up gibbeting 'round here?" Clay smiled, but it didn't quite reach his eyes.

Which was fine, 'cause Long's didn't reach his neither. "That'd be Simon Ratchet. Murdered a family a couple miles east of here. Was a revenge killing—black man killing his former master. Had a few incidents of the like the last couple years. The locals took care of it, though. Strung him up before I had to."

"You allow vigilantes 'round here?" Clay's eyes shot to his hairline, but Long simply shrugged him off.

"Nah, just never found out who done Ratchet in is all, but I'm not gonna look a gift horse in the mouth. Did my job for me." Long paused. "And they seem inclined to let him hang 'til he rots off the rope, and I'm a humble public servant."

Clay had *opinions*. No way in Hell was he going to believe that Ratchet got a fair shake, nor did he believe Long cared much who lynched him. Black men didn't get the same justice as white men, not before the war and not after.

"It's just a shame is all," Clay said, keeping his tone flat. "Beautiful town other'n that, Sheriff."

"Beautiful town anyway," Long replied. "We don't let criminals run this place. There's no shame in advertising a no-tolerance policy."

Clay wasn't going to get anywhere with the sheriff and he knew it, but he'd be damned if he let a corpse linger by the road like that. An animal didn't deserve an end like that, never mind a man. "Fine enough. I'm gonna cut him down and bury him myself then. Thank you for your time, Sheriff."

Clay turned to climb back onto Squirt, but Long called his name, sharp and without the pretense of hospitality. Clay's fingers inched toward Gayle just in case the sheriff decided to push the issue. He didn't look that dumb, which was good, because Clay didn't fancy writing Washington and explaining why the leprechaun was still bashing in people's heads while the sheriff of Little Rock had a bullet hole in his face the size of a saucer.

"You don't have jurisdiction here, Marshal. This is a local affair," Long said.

Clay peered at him for a long moment before reaching into his coat and pulling out his tobacco bag. He pinched leaf into his papers and tucked the cigarette between his lips. Long shuffled his weight back and forth, growing irritable that Clay hadn't answered him yet, but that only encouraged Clay to go twice as slow. He lit up and took a pair of draws from the cigarette, his eyes narrowed to thoughtful slits.

"Here's the thing. Only people with more jurisdiction than me live in fancy houses in the capital. You can write them if you'd like, but that's a lot of effort to get ignored. 'Sides, this ain't about jurisdiction. This is ethics, and last I checked, I'm well within my rights to do a human deed no matter my job title." He blew a cloud of smoke in Long's direction before swinging his aching body into the saddle.

—

Clay bought a shovel, but it was a waste of a nickel. Two of Long's deputies cut him off on the road to cut down the body. Clay suspected that might happen; wouldn't do any good for the locals to see the outside officer burying the hanged man. Now Long could say he brought Ratchet down of his own accord. The other way, he looked like he was bullied by a fed.

Which he was, but it was about saving face.

Clay was fine with Little Rock doing its own dirty work. He was tired enough without having to plant a corpse, too. Hell, that would have taken him past sundown, and he wanted to clean up, eat, kiss his gal, and go to bed—in that order. He'd report the unethical fuckery he'd witnessed to Washington next time he was in a city near a post, but there wasn't much he could do about it 'til then.

He followed Cora's path to the hotel, handing Squirt over to the stable boy. Clay tipped the kid a shiny new shovel for his troubles, figuring a shovel was a useful thing to have when your business was hauling horse shit. The kid didn't look too impressed, so Clay gave him a nickel, too, which went over far bigger.

Shovels were underappreciated gifts.

The moment Clay walked into the hotel he all but melted with exhaustion. The innkeeper pointed him upstairs, and Clay dragged his sorry carcass up the steps, spurs clanging with every heavy footfall. There wasn't anything fancy about the place—it bordered on rundown with its squealing floorboards and bevy of cobwebs—but as long as the beds were bug free, he'd stay. His ass would fall off in protest if he attempted another minute in the saddle.

He bumbled his way to the last room on the right. It wasn't pretty, but it was spacious and had the necessities: a bureau, an end table with a lantern, and a desk Cora had covered with her tinkering tools. The cats were on the floor picking at a plate of shredded chicken while Frederick dangled from a curtainless curtain rod. Cora sprawled across their big, lumpy bed without a stitch of clothing on, her pale hair coiled around her hips in wet ropes.

A big wooden tub steamed in the corner.

"I've died and gone to the angels," he said, tossing his hat at Cora's flank. It landed on the curve of her left cheek, perched at a proper, jaunty angle.

"I thought you'd like that. Everything settled?"

He stripped down and climbed into the tub, whimpering as warmth enveloped his aching bones. "Yep. The man's getting a burial. Sheriff don't like me, though."

"Lots of people don't like you, but that's never bothered you before." She slithered off of the bed and walked around to the back of the tub to soap his shoulders and neck. "We won't be around long enough for it to matter. You'll ask around about your leprechaun, I'll do a little business, Doc can shop, and we'll be on our way to Sterling's by tomorrow evening."

Clay stiffened at the mention of "business." He knew she was running low-profile cons here and there, something she'd started up again over the last few months. He didn't know if it was her way of saying he couldn't tell her what to do or if she was putting the money away for a rainy day. Whatever the case, he didn't press her on it. She wouldn't be forthcoming—had no intentions of being forthcoming—so he tried not to think about it too much to keep the peace.

After that first altercation at the cottage, a lot of new-love giddiness fizzled in the face of the harsher realities. Cora called thieving an idiosyncrasy; he called it immoral. There'd be no marriage and probably no kids. She had more secrets than a wishing well and wouldn't commit to walking across the street for fear of some terrible repercussion—not that she'd discuss that terrible repercussion with him. He just had to live with the knowledge that some nebulous evil cast a shadowy pall over her—and him by association.

It wasn't always easy to live with, but as Doc had counseled over two bottles of booze and side-by-side pukings in a gutter, all relationships had their trials. Clay's trials just so happened to be a flighty fairy who liked to pilfer. He could have found some other pretty thing to warm his bed, but he'd spend every day comparing her to Cora, and any gal nice enough to let him play with her wet-and-naughties deserved better than that. Or so Doc claimed, though when she said it, it sounded more refined with no mention of cooter.

"I got you dinner," Cora said, her sudsy hands sinking into his hair. His shallow-yet-deep thoughts about their relationship dribbled out his ears; the massage was soothing in spite of the zaps and shocks streaking over his scalp.

"You feed me 'cause you're a wonder."

"I am. I took care of everything—even Doc. I think she was asleep before I left her room. Poor thing was exhausted."

"We all are."

Cora rinsed him, toweled him, fed him, and was even kind enough to climb on top of him before they slept, letting him lay back and watch as her roundest parts did a hypnotic, wobbly dance. Spent, there were sweet words and entangled legs, and soon after that, a small army of cats and squirrel sprawling over their bodies in a snuggle pile. He wasn't too keen on that part of the equation, but it was a small price to pay for everything else going right.

He slept long and hard, too tired to care that the mattress had an ass divot from an army of previous patrons. Usually, he was up with the roosters, but that morning he drooled into his pillow far past the normal hour. It wasn't until Frederick sailed in through the open window and chased a cat across the floor that Clay stirred. He grumbled and hauled himself out of bed, frowning at the distinct lack of Cora. He knew what she was doing, and the desire to chase her down and tell her to stop was there, but he had other things to worry about.

Like catching a homicidal leprechaun.

Which was still damned funny in a macabre way. A short man wearing all green hopping up and hitting folks in the head with his gold sack? Hell of a mental picture. What did he do? Get a foot stool? And did folks just stand there waiting for him to get to higher ground so he could whack 'em dead?

If so, they were dumber than pig scat and prolly deserved whatever they got.

He dressed simple for the day, in a white shirt, suspenders, and black trousers. No coat or vest because it was hotter than a whore's drawers. Gayle rested on his hip. His star was clipped to his belt so folks knew he was on official business. He didn't have many leads to work with—the leprechaun's last sighting was north of Little Rock three weeks back—but he'd search because it was his job to search. And when he determined it an official waste of time, he'd write Washington and let them know the little green man slipped his grasp because shit happened a lot in the weird business.

He collected Squirt from the stables. A few hours of wandering north yielded nothing, not even near the woods where the leprechaun was last spotted, so he spent his time being lazy, guiding the horse from shade patch to shade patch and enjoying the breeze. It was pretty country, so he circled back to Little Rock the long way, giving three hours to the murderous li'l bastard before determining lunch was a more pressing matter than a cold trail.

He'd just spotted the church steeple when he sensed Cora's magic. She'd warned that she'd be at her nonsense today; he avoided her when she was thieving, but circumstance had brought him near, and if he was near, he might as well give a peek. She stood by a hillside cliff, her hair pinned to her head, her body hugged by a dress the color of daffodils. Who knew how she'd glamoured herself for her forty or so gawkers, but her natural self looked beautiful to him, all delicate and summery.

It annoyed him. If she was going to break the law, the least she could do was be ugly while she did it.

He stopped Squirt thirty yards from the gathering. He couldn't make out anything Cora said, but he didn't need to neither. Cora foisted that ugly bladed parasol over her head. She pointed at it, talked about it, and then she stepped off the edge of the cliff, the blades whirling as she floated like a leaf on the wind.

The people looked amazed, and to a point, they should have been. There was a gal buoying over a fifty-foot drop with only a machine to hold her aloft. Knowing she was an air fairy and couldn't splatter eased his mind, but what came next bothered him. A lot. He watched Cora step back onto solid ground and offer the parasol to the crowds. A young man was first to come forward. He handed her something Clay assumed was a coin and then neared the cliff, hesitating only a moment before holding the parasol above his head and taking a leap. He bobbed gently mid-air, the combination of machine and Cora's magic floating him.

Seeing one of their own aflight, the people of Little Rock scrambled for a turn. Clay's hands clenched around Squirt's reins as three and then four people stuffed money into Cora's palm, accepting her parasol and gripping onto it as it floated them over the ravine. A few people were sensible enough to back away, mothers holding their little ones close as they watched this amalgam of science and magic with distrustful eyes, but they were the minority. In twenty minutes, Cora had made herself a few dollars at the very least, that damnable machine of hers a perfect way to siphon money from strangers' pockets into her own.

Clay was pissed.

He turned away with a clenched jaw, ready to find himself something to eat so he didn't march over there and snap her contraption in half, but a woman's yelp stopped him short. He jerked his head around in time to see a little boy running at the cliff, having torn away from his mother's side. She reached for him, as did Cora, but the slippery scamp dodged them and lunged for the man holding the flying machine.

The little boy flew for a moment, utter joy on his face before his hands swung wide, completely missing the man with the parasol. The man tried to catch him, but there was limited mobility with the device, and his grasping fingers could only reach so far. A small squeak, a barely audible cry, and the boy plummeted past the ledge to the ground below. Clay couldn't see the result of such a fall, but by the immediate sobs and gasps of the collected crowd, it was bad.

Cora didn't get him in time.

Her scream was echoed by the child's mother. Everyone came alive with frantic concern, men running along the cliff side to get to lower ground to help the boy, but Clay froze. He'd seen a lot of tragic things in his line of work—people shot down too young over something stupid, people maimed by monsters or monsters maimed by people—but none of it had involved a child. It was an altogether different type of ache, a despair that hit square in the belly and sat there like a cold lump.

It was needless.

All of it was so very needless.

Cora helped the last floating man to the ground and reclaimed her parasol. She must have seen Clay ride up because she pushed her way through the crowd to get to him, her face stark white and covered in tears. He licked his lips, torn between sadness and anger. She never thought these things through. Sure, she never could have seen a kid running over a cliff because of her invention, but if she wasn't conning people in the first place, he'd *be unharmed.*

She was almost clear of the locals when someone grabbed her sleeve. She shook them off, but another set of hands took the first's place, these ones fisting in her skirts and jerking backward. Cora squawked, Clay watching in horror as a half-dozen people pulled her to the ground, their bodies forming a wall around her.

"Hold her. Hold her for the sheriff!" someone cried, and Clay kicked Squirt into a full run, pulling Gayle from her holster and firing a warning shot before any of them got to kicking or tearing or doing who-knew-what to the woman he loved. Cora could defend herself, but he doubted she'd go so far as to use her magics against humans unless absolutely necessary.

She knew the laws; they rarely favored the weirds.

"Leave her alone," Clay yelled, slowing Squirt when it looked like she might plow down folks. The moment Cora was in reach, he slid from the saddle and forced his way through the bodies, people yelling and shouting all around him. He found Cora huddled on the ground, knees drawn to her chest, eyes closed. She looked fine—mussed and dirt-smeared—but otherwise intact, and he pulled her to her feet before jerking her against his chest.

"The Sheriff's coming," he heard someone say.

Clay winced. When Long discovered Cora was Clay's woman, he'd no doubt drop every bit of weight he had on her head. There was a score to even thanks to the hanged man, and Cora couldn't have made it easier for him unless she'd waltzed up to the town's preacher and struck him dead with lightning.

"CLEAR IT OUT. GET BACK," the sheriff hollered. Clay shoved Cora behind him so Long had to go through him to get to her. She jabbed him in the back and promptly stepped around to his side, her head high despite the tears raining down her cheeks.

"This is my mess, Clayton. I should be here."

"Fine, but let me do the talkin' so you don't get yourself into anymore shit than y'already have."

She didn't like that, but frankly, he didn't care. He held Gayle in his hand, not bothering to holster her. The tension on the air was thicker than biscuit gravy. People were mad. People were scared and sad. Somewhere nearby, the child's mother wept. Clay would defend Cora to this lawman because he loved her, but in his heart, he knew a line had been crossed. She didn't murder the boy outright, but she played a part in his death, and that made her guilty of something. He couldn't name that something proper yet, but it was there.

The crowd parted like the Red Sea before Moses. Long appeared at the end of the tunnel, his hands hovering over his guns. His deputies stood sentry behind him. Clay recognized them from the previous day. They'd been the two sent to remove Ratchet's corpse.

"Neville Anders is hurt real bad. Jumped off a cliff after seeing that lady's machine at work," a helpful citizen offered, one of them poking Cora in the side and making her cringe.

Clay's free hand snagged the perpetrator, giving him a none-too-gentle squeeze. He locked eyes with the man—a short, bearded individual with a bald head and a green shirt—before thrusting him away. "You don't touch her or I touch you, and my touchin's meaner."

Long surveyed the crowd and motioned at one of the men Clay'd seen suspended from the parasol not fifteen minutes ago. Long barked questions at him, and the man answered to the best of his ability, not embellishing but not withholding information either, which made Clay uncomfortable. Mostly because in Long's shoes, Clay would have taken Cora into custody. It came as no surprise when Long pulled out his handcuffs and motioned at his deputies to flank her.

"Nope. Not gonna happen," Clay said.

"A crime has been committed today," Long said, his voice full of flint. "You can't dispute that."

"I don't dispute that. But *you* ain't taking her in."

"That so?"

Clay eyed Cora. "Show 'im." He didn't need to say anything else—he didn't have to. She understood. Her magic grew. The gentle thrum he felt standing beside her turned to an electric jolt that ripped over his skin and set his teeth on edge. The people around them gasped, and though she looked the same ol' Cora to him with her pointy ears, blue tipped-hair, and blackened fingertips, he guessed she looked totally different to everyone else. She'd stripped her glamour for them.

"Fair folk, which makes her mine," Clay said. "Fair folk are federal jurisdiction."

"No." Long's hands slid for his guns. Clay wasn't even sure if he was going to pull them, but he wasn't going to take his chances. He swung Gayle up and pointed the barrels at the Sheriff's heart, his legs braced in case he needed to drop or roll or somehow make a play to get away. There were lots of folks around and only him and Cora. She could probably flatten 'em all if need be, but Clay'd not live to talk about such a spectacular display if it came to pass.

He'd like to avoid death if at all possible. Dyin' wasn't as much fun as livin'.

"I'm takin' her in myself, sheriff. And for all that I got the gun on you, I'm not your biggest problem if you pull on me." It was eerie how fast the clouds overhead morphed from white and fluffy to steel gray and angry. Thunder rumbled as a storm swept in at Cora's behest. It was immediate and absolute, a beautiful day washed away in seconds. People shrunk away as fat droplets of rain sprinkled their heads, every wet splash a tiny warning of what Cora *could* do if she so chose.

Water rolled off of Clay's hat brim to leak down onto his shirt. Under any other circumstance, he would have appreciated the reprieve from the heat.

Not today.

Long muttered an oath, his hands sliding from his guns, palms up to show himself unarmed. His deputies followed suit. "Go then. But you give me my word you'll see this wrong righted. No baby killer's gone free in Little Rock before. The first won't be under my watch."

"I'd never! He's not dead, I don't—"

"You got it," Clay said, interrupting Cora before she could argue the semantics of her guilt. The townsfolk took a reluctant step back when the sheriff did, and Clay grabbed Cora's wrist to pull her toward the horse. He lifted her into the saddle and slid in behind her to get back to the inn as quick as Squirt could carry them. Cora broke down sobbing halfway there, slumping against his chest, but he didn't acknowledge it, his eyes fixed dead ahead, his molars grinding.

He knew what he had to do. He didn't want to, and it would break his heart in the end, but he knew what he had to do. Beyond Long, he'd made a promise to a metal-armed man in a Charleston infirmary all those years ago. Clay wasn't the type of man to break his promises. All he could hope was that Doc understood, and that one day when she looked back upon what had happened in Little Rock, that Cora would understand, too.

—

Cora cried for hours. He didn't know what to say to her, so he held her in his lap and stroked her hair, waiting for the storm to pass. It seemed that's all she needed from him, which was good 'cause it was all he was capable of offering. Emptiness had settled into his bones. He felt emotionally detached from everything and everyone, like Cora's distress and the mother's sadness and Long's anger were someone else's problems. Doc would probably say it was his brain protecting him from the shitstorm that was his relationship, but Doc liked all that science babble too much sometimes.

By the time Cora stopped her weeping, the moon was high and the cicadas were well into their choruses. Clay lit the candles so the room wasn't cast in total darkness. Even in the dimness, Cora looked wrung-out; her nose was red, her eyes swollen. She moaned about her head hurting, but that shouldn't have surprised her. She'd cried enough to flood the Arkansas River twice over.

"I'll go see if Doc has something to help," he said. But he was saying it to Cora's backside. She'd flung herself off of him to collapse back onto their bed, her arms wrapped around her pillow. He could hear the muffled snivels as she broke into a fresh torrent of sobs.

He should likely feel sorry for her. He didn't.

Doc had heard her through the walls earlier and rushed over to see if everything was all right. Clay'd given her an abbreviated explanation of the day's disasters, fully expecting Doc to sail to Cora's side and fret and fuss over her, but the good doctor refrained. In fact, the play of emotions across Doc's face suggested that she was repulsed by the situation. Doc had never minded Cora's devilish side before, but it was clear that she fell into the Clay side of thinking on this one—that some fairy tricks were too damned dangerous. Cora hadn't thought through the risks, showcasing her parasol over an open cliff like that. Sure, it was a more dramatic display there, but too much shit could have gone wrong.

And did go wrong. If she'd just done it on flat ground, the kid would have been fine. Hell, if she'd just not done it at all because swindling was immoral, the kid would have been fine.

Hindsight.

Goddamned hindsight.

Clay knocked and walked into Doc's room without waiting for the invitation to come inside. For once, Doc didn't rattle his cage about it. She was too busy lying in bed with a book on her chest, her spectacles pushed to the bottom of her nose so she could read by candlelight. Her suspenders were off her shoulders and dangling from the bedside.

"Need a couple'a favors," Clay said.

"Of course." Doc hesitated before adding, "I attended the Anders boy, by the by. He'll live, but I'm not sure when he'll walk again, if ever. He has no feeling from the waist down."

Goddamn it, Cora.

"Hell. I'll send money to the family. That woman, I swear. I don't know what goes on in that pretty head'a hers sometimes." He ran a hand down his face and sighed. "Look, I know she don't deserve doctorin', but Cora's head's killin' her. All the cryin'. You got anything that'll fix it?" Clay asked this while making his way to Doc's desk. There were various books and papers there, and he rifled through to find himself a blank piece of stationary. He stared at it awhile, feeling how that asshole Judas must have felt before handing over Christ to the Romans. But that didn't stop him from sinking into the chair and scrawling a note, his fingers trembling with every word.

"Laudanum, but that's it. I could give her a small dose."

"If it'll put her to sleep, do it. I can't take the weepin' any more than she can." Clay finished his letter and folded it twice, not bothering to skim for errors. The message was there, with or without spelling mistakes, and damn him for writing it at all. But he had to. *He had to*, he kept telling himself, because if he didn't keep reiterating it, he'd let her off the hook.

And I've given my word. Twice now. What good is a man without his word?

"Need you to get this out to Sterling tonight," he continued, his mouth grit dry. "Please. Send the stable kid maybe. I'll pay good money for it to get there quick, but I need a response before sunrise. Need to know..." Clay swallowed and rubbed his brow with the back of his hand. "Need to know what Sterling wants to do about all this. I think I know, but... hell."

"I see," Doc said. She put the book aside and sat up, her legs swinging to the floor. Clay watched her wriggle her feet into a pair of soft, leather boots, her thin fingers lacing them. "I'll go myself. I know it'll get there that way."

The significance was not lost on Clay. Doc hated the wilderness and despised riding horses, but neither of those things stopped her from changing into proper riding clothes and donning a bowler hat to venture out in the middle of the night. It was rare for her to travel with a gun, saying it was for "unsavories and those who can't battle with their wits," but for Clay's grimmest task, Doc strapped herself with a pistol. Clay didn't have the faintest clue if she knew how to use it, but sometimes having the weapon was enough to deter trouble.

"I know she's your friend, Doc. You don't gotta—"

"I'm quite aware of what I do and do not have to do. I am choosing to do this because I think it's the right thing to do. But this does present a problem. How do you think Cora will react when Sterling arrives? More to the point—" she paused to eye Clayton over the tops of her spectacles. "—do you think you ought to be here for it?"

The answer was "no." Clay knew it, Doc knew it, and he looked at the wall between Doc's room and his own feeling like he would be sick. He wished today hadn't happened. If he could just go back to yesterday, he'd steal that stupid flying machine and destroy it before Cora got her con going. But time didn't work that way, and there he was, holding the letter in his hands that probably meant the end of his relationship with the only girl he'd ever loved. Maybe she'd calm down and come back to him later—her temper bloomed bright and fizzled fast—but if he stayed, he risked getting his testicles fried off by a lightning strike.

He glanced at the letter. He could still change his mind, but what would he think of himself if he did?

"Clayton." Doc's voice was quiet. Clay lifted his chin to peer at her, trying hard not to show how upset he was. It wasn't working. Doc crossed the room to put her hands on his shoulders, giving him a faint squeeze. "I'm going to give you enough laudanum that she'll sleep through to the morning. Pack my things. I'll bring Sterling back with me. You and I can leave before she wakes."

It wasn't very brave, but he found himself nodding. Yes, being gone before she woke would be good. He'd write her later and explain it all, and maybe with some time apart she'd see why he did it this way. He had to protect himself, but more than that, he had to be gone so he didn't tell Sterling he'd changed his mind. So he didn't threaten to shoot the very man he'd called out of retirement to do his dirty work for him.

Doc thrust a dose of laudanum in his hand.

"I'll see you soon," she said, shrugging into the traveling coat of her boy disguise and walking out the door.

Clay sank into the chair by Doc's window and stared out the window, doing his damndest not to weep like a baby.

CHAPTER NINETEEN

NOW

Sterling announced they were only welcome for two days because "time is a-tickin' and Clay needs to get this Cora nonsense sorted." Clay was disappointed that Sterling wouldn't let him hole up and die in his spare room, but the old man was adamant he keep on living. Hell if Clay knew why. Maybell was going to catch him sooner or later and smear him across the ground like a turd off a boot heel. Dying from a blood curse had to be better than whatever fiery rectal torture the eldest Lynch gal would inflict upon him.

Sterling's heart was in the right place even if his head was up his ass, but Clay had better things to do than argue with the old man. He spent the day in a wooden chair by the pond, drinking gin with Doc and Sterling and staring out at the sapphire waters. The three of them reminisced about simpler, soberer days until dusk, at which point Clay abandoned them to visit his horse. She was rolling in the dirt in her paddock, but when she spotted him, she got up and trotted his way, bashing her forehead against his arm in a silent demand for treats and affection. He produced both with a tired, sad smile. Squirt had been biting him, farting at him when he picked her hooves, and stomping all over his toes for years now, but she'd carried him well. He would miss her dumb ass.

A mosquito the size of a condor stabbed him in the neck, and he took that as his sign to seek refuge. But first he watched the mosquito float up—too far up—his cursed blood sending it careening towards the clouds. Good. Served the little blood-sucker right. Clay hoped it smacked right into the moon.

He returned Squirt to her stall and meandered into the house. He promised Marie he'd research draugr, and that's what he did, yawning damn near incessantly the whole time. As sad as it was to admit, he'd been going to bed before sundown lately, but he forced himself through the weariness for Marie's sake.

Clay sketched out a pair of letters and tucked them into his saddlebags before staggering to his borrowed bed. Morning came too fast for his liking, Sterling whacking at his bare heels and waving a plate of eggs and hash in his direction. "Get up, eat, and get out. You have dying not to do. Not going to let you rot on my doorstep." Clay grunted at him and threw on his clothes, grumbling when his pants fell too low on his hips and he had to poke another notch into his belt. If he gave one good goddamn, he'd get them tailored proper for his new, skeletal physique, but that required effort.

Effort was hard.

He ate and went outside, his hand blocking the sun so it didn't stab him in the eyes. Sterling took pity on him and produced one of his old hats, a beat-up brown thing with a lopsided brim. It wasn't much to look at, but neither was Clay these days, and he accepted it with muttered thanks, grateful for the reprieve.

"Just remember this is all a temporary setback, son," Sterling said.

"Of course it is," Doc said, throwing a small leather sack into the back of the cart. "Temporary and manageable."

Clay itched to tell Sterling that Doc was full of manure, that on the way to his house she had Clay dead and buried, too, but climbing into the cart took all his concentration. Not only did the movement make the darkness in his vision rise, but there was dizziness, too. The scenery revolved around him, a carousel of bleeding color, and he likened it to the morning-after-drunk he sometimes got from too much whiskey. But unlike whiskey, he couldn't simply imbibe more to make it right again.

He clung to the rails of the cart, waiting for his balance to return. Sterling came to the rescue, his hands gripping Clay's waist and pushing until Clay was properly situated on the bench. It was more than a little unmanning—Sterling would do the same for a gal or a small child, which made Clay think it was time to turn in his twig and berries. He wasn't sure what kind of sick fuck would want 'em, but if weird marshaling had taught him anything, it's that there were all kinds of people with all kinds of proclivities out there.

"Thanks," Clay mumbled.

"It's nothing. Now, I'm holding your gun and your horse here, but it's temporary. You hear that, son? Temporary," Sterling said.

"You keep repeating yourself. How could I not?"

"Well, you said your eyesight's bad. Didn't know if your hearing was going, too." Sterling chuckled and gave him an affectionate slap on the thigh. "Doc, good to see you. Take care of Princess, and if you need anything, send a runner. I'll come."

"I will. A pleasure to see you again, Marshal."

"None of that. I'm retired. Sterling."

"Sterling then. And I'll—*we'll*—see you soon."

"You better."

Clay waited for Doc to climb in beside him. The cart was significantly lighter than before, the back near empty save for some basic supplies. Part of that was so they could travel faster. The other part was that yesterday when they were sitting by the pond, every time the wind blew or grass grew or a bird had the gall to come within a half a mile, Doc ducked out to check on her wardrobe, insisting that the trunks weren't proper protection after so many weeks exposed to the elements.

After Doc's fifty-third insistence that Mother Nature was a heinous bitch with a corset vendetta, Sterling offered to stow the luggage in his back room. Doc was most appreciative, even if putting everything away left her with a single pink gown. Clay was dubious that'd satiate her hunger for lace and ribbons, but what did he know? He wasn't a woman with a dress fetish.

They set off mid-morning, an amicable silence stretching between them. Unsurprisingly, Clay couldn't stop thinking about Cora. Sterling's notion that she had no intention of killing him left him conflicted. On one hand, he felt he should go right on trying to hate her. Sometimes, he succeeded, like when he thought about Addy's fate at the hands of Thomasine Lynch. It was evident that Cora hadn't learned a damn thing after Little Rock. She did whatever the hell she wanted with little regard for how it could go bad. It was like something inside her couldn't reason out the effects to her causes.

On the other hand, he wasn't sure he had the right to hold that against her. It was like holding the spots against the leopard. From the beginning, Clay knew Cora was an impulsive girl who liked to skirt the edges of propriety. Their introduction proved that, what with the fake wind machines, and after that it was the carnival in Atlanta, and then the bogey attack in Louisiana. His first impressions of her were fairly accurate; she was rash and immoral. She put fun over responsibility and always would. The fearless demeanor was a ruse, but still… Cora wore her personality on her sleeve. He'd fallen in love with her in spite of it.

So then why was he so damned surprised she kept right on being her?

"Got a question for you," Clay asked after a time. He pulled out a cigarette and plunked it between his lips. Sterling had seen him struggling to assemble one at breakfast and rolled the rest of his stash out of pity. Clay counted fifty smokes fattening his tobacco bag. It was the one thing to go right this pissant week.

"Mmm?"

"Why'd you side with me on the Cora thing in Little Rock? You two were friends before I came along." Clay lit his cigarette and crinkled his eyes, the wind blowing in such a way that his own smoke struck him in the face.

"For one, I saw what happened to that little boy's legs, and it was awful. For two, you were merciful while sticking to your principles." Doc shrugged her shoulders. "You could have left Cora to that awful sheriff, but you gave her into Sterling's care instead. She served two weeks for theft, and the charges against her regarding the boy's injury were dropped after she paid a fine. I think you handled a difficult situation with grace. You're something of a cock, but you had a good moment there, Clayton."

"Two weeks, huh? I spent so much time trying to not think about her after she kicked me aside that I didn't ask questions 'bout her sentence. Figured I'd hate the answers."

"I knew that, which is why I didn't mention her or the letters she sent me. It would have hurt you to hear her name."

"I suppose, but—" Clay's voice fell off. If Doc had simply informed him that Cora was in and out of jail in two weeks, Clay would have been spared innumerable sleepless nights. All he'd pictured was Cora burning in iron shackles in a windowless jail cell somewhere. The truth was she'd waltzed in for a two-week sojourn and waltzed out as whole as she'd been before her incarceration.

It was pointless to be pissed about it so much time later, but that didn't stop him from spitting his cigarette out onto the road beside him and watching the wagon wheel crush the stub.

Everything about this situation can suck a dead mule's ass.

"I also didn't say anything because—I almost hate admitting this—I thought you two would reconcile." Doc's fingers tightened on the reins, snapping them to spur the horses into a trot. They'd just reached the flatlands that would take them out of Little Rock and toward the river. Pushing the horses now meant they could rest them at the confluence of the Arkansas and Mississippi. They'd get downtime on the transport barge. "Foolish to say with the curse business afoot, but I had this fanciful notion that you and Cora were better torturing each other than two unsuspecting, normal people. I didn't want to share angry words or news to compromise your reunion. Had I realized it'd go so foul so fast…"

"I get it. Don't like it, but I get it," Clay said. "If it's any consolation, I thought she'd come back, too. I said to her one time that I'd rather be miserable with her than without her, but now—Hell. I don't even know what to think. I'm mad at her, I hate her, I don't hate her, I love her. I feel all of it every minute of every day. The only bright side I can see to this whole damned mess is that Sterling got to capture his white fish."

Doc's eyebrows knitted together so tightly it was hard to see where one fuzzy strip ended and the other began. "Pardons, I don't mean to be dim, but white fish?"

"Cora. She's his Moby Dick. White fish. He told me all about it once."

"Whale. White whale, you imbecile."

"Yeah, that. Fish, whale—all the same."

"They are not. One is a mammal and the other—"

Clay reached out to poke Doc in the side, wedging his finger into the tiny fat pocket above Doc's brown pants. "Ain't the point, Doc. My point is it always bothered me that I dragged him out of retirement to do my dirty work. Felt cowardly, but I couldn't bring myself to do it. Only good thing that came out of the whole mess was Sterling got to be Moby Dick for a day."

"Ahab," Doc murmured.

"What was that?"

"Nothing."

They both knew it wasn't nothing, and Clay had heard her perfectly well, but they weren't going to discuss it because that'd kill the conversation. Doc moved the reins into her left hand and removed her hat to fan her face, quickly deciding that was a bad plan and stuffing it back onto her head. "Well, I can say she wasn't angriest that she was arrested, but that you had someone else do it. She called it a breach of trust. Perhaps if you'd discussed your reasons with her first, it would have made a difference, though things were so volatile after Little Rock, I doubt that. Tensions were too high."

"A breach of trust?! Oh, ain't that something coming from a conwoman." Clay hunkered down on the bench, his chin touching his chest and his eyes fixed on the road. His temples throbbed, though he wasn't sure if that was agitation with the conversation or symptomatic of his new friend vertigo. "Because of her, I'm near dead, the Lynches are almost all dead, Addy got skewered…Christ, she sicced a monster on a helpless old lady! That's all fine, but have a mutual friend arrest her because I love her stupid ass too much, and I'm the asshole? That's rich, Cora. Real rich."

There was a heartbeat of a pause before Doc said, "Did you just call Marie Laveau a helpless old lady?"

Clay should have been annoyed at yet another tangential aside, but thinking about it, he grinned, too. "Think I did."

Doc shook her head. "You are a bloody idiot, Clayton Jenson."

Clay tipped his borrowed hat to his friend in spite of his swirling head. "Why thank you kindly, Irene. An imbecile and an idiot in short order. I'm right fond of you, too, bitch."

—

Once they hit Brookhaven, Clayton took the reins. He wasn't dizzy anymore, but that's because he was smart enough to not turn his head. Seemed that was what sent everything whirly, but if he let his eyes do the moving, he was all right.

He'd only been to Cora's cabin a few times, but he remembered the directions clear. He took a left at the willow tree near the red barn and followed the path four pines down on the right. Doc had never been out to the cabin, and watching the last vestiges of civilization fade behind them, she expressed nature-phobic consternation that they would die to indigenous fauna. When a bee buzzed near her head, she cowered on the bench like a child, practically flattening herself to the wood.

"Oh, stop. Bee don't eat much," Clay said.

"No, but they hurt if they sting."

"You'd live. I got stung in the neck by three wasps last summer. Hurt like Hades for about ten minutes, but after that, it was nothing."

Doc sat up with her hat in hand, ready to swing if another yellow and black terrorist soared her way. "I'd rather avoid the ten minutes."

"Pansy."

"Your point?"

"Touché."

Clay guided the horses into the heart of the woods, the edges of the cart so close to the trees he could hear the lowest branches raking over the side panels. It was more overgrown than the last time he'd visited, which is why it took him longer to spot the stone path that curved its way to the cottage.

Well, that and he couldn't see worth a shit anymore. Made finding hidden things difficult.

He pulled the cart to the edge of the property and peered at the fairytale cottage. It was so unchanged; the windows were open, the shutters thrown wide to welcome the sun. One of the three cats perched inside the window box of flowers, its legs tucked under it to give the appearance of a fluffy gray loaf. Every once in a while it tilted its head to gnaw on a daisy. Another cat tiptoed along the ledge of the well, peering into the darkness and courting an early demise. Clay couldn't see the third one, but he *could* see a speck of silver in the shrubs next to the house.

He smiled in spite of the sick in his guts.

"Frederick," he said, pointing.

"So she is here. Good." Doc climbed down and fussed with her hair, her fingers streaking through the sides before she tied a red kerchief over it. She offered Clay a hand, and Clay remembered all the times he'd assumed a similar posture for Irene when she needed help.

Oh, how the tables had turned. Clay took her fingers and descended to the ground, his weight balanced against Doc's shoulders. He swayed a little, and Doc steadied him with her arm around his waist.

"You are too thin," Doc murmured.

"Welp, blood curse will do that to ya. At least I'm still able to hold my own pisser."

"Charming, Clayton. Simply charming."

She helped Clay to the door, pausing a few feet away, her brow furrowed with concern. "I'll leave you two alone to talk, I think. Unless you need me?"

"Nah, but do me a favor. A couple of favors actually." Clay leaned against the house front so he didn't fall on his ass. Not only was everything spinning around him, but his muscles were weak, too. Didn't seem right that his body would wear out so quickly while his mind stayed razor sharp.

"Yes?"

Clay ran his fingers down his face and grunted at the thick stubble there. If he tried to hold a straight edge, he'd cut his own nose off, but the notion of asking Doc to act as his barber bugged him. Scrawny, nearly blind, and frail, sure, but his pride still worked just fine. "I know this ain't the best time to mention this, but two things. One, if I don't make it—and I don't mean out of Cora's cottage 'cause I sincerely doubt she's gonna kill me any worse than Betsy already has—but if I don't make it *period*, go be happy with that fella in N'Orleans. Hell, go even if I do make it. It ain't fair that the best person I know spends her days miserable and alone, or, if not alone, hauling ass around the country with the likes of me."

Doc stared at him for a minute and then cleared her throat. Clay could see a few tears dribbling down her cheeks from behind her spectacles, and on another day—on a healthier, better day—Clay would have given her shit for it, but not then. Then he waited until Doc collected herself and nodded, her small hands gripping her suspenders like they held up far more than her pants. "I will. And the other?"

Clay motioned at the cart with a limp flick of his wrist. "Two, I wrote goodbye letters to my parents and sister when I was at Sterling's. Make sure it gets to them if need be. Also a letter for Marie about her draugr, so get that out, too."

Doc made a high-pitched squealing sound that left Clay with the distinct impression that she was going to weep if Clay kept talking, so Clay stopped talking and walked into Cora's house, afraid and tired and unsure of what to expect. It wasn't until his boot crossed the threshold that he realized something alarming. Cora sat in the corner chair peering at him with the third cat sprawled across her lap, a crocheted shawl over her shoulders. *And he hadn't felt her.* He hadn't felt a damned bit of her magic. Either he'd rotted so bad inside his witchsniffer didn't work no more, or...

There was no more. It was another part of him that was broken.

He peered at Cora, or at least her foggy caricature, and she peered back. As far as he could tell, she looked the same, timeless and princess-like with her flaxen hair and peach cheeks. She wore a lavender dress, and he could see her bare feet peeking out from the bottom hem, the undersides of her toes green from walking barefoot through the grass. She was as beautiful as ever, and didn't that just make this all the shittier, because all he wanted to do was grab her and yank her into a hug.

Too bad he couldn't even walk across the floor to get to her.

"Cora," he said. "Looking lovely, as usual."

He slipped his hands into his waistband and eyed her. He had no idea what she might do with him there. He was sure she was expecting him. The wind talked to Cora, and Cora talked to the wind, so it must have heralded his arrival, which meant she'd had time to prepare. Screaming was likely, throwing things was also a possibility, though a much more alarming one now that he wouldn't be able to dodge. Maybe there'd be lighting or wind. Maybe there'd be tears. Anything was possible, but the only thing he could do was stand there like a dumbass and wait for her to make the first move.

Cora's eyes skimmed his face and body, her hand creeping up to clasp her throat. Color flooded her cheeks and splotched over her chest. "You look terrible. What happened?"

"You. Betsy-fucking-Lynch. Then three more Lynches after her. You know, the usual," he replied, his voice even. His legs wobbled, and he reached out to steady himself on the table, using it for purchase so he didn't end up a boneless heap on her floor. She sprung from the chair to help him, the third cat scrambling as she ran to his side, her arm looping around his waist the same way Doc's had. There should have been electricity when she touched him, and there was nothing.

It was like any other touch.

But it's not, is it? Because it's Cora, and even without the magic, she's the most special...

Damn it.

Even knowing what she'd done to him, he had to fight the urge to bury his nose in her hair and hold onto her until his body gave out. He reminded himself she got him afflicted, that he should be shaking her until her teeth rattled right out of her head or screaming at her until she apologized, but he couldn't bring himself to do any of it. Instead, he let her guide him to her vacated seat.

Caring for him was so contradictory to cursing him in the first place, but that contradiction was what *made* her Cora, wasn't it?

He slumped into the seat and waited for the spinning room to still. Cora's hands reached for his furred cheeks, cupping them so she could peer into his gaunt face, her thumbs skimming along his jawline. "It wasn't supposed to be like this. I talked to Betsy. I told her… this is wrong," she whispered. He could still feel the warmth from her ass where she sat, and he wriggled into the cushion. "You're so sick, Clayton."

"Yeah, I am. And I'm not gonna lie, it sucks worse than a fat man at a chicken bone."

She lifted her head to peer out the window, her hands sliding to his shoulders and squeezing. "I thought I heard Doc. Maybe she can…"

"Ain't nothing Doc can do for me. Only one who can fix me is Marie Laveau, and we know she can't because WHAT THE FUCK WERE YOU THINKING?" Well, there was a scream, though it was less anger and more raw frustration and sadness that they'd gone from loving each other so hard to this. How? How could two people who were so happy fuck it up this much? "What happened to you, Cora? You sic a crazy-ass witch on me, sic a nightmare monster on a nice old lady who's treated you fine. Addy got stabbed with a fucking iron spit. The Lynches are almost all dead. I understand being pissed at me, but what'd Marie or Addy do to deserve—"

His voice stopped mid-tirade because he caught a flash of something large and orange moving in the room next door. He leaned forward despite what it'd do to his balance. When his vision adjusted, colors formed shapes and shapes became a tiger with enormous golden eyes and a whipping tail lying on the bed. He stared at the cat, and the cat stared back.

Clay couldn't help but cock a smile.

"Montague? That you?" He carefully craned his head to look at Cora, ignoring the way her fingers rubbed together like she wanted to reach out and choke him. "Does that mean Addy's alive? Or did you inherit him 'cause she—you know…"

"Quite alive. She recovered fully in Fairy. I'm surprised you didn't realize it already."

"Realize nothing. No one tells me anything." Clay sank back into the chair, taking his time so he didn't suffer the consequence of too much motion. Hearing that Addy was still kicking made him happier than a fox in a henhouse; he might be screwed two ways to Sunday, but at least his friend could get back to her boozin' and whorin' in short order. "She saved my life at least once these last few months. Tell her I said… well. Just tell her I was glad to hear it. I'm real happy—thrilled. S'good news."

"One less thing for you to scream about. Good!"

He eyed her from beneath his brows, his beleaguered sigh ending on a grunt. "I don't want to shout, but I think I'm entitled to some upset, Cora. I'm rotting over here. None of my parts work right. My piss floats and nearly hits me in the face. I can't feel your magic no more, and that's something I've been able to do since I was dragging on my mama's tit. So pardon me if I'm having a hard time seeing your two weeks in jail warranting my slow and painful death. Don't exactly feel even."

"It was more than just the jail time, you idiot!" Cora took a deep breath, muttered, and then paced across the floor, her irritation manifesting in a violent wind that clapped the shutters against the house. The cat in the window box skittered in to hide under the bed despite the presence of a much larger feline on the mattress. A small silver rodent sailed in to land on the table, skittering across the surface and nearly plummeting to the floor. Seeing Clayton, he paused, chittered, and launched himself at Clay's trousers, climbing the folds of fabric to sprawl across Clay's knee. Clay peered at him and smiled, his finger tapping along Frederick's metal back.

"'lo, little buddy. Cora, don't get too pissed. Doc's out there with the horses. You electrocute my best friend and you've officially ruined everything I give a shit about."

She paused and swallowed hard, taking a deep breath to calm her raging temper. Her hands rested on the back of a kitchen chair, and she dropped her head, her hair obscuring her cheeks like a curly, blond veil. "Betsy wasn't supposed to do this to you. It was supposed to be something inconvenient for a while, something you'd need help reversing and have to come to me for, but she must have taken it too far. I don't know why."

"Oh, I got a pretty good idea why." Cora lifted her head, and Clay pointed at the single cat still in the room. It bristled at his attention, its tail twitching in invitation of a pat. He ignored it because fuck Cats. "You had me steal her critters."

Cora frowned. "I was saving them, not stealing from her. She had to know that."

"Did you meet the same Betsy Lynch I did? Kinda sweet but also real damn creepy? I'm not sure she understands normal. Understood. Past tense now." Clay sighed and narrowed his eyes, the pad of his finger streaking over Frederick's smooth body. If the purring was any indication, the squirrel liked it. It was weird, but he *had* been spending a lot of time with cats lately.

"If that's the reason she did this, I—" Cora groaned and dug her fists into her eyes. "—I underestimated her. I didn't think she was malicious, but I suppose… I was wrong. I know it's hard to believe, but it all made sense at the time. You'd get afflicted, come to apologize. The fairy on Marie was to watch, not to hurt. I was so upset you gave me to Sterling. I remember telling you in this very room how much I valued my freedom, that it was the most important thing to me. And then you went and handed me over to someone else without considering what that might mean to me."

Clay hadn't quite thought of it like that, though if he was being honest with himself, it didn't really matter. Even if the freedom thing had occurred to him, he would have done it the same, maybe with a dialogue beforehand to soothe her nerves. Course, he wouldn't have put it past her to hightail it out of town when he announced Sterling was on his way to arrest her.

It wouldn't have mattered. None of it mattered.

"I couldn't do it," he said. "Only reason I didn't arrest you myself was I loved you and couldn't do it. Figured if Sterling did it, you might hate him more than me for a while and we'd get past it. I guess I figured wrong."

"Very wrong. I lost a lot of respect for you after that. You had someone else do your dirty work."

He tilted his head to eye her, his expression as neutral as he could make it so *maybe* she wouldn't electrocute him. "You mean like putting Betsy Lynch on me instead of coming after me your damned self?"

"Actually, that was the whole point of it. I wanted you to see how it felt to be hurt by someone else because the love of your life… " Her voice fell off on a moan, her hands covering her face as she sank into the kitchen chair. He waited for her to speak again, but she sat there, silent, trembling and hiding, her shoulders hunched.

"Addy said you cut a bad deal for the draugr," he said after a while.

She nodded, not quite lifting her head. "I did. I was so angry at you that I… I didn't think. I was upset about the jail thing, upset that you didn't come back to fix things. Nichnevan's court is mostly made up of pixies. I haven't the foggiest idea why she sent a draugr to Marie. I should have been more specific when I made the deal, but—it's all such a mess."

"Yeah, it is. Addy said bargaining with Nichnevan's put you in a world of trouble. I hope for her sake she's wrong, but you gotta use your brain, girlie. You can't just go willy-nilly crazy 'cause you got your dander up. And in my defense, I would have loved to reconcile, but I was told you never wanted to see me again. In fact, you threatened to strike me dead if I showed my face near the jail. Figured that meant we were done. Murder is generally the end of the line for most folks," he said.

She stiffened, her jaw clenching hard enough the veins popped in her neck. "Nichnevan is my problem, not yours. I'm not going to worry about it until absolutely necessary, and for now, she's quiet. I'm quite content with that." Clay knew a Cora-flavored "mind your business" when he heard one, but he frowned at her all the same. She ignored him to keep talking because that's just what Cora of the Gales did a lot of the time.

"And you know I never would have hurt you," she said. "Well, not with lightning. The curse was different because it wasn't supposed to make a point. I wish I'd realized—well, I suppose it doesn't matter now. Betsy's dead." She winced and shifted her weight in her seat, squirming like she couldn't get comfortable.

Good. He hadn't been comfortable for three states.

Petty? Yes. Did he care? No.

Clay lifted Frederick off of his lap to put him on his shoulder. The squirrel yawned and sprawled, his paw twisting in Clay's collar and giving it a tug.

Cora watched them, a pained smile on her mouth.

"You know what's saddest?" She motioned at Frederick. "Well, besides how much he missed you. But how many years did we dance our dance before we finally got to hear our song? And then we threw it away over something stupid."

"You don't have to tell me it's stupid. I'm the one dying over stupid, and don't that make me feel special."

"Oh, Clay." She rose from her seat to kneel in front of him, her fingers interlocking with his. He considered pulling away, but the truth was, he liked the contact too damned much. There was comfort in it, in the way her warmth felt sliding over his. He almost missed the electricity, but this worked just fine for the time being. "I'll help you," she said quietly. "To get back to Marie and get cured. I know it doesn't mean much, but Betsy didn't do what I asked. This wasn't what she was hired for. I wanted something simple and stupid, but this… I'll do what I can to make it right. I know there's probably no us anymore, and that's something I'll have to live with for the rest of my life, but I'm sorry. I'm so, so sorry for everything I've done."

Clay rolled his eyes to the ceiling, his heart bobbing between chin and shoulders. He forced a smile, though, and held back his blossoming tears.

Because that's just what Clayton Jenson did a lot of the time.

CHAPTER TWENTY

THREE MONTHS AGO

Lola rolled off him to stare at the ceiling of the Rattlesnake Saloon, her cheeks flushed, her neck sporting a suck mark she'd gotten from another man. Clay lit his cigarette and closed his eyes, his hands sliding behind his head like he didn't have a care in the world. It'd been a good way to end the night—better than most lately, anyway. He'd taken up a new hobby Doc called Put a Hole in It, wherein he'd drown his memories of Cora with one of Eagle's top shelf liquors until he couldn't walk right.

The holes, Doc informed him, were what would appear in his liver in a few years if he didn't slow his drinking.

Doc never let him have any fun. Good thing she wasn't here tonight or she'd have sent all the whores to church. Clay's pecker had needed a little exercise. Any more abstinence and it would have walked off and attached itself to another gentleman.

"Sainted Mary in heaven, that was amazing," Lola rasped, her hands sliding over the curves of her breasts. Clay thought that was real enticing for a moment, but then he realized it was so she could pick up each of those bodice-fillers and wipe the sweat out from underneath. That was a fair bit less attractive.

"I told ya."

"You did. And I guess that means you get your dollar back."

They'd made a friendly bet downstairs that if Clay could make Lola come twice, she'd refund his money. She was good on her word, rolling over to the bedside table to stuff the bill back into his pants pocket. It was sort of ironic, really, because everything he'd done to Lola another whore'd taught him years ago, a gal down in Atlanta named Bridget. He'd been the typical seventeen-year-old sticking himself in anything that moved, Bridget included, until she told him that he was plenty good on the eyes but an absolute wreck in the sack.

It'd cost him almost ten dollars to spend the weekend with her, but by the time he'd left Bridget's perfumed embrace, he was an educated man. No lady fold was left unstimulated. No bits, buds, or otherwise escaped his attentions.

Clay finished his smoke and got dressed so Lola could get back to doing what she did best, which was working an ass divot into her mattress. Clay was a little drunk, but if he went downstairs and sat at the card table another hour, he could get very drunk, and he liked very drunk. Very drunk was good. Very drunk meant dreamless sleep and no worries about the woman he left in Little Rock. Or, more accurately, the woman who'd kicked his ass aside in Little Rock.

Fucking Cora.

"You can stay if you want," Lola said, making her way to the basin to wash herself. Clay tried not to watch how she hauled her foot up against the wall near her head and scrubbed herself clean with no thought for dignity or privacy or—damn, she was flexible. That was impressive. There was a contortionist in Atlanta who could do that, too. Who'd a thought he'd find it in Houston someplace besides a circus tent?

"Nah. Got a little more gamblin' to do. 'Sides, you had some fellas downstairs looking to ride. Don't want to interrupt the flow of commerce," he said. He rebuttoned his vest and replaced the Stetson, leaning over to let her kiss him on the cheek when she stood on her tiptoes.

"Any time you want to wager, I'll wager with you."

"I'm a lucky man." When she wasn't looking, he plucked the refunded dollar from his pocket and added two more, slipping them beneath her pillow and ambling for the stairs. He passed the Rattlesnake's resident madam, Delilah, on the way. She sat near the stairs reading a Bible, which seemed odd until you considered the Jesus and Mary Magdalene business. In his experience, whores were a good-hearted lot. Some did it 'cause they enjoyed the work, but others weren't so lucky. Some of 'em were sold into it. Some of 'em were abandoned by their men and had to support themselves and their kids the only way they knew how. When that kind weren't turning tricks, they turned to the Lord because the Lord said He loved them no matter who they took to their beds.

Delilah grinned at him over her well-worn copy of the Good Book. "Finally got you into one of my girls, Marshal. I think I'm proud of Lola."

"Don't be. She made a bet with me that if she liked it, I didn't have to pay."

"And did you pay?"

"Won the wager, if that's what you're asking. Left her a tip either way. It's just polite." She cackled, and he tilted his hat to her, his hand on the railing so he didn't fall down the stairs. Maybe he'd had more whiskey than he'd given himself credit for. His legs were rubbery and the room tilted in that pleasant, too-many-drinks way. A poke usually helped clear the buzz because—as he explained to Doc once—"You shoot all the drunk right into the gal, I swear."

But even post-coitus, his head felt fuzzy.

That could mean only one thing.

More whiskey.

Clay made his way to what had become his stool over the last month and settled down. Eagle was hauling beer at the other end of the bar but abandoned his customer to deliver a fresh bottle and a glass to Clay. Clay grunted his appreciation. They had a good thing, he and Little Eagle, and though Clay would have to return to that whole marshaling business sooner or later, he had a home away from home here with the Native gentleman and his limited selection of alcohol.

Clay'd just poured himself a fresh one when the swinging doors squealed open behind him. Irene fluttered into the room, her icy blue dress with pink accents reminding him of a garish butterfly. The tall, silvery sticks wedged into her blond wig even resembled antennae. She held a fan over her face, as much to play lady-coy as it was to protect herself from would-be critics, and drifted to Clay's side.

"This arrived at the inn," she said, shoving an envelope with Clay's name scrawled across the front into his hand. "A special delivery, so I thought you'd want to open it."

Clay eyed her and then the envelope, not recognizing the terrible penmanship. Some of the letters were backwards, and Marshal was spelled wrong, making him think it must have come from a kid. Only kid he knew well enough to write him was his sister Elise, and she wrote a damn sight better than this. Hell, she used words Clay didn't even know. She was eleven and she dropped "abhorrent" on him in their last correspondence. It made him proud and worried at the same time. What if his sister was already smarter'n him?

That'd be just like a woman.

He ran his thumb under the envelope flap to pull out the thick, costly stationary. It was good quality, something he normally saw coming from the government, yet the note was distinctly *less* professional than anything hailing from Washington.

Marshell -

I wood like very much if you visited me tomorrah. My sisters are away four the week and I coud use your assistence with a privut matter.

Yours,

Besty Lynch

"Special delivery, huh?" Clay said, showing Irene the note.

"Yes, it came in when a raven flew—" Doc paused as she skimmed the note. Her brow furrowed, and she tapped her lower lip with her fan. "—a raven flew in through the front door. The innkeeper gave it to me to pass along. This makes no sense. Maybell doesn't leave Betsy behind. She takes extra care, as you know."

"Suppose that means I oughta go then, if Maybell's outta town. Betsy mighta done something dumb." Clay eyed his drink and frowned. If he had to travel tomorrow, he probably shouldn't ride hungover, especially not if he had to deal with Betsy. She was nice-ish, but Clay'd had enough exposure to her to say there was no bell in that church's particular steeple. He needed to be functional to handle her flavor of not right.

"I hate goin' out there," he grumbled.

"I know, but the Lynches adore you so."

"Suppose."

After that initial tea-and-sandwich luncheon, there'd been numerous visits to the ranch, the cat kidnapping never mentioned again by either party, thank Christ. Clay would have rather slept or worked or waxed off his butt whiskers than go, but Cora insisted he accompany her on account of her blossoming friendship with Maybell. Her reasoning was that if she was invested in something or someone, he ought to be, too. He didn't care for the philosophy, especially since it didn't cut both ways. If he tried to get Cora to gamble, she'd tell him to piss in his hat, for example. But he went along anyway. The Lynches were well-connected in the weird community, and for all that their lady blather bored him to tears, whenever he had a question about a monster, they were always willing to help.

The thing with Betsy was that she could go an entire day being sweet and friendly, but inevitably, she'd let some comment slip that was just plain awful. Everyone would stare, and Clay'd wish he was anywhere other than in her presence. That's why he spent much of his time at the Lynch ranch avoiding her; he always expected her to go strange, and he didn't want her to go strange *on him* for stealing her test subjects. Cora told him not to worry about it so much, that Maybell had assured her in private that Betsy didn't even remember it'd happened, but Clay likened the incident to a fart that hung on the air. Everyone knew it was there, everyone breathed it in, and no one had the balls to bring it up.

Cora hadn't liked that metaphor. Said it was disgusting.

Good.

"I'd go, but she says a matter of privacy. I don't want to—hrm. I'm not sure. What do you think?" Irene glanced at him, looking worried and confused and maybe a little gassy, though that could have been the way she'd applied her lipstick, too. She sometimes drew on her face in such a way that it did strange things to her expressions. One time her eyebrows were halfway up her brow, making her look like she was in a perpetual state of shock.

"Think I'm gonna finish this drink and go to bed. Tomorrow, I'm gonna visit a creepy-ass witch because she asked me to, and don't that make me an idiot."

"Yes, but do you want me to go with you?" Irene pressed.

"Nah. S'Betsy Lynch, what's she gonna do to me?"

Irene frowned and ran her hand down the front of her gown, straightening wrinkles only she could see. "That is the question, isn't it?"

—

Doc, back in her man-form disguise with a dark ring of makeup under her eyes because she hadn't washed off her kohl before bed, joined Clay at breakfast the next day. Clay's head hurt in spite of his abbreviated drinking night, which meant his greeting consisted of a groan and another haul off his spiked juice. No point in venturing out into the middle of the desert all surly-like. A little medicinal whiskey made everything better.

"You're sure you don't want me to go? I'll ride a horse if need be," Doc said, shuddering as soon as she made the offer.

Clay stopped shoveling eggs in his face to peer at her, a half-smirk stretched across his mouth. "*You're* offering to ride? Thought you said riding was unsafe? Oh, and horses are dumb and unsanitary. You insulted Squirt with that one, you know."

"I did not insult Squirt because Squirt is too stupid to know when she's being insulted. I stand by my statement. They are unsanitary, unsafe animals. You have no idea how many arms and legs I've set because a rider was thrown when their horse spooked."

Clay stabbed a piece of sausage with his fork, savoring his last, precious swallow of spicy gristle. "Yet you're offerin' to get on one knowin' all you know. I ride because I can claim blissful ignorance of the hazards."

"No, you can't. I've educated you more than once about—"

"You stay here. I got Betsy," Clay said, interrupting before Doc could take off on another rant. "Betsy said private. I'm gonna respect that."

"You're quite certain? It's just so odd. Her being alone is odd. Her writing you is odd. I don't... not to say I anticipate trouble, but I... "

"Anticipate trouble. I get it," Clay finished for her. Doc nodded, and Clay pushed himself to his feet, his eyes drifting outside. It wasn't too hot out, though that'd change once he got to that arid patch of shit separating Houston and the Lynch ranch. If he wanted to get home before nightfall, he had to leave now. He reached into his coat and produced his flask, taking a haul of liquid lightning before fumbling for his tobacco bag. "I'll be fine. Worse comes to worse, I can shoot her."

"Clayton!"

Clay let out a guffaw as he moseyed toward the door. "I'm yanking your chain, Doc. Calm yourself and I'll see you tonight."

"Be careful!" Doc called after him. "I'll be in my lab if you need anything when you get back."

Clay saddled Squirt and set off in the opposite direction of civilization. There wasn't much to see along the way, and so he hummed awhile to keep his mind from drifting to Cora. It was difficult not to obsess over her, though; she'd been a fixture in his life for ten years. The wench had hooked him the moment he saw her, and she hadn't let go until her murder threat some weeks back. It would have been kinder if she'd just shot him in the...

Damn it. He was thinking about her again. He was supposed to be singing, not regretting following Frederick through Atlanta that hot summer day a decade ago. Of course, telling himself not to think about something only made it worse. There was a reason he drank so much. Keeping his treacherous brain from doing whatever the fuck it pleased, whenever the fuck it pleased, was a job for whiskey.

By the time he arrived at the Lynch place, he'd smoked ten cigarettes and was hoarse from shouting at cacti. He'd pretended they were Cora and found a strange satisfaction in telling them exactly how much he thought they sucked, and not in the fun way. He removed Squirt's saddle and swung it over the fence, bringing her to the nearby pond to graze. He'd rub her down before he left again, but for the time being, she'd earned herself a rest and a snack.

He approached the row of Lynch cottages, taking note of the closed doors and windows along the line. The only one open for business was Betsy's. She actually was by herself, and he likened that to Maybell leaving a toddler alone in the kitchen with matches. Sure, she was eighteen on paper, but if her mind hadn't caught up to her body, how old was she *really*?

"Betsy? It's Jenson. You around?" he called out. For all that he'd been there half a dozen times, he'd never seen the inside of Betsy's cottage. That was about to change, for better or for worse. She threw her door wide with a big, yellow grin.

"Hi, Marshal!"

She wore a brown dress, a shapeless thing that looked to be made of burlap, and beckoned him in with her thick fingers. They were stained with mud—well, he hoped that was mud or Betsy was rank on top of ugly. The shape and color reminded him of the sausages he'd eaten earlier that morning.

He really wished his mind hadn't made that connection. Sausages were delicious. Betsy Lynch's fingers, not so much.

"Come in, come in, come in," she chanted as she ducked inside. There was really no way to avoid following, and he trudged after her, wishing he was forty million other places than at the Lynch ranch alone with Betsy. His hand hesitated on the handle of the screen door. It was so dark inside he couldn't see much outside of a table covered with herb clippings, and that made him uncomfortable. He glanced over at the windows, and sure enough, they were covered by ragged swaths of cloth to keep the light at bay.

"You practicin' for the dark days?" he asked.

"No. But herbs keep better in the dark."

That sounded almost logical, and so he pulled open the door, the hinges whining for oil. The moment he stepped into her house, he felt her power—or smelled it, really. It was baked goods and spun sugar, and he glanced around to be sure she hadn't just made a pie or a cake that'd account for the cloyingly sweet odor, but there was nothing, only Betsy, and he rubbed at his nose as his eyes adjusted to the dimness.

The walls were covered in crude wooden shelves, each shelf packed with all manner of oddities. One shelf was covered entirely by tiny skulls, and he flinched to think about the hapless furry victims that'd fallen prey to Betsy's magic. Another shelf had potted plants, and another had jars of clear liquid with stuff floating in them. He peered at those awhile, but promptly looked away when he realized there were eyeballs in one and toes in another.

The ceiling also had lots of things on it that he'd rather not think about: rows upon rows of shed snake skins, pelts, tiny bird bones strung to click together like wind chimes. There was no escaping the weirdness of the place; everything was dark and glum and so very witchlike.

Except for Betsy's cookie smell, that was. That definitely wasn't witchlike. *That* was just plain bizarre.

"So where are your sisters at?" He slid his hat from his head.

Betsy motioned him at a rickety chair next to her table. He didn't want to sit, but she practically forced him into it, using her girth to herd him like a shepherd with sheep. "Gettin' Mama's ghost back. It escaped again."

She turned away from him to assemble what looked like a pair of sandwiches. The only thing worse than being inside of Betsy Lynch's cottage alone with her was eating something she'd made. What if she'd gotten a piece of dead kitten in it? Or if a piece of snake skin had fallen from the ceiling? She already had those dirt-crusted sausage fingers. Who knew what else could lurk between those two slices of crusty bread?

"Not hungry, Betsy, but thank you. And what do you mean your mama's ghost escaped?"

"Oh, it does that from time to time. Mama doesn't like being cooped." Betsy pretended she hadn't heard him and slapped a plate before him. He peered at her creation, his thoughts divided between not wanting to eat this pink and green sludge and the terrifying prospect of Eloise Lynch's restless ghost running rampant across Texas.

"They need help, do you think? I could offer my expertise. Know a thing or two about weird control."

"No. Mama does this from time to time. Maybell will get her back. Especially with Elly, Tommy, and Augustine there." Betsy settled into the chair opposite him and lifted her sandwich in salute. She bit into it, yummy groans warbling from her throat, eyes fluttering closed in delight. A gob of the hideous goop slithered down her chin to plop onto her sack-dress. "It's chopped ham and pickle. My favorite," she said.

Knowing what she was trying to feed him, he felt less terrified of it, but there was still that whole thing about her making it with those dirty hands. He wondered how he could get out of eating it and still be polite, but everything he came up with in his head sounded rude. Maybe if he took a bite or two, she'd be satisfied.

Hell, it was just a little dirt. What harm was there in that?

He picked up the sandwich and stuffed it into his mouth before he could talk himself out of it. Betsy paused to grin at him, that unright smile spreading across her plain, warty face. He ignored it to take his second bite, marveling that somehow this wasn't the worst thing he'd ever put between his lips.

"So why'd you call me out here? This is delicious by the way. Thank you," he said. He'd intended to stop eating already, but this was so tasty he couldn't see the harm in finishing it. Dirt or no, Betsy Lynch had made him a chopped ham and pickle sandwich, and he'd eat it because—

Well, he'd eat it because it turned out to be not awful.

"To make you a sandwich," she said.

He smiled at that, thinking it sweet in a vacant, Betsy-like way, but then two things happened to alter that perception. The first was that her eyes narrowed. He couldn't recall Betsy ever looking more *aware*, the childishness evaporating because she had a plan and him eating that sandwich was part of it.

The second was he found the first long hair. It was brown-colored and long, curling slightly, and he spit out his mouthful to tug the hair from between his teeth. He shuddered as it slid free. Peering into the remains of his sandwich, he spotted a whole jungle of little hairs then. They were everywhere, as much a part of it as the pickles, and for all that he'd like to pretend that it was disgusting circumstance, he knew better.

He was dealing with a witch who liked to play with curses.

The smell of cake and cookies grew strong, the whole cottage reeking like a bakery. Betsy stared at him, he stared back at her, and before he could do a thing about it, her hand snapped out and her thumb pressed into the middle of his bare forehead.

"WITHER!" she screamed, erupting into a torrent of insidious giggles. Clay reached for her forearm, managing to snag it before she pulled away, but it was too late. Something strong and ugly hit him like a brick. He felt strange all over, his body going hot and cold in short order. First he boiled alive, a fever blossoming in his head and covering him with sweat, his clothes sticking to his saturated skin like he'd been caught in a rainstorm. Then came the cold, a shiver rushing through him like he'd been thrust into a tank of ice water.

He wrenched himself from the table, the chair clattering to the floor behind him. His hands were still on Betsy's wart-ridden forearm, and he gave it a yank, half-pulling her across the table and smearing her bosom into her own sandwich. "What'd you do, Betsy?" he demanded, his heart pounding hard enough the pulse in his ears beat like a drum.

"For Miss Cora. And for me. You weren't very nice to me, but you were especially not nice to Miss Cora! You are a very bad man, Marshal Jenson! A bad, bad man."

He couldn't remember ever not being nice to Betsy. He'd kept every ugly, warty comment he'd ever thought to himself, but Cora... what did Cora have to do with anything? "What do you mean I wasn't nice to Miss Cora? That's between her and me. You got no stake in this. Now fix me."

"No, no, no, n-no!" she squawked. "She told me to give you the bad magic. I did. You have it, now. The blood curse. Bad blood, bad blood!"

Clay didn't want to believe it, but why would Betsy lie? The notion of Cora marching onto Lynch property and involving Betsy-goddamned-Lynch in their mess was nigh unfathomable, but what other possibility was there? Betsy wouldn't come up with this alone. She might have had a single moment of cunning getting him to eat the sandwich in the first place, but not a minute later she would be back to that pie-eyed creeper that made his skin crawl.

"Fix me," he repeated, shaking her.

"No. No, I won't. You need to make it up to her. To me."

"What do I need to make up to. What do you mean to you?!"

She wouldn't answer him, her guppy-mouth flattening into a mutinous line, and he pulled Gayle from her holster and pressed the twin barrels right to Betsy's forehead, giving it a little shove so she could feel the metal grinding into her flesh. Betsy whimpered before her eyebrows dropped over her eyes in a deep V.

"You'll rot, Marshal. You'll rot from the inside! Let the worms have you!"

"Fix it, Betsy."

"No!"

"I AIN'T FUNNIN'. FIX IT, BETSY," he shouted.

Come to find out, Betsy wasn't funnin' neither. He saw her free hand swing up from her side, strange light dancing over those fat, soiled fingers. He acted before he wasn't given the chance to act. He pulled the trigger. Gayle erupted in a deafening blast, and Betsy's forehead exploded apart, the close proximity sending bits of her skull sailing back to splatter the wall and table with crimson rain. The youngest Lynch was jerked from Clay's grasp, her body flying in an unnatural arc to strike the wall before it tumbled to the floorboards with a heavy, wet thud.

He'd joked about it earlier, but it was no joke now.

Clayton Jenson had shot Betsy Lynch dead.

Hell.

CHAPTER TWENTY-ONE

NOW

The matter of whether or not he should take Cora with him wasn't something he pondered overly long. Maybell Lynch was coming, a shadow on his horizon, and Cora was one more line of defense against a splattery, disemboweled end. Sure, this was all her fault, but if he focused on righting his illness, her company was a boon. It might piss off Doc, but she'd get over it eventually.

"Fine. Only concern I got is if I'll make it back to Marie. It's a longish trip, and I ain't—" He frowned, his eyes straying to the window. "—ain't thinkin' I got long. I'm fallin' apart."

"If it comes to it, I can sneak you through Fairy, though they don't like outsiders. Your fairy blood will help, but you're still human. Excuse me a minute." Cora got up to look into her bedroom, her hand thrusting the door open. "I could really use you in this discussion."

He didn't dare to glance over, instead waiting for Cora to reappear. When she came, Montague leaned into her side, his tail lashing. The cat looked at him, looked at Cora, and then it shimmered like a quaking sun. It was so bright he had to shield his face, his vision swimming once more as the tiger stretched tall, then narrowed, then turned into a beacon of white light. Orange fur became red hair, paws became hands and feet, and black stripes stretched thick and long to bloom into a black silk gown that clung to heavy, exaggerated curves.

Montague was no more. In his place stood a fat lady fairy with her hands on her ample hips. Clay grinned at Addy, Addy grinned back, and before he could prepare himself, she launched herself into his lap to hug his neck, her lips smacking against the cut of his cheekbone over and over again. "I wanted to surprise you. Thank you. Thank you so much for everything you did. You saved my life," she said.

"Weren't nothing, Addy. Don't you—seems weird that you thank me when you were the one to put your ass out there for me in the first place. I should be thanking you." Addy squeezed him tight, his face squishing in between two gigantic melon tits that smelled like cinnamon and vanilla. It was a pretty nice place to be, though the lack of oxygen quickly grew alarming. Maybe if he went slack and let it happen, he could die a happy death after all. No shame in a dying man appreciating Addy's ridiculously plush form.

"Would you please remove his face from your bosom," he heard Cora snap, though it was muffled thanks to the mountain of warm flesh beside his ears. "I understand we're estranged, but that's not an invitation for you to be so... so you-like."

"Isn't it, though? You've practically killed him." Addy pulled away so she could wink down at him, her hands braced against his shoulders. "I'd say he's fair game now. In fact, if I wanted to take him into the other room and have him two ways to Sunday, there's really nothing you could do about it," she said. He had the feeling she wasn't serious, especially since he couldn't walk, never mind properly bounce a mattress, but she was making a point to her sister. It was salt in the wound.

On one hand, he probably shouldn't encourage her.

On the other, Cora'd been an asshole.

"I get it, Adelaide. I've made my apologies," Cora snapped.

Addy rolled her eyes. "Oh, because that's sufficient. I'm sure 'I'm sorry' rights all the wrongs. Don't be an idiot, Cora." She leaned in to press another kiss to his forehead. "You know, I thought tricking you with glamour for the first time would be fun, but it doesn't count when you have one foot in the grave."

"Guess that means you'll have to try again if I get better," he said.

"*When* you get better, and yes, it does."

"You sound like Sterling. Son of a bitch won't let me die proper."

"Smart man, that Sterling. I ought to give him a little sugar next time I see him," she said.

Cora groaned and sank back into her chair, her arms stretching out over the table before her. Clay expected her to contribute something to the banter, but she was lost to her own thoughts, her expression a combination of misery and concentration. Seeing her so despondent, Frederick peered at Clayton as if asking permission to go to her, and Clay flitted his fingers in dismissal. The squirrel tore down his pants leg to climb Cora's gown, sprawling on his back in the nook of her elbow. Cora petted him, but there was no heart to it.

"Where's my friend Montague?" Clay asked. "And why didn't you tell her I was sick? Seems like the sort of thing you oughta mention."

"Montague's with a friend. After his last venture into Fairy, he refuses to go back through the portal, which I think is the reason Cora outed me just now. To explain about Fairy." Addy paused to cast a glare at her sister's slumped shoulders. "No one hurt him, but it's chaos in there. It makes no sense, and it's not terribly kind to a simple cat mind. Humans don't fare much better. Fairy can pluck your dreams and nightmares from your head and make them real at a whim. I'd avoid it in your condition. There are too many things there that would toy with you for no other reason than they can.

"As for the second question—" She paused and glanced at her sister's back. "—words are easy. She had to see what she'd done with her own eyes. There are some things that shouldn't have their impact diminished. Because nearly killing both your sister and lover in a matter of months because you're cocked off isn't all that forgivable."

Cora sighed from the table, clearly not pleased with the explanation, but Clay didn't give a damn about her tender feelings. Addy had the right to be a bitch. An honest bitch, but a bitch all the same. "Makes sense," Clay said. "Let's hope traveling by Fairy's not the only way to get me to N'Orleans before I expire. Don't reckon I'd much like having pudding brain 'cause of the weirds."

"No, you wouldn't. And on that note, when do we want to leave? Today? Tomorrow?"

"Tomorrow, if there's still reason to go," Cora whispered. She glanced at the front door right as the wind kicked up. The tree branches rustled outside and the lace drapes twisted around themselves. Cora shriveled in on herself, a grape gone to raisin, her arms wrapping around her middle to hold herself tight. "The wind says she's near. She must have followed you, Clayton. I wish we had more time, but we don't. I hope she's—maybe she'll listen to me. This is my fault. I'll take the brunt of it."

He didn't have to ask who "she" was. Addy groaned, and Cora stood from the table, resigned. Clay tried to push himself to his feet but promptly lost his balance and slumped back into the chair.

He swallowed past the panic in his throat and growled, his eyes closing so he didn't have to watch the world tilt around him. "Ain't all your fault, Cora. Mostly, but not all. I killed a whole bunch of Lynch gals between then and now, and I'm bettin' that's what's got her most riled. Get Doc in here and get the horses behind the house in case she comes in blazin'. Not their fault Maybell wants blood."

He could hear the sisters walking by, their dresses swishing as they readied themselves for the approaching danger. When he was fairly sure he could see without the inside of the cottage spiraling, he cracked an eye. Addy braced by the window, watchful. Cora stooped over her tinkering table. He didn't know what she was up to, but he wasn't given long to think about it. There was a scream from outside followed by the front door being thrust wide. Doc stood in the doorway, a frantic expression on her face. Well, Clay had to assume that was frantic, but he couldn't be sure because Doc was only half-done putting on her makeup, which skewed her expression. One eyebrow was drawn on; the other was not. Her powder was set, but her lips were not, nor were her cheeks. There also wasn't a wig yet, so her real hair was slicked back awaiting an ornate coif that remained in a box.

"There's something in the woods that's buzzing. Many things buzzing," she announced before turning her attention to the fae sisters. "Hello, Cora. Hello, Addy. Glad to see you're not expired."

Cora nodded at her. Addy winked, the she-devil.

"You sure it ain't just a bee?" Clay demanded.

"Do you think I'd run inside for a single bloody bee?"

Clay blinked at her.

"Shut up, Clayton."

"Didn't say a word."

"You don't need to!" Doc slammed the door behind her and raced for the windows to latch the shutters, her fingers trembling while she played with the hooks. "Yes, all right, I would, but this is... can't you hear that?"

Now that Doc had said something, Clay could hear a strange sound, like a chorus of voices all humming a single note at the same time. It came closer and closer, increasing in volume, and Clay sat up straight, cocking his head to listen. There was a hard smack against the cottage side a moment later followed by another and then another. Each one reminded him of popcorn inside of a kettle—*Pop! Pop! Pop!*—until too many came at once, the stone cottage getting bombarded by whatever strangeness Maybell sent their way.

Cora tilted her head back and muttered. Doc dove for cover under the kitchen table, taking refuge with Frederick and the cats. Addy positioned herself in front of Clay in case the onslaught broke through the doors and shutters. Clay could see the wood bowing as something pushed on it from outside, the pressure making it quake on its hinges. Cora lifted her hands, palms turning to the sky, and a moment later there was a crack of thunder outside followed by the howl of vicious wind. Rain sloughed onto the roof. Tree branches snapped as a furious storm rolled in at Cora's behest. Soon, the tumultuous weather was louder than the buzzing. Soon, the door and shutters stilled, Cora's lightning and wind overcoming Maybell's thrumming harbingers.

Cora let her magic go. The rain diminished to a steady drizzle, the wind dying to a soft, summer breeze. Clay's immediate concern was for the poor horses left outside. Those pack nags had been with him for months, and they deserved better than to die to Maybell and Cora's dueling magics.

"You kill my horses?"

"No. I kept them in a pocket of air so they were spared," she said. "They'd thank you, but as Doc said, horses are stupid. Would walk right into a glue factory, so you'll have to take it from me." She blinked at him, incredulous that he'd jest even now, but he just shrugged. If he didn't have his humor, he had nothing left. They could pry his shitty jokes from his cold, dead fingers.

Addy was the first to approach the window. She worked the fastenings and then had to shove with both of her hands to get a single shutter open. The reason for the resistance became plain when a wet plop of insect bodies tumbled in to land on the floor by her feet. It wasn't just bees, but butterflies, flies, and locusts, too, the wad of bugs all dead thanks to Cora's storm. Addy looked out at the yard, and Clay followed her gaze. The once-green grass was hidden beneath a thick, crusty layer of felled insects that extended as far back as the stone path in the woods. It was a segmented, carapace-covered blanket as black as an evening sky and easily two feet deep.

"Oh, that's gross," Addy said, snagging the shovel from the fireplace to scoop the carcasses from the floor. She flung them outside, shuddering all the while. Doc let out a shrill whistle that spoke of untold traumas, and Clay suspected the good doctor would never again travel beyond a city line. The countryside was full of too many things that'd haunt the nature-phobe to her dying day.

To be fair, the visual would stick with Clay a long while, too. It was high on his list of disgusting shit, and he'd seen some things in his time.

"Someone's coming," Addy said, leaning out the window to take a better look. "Must be her."

Cora slipped her bare feet into a pair of worn leather boots and made her way to the door. It wouldn't open with her weight pushing alone, so Addy stepped in beside her, the two of them shoving against the resistance of piled-high bug bodies. When they'd made a crack a foot and a half wide—big enough for Cora, but a tight squeeze for Addy—Cora motioned over her shoulder at her bedroom, her expression grave.

"Doc, take him away from the windows and door. I'm going to try to—"

"No," Clay said. "I ain't being hidden away."

"Clayton."

"Nope, ain't gonna do it. She's pissed at me for killing her sisters. I'll take my lumps."

"And you wouldn't have killed the sisters if I hadn't sicced Betsy on you in the first place. So let me do what I have to do and—"

"Nope."

They glared at each other until Addy hip-checked her sister out the front door. Cora was forced into the bugs, the hard insect shells crunching beneath her feet. "You two can argue later," Addy said.

"When there's not a homicidal witch in the front yard. Clay, you can't handle a flat floor never mind this mess out here, so prop up by the window if you must, but stay inside."

She was right, and he hated it. He hated, too, the idea of Cora and Addy going out there in his stead, but what purpose would he serve if he followed them? He had no gun, and he couldn't run. He'd be a lump of useless meat—just one more thing for them to have to worry about. More and more he was feeling like a burden. Where once he was a skilled, capable man, now he was a drain—a drain and a danger to everyone he cared about. Maybe the right thing to do would be to go out and hand himself over to Maybell. It had to be better than risking their lives again.

"Stop that," Doc said, interrupting his thoughts.

"Eh?"

"Thinking that way."

"Thinkin' what way?"

"You know exactly what I'm talking about. Stop being obtuse." Doc crawled out from under the table to offer a shoulder. Clay accepted, his arm looping around his friend's neck so he could sag into her side. Doc guided him across the room, taking small steps so Clay wouldn't lose his footing. Clay felt a little stronger since he'd rested his legs in Cora's chair, but it wasn't enough.

Nothing he could do was enough.

"I'm sure I ain't got the faintest idea what you're talkin' about," Clay said.

"No, of course not. You were not at all thinking about walking out there and handing yourself over. There are a few things I think we can both agree on at this late stage of our friendship, Clayton. One is that you are a better shot than I am. You're also better looking and more charming, though I have no idea how and why on the last as I think you're a brute, but women seem to love you." Doc paused to grab the chair by the table, kicking it hard enough it skidded the rest of the way to the window. "However, I think it is safe to say I am smarter than you, and I always will be. We're helping whether you like it or not. Now stop being such a bloody martyr or I'll drug you, and you can spend the next three or four hours drooling into a pillow."

Doc's voice was flinty enough that Clay knew she meant every damned word. H he sank down into his seat with his teeth clenched on the sides of his tongue. "Fine! Fine," he growled, rubbing his eyes until he could see straight. He blinked to clear the last of the blurriness and looked out the window. Maybell stood at the edge of the property, her hands gripping a tall, oak walking stick. She'd dressed in black—likely a sign of her mourning—and her hair was tied up into a tight bun that made her look older than she really was. She'd always been a severe woman, but she looked twice so now, her grief evident in the stiff set of her shoulders and the tilt of her chin.

"I forgot you could do that with the weather. Had I remembered, I wouldn't have wasted so many insects," Maybell said in greeting.

Cora forced a smile, her toe kicking out to send bug carcasses flying. "Everything about this trip is a waste. I'm not going to stand by and allow you to take him, but I think you knew that."

"No, I didn't, as I thought you wanted him dead. But it changes nothing. He's coming with me whether or not you allow it." There was no inflection to Maybell's voice, like her words came from a very cold, hollow place. Clay dug his fingers into the window sill, his heart beating fast. Cora shouldn't be out there with her. She was good with her air, but Maybell was good with everything, which put Cora at a disadvantage. A specialized magic versus a universally capable one wouldn't fare well. At least Cora had her fairy resilience, but Maybell was crafty enough to know the iron trick. She'd know the fairy weak spot.

Cora's hands dropped to her sides, and she shook her head. "No. Your problem is with me. I sent Betsy after him. He defended himself. And I think you and your sisters can take credit for the rest of your troubles. If you'd left well enough alone, there would have only been the one loss, but instead you kept going. At what point is revenge no longer worth it?"

Hearing that, Maybell's jaw clenched, an angry tic starting along her cheek and extending down to her throat and neck, corded veins appearing where there had been smooth skin before. "You don't know what it's like to lose everything. Your entire family. My mother, my sisters. I have nothing left but my revenge."

Cora took a deep breath before she spoke, her voice so quiet Clay had to lean forward to hear her. "You're wrong. I do know what it's like. Revenge is anger, and I can tell you from firsthand experience acting out of anger hurts everyone. Betsy died because I lost my temper. Your other sisters died when they sought retribution. My sister suffered in ways I can't. I owe her. I will always owe her a debt for that. And Clayton is the only man I've ever loved, and he's disintegrating before my eyes. All because of revenge. Don't do this, Maybell. Please, be better than me."

Clay swallowed a groan. It was everything he ever wanted to hear from Cora's mouth, and as per her usual pain-in-the-ass nature, she had to go and say it at the worst possible time. Why did it take near-tragedy for her to understand how every rock thrown into a pond creates ripples, and those ripples needed to be considered beforehand, not when the world went to Hell? The idea of her finally coming around to his way of thinking only long enough for him to die was cruel. Unfair and cruel, and it made him so mad he didn't know what to do.

But for every bit of anger he had, for every bit of annoyance and aggravation she'd caused him over the last few months, there was one thing he knew for sure—that impossible, stubborn woman was the only thing he ever wanted in his life. She was the only thing that made him happy even when she made him miserable. He'd rather die fighting with her than holding someone else's hand.

Hell.

He shook his head and peered out at the women in the yard. Maybell and Cora continued to stare at one another, both of them miserable and contemplative and unsure of what to do. They'd been friends once, but that was over. Clay didn't know how to contribute without making it worse, so he said nothing at all, which was when Doc took it upon herself to step outside. She approached Addy's side to take her hand, squeezing her fingers in a gesture of comfort.

"Doctor," Maybell said in empty greeting.

"Maybell. If I may speak with candor?" She said nothing, which Doc must have taken to mean consent because she continued with little hesitation. "I've traveled with Clayton these months, and I will swear on anything you or I hold dear that he never instigated with your sisters. They brought the violence to him. In one instance, Clayton could have harmed Augustine, but he dropped his weapon and told her to go home. When he turned his back, she thrashed him to ribbons. Those are scars he will always carry, whether or not Betsy's curse finishes him, and there is a very real possibility it will.

"I would not stand here and plead for what remains of Clayton's life if I didn't believe he deserved it. I would have much preferred to stay out of this altogether considering our association, but I can't. I couldn't when I saw Elmira attack not only Clayton but Adelaide, too. This situation is out of hand. As a woman who stands to lose two very dear friends, I beg of you. Go home. Please."

For a minute, Clay thought Doc's pretty words had resonated. Maybell dropped her head, her tears sparkling in tracks down her cheeks. She looked damn near tragic, like the weight of her losses would crush those broad shoulders. But then she shook it off and stood straighter, her face lifting to regard first Doc and then the fairies. Finally, her gaze drifted to the window, and seeing Clay there, she frowned. "I didn't agree with going after the marshal. I told them not to go, that we were at fault for leaving Betsy alone at the ranch that day, but Elmira didn't listen. And then the twins didn't listen.

Regardless of the circumstances, that man has buried four of my sisters. I have no family anymore, so what is left for me? To live in the desert by myself? To remember my sisters every day while I stare at their empty houses? They're all I ever had. I do understand, Doctor Miller, but I can't..."

She never finished her sentence. Her hand jerked up, and she closed her fingers like she was choking an invisible neck. Doc flew from the ground to sail Maybell's way, colliding with her chest in the most violent embrace Clay'd ever seen. Doc was forcibly spun so her back was to Maybell's front, Maybell's fingers jabbing into the tender flesh beneath Doc's jaw. Doc let out a terrified squeal and Clay shot to his feet, his hand going for a gun that wasn't on his hip. Worse, he couldn't even stay upright without clutching the windowsill, his legs quivering like jelly.

He wanted to kick and spit in his frustration, but he couldn't. Maybell had Doc, and Doc shouldn't suffer for Clay and Cora's sins. "Let her go, Maybell," he called "It's me you want. And killing me won't bring your gals back, but maybe it'll give you peace or whatever the shit you're looking for."

"I don't take her to harm her. I take her as insurance. If lightning strikes me, lightning strikes Irene," she said. Her eyes fixed on him, but her words were for Cora.

"No need for any of this. This is stupid. Addy, come help me out," Clay called. "I'm dead anyway. Ain't nothing she's gonna do that's not gonna happen soon here anyway."

Addy came as he asked, but as soon as she guided him away from the window and behind a stone wall, she flared bright and transformed. It was Gemma Sanderson's place all over again because she'd taken his countenance for her own, and damn if he wasn't ugly as sin. She'd copied everything from the skeletal angles of his face and his long, chicken neck to his too-big clothes and scraggly beard. His hair even looked greasy, which was a sight embarrassing, but nothing he could do about it now.

The only difference between the two of them was the presence of Gayle on Addy's hip. For some reason, she'd added that, which made him wistful for the weight of a weapon he couldn't actually lift.

"You can't do this, Addy," he whispered. "You done enough for me already. I won't have you dying on me again."

"Listen to me. There is nothing she can do to me that'll hurt me outside of iron, and even then there's a fairy ring beneath the bugs. The mushrooms. I can offer a distraction, but only for so long. Can you shoot at all?"

"Not well. I'm all blind and shit."

"Your 'not well' is still better than other people. Just a moment." She left him clinging to the wall while she approached Cora's workbench. She rooted through a pink purse covered in shiny beads, pulling out cosmetics and brushes and various pieces of jewelry. His eyes skipped to the rest of the table, and he immediately spotted the bane of his existence. Gleaming silver and looking pointy and hateful was the flying parasol. He wished it'd gone over the cliff with the kid in Little Rock, but no, somehow Cora'd gotten it back after her incarceration. It laid there taunting him, letting him know that he might go outside and get blown to pieces, but it'd prevail anyway, the rude thing.

He wanted to throw it against the wall. He probably couldn't because he could barely walk, but thinking about it made him feel better.

"Here," Addy said, shoving a two-shooter into his hand. It was tiny, no bigger than his palm, but it had bullets inside it, and that's what was important. "Do what you can," she said, and before he could grab the sleeve of her shirt and hold her back, she staggered toward the door and threw it open, doing her best impression of his sick walk.

"I'm here," she said in his voice. "Now let Doc go."

Clay couldn't see Maybell, but he heard her snort with derision.

"I want to see both of you. I'm not a fool."

Clay had to go outside. The problem was getting there and staying upright. He looked around for something he could cling to—something sturdy and yet not too big that'd act as a proper walking stick. There was nothing. Well, almost nothing. There was that stupid goddamned parasol. It was collapsed now, its blades tethered to its body with a metal wire that hooked on a latch. It was as light as he remembered when he pulled it from the table, the tin hammered to thin, flat sheets. In spite of that, it was sturdy. He could easily rest his weight on it.

He tottered to the door and took a deep breath, easing his thin body through the crack so he could stand behind his friends. Maybell peered at all of them, her eyes narrowed, her mouth pinching into an Elmira-type frown. It was one of the few times he could see the resemblance between the gorgeous sister and the pointy-faced one.

"Cute, Fairy. I don't want to play games. Give me what I came for and I'll leave."

Cora glanced behind her and to her side, looking confused and then irritated in turn. She glowered at both versions of him before shooing them back toward the house. "I told you to stay inside."

"Nope," both of them said in tandem.

"Stop that!"

"Nope," they said again. Clay shared a grin with Addy, and they winked at one another. Cora groaned and spun around, lifting her hand to do… Clay wasn't sure what. Instigate, get this over with—it didn't matter. She went after Maybell. She wouldn't use lightning, not with Doc crammed up against Maybell's body, but she called her magic all the same. She never got the chance to cast anything. From the ground by her feet, thick, long roots jerked up through the bug bodies to wind around her ankles and wrists, wrenching her off the ground and whipping her back and forth like a flag.

Everyone shouted at once, both Addy and Clay reaching for Cora's hands, but she was lifted too high, at least seven or eight feet in the air. Clay couldn't exactly jump up to grab her without falling flat on his face in a carpet of bugs. He would for Cora—he'd eat every bug here if it'd save her—but the more pressing concern there was that he'd be prone in front of Maybell Lynch. It wasn't the best idea given the ultimate purpose of her visit.

Clay turned to glower at Maybell right as Addy ripped her version of Gayle from her hip and pulled the trigger. It boomed out a fake bullet, and Maybell ducked, dragging Doc down onto the ground with her. Doc went deadweight, forcing Maybell's fingernails up into her chin and cutting her, but that didn't stop her from flailing her elbows back and striking Maybell in the shin. It loosed the witch's grip enough that Irene could fall forward onto her hands and knees, her foot striking out to bash into Maybell's knee again and again.

Addy ran to the left, wading through the sea of insects to lift the gun, readying another shot. Maybell was torn between regaining her hold on Doc and flinching from Addy. When Addy fired a second bullet, Maybell let Doc go to create a magical shield that curved around the front of her body, as tall as her bun and as wide as her elbows. It shimmered pale blue, like she'd ironed a sapphire flat for protection. It caught no bullet because there was no bullet, but she hadn't registered that as odd yet—she must have assumed the shot went wide. A part of Clay was offended by that; Clayton's reputation for sharpshooting was something he prided himself on. Didn't she know he'd never miss?

Which promptly reminded him of the gun he did carry. It wasn't much to look at, and the bullets were small, but shot somewhere vital they'd do a fine job of getting Maybell dead. The problem was even when Maybell lifted her hand to cast another spell, sending a giant felled branch Addy's way that Addy dived to avoid, the shield never disintegrated. She wasn't a one-spell-at-a-time kind of witch. She could cast multiples at the same time, somehow maintaining the roots around Cora, her defenses, and tossing tree limbs all without breaking a sweat.

It was a testament to her skill. And her scariness.

Clay knew he couldn't shoot her from the front without that shield up, and getting behind her with all those bugs would be a problem. He wasn't sure what to do until Frederick gave him an accidental idea. The little squirrel was climbing the roots to get to Cora, stopping every few feet to nibble on the flora, but when one particularly hard thrash flung him off, he sailed toward Clay, his arms extending so those flaps of leather beneath his arms would carry him on the wind. He landed on Clay's shirt and used the fabric to tug himself up, perching on Clay's shoulder like he'd been there all along.

Flying. He'd *flown*.

If Clay could get over Maybell, there'd be no shield.

Clay loathed Cora's flying machine more than anything in the world. It was easier to blame the device than it was its maker for what had happened in Little Rock, but that didn't mean the confounded thing couldn't serve a purpose now. It'd done enough harm, and maybe it was time for it to do some good in the world. Clay lifted the parasol and unlatched the wire around it, letting those long, bladed cleavers loose.

"Cora, gal. Can you hear me?" he shouted. She looked at him, groaning as the roots twisted her around. He motioned at the parasol, not wanting to call any more attention to himself than necessary. Maybell was busy advancing on the other Clayton, flinging projectiles, which as far as Clay could tell, hadn't hit yet, but he couldn't find Addy to determine one way or the other. Either way, that fight provided him a small window of opportunity to shoot if Cora could get him off the ground. Addy hadn't given him the derringer for nothing.

It took Cora a few seconds to get her wind flowing, but trying to work while a bunch of roots shook her probably wasn't easy. The blades above him whirred around, circling so fast that the contraption vibrated. He reached up with both his hands to cling to the hooked umbrella bottom, hoping his arms were strong enough to support him for the few seconds it'd take to get him aloft. The air stirred, some of the dead bugs whipping up to smack him in the thighs as his feet left the ground. Oh, he didn't like it, not even one bit. The first few feet weren't too terrible. It was the fifth, sixth, and seventh feet that worried him, his arms extended over his head, fingers clasping frantically to the curved handle. He wasn't sure if he wanted to piss himself or puke. Little bit of both, probably, especially when he felt his palms go sweaty and that tiny gun shift between his fingers just enough that he thought he'd drop it. His arms started to tingle, too, which meant he wasn't going to last up there for very long. He was weak, and weak men couldn't hold their own weight long.

He nearly fell when Cora jolted the flying machine in Maybell's direction. He'd hoped he'd be able to sneak up on the witch, maybe fly right above her with the umbrella and shoot down at her, but she jerked up her head right as he got positioned. He watched her jaw clench and her hand lift in his direction to cast some horrible spell or another, but Clay decided to surprise her. He let the umbrella go and dropped, trying to angle his body at hers so when they collided, both of them would end up in the bugs.

He landed mostly on her, his weight pushing her face forward while he sailed backward, his legs straddling her hips like she'd become a pony. The only good thing about having so many bugs in the yard was they acted as a strange sort of mattress, cushioning his fall and preventing him from shattering upon contact. It wasn't comfortable, and Maybell certainly wasn't comfortable with the whole face-in-bugs thing, but that was negligible next to the damage the fall could have done to both of them. The only real problem Clay had to contend with was the vertigo. The hard impact made his head snap back, and for it, he felt like he'd walked into the middle of a tornado, the whirlwind making his temples throb and his stomach drop to his knees. That liquid inkiness crept along his vision and sloshed, rising and sinking back down like a black tide.

He groaned and narrowed his eyes to a slit. He could see Maybell struggling for purchase in front of him, her arms and legs flailing to grab something solid so she could turn around and murder him proper. When she thrashed hard enough that she damn near knocked him in the giblets, he scampered away from her, nearly losing the little gun in the process. He caught it before it could slip away, though, carefully cradling it to his chest while he waited for his window to shoot.

And he really wished that opportunity was now, because Maybell was upright picking bugs from her hair and screaming. A moment later, she was throwing herself at him.

He couldn't see right, and with only two bullets, there was only so much chance he was willing to take, but even when she landed on top of him, he didn't dare take the shot. He didn't know if she had that shield up to protect her front. He was also afraid that once she saw the gun, she'd do something that'd prevent him from shooting it, like turning it into a tuna. And really, tuna was delicious, but it wasn't a proper killing weapon.

She snarled before reaching for his throat. He wriggled beneath her, keeping the gun tucked in close as her fingers manacled his neck. He thought she was going for some good old fashioned choking, which wasn't all that pleasant, but at least it wasn't a poisonous enema. Then her hands went frigid. This wasn't no normal cold neither; it was bone-shattering cold, and he felt a sheen of magical ice sprouting from her fingertips to crawl over his beard. It traveled to his mouth and forced itself between his lips, the ice spreading over his tongue, over the insides of his cheeks to coat his teeth.

It was an unusual agony, one that made him breathe heavy and thrash in desperation. He lifted his arms to shove at her, still holding tight to that gun and waiting, but how much longer could he go on that way? How long before that ice blocked off his throat and nose? He whimpered and kicked up at her, but Maybell pressed down, shoving him harder into the nest of bugs. He bucked, and she forced that ice toward his windpipe and tickled his gag reflex.

He lifted the derringer and shoved it into Maybell's side, angling it in such a way that he could stun her if not outright kill her with one shot. She ignored it, pressing her magic upon him and making him see stars. He wedged the little gun as deep into her guts as it could go and pulled the trigger. There was a muffled bang followed by the smell of a fired weapon… and that was it. Maybell kept pushing her advantage. The shield must have still been there, swallowing the bullet to protect her. More ice slithered down his throat, a frigid serpent intent on stealing his last breath. The blackness in his vision rose, but this time it had nothing to do with the curse. She was suffocating him. His lungs burned, his eyes stung, and the gun dropped into the insects surrounding them as his fingers dug into Maybell's dress.

Is this it?

Am I done?

Is it all just cold and blackness and then you're snuffed out like a candle flame?

Oh, Cora.

"DOWN, CLAYTON. Keep your head down!"

Doc's voice, loud and horrid and wonderful all at the same time. Clay didn't know what was happening until he saw Doc walk up behind Maybell with a shining, whirring silver thing in her hand. Recognizing the parasol, Clay's eyes grew big. He had no idea what Doc planned to do with it at first, but Doc's intent became gruesomely clear when she brought it up over her head only to bring it down on Maybell's back a second later. The device's metal may have been thin and pliable, but those blades were sharp, and at the speed they traveled, Doc wielded a weapon of utter destruction.

The first splatter of Maybell's blood hit Clay bald in the face. After the second gob of viscera landed on his cheek, he brought his hands up to protect himself best he could, trying not to think too much about the horrid thing happening just above him. Maybell never got the chance to scream. Doc's first swipe dug into her back and severed her spinal cord. The second and third shredded her flesh and sliced her organs, tearing pieces of her away in a wash of blood and gore.

Maybell Lynch was dead within seconds. It was messy, yes, but there was a brutal efficiency to it that bordered on kindness, too.

Maybell went slack above him. The ice receded from his windpipe, the aftereffects leaving him numb and short for breath. A few gulps of precious oxygen later, Clay dared to open his eyes. The witch's face hovered above his, her eyes closed and her mouth tilted in a strange, final smile. From where Doc stood, Clay was sure it was a different, sloppier story, but from underneath, she looked like she was at peace. It was over for her, even if it wasn't over for him.

He understood then that Maybell hadn't really come to the Mississippi woods to kill him. Sure, that might have been an added bonus, but this trek had been less about murder and more about suicide. Maybell Lynch would have rather died than to live without the people she loved.

And that made a whole hell of a lot more sense to him than he ever wanted to admit.

CHAPTER TWENTY-TWO

LATER

The smell of lilacs woke him from his dream. There was the feeling of lace gliding over his bare chest, followed by exaggerated wipes of a damp cloth. He remembered a scene like this from long ago, after the bogey had burned his skin raw at the auction house. Back then, he'd assumed it had been a repentant Cora doctoring him after he'd nearly died. Now, he knew better, and he smiled despite the dull ache in his head.

"'lo Irene."

"Oh, good. You're awake. Marie's been asking about you incessantly. I assured her you were too stubborn to die. I'm glad I wasn't wrong in that," Doc said.

Marie's. So they had made it to N'Orleans, though he didn't remember the travel. The last thing he could recall was the aftermath of Maybell's death. Cora'd dropped from her vines, Addy'd risen from the bugs with a dance of disgust, and Doc had pulled Maybell off Clay to help him to his feet. Cora'd brought the wind to clear away the insects, they'd burned Maybell's body, and Clay had gone to nap only to not wake up again that day.

Or the day after that. Or the day after that.

"You people are the balls, you know that? Bringing me here like this. Just the best danged folks," Clay said, his eyes fluttering open. His voice was raspy from misuse, but that didn't stop him from talking. He had a lot to say all the time and in all the ways, even if not everyone wanted to hear it. Irene seemed fine with it, though. She sat on a stool by his bedside, a black wig with pearls adorning a bunch of intricate braids covering her head. Her makeup was perfect, her fake mole in attendance, though on the opposite side of where it had been drawn the last time Clay'd seen it.

"It's no different than what you would have done for us," Doc said.

"Oh, I dunno about that. I may have been done the moment the bugs showed up. Won't even blame you if you never set foot outside of city limits again." Doc smirked and leaned over him to wash his other arm. Clay took that time to peer around the room, taking note of the tall windows, the silk cloth tacked to the walls, and a bunch of fancy art. It seemed they hadn't just made it to Marie's house—they'd stayed *at* Marie's house after their arrival. If anyone would have rooms to spare, it was a lady with nine kids, he supposed.

"I'm glad you mention that, because I might not—well, for a time anyway." Irene smiled and sat back down again, pulling a fan from inside of her pink bodice to wave it at her face. "Jacque has asked me to visit his summer cottage on Lake Pontchartrain. I'm thinking of going. After you feel better, of course. And if you don't need me wherever you travel next."

Clay settled into his pillows with a grin. It was a big bed, a good bed, the linens more comfortable than anything he could recall in the near-distant past. "Nah, you deserve a vacation. And if you wanna go ahead and live with Jacque until you're both shriveled up and old, I won't bitch too much, though the road'll be lonelier without you."

"Oh, I won't be gone for good. It's just a break. I don't think I could live without your particular charms for too long. I'd grow despondent."

"M'sure of it. Because I am a charming fellow, as you've pointed out so many times."

Doc smirked and leaned over to close her medical bag. "You are. A curse-free charming fellow at that, I'm happy to tell you. And just barely. Marie said if we'd gotten here two days later, you'd be dead. You can thank Addy when you see her next for insisting Cora drag you through Fairy to expedite the trip. At least you weren't awake for it to scar you."

"Then how'd you get here?"

"Oh, through Fairy as well. They put me in my own trunk for safe travel. I wasn't pleased with the arrangement, but at least I am unscathed."

Clay smirked at the mental image of Doc being squished in with a heaping pile of her own silk and lace. She was lucky she hadn't drowned in it. "Well, you got here. That's the important part. And where'd Addy go? She say when she'd be back?"

Doc snickered and fanned her face, her eyelids fluttering in a way that suggested she was far too delighted by what she was about to say. "Oh, she went to visit Sterling to thank him for everything he's done. I sincerely doubt we'll hear from her for a little while, though I did ask her to collect Squirt and Gayle for you. After she was done abusing Sterling's person, that is."

"He's old. What if his heart gives out?"

"He'll die a happy man?"

Clay couldn't argue that logic, and so he chuckled and stretched inside his bed. His body felt better than it had in ages, though he was still plagued by a weariness he hoped would diminish sooner or later. He wouldn't push it for now, though. He'd rest, relax, and hopefully figure out what the hell he was supposed to do with himself now that he wasn't dying.

"On a more serious note," Irene said, her hand reaching out to take his. "Cora's been here every day sleeping by your bed, feeding you. I know before I said all manner of angry things about her, but… if you were to decide to forgive her, I don't know that I'd mind. Or I won't mind as much as I would have before. That's up to you, though. I'd never impose upon—"

"I love her," Clay said, cutting her off. He didn't mean to be rude, but there was no sense letting Irene go on and on about something he'd already made up his mind about. Clay wasn't Clay without Cora, even during the really bad times—and there'd be more bad times ahead because the two of them were idiots, but they'd be idiots together. A long time ago, Clay'd asked his father why he was willing to wait around for his mother to return from Fairy every ten years. Harland's ineloquent response had been, "Love's where you find it even if it's up a pig's ass."

Well, Clay was up a pig's ass with Cora, whether or not he liked it.

Doc nodded and stood, her fan whipping out to motion at the door. "I'm glad to hear you say that, I think. Let me go tell her you're awake. She's been eager for your recovery."

Doc swished out of the room in a dress so full of petticoats it almost didn't fit through the door. Clay watched her outline disappear down the hall, his stomach jittery and off. He wasn't sure why that was. He especially didn't know why it worsened twofold when Cora appeared, looking pale and tired and generally frazzled. Doc must have meant what she said about Cora staying by his bed, 'cause the gal looked like she hadn't seen sheets in weeks.

"Hello, darlin'," he said, forcing himself into a quasi-upright position. Cora peered at him, he peered back, and without much care for the fact that he smelled like Irene's lilac water, he opened his arms to her. Cora didn't hesitate. There was a muffled sob, and she threw herself at him, her body colliding with his as her lips skimmed over the stubble on his cheeks. She must have shaved him while he was out, and wasn't that just plain sweet of her. For all that she nearly murdered him, she could be considerate on occasion, too.

She kept right on kissing him after that, her mouth skimming over his lips, his chin, his nose. Each bit of contact resulted in a little zap that made him grin. Seemed he'd recovered enough that his witchsniffer was back and fully functioning again.

No man had ever been happier about being electrocuted.

"I'm s-sorry. So sorry," she said over and over again, and Clay stroked her hair and smiled, not really caring as much about the curse as he probably ought. He was alive—that was the important part—and she was here alive with him. After all was said and done, that was really the only thing that mattered to him. Them alive. Together. For better or for worse.

"I know y'are, but you can spend the next few months making it up to me if you'd like. Breakfast in the morning, dinner at night, and then after dark, I get two pokes if I want, even if you're not in the mood. Hows'at sound?"

"Marvelous. Wonderful. Gladly, even." She lifted her hands to hold his cheeks and peered at him, her gray eyes watering in spite of her smile. He reached up to brush away the tears, and she leaned in to kiss him again. He found that right nice of her considering his breath had to stink like rotten garlic. "The draugr's gone, and I've apologized to Marie. She... she was so nice to me, Clay. I didn't deserve it."

"No, you didn't, but Marie's good folks. Just remember that the next time I piss you off. All right?" She dropped her head onto his chest with a shudder. He rubbed his chin against the silk of her hair and wrapped his arms around her. His stomach felt better. No more fears or trepidation. There was only contentment laced with post-curse weariness.

"You know," he said after a time, his lips drizzling across her forehead. He worked his way across the planes of her face, relishing the softness of her cheeks, the tilt of her nose, and the bow in her upper lip. "I heard you say you loved me when you talked to Maybell. I thought you couldn't do that or you'd get eaten by something in Fairy?"

"I probably shouldn't—well. I should have, but not..." Cora sighed and took a ragged breath, her head tucking under his chin once more like she didn't want to look at him when she spoke. "The wind carries words. Saying you love someone is a promise, and promises hold power. I didn't want my father to find us because he is clued into that power."

"I see," Clay said, though he didn't, not really.

"My father arranged a marriage for me a long time ago," she said. Her offering information freely was a momentous occasion, so he sat quiet and listened, his fingers threading through her hair, the tips skimming over her pointy ears. "I hated the man he'd betrothed me to and left the Seelie Court so I could escape him. Addy refused her own betrothal, and we've been running ever since. The money we take is to pay back our dowries. We want to pay off our debts so our father frees us from our bonds. He said he'd let us go when and only when we'd bought our freedom. It's a high price, Clay. I... it was going fine until I met you. You changed everything. I fell in love, and I had to protect you—us. I wouldn't risk making promises. I didn't want my father coming for me before I was ready to be rid of him for good. Do you understand now?"

It explained so much. It still bruised his ego that she thought he was so fragile, that she felt she had to protect him from her father, but it wasn't worth bringing up. They'd just tackled one enormous problem in the course of their relationship. This one could wait for another day when they weren't liking each other so much, which—knowing them—would be sometime next week.

"I do. And all I'll say on it is this—if we can survive five witches and a death curse, there ain't a lot that scares me anymore. So do with that information what you will," he said.

"Thank you, Clayton," she said, quietly, like a prayer.

"You're welcome Cora."

"I love you," she said.

His grin stretched to his ears.

"I know. And I love you back."

ABOUT THE AUTHOR

Hillary Monahan is the critically acclaimed *New York Times* bestselling author of the *Mary: The Summoning* series for Disney-Hyperion, among other titles. She lives in southeastern Massachusetts with her family of some parts humans, some parts fur kids. She's a feminist, a queer advocate, and a professional gloom cookie who can (and will) recite Young Frankenstein from memory for you if you ask nicely.

CPSIA information can be obtained
at www.ICGtesting.com
Printed in the USA
BVHW031826201118
533647BV00001B/80/P

9 780998 778372